SATYRDAY

by the same author

Drug Tales
April Ashley's Odyssey (with April Ashley)

SATYRDAY

Duncan Fallowell

MACMILLAN

First published 1986 by
MACMILLAN LONDON LIMITED
4 Little Essex Street London WC2R 3LF
and Basingstoke

Associated companies in Auckland, Delhi, Dublin, Gaborone,
Hamburg, Harare, Hong Kong, Johannesburg, Kuala Lumpur, Lagos,
Manzini, Melbourne, Mexico City, Nairobi, New York, Singapore
and Tokyo.

British Library Cataloguing in Publication Data

Fallowell, Duncan
    Satyrday.
    I. Title
    823'.914[F]   PR6056.A5/

    ISBN 0-333-42240-6

Typeset by Rapidset Ltd, London
Printed and bound in Great Britain by
Anchor Brendon, Tiptree, Essex

To my mother and father in their
44th year of marriage

Many say that when Catiline bound his associates
by oath to his criminal deed, he mixed the blood
of a man with wine and passed it around in a
bowl; when all had uttered a curse and had drunk
from the bowl, as is the custom in holy rites,
he revealed his plan.

Sallust, *Catilina XX*

There is a point in space between the Earth and
the Moon where both appear to be of equal size
and therefore equally distant. But it is an
illusion.

James Thorne, *The Meaning of Meaninglessness*

Contents

Part One

– 1 –

The Flat

'Doctor, I was lying in bed last night and a terrible panic overcame me, a terrible confusion and distress, sweating, dizziness, fear, which somehow resolved itself into an intense muscular constriction of my chest and stomach – as if I was being wound up tighter and tighter and when the limit of tightness had been reached it didn't stop, it went on getting tighter – then I started having these really horrible plunging sensations, as if the floor was giving way under me – and I became very afraid, so afraid that I thought my body would break apart – and then cold – and then finally I became indifferent to myself because the experience was so terrible that I lost my fear of death – death was not more terrible – I suppose eventually I fell asleep from exhaustion. Is this normal?'

To the north, south, east, and west, into the mist that rolls on distant slopes or drifts to a halt in hushed woodland, spread the limbs of the great city. Its limbs were dark with bruises, prickly with fever, the great city on its back like a Titan, bemused, breathing heavily with heart thumping, eyes blinking, mesmerized from time to time by fragments of history which float past in slow motion like exotic aerial plants, stunned by brick and concrete wreckage gathered up in immense heaps and blackened by smoke borne on a screaming wind. A disparate and excited population communicates, one to another, resembling castaways frantic at the crests of mountainous waves. New structures bristle from the flesh of the great city: metal arrows, glass knives, devices of ingenious torture and entertainment. The air everywhere is tinged with apprehension. A hush congeals out of hubbub. Tiny splashes of nervous laughter burst fitfully from the rigour of suspense. And lo! The Titan stirs! The blood of its capillaries turns an electronic purple. In the shadows of stabbed thighs and flanks, beneath the wounds of the fallen back, in tilted rooms and ruptured gardens, choked streets and flyovers swooping into emptiness, among turrets of glass and cabins of wood and plaster, in sliced-up palaces and under flows of rippling tarmac, activity renews itself, and the whole begins to glitter with the refulgence of a beautiful complexity as now, beneath the slowly opening eyelid of the moon, the night comes forward in unearthly surges.

Kate was eating pink jelly in front of the video while Guy was vomiting in the kitchen. On the screen a group of glossy humans was sitting in the sun, picking over the entrails of a young decapitated female with long slim dinner forks and occasionally eating something. The television set was housed in a cube of aluminium. The group on the screen paused – one of their number urinated into the entrails – they continued. The sounds in Guy & Kate's warm flat in the great city were primal: the sound of eating: the sound of vomiting: the sound of urination on the video had now given way to the sound of sexual congress.

Guy appeared in the doorway wiping his mouth with a towel. 'What's that filth you're eating?' he asked.

Kate ate some more and said 'I just don't believe this film, Guy.'

Guy spat into the towel and said 'Where are your nail scissors? I want to cut my toe-nails, they're making holes in my socks.'

'What made you throw up?' asked Kate.

'Don't know.'

'Oh God, this film, Guy, where did it come from?'

'Someone dropped by the studio with it. Pretty sick.'

On the screen a woman was defecating into a freshly scraped skull. 'A girl I knew at school,' said Kate, 'used to keep her mother's skull in the garage. I don't like this.'

Guy wandered into a room, fiddled with a computer, couldn't get it right, got angry with it – eventually a small puff of smoke appeared at the back – it was broken. Kate said 'A computer's only human, Guy. It too can break down.'

4

'Are you coming to this party to-night?' he said.

'I might,' she said. The phone rang, she picked it up and started talking.

Guy went into the other room and looked out of the window: a soft drizzle on brick and stucco emptiness. He looked into his mind and saw something similar, grey sand to the horizon being drizzled on . . .

– I have got to use my will-power, he thought, because I have no desire.

A want and a desire are different things. Guy wanted to go swimming. He also wanted to chase up a man who owed him some money. He also wanted some sex. He also wanted to buy some new underpants – he liked buying underpants, he got a randy feeling off it. He wanted to read some more of a book someone said he should read, although he wasn't actually enjoying it. He wanted, vaguely, to go to the loo. He wanted to phone his mother and father because he hadn't spoken to them for ages and it was beginning to hang over him. He wanted all these things and he wanted them now, all at once, simultaneously – in consequence he was paralysed by indecision and life itself overhung him. He stared out of the window at the evening rain and the clock slid slowly round and time fell over the horizon in specific amounts, gone, gone, gone in little puffs, puff-puff-puff . . . and nothing happened to him.

A couple of days ago. The Young Die Screaming phoned up from Geneva – they were a pop group he was connected with. 'We're stranded,' they said.

'Oh Jesus,' he said.

'What do we do?'

'Oh fuck off.'

'But Geneva's awful.'

Guy put the phone down and picked up another.

'Is that the Studio?'

'Yes.'

'Oh Guy, it's you. I didn't recognize you. You sound so far away. Have you been hiding from me? No, I know, you're working hard – that's what they all say. Look, what I rang about is – I'm having a little party the day after to-morrow – can you come?'

'That's nice, is it—'

'The printer's totally,' Margot Ingot drew in a deep breath, '*fucked* the invitations, so I'm having to phone round. I've been at it for yonks. Deeply boring.'

'Is it your birthday? I'll bring a present.'

'No, it's not.'

'I'll bring one anyway.'

'James Thorne's got a new book coming out. And it's time I gave another bash. I've also discovered it's the day Bartok was born and Debussy died. So it's more of a festival. Be joyous, dress gallantly. Bye.'

The phone rang.

'Is that Mr Manners?'

'Yes.'

'This is the Inland Revenue.'

'No.'

'What?'

'Glug-glug-glug!'

'What?'

Guy slammed down the phone and picked up another which was ringing and put on a funny voice – the person at the other end hung up. Then it happened again – the person hung up at the other end. 'Someone's playing silly buggers,' he said to no one because there was no one else around – even Kate hadn't come in to help out, even the pop types hadn't come in to hang out. Larry's secretary phoned asking for Mr Manners – Guy put on his funny voice again and said he was elsewhere. He didn't want to be around. The phone rang.

'Hullo, this is the Inland Rev—'

Guy slammed down the phone, slammed down the stairs, shot into the street and into a cab. 'Heathrow!' He sat in the airport trembling, had a port & brandy, trembling, had another, and when the trembling stopped he came home on the bus – he wanted to be very ordinary for the moment, very banal. Upstairs on the bus he overheard 2 old ladies talking. One was saying 'And I had such a funny turn, I thought I was going to pass out.' The other one said 'I get funny turns too.' Guy felt much better.

'Who was that on the phone?' Guy asked Kate.

'Rory.'

'Rory again?'

'Can't I talk to Rory?'

' . . . . . '

'I wish you weren't so possessive.'

'You make me want to spew half the time. But I love you.'

'Then don't be so possessive.'

'But I want you.'

'All right, Guy, all right, but just . . . don't be so possessive.'

'Can't you say anything else?'

'What do you mean?'

'You're terrified of getting close to anybody.'

'Anybody?'

'Me. Why can't you be possessive about me?'

'Ah . . . ' muttered Kate precariously.

'Well?'

'Guy, stop being so . . . '

'Possessive.'

'Aggressive.'

'I just want to—'

'You just want to stick your fingers up me and stuff the whole bloody time!'

'It's not just that.'

'It is.'

'It isn't.'

'It is.'

'IT ISN'T YOU FUCKING BITCH!!!'

Kate was playing one of her games: sexual humiliation. He hit her and she bled and he cried. And she laughed in his face. Guy slammed the door on his way out, causing a small glass figure of Vishnu dancing on the mantelpiece to jump off, float and turn in the air for a few moments, then hurl itself with great deliberation against the floor.

Across London town in the gathering night the clouds heaved greenishly like the bellies of toads. Helicopters came out of them, flapping and blinking like predatory night birds, and went back into

7

them again. The orange sodium streetlamp came on outside the window. Kate stared into the bowl of jelly and saw disconcerting things there. She saw . . . nothing. Then she saw . . . something, a dim huddled shape, a young shape, herself seen from behind sitting on the edge of a bed. She saw her back in a navy blue sweater hunched over something, hunched over something important, something crucial, hunched over a . . . bowl of jelly and in this bowl there slowly developed the image of her mother's face. Her mother was crying and the tears welled up in the bowl and overflowed across the bedroom floor in a thin pink ink. Kate shuddered and, as though an old indestructible memory had suddenly been loosed from its bower of obscurity, down from the misty hills far away there came the long howling of wolves like a streak of black light into the very heart of the fluorescent city.

Guy looked out of the window. It was night. It was wet. He looked at a desk in the corner. Paperwork. His little record company. Visions of Greatness Records. Shaking All Over Records. Fistdisc. Precipice Productions. The incantation of the names produced an unpleasant numbness in his head which could go on for hours, for days, unless focused and knotted into the belly. He was learning to pull the anxiety down out of his brain where it was dangerous and into his belly where it was less so. The Abused, Torture Chamber, the Flying Rectums, the Young Die Screaming, these groups had done nothing for his sense of security . . .

Larry's face leered up at him: a recent promotion party at the Hilton Hotel. He was in debt to Larry for a substantial sum.

'Come down to the house,' said Larry who owned a 19th century Tudor style manor in Sussex and peopled it with his creatures. Edward VII had shot there. Larry had been shot there. It had a 19th century Tudor staircase with a continually moving 2-way escalator built into it. When people passed out at parties on the ground floor they were slung on at the bottom and were delivered to the bedroom floor where someone else, usually an employee, would haul them away. Larry didn't believe in servants. He believed in employees. Larry owned 3 very big pop groups, 2 even bigger sports stars, and sniffed cocaine as fine as the foam of champagne. He was rich, violent, and ugly. He ate too much, drank the best wines, smoked cigars from Lewis's and cannabis from the foothills of the Himalayas and dope pollen from Colombia. He was large, loud, confident, generous, cruel, and farted without embarrassment in the presence of women. He had some principles. He had no truck with heroin and thought those who did were inadequate. He looked up to degenerates but despised inadequates.

'Can't, Larry, going north that week-end, thanks all the same.'

'Look, I don't want to get . . . ' Larry put his arm round Guy who caught a whiff of Penhaligon's English Fern from Larry's thick greasy neck. '. . . don't want to get . . . '

'Amazingly heavy.'

'Ha, ha! I like your style, Guy. Always did. Look, man, there's trouble and there's trouble. You've only got the first. Believe me, you don't want to catch the second. Please sort out your bills. And soon. That's all I want to say. It's the principle of the thing. If I let you off they'll say Larry Perkins is getting soft, Guy put one over on Larry Perkins, and I can't have that, can I? It's not as if we're related or anything, is it, know what I mean?'

The point about Larry was that he didn't want to have Guy snapped in 2. He really didn't like resorting to the Fundamental Law. He would feel genuinely upset in having to pick up the phone and send in the boys. This was Larry's charm – he had a heart. He was also very street-wise – unintelligent but street-wise, quick to pick up on the ideas of others.

'Shame you can't come. Wanda'll be there. She likes you, does Wanda.'

'Going north, Larry, going to Henry's. But I'd love to next time.'

'So you're sure you're going to last that long? Ha, ha, ha!'

Larry spotted Beryl Finch, the lead singer with crusty lacquered hair and spotty back from a new tinsel pop act, and went off to make a very important suggestion about her going solo. The magnate touch. The touch Guy didn't seem to have. Guy put out these frantic records on his desperate little labels because it was a way of getting something off his chest – even so, always driving him on was the vision of greatness shining like a great revolving sun at the end of an avenue of white pillars . . . the Hit . . . the strike, the big one, the thing which made it, which tore and broke right through the slippery, yielding but maddeningly resistant membrane which divides failure from success, umbra from refulgence.

Going north, going north. To Henry's. Was he?

He picked up the phone and dialled. 'Henry?'

'Yes.'

'Guy.'

'Hi. I didn't recognize you.'

'I thought of coming up next week-end.'

'Do.'

'For a break.'

'Do, do. There's nothing happening. Pop's in London for some party. Do. Come Friday. Come Thursday indeed. In fact – come now. Nothing's happening here. Nothing whatsoever. I could do with a conversation. We could discuss something. Anything. So long as it's not business.'

'OK, I'll see you then, then.'

Henry, the Viscount Mountsavage, was Guy's 'sort of' partner. But basically Henry Mountsavage's big interest was radio – he was a radio ham, an overgrown schoolboy who wore old tartan slippers into the village sometimes.

Having swept up Vishnu, Kate sighed and picked up the evening paper. *The leader of the Opposition Party announced to-day that he would be having a sex-change operation. He said this would not affect the quality of leadership but he hoped, he said, to be 'able to serve the party a bit more graciously in future'. Mark will be taking the name of Marjorie. The leader's wife, who was told some time ago, said, from her home in a depressed post-industrial area of the north of England, that she was shocked 'but perhaps it can save our marriage'. The leader's son, who is away at school, hasn't stopped giggling for nearly 2 weeks and doctors are getting anxious.*

'We must accept that some people are like this,' said the Archbishop of Canterbury.

'We can accept such people,' said the Prime Minister, 'but we don't have to vote for them. I hope the general public will not be taken in by what is clearly a cheap vote-grabbing stunt 3 months before the local elections. It's things like this which make me seriously consider abolishing local elections – they prevent the people of this country from concentrating on the major issues.'

10

The day had begun with a thud: the sound of something hard hitting something soft. Oh urine dawn! . . . Guy thought it would always be like this. Whether he slept with someone or slept alone, seemingly the day would always begin with a thud, a piss, a sense of oppression and fatigue. Last night he'd slept alone. He'd got back late, a bit the worse for drink. He didn't want to wake Kate. Look – he wasn't a drunkard. He remembered the day he discovered he could enjoy himself without being drunk – a Sunday – they'd gone to a new club which hadn't yet got a licence to sell alcohol on Sundays. He was shy of dancing. He shuffled about self-consciously in his seat. Then he thought – fuckit. He simply stood up and pushed himself onto the dancefloor and danced. It was wonderful, it was freedom, freedom of action. He could dance without being drunk, smashed, ripped – what an astonishing discovery. And there were so many other things apart from drink. For example, pills. His favourite was pink and black. It made you happy without making you trivial.

The day had begun with a thud. And had continued in thick unfocused fashion. He hadn't been to the office to-day. 'Studio' they called it. He hadn't been to the Studio. And at the flat the phone had been off the hook.

'What if someone wants to get hold of *me*?' said Kate.

'Nobody will want to get hold of you until after 6 o'clock,' said Guy. 'We'll put it back on at 7.' Then Guy felt guilty about Kate.

Kate saw 2 bags of washing in the corner asking to be dragged out to the launderette, washed, dried, dragged back, and ironed. The woman who used to do it – it all got too expensive. Kate thought – What am I doing with a drip like him? – Why did we never buy a washing machine? She was hot and angry but remained silent. Then she felt guilty. She looked at Guy. He was very downcast. He looked really upset. Suddenly it had dawned on him that it was possible to live an entire life without ever seeing a Zulu or hearing the creak of a glacier or touching the walls of the Potala Palace or being able to forget the name of your bank manager.

Guy went to lie on the bed. He was tired. He wanted to go to a land where women didn't shave their armpits, where they blew sweet air on closed eyelids with warm breath. He didn't want to work, push, insist, work, hunt, catch, shove it in, push, push, push. He wanted to lie on his back with arms and legs outspread on the bed while a dusky girl, with a slim body like a chocolate slipper, curled and slid all over him. That was it – he wanted to be done over. That would be nice.

The fogs and swamplands of Guy's mind resolved into 2 options:

1) He didn't give a damn about it all
2) He gave a damn about it

His attention considered first the advantage of one, then of the other, and back to one, whence to the other, to one, to the other, to one, t'other – – a helpless oscillation established itself. He began to sweat, grow confused. He felt the panic mount like lava up the throat of a volcano. His eyes snapped open. He stood up. The floor moved underfoot like the floor of a boat, then it turned spongy beneath him. On liquid legs he went into the bathroom and splashed his face with icy water, looked at himself in the mirror, looked at a haggard stranger there, splashed his face again, took off his wetted shirt, looked biliously about, found a cigarette, lit it – anxiety flowed everywhere like yolks spilling from broken eggs.

Kate was standing in the window of the sitting room. He approached her from behind and put his arms round her waist, rested his head on her shoulder. 'You silly boy . . . ' she said. Kate lit a cigarette. Guy stubbed his out in a souvenir ashtray, souvenir of one heavenly high-focus champagne morning at the Dorchester Hotel in the springtime with a view of new daffodils in Hyde Park – Kate had slipped the ashtray into her handbag for him. An Arab boy, with no legs and dumped on a sofa, saw her and laughed. Guy now lit another cigarette. Kate stubbed hers out in an old pot ashtray, souvenir of nothing at all, quite barren of cloying suffocating connotations thank God, she thought, redolent of nothing whatsoever except the accumulated dinge of the coming and going of lots and lots and lots of ash. Kate lit another cigarette and stubbed it out immediately.

– We don't light our cigarettes at the same time any more, she thought.

Regardlessly, in a world of its own, the video clicked off.

'I think I'll cook a bit of fish – do you want some?' asked Kate without relish.

'No.'

– The flat will stink of fish all night, he thought, and there'll be mountains of food at Margot's party so obviously Kate's not going to come.

Kate was thinking – Oh God, if I don't have something solid to eat I'll faint and never make it to that damn party which I'll probably go to because it'll do me good.

Neither of them moved just yet. Kate stared at the fair hairs round Guy's navel and thought of love. They hadn't made love for a while. They hadn't even had sex this week. The last time – it wasn't love, it wasn't sex, it was some kinky thing, it was terrible, he'd gone crazy. 'I hate you,' he'd said, 'HATE you. I hate the way you walk, the way you fucking walk in those silly shoes, and your smell, I hate that, your stink, the stink of you with that nauseating perfume, God how I hate that! and that stupid look on your face when you think no one is looking at you and I'm looking at you, the fucking stupid gormless look like you were waiting for Jesus to come along and SHIT on you – well, he did, he shat on you, and you just sit there taking it. I hate the way you move about the room with your silly body and bloody elbows sticking out and stupid pop eyes when I say something, pretending to be surprised, pretending not to understand – did you say that to me? Oh my, what do you mean? – the pretence, I hate it, you, that fucking mimsy way you, you, I hate the way you fucking – fuck! I really hate that, like someone spilled a cold cup of tea in your lap, like someone knocked a glass off the table by accident, oh my best glass never mind, never mind – you screw like it was unnatural, like it was a disease, oops, oh sorry, everso, everso sorry, no not there, please not there Guy, *not* there Guy please, you screw like a weed, like you were keeping it in curlers for a rainy day, you fuck like dear me, oh everso sorry, wipe it up quickly, oh you fuck like – well, what I'm trying to say is you won't do it with me why not why not? You have these little indiscreet discharges, these little hot poisonous comings and goings and wafty tremblings and sometimes an irrepressible twitch which is the fuck trying to escape out of you but you won't have it, you won't allow it, you won't give it, and I hate the way you mess up all that and I bloody fucking hate YOOOO!'

She tried to say . . . 'I don't understand what you're saying. What do you want, Guy?' but an invisible cord muted her. She'd always thought the love-making was the one thing they'd got right, the one place they could always retreat to.

13

'I want you to get hot and wet and pumped up and I want you to, want you to get, I want, I – want – want – I want—' He shot spunk all in her hair, gunks of it jumping into her mass of brown hair and one big jellyish gobbet sliding down her cheek. He loved the sense of smearing her – this side of their relationship had obviously been neglected. And she sat on the edge of the bed white as death, crying in a funny dry choked uneven hysterical way.

The doorbell to the flat rang. It was Jill from the ground floor, with whom relations were amicable but she didn't come upstairs very often. Her hair was short and done up in a colourless frizz. This, combined with thin lips and a long sharp nose in a grey complexion, gave her a harsh, rather lesbian quality. But there was something athletic and firm about her body which was very attractive. She worked at the National Computer Monitor in north London. If it were raining at lunchtime and she didn't feel like going out, she would look up in the Citizen Databank the particulars of people she knew or had heard of and have a good laugh while eating a lunch of salmon & cucumber sandwiches with brown bread.

To-night her eyes shone. The glow was within and coming outwards. What she said was 'Guy love, can I borrow a cup of red wine to put in Trevor's stew?'

'Come in, Jill. Kate, darling, it's Jill! Oh, Kate's on the phone, she lives on that phone.'

'How are your mother and father, Guy?'

'They're OK. They're at home somewhere.'

'Saw that Margot friend of yours in the papers with some young bloke at some party. She gets around a bit I daresay.' Jill gave a resonant laugh. The laughter hung around her in the air for a little while after the noise had stopped, the laughter and something else, an excitement? a fear? Jill pulled a funny face. 'I've got to go out,' she said. 'I just wanted to liven up Trevor's stew . . . bless him. He's swimming. He'll be hungry when he gets in . . . Guy?'

'Yes?'

'Er . . . oh nothing. Just a drop of wine.'

14

Kate often worked in Guy's office. But humping boxes of pop records about as a team member of Guy's assault on the Matterhorn of success was not her idea of fulfilment. Something was lacking which also wasn't found, it transpired, in the Russian evening classes to which she turned in a mood of desperation. In her search for some individuality of expression, to demonstrate that the flame of creativity burned within her too, that she was relevant and irreplaceable, Kate had entered an ice-cream making competition. The prize: a week for 2 in Cremona, Italy, where ice-cream was not invented but first developed (from one of Marco Polo's Chinese recipes). 'If I win,' she said to Guy, 'I'm going to ask them if I can stay for 2 weeks if it's just me who goes.' He looked at her. She was serious. He swallowed before he spoke. He said 'I should've thought that 2 weeks in Cremona was 10 days too much.' But Kate lost, despite her jetblack ice-cream (flavoured liquorice).

'I'm going up to see Henry next week-end. We've got a few things to sort out. Coming?'

'Oh darling . . . no.'

'Go on. It'll do you good.'

'Ya ya, but with his father there . . . the old fool wouldn't stop making passes at me last time. He asked me to live with him. I said "Aren't you a bit set in your ways for a new affair, Lord Flamingfield?" and he said "I recall that Cato the Elder began the study of Greek at the age of 80." Then we had a row about politics.'

'I suppose he's very lonely in that big old place.'

'He's got Henry living there,' said Kate.

'They're both lonely together. Anyway his lordship may not be there.'

'Lady Flamingfield – I'd like to have met her,' murmured Kate. Henry's mother, Rapunzel Flamingfield, the Countess, had been killed in a car crash while he was still at school. A lorry had been driving steadily along a motorway bearing a stacked load of corrugated iron sheets. Behind the lorry rode a man on a motorbike. The top sheet of corrugated iron was loose. It shook itself free and slid off the back of the lorry. The sheet, being heavy, shot vigorously backwards and decapitated the man on the motorbike. The lorry driver, unaware of what had happened, continued on his way. In its death spasm the body of the motorcyclist clenched. This clenching caused the hands to twist the accelerator on the handlebars. The motorbike accelerated and overtook the lorry. The lorry driver, glancing out of the window, saw himself being overtaken by a headless motorcyclist. The shock of this produced a seizure. The lorry driver had a heart attack, the lorry swung out of control, crossed the central barrier, and crashed into several oncoming cars. One of these cars was being driven by Rapunzel Flamingfield.

Trevor sat greyly, pastily behind the counter at the bank and processed small amounts of money hour after hour all day long. Sometimes he thought his head would burst like a bladder of hot pus. So long had he sat only half hearing people through the glass partition, that he now didn't listen to them at all and conducted intercourse with the other side in random platitudes of general application.

'That's half the battle isn't it,' he'd say in reply to God knows what.

'Burble burble.'

'Still, what can you expect these days?' he'd say.

'Rumble rumble rumble.'

'And it get's worse doesn't it.'

'Cluck cluck!'

'Get's worse, yes.'

'Young man,' squawked Mrs Shadbolt, 'I say the service in this bank is simply terrible and you calmly tell me it's getting worse! I'll have my money in tens. I also want a new chequebook, and I want to see the Manager!'

It was occasionally Trevor's misfortune to be woken up. His real attention lay elsewhere. In dreamland. In El Dorado. Not in footling transactions but in the real stuff – piles of gold. Inside the bank, money was characterless, like drugs in a hospital, but outside . . .

He felt that he and Jill got on. They embraced each other and took on life from there. He was mad about her. He was always saying 'Have you met Jill?', 'I'll bring Jill along', 'I can't, I'm going out with Jill', 'Jill doesn't mind', 'Jill likes that', 'I can put Jill off, she understands', 'That's just like Jill', 'Jill would love this', 'Jill should have a nose-job'.

The nose-job was just about the only point on which they parted company – because Trevor felt that with it Jill would be completed. 'That conk of yours . . . ' he'd say. Jill would go all funny at this. Crying didn't come easily to her, it wasn't her style, but sometimes she wished it were because she felt like crying now. Instead she went all funny. 'This operation, Jill, it's nothing,' he'd blunder on. 'But, Trev, I don't want to, honest I don't. It would make me different. It makes me nervous.' The idea of being completed terrified Jill. It was like being buried. Coping with her nose kept Jill's feet on the ground. She thought – Besides, Queen Frederika of Greece died from a heart complaint which developed after an operation on her eyelid. Some women are very sensitive. 'Give me a break,' she said. Trevor's lower lip sagged with disappointment. She touched him below the waist. 'Right?' she said, lifting her eyebrows. The television has replaced the fire as the domestic hearth – Trevor and Jill started licking each other's genitals in front of the television.

Trevor sat greyly, pastily behind the counter etc but when in the evening he went to the swimming pool, slipped out of his clothes and into the water, he was transformed. His body was perfect. It was more than perfect – it was impressive.

'When you take your clothes off,' said Jill, 'it's like Superman coming out from behind his tweeds and specs.'

'Leave it out, Jill, I'm not even 6 foot,' said Trevor, screwing up his rubbery face and rearranging his heavy genitals inside the swimming trunks.

'You are to me, love,' she said, rearranging her heavy creamy bosoms inside her bikini top. She said it matter-of-factly.

'Jill – come ere.'

'Trev, not on the surround . . . '

Among the many things banned from the Swimming Baths by notices ubiquitously posted – no running, no smoking, no flippers, no bombing, no pushing, no ducking – was *no petting*.

'Ere none of that!' the jocular voice of the lifeguard echoed in the arched and brightly lit blue length of the Edwardian pool. But Trevor was embarrassed to unhug Jill because his penis was sticking out of the top of his swimming trunks. Later at home they made love in front of the television and he entered her anally with the help of a little corn oil from the kitchen cupboard, which was one of the things they loved to do in their private non-verbal space and never never

never mentioned to anyone, not even to each other, least of all to Jill's mum who lived a dogged life in an East London towerblock.

Now, to-night, in Guy's flat, the phone rang and Guy picked it up and said 'Yes?'

'It's Trevor. I'm ringing from downstairs. Have you seen Jill, Guy?'

'Yeah, she was here not long ago. She left.'

'She's not here. I don't understand it. She's always here when I get in unless she leaves a note.'

'She said she was going out. I expect she's left you some food.'

'Oh yes. But – OK, sorry to bother you. How's things, all right?'

'Yeah, fine. And you?'

'I wish I knew where Jill was.'

Guy was looking this way and that in the bathroom mirror, trying his hair this way and that. He wanted to look good. He needed to look good. One thing he certainly didn't want was to look how he felt because he felt like a chunk of foot fungus.

This way?

Or that way?

The discrepancy between feeling and appearance was increasingly a problem. Oh Christ, he no longer knew how he looked – yes, *hysterical* foot fungus! That was Guy . . .

– Kate doesn't love me, Guy thought. Yes, she loves me. Do I want to be loved? I want . . . People have a rotten knack of not fitting in with one's plans. This is the basic fact. You discover it the moment you challenge inertia. Why are people so bloody inconvenient? Guy sympathized with the problems a government has in trying to co-ordinate a volatile population. He understood the Government Health Warning: *Citizens, Beware! Ideas May Strike At Any Time!*

He started to shave and his spirits rose. He thought – I don't want to be loved. I want to be worshipped. Having someone sprawling abject at my feet brings out all my best qualities, all my strengths. Out of my fucking way, you bastards! Do what I tell you! Let's get a bit of action around here! . . . but they didn't take any notice of him.

Meanwhile, over at the dressing table in the bedroom, Kate was

18

playing with a half empty pill bottle. 'I hate it, I hate it!' She found herself saying it aloud, heart beating wildly, flashes in front of her eyes. A memory from way back slotted into the viewfinder of her brain and was projected against the front of her skull. In this memory she was a young girl, standing by a telephone in a hallway. She'd just slammed down the receiver. She was saying 'I hate him, I hate him!', all hot and flustered with tears burning on her cheeks. Some other him. A long time ago in some other place – her uncle came into the hall and said 'You have learned that it is often the things we don't like which have the greatest hold on us. Now come and have a cup of tea with your auntie in the front room.' Schoolgirl Kate stared at her uncle, then stared into space. Before her the great challenge of life rose up like a massive pair of baroque iron gates, wondrously constructed, dripping with shit.

Guy wanted to live somewhere else. He'd gone off the flat. Gone off the street, gone off the yellow sodium light being so 'interesting' right outside the window.

– We don't need a flat, he thought. What we need is an urban living space in a post-industrial conversion, something we can do things with, struts you can treat as pillars, vaults of brick you can put Italian spotlights in, whole stretches of floor you can leave empty. I've gone right off flats with rooms. I want a place I can *run* across. Leap about in! Extend myself into. Like Anthea's place. [Anthea van den Clack, daughter of a diamond merchant, living on the river in part of a converted Liquorice Allsorts factory.] I like Anthea. I should see more of her. She fancies me, I can feel it. Great place she's got . . and great knockers . . .

'What did you say?' Guy breezed in naked.
  'I said I hate it.'
  'Ya, it's horrible, isn't it.' He came up behind her and tucked his member into her armpit. Her head fell back, her eyes rolled back, and he rhythmically stroked her vocal cords. 'Jill popped in, then Trevor rang, and – oh, who were you on the phone to earlier? Rory I suppose.'

19

'Actually, it was the British . . . Museum.'

'Good God, what did they want?'

'They wanted to *know* if Charles was here. Apparently he's vanished.'

Charles Robinson was Guy's only friend who survived from schooldays, the one man (Guy felt) who would harbour him if he'd committed a murder – Charles had that kind of depth. At school Charles was the glamorous boy who did nothing, whose tie despite regulations was always loosely knotted over a loosened collar, who leaned against walls with one leg up looking as if he'd just put out a cigarette. His eyes had a violet tinge which suggested a personality both contained and dangerous. Charles would become, if he cared to become anything at all, a film star, a spy, a playboy with a string of adoring silly women, or an eccentric biochemist, or something which demanded a recondite knowledge of South American capitals or a casual familiarity with the latest firearms. Then one day, still young and impressionable despite the opinion of his peers, Charles had stumbled across a copy of *The Egyptian Book of the Dead* in an old garden hut among yellow newspapers, dried-up flowerpots and rotten wooden planks. With growing astonishment he read this dismal tome. He was riveted by it. He said 'Stupidity on this scale is absolutely fascinating. I must find out more about this inane race of men.' Eventually, via an unusual route which involved a spell at the University of Saudi Arabia, Charles Robinson had become the Keeper of Middle Eastern Antiquities (which excludes the Egyptian Collection) at the British Museum. He was also an expert on the buildings of Borromini and the symphonies of Bruckner and the paintings of Giorgione – he had written a controversial article proving in just 24 pages that not one of the extant Giorgiones was genuine. He also had access to the most arcane video films at the very limit of human bestiality, though preferred it not to be known. 'Don't tell Kate or anyone like that,' he said as he handed Guy a small parcel at the Studio. It was almost a joke at first.

The Assistant Keeper of Middle Eastern Antiquities's assistant entered the Doric office of the Director of the British Museum and said 'You probably haven't heard, sir.'

'Heard?' The Director stopped doodling on his blotter, looked up at young Filbert, and started fiddling with a piece of hair behind his ear.

'Robinson seems to have gone.'

'Gone?'

'Er, yes, I mean – really gone. Hopped it. With . . . '

'With?' echoed the Director blandly.

'With . . . '

'With?' echoed the Director waveringly.

'With—'

'With what, you cretin?'

'With – with – with the Nineveh Codex . . . sir.'

Silence fell suddenly and heavily like wet cement, and set. The colour drained entirely from the Director's pink fingernails. His large Adam's apple, daily and sorely scraped of the hair which grew down to it, disappeared below the level of the Director's hard white collar in an immensely traumatic swallow, causing the collar because of its tightness to bob upwards. The Director, though only 40 years old, always wore hard collars and tailored suits of great exactitude, as if punishing his character for its unacceptable inclinations (which included mint tea, gym instructors of either sex, and a failure to believe in God). At the end of each day a raw red ring encircled his neck and sometimes a little blood. Once only had this armour failed him and this was when the Queen made a visit to open a new room of Greek pots – she'd asked 'I hear you are an agnostic, Director.' Hideously, upon realizing that this was her way of apologizing for the King's being unable, ever, to accord him a knighthood, he'd peed in his pants, though fortunately it didn't show because of the sobriety of the cloth.

The Director said 'I don't believe you, Filbert. How dare you!'

'Honestly, sir, it's so.'

The Director was about to say something again but he saw by the vivid glitter in Filbert's eyes, a glitter which was akin to that of sexual excitement, that he told the truth. The Director in utter panic checked the facts over several intercoms – the police were already on their way and then an interval grew like a black hole in the rubber sheet of space–time.

'Director?' whispered Filbert.

' . . . the Nineveh . . Codex . . . . . ' eventually stirred on the Direc-

tor's lips which were blue. His cheeks were green. ' . . . Help me . . to
the couch . . . ' hissed faintly this withered creature who only 5
minutes before had been in the prime of life and at the top of his profession. No one is safe from disenchantment! ' . . say you're all joking . . . ' was the piteous plea.

'I'm not joking, sir,' said Filbert cockily – God, how he loved it.

'The gin . . . the gin – quickly . . sssss . . . '

The Director, shaking, poured himself a tumbler of straight gin
and drank it, spilling much as he did so. 3 or 4 violent shudders
twisted his body, after which he seemed more his old self. ' . . The
little *cunt* . . . ' he murmured venomously. 'Join me, Filbert?'

'No thank you, sir. I'm on a diet,' replied Colin Filbert who was
small and slim and bright.

'You little c—' The Director knocked back another tumblerful, sat
upright on the chaise longue, and straightened his jacket and tie. An
extreme malevolence gripped his face. 'When I find him . . . I'll *kill*
him.'

'Vanished?' said Guy, tickling Kate's hairline.

'Gone. Poof. Nothing. His office simply abandoned, like the
Mary Celeste. Except that some priceless manuscript was missing
too.'

' . . . Christ . . . . ' Guy's member fell out of her armpit.

'He stole some horrid old Babylonian thing. Good. I'm glad. I
hope he burns it, wipes his arse with it, sends it back to them strip by
strip! I hope it disintegrates in his hands, I hope the whole bloody
museum caves in, the whole bloody shithouse.' Then she said, with
tremendous vehemence, 'Oh God, I hate the past, I *hate* it!'

– 2 –

The Party

Margot sat at the dressing-table, exfoliating. 'De-ageing starts here' affirmed the pot, as she abraded the surface of her face with crème de sandpaper. Then she emolliated.

She shifted on the dressing-table stool to examine herself and squirted something extremely expensive up her 'gin gin' as she called it, something which the manufacturer claimed did not produce a nasty effect in the mouth if tasted. Lovers had sometimes complained that her armpits – not only her armpits, her pits in general – were overchemicalized. This was because she was getting old and no longer had body confidence, not that deep confidence. She felt that a funny smell here or there would put men off, would be interpreted as the old-woman smell of crusty decay. And yet . . . she wanted to avoid setting men's teeth on edge if they kissed her between the legs. Was this new spray the answer to an old problem?

Margot depressed a button and said into an intercom 'You can come in now.'

Joyce, the housekeeper/personal maid, came in and pursed her mouth. 'With the emeralds, do you need a green belt? I'll get a black belt.'

– She's got me all in black again, thought Margot and decided to pile on some extra emeralds for compensation. 'Have some champagne, Joyce.' Debussy piano music played softly in the bedroom from concealed speakers. In a little while Margot said 'Can you take your champagne outside, Joyce? I'd like a few minutes alone. Tell Mr Wilkinson I'll be down directly.'

Margot tidied up some magazines on the end of the bed. She

thought – Should I wear one breast exposed in the current fashion? – better not – I've got a suntan mark.

She positioned herself regally in a chair, closed her eyes, and tried to let the breathing come as naturally as possible. It wouldn't. Her heart was quite thumpy, like doors constantly opening and closing inside her. She took another few sips of champagne, swallowed a tranquillizer, got into her high heels and was ready to descend. She thought – I'll greet the guests in the hall and mingle later.

'Now remember,' said the ½ French caterer, 'this is England. It doesn't matter how good or bad the food is. What matters here is that hot food should be HOT and cold food should be *warm*.'

Jean-Pierre Wilkinson, an interesting case: his father was an Englishman who fled from debts to Paris; his mother was French; Dad fled Paris one night leaving Mum with baby Jean-Pierre who was consequently brought up to hate Dad in particular and the English in general; he now made a fortune in London as caterer with brilliant food, preying on the ambivalent attitude of the English upper class towards France.

'Is everything all right, Monsieur Wilkinson?'

'Lady Ingot, the house – stairs, stairs – up and down, up and down – we don't have enough time for all these stairs!'

'Your boys and girls look very fit. As indeed do you.'

He smiled, appeased – like all food freaks he couldn't resist a personal compliment.

Margot was heroically rich. The luck began with her grandfather's fortune – most of Edwardian England sat on his lavatory pans – and reached a climax with the electronics millions of her 2nd husband, Sir David Midland: The Man Who Took The Hiss Out Of Tape. 'The whole idea of magnetic tape,' he said, 'goes back to the Ancients – a roll of parchment wound on 2 sticks. Now rethink in terms of a 3 dimensional memory bank, laser search and micro-circuits, housed in a cartridge the size of a cough pastille. You feed the player like feeding a slot machine with a sovereign. The one

24

drawback is packaging. What will happen to packaging?' But he underestimated the relief with which the public found it was possible to have all Beethoven's symphonies in a cough pastille. It went like a bomb, worldwide. He was knighted and died of a heart attack in a taxi on the way back from Buckingham Palace.

'People never believe it,' said Margot at the champagne wake after his funeral, 'but to David I was faithful . . .'

Afterwards she reverted to her maiden name: Ingot. She wanted young lovers she could have fun with, and boss a bit. She had them and felt older, not always happier. She loved dirtying chiffon and silk in bed. She had only one rule: Don't fuck with your bodyguard. She had also become one of the richest women around, with lots of places to live in. The flat in Rio de Janeiro she hadn't yet visited. She'd heard that in Rio taxi drivers won't stop at red traffic lights after dark, for fear of being shot and mugged. She wasn't usually nervous about this sort of thing – she often went shopping, with Solon the bodyguard at hand – but what with David's taxi death and oh Rio, such a long way to go to get shot at. Her parents had lived all over the place too. When Margot was 23, Mummy and Daddy were killed. They shot over a cliff in a sports car on their way to the Monte Carlo Opera House.

'What a heavenly sunset,' Mummy had said.

'Oh wonderful,' said Daddy who was still gazing blissfully at it when the road made a sharp left . . . .

It was part of the legendette that as a baby Margot's first word was 'ritz'.

'Oh really? How ultra *ultra*! Me too! Biarritz, St Moritz, St Tropez – anything with "ritz" in I adore!' gushed Sophie Shatner as she arrived at Margot's party that night dressed in a tube of pink rubber. Lots of people were already there.

'St Tropez doesn't have ritz in,' said Venetia Vane-Tempest-Wormold in a more tasteful green rubber tube.

'It almost has. Christ, Venetia, don't be so bloody *literal*. Have you got any of that stuff? It was really excellent.'

'I hate cocaine.'

'No, I mean that other . . stuff. My tube's killing me.'

'Oh that other stuff. No, I haven't. I hope this party's going to be sick,' said Venetia. 'I fancy something really brilliant and sick.'

Mary Yodel was talking to millionaire Dick Tring in a Venetian

window. Mary's husband had been Minister of Employment until
he was sacked a year ago, an event Mary felt quite happy about.
'Now we'll see *more* of each other,' she'd told him. Her husband hit
the male menopause like a rotten old canteloupe dropping schlup! off
a lorry. He sat in the vacuum of his favourite chair in the spick and
span front room for months, immobile, rainwater dripping down
the blurred screen of his eyes, while Mary fiddled about in the
kitchen with eggy things humming along to the radio. 'It's so lovely
to have him home,' she hummed. 'Now, let's try this new Super
Triple Chocolate Goo Goo Instamix!' Just one of the mouth-water-
ing whisk-me-ups from Ultragunge! Be Queen of the Powdered
Puds with Ultragunge! . . . Mary said 'There, there, diddums,' and
lifted a spoonful of the pale brown slop to her husband's flabby lips.
Then she wrote a bit of novel.

'Give Fred my regards,' said Dick Tring. 'He was a good man.
Incorruptible. And I know, because I tried corrupting him a few
times – ha, ha!' Dick Tring was in a big generous open mood. He had
just pulled off a mighty personal coup, the ramifications of which
were to involve in varying degrees many of Margot's guests this
evening. To-night – and secretly! – Dick Tring was an exalted man
who felt that all the glories of the known and unknown universe
were his . . . for the taking.

A group of people holding glasses said:
'Jean-Pierre Wilkinson's doing the food.'
'Yummy. Only the French could've invented French dressing. In
fact I think it's true that French culture is superior to English culture.'
'Oh, that's fearfully exaggerated. I mean, they're good at food and
designing wallpaper and that sort of thing but, well, I've had some
appalling meals in France quite frankly, and of course they don't have
a sense of humour, do they. They've wit but not humour, not
warmth, which is a great cultural defect in my opinion and it produces that terrible sort of French impatience.'
'I always thought it was the Germans who had no humour.'
'No, it's the French. The Germans have it – but it's a loutish barbar-
ian humour the Germans have.'
'They overdo everything the Germans, don't you find? My cousin

26

stayed with some Germans and they had, can you imagine, cheese and garlic sausage for breakfast.'

'It's because they weren't part of the Roman Empire.'

'You can always tell which parts of Europe weren't part of early civilization. I'm always deeply happy that England was part of the Roman thing.'

'So am I. *Deeply.*'

'I can't stand the Italians. O sole mio and all that. The men are always playing with their . . . things.'

'What about the English? So awkward at sex.'

'I find that very sexy, the way the English are awkward at sex.'

'Why is the orgasm in England subject to police surveillance?'

'The French talk a lot during sex.'

'And the Americans read a lot. Sexually, Americans will try anything – so long as they've read it in a magazine first.'

'Has anyone had a Japanese?'

'Oooo – I wonder what a Japanese is like to have.'

'Very polite, very unworried, apparently. Sounds really excellent.'

'I hear the Koreans are the sexiest people in the east.'

'I read a Japanese short story with the title *He Followed His Friend into the Other World, after Torturing Him to Death.* That suggests something, I think, about the Japanese.'

'I hate Japanese food. It's like eating little ideas. And no flavour.'

'I feel the French are still interested in flavour.'

'Bloody rude the French.'

'I was mugged on the Riviera.'

'So was I!'

'*Deeply* boring that whole thing. But I wasn't frightened in New York.'

'The place I was frightened was Glasgow on a Saturday night.'

'The Scotch are rough – which brings us to the Roman Empire thing again.'

'What about English football hooligans?'

'I go to football a fair bit and the only time I saw any unpleasantness was in Barcelona. An all-Spanish crowd.'

'Very unpredictable the Spanish. A very morose lot.'

'Like the Greeks.'

'Yes, the Greeks have gone right off since Alexander the Great.'

27

'The Portuguese are *much* nicer than the Spanish.'

'Yes, but stupider – didn't you find that?'

'For thickness the Irish still take a lot of beating.'

'That's what Germans say about Poles.'

'And Poles say about Russians.'

'God, the Russians – is there hope there?'

'I think we're all terribly terribly unfair about the Russians.'

'You see, the thing about the Irish is that they'd rather be polite than tell the truth.'

'Just like the Indians – the Indians of India, that is.'

'Oh *just* like the Indians of India – spot on – I was in India.'

'I didn't know you were in India. I thought you were in Africa.'

'Ya, I *was* in Africa for a bit. And it's true what they say about black men. Enormous dongs, some of em.'

'But such happy, simple people, always smiling, always dancing.'

'Always fucking. Endless children. And who has to pay? The tax-payer. We have to pay to feed them, to educate them, to support them on the dole, and when they start mugging we have to pay to keep them in prison.'

'My niece married a black. But they got divorced.'

'I've just heard that a niece of mine has married a traffic warden.'

'I've never met anyone related to a traffic warden before.'

'The French are terrible drivers.'

'No, they're not. They're fast, very aware and liberated on the roads.'

'They're very liberated everywhere on the Continent. Have you noticed how free they are with themselves?'

'It's from having great armies marching backwards and forwards across you all the time.'

'It's a fallacy they're liberated over there. If you were a peasant girl in Italy with Mama, Papa, the Church and the Mafia all breathing down your neck I don't think you'd feel very liberated.'

'The European boys consider the English girls the easiest to sleep with.'

'Oh, no . . .'

'The problem with the French is they can't bear to be laughed at – so they never realize when they're being ridiculous.'

'You've hit something frightfully true there.'

'We're off to France next week to stay with the Smiths at Cap d'Antibes.'

'Oh, I'm madly jealous.'

'We're off too next week – to Italy.'

'I prefer Italy.'

'Do you? We prefer France.'

'I absolutely *loathed* China.'

Lord Flamingfield, confined by his wheelchair to the ground floor and irritated because he felt more significant conversation to be going on overhead, blurted out to nobody 'Who's that bloody fool talking to Margot?' It was James Thorne, the philosopher, who was saying 'Is the old boy a war victim?' Lord Flamingfield liked people to believe this – but it was in fact bicycling in Kent, hit by a car coming round the corner. He stood up once a year, at the Christmas Dinner in the hall at Risingtower, to toast the Royal Family. He could maintain it for 15 seconds, supporting himself with his hands on the table, before flopping back into the 'chariot' as he called it. The Earl developed a tendency to feel up ladies' skirts in public places such as shop queues. In the chariot he was well-placed to do so. They never prosecute a war wound. Loudly proclaiming 'What a shower! What a bloody bunch!', he sped towards a source of champagne where the presiding noise was James Thorne.

'My book isn't published until next week,' said Thorne. 'Margot got the date wrong. It's called *Discourse on Pure Ridicule*.'

'I haven't quite finished your previous one,' said Lord Shropshire, chairman of the Dockland Development Board.

'Don't bother. It's out of date,' said Thorne philosophically.

'Oh, all right, thanks.'

The Earls of Shropshire and Flamingfield were good friends, bonded by secrets. Shropshire knew all about Flamingfield's bicycling accident. Flamingfield knew Shropshire only had one ball – he'd felt it at school. ('Good God, Shropshire, you've only got one ball!' 'Sh, not so loud, Flamingfield.') Sometimes, late at night beside the fire, after a few drinks, Shropshire would mutter 'I wish I had the pair . . . ' To compensate, his wife produced twins, 2 boys, Tristram and Dominic, and in due course 4 balls popped down, 1!2!3!4!

Philosopher Thorne turned to the Countess of Shropshire who was in trade, the rag trade, and said 'You see, modern man doesn't know who he is and therefore can easily be persuaded that he's some-one else.'

'Ugh . . . ' glugged Joan Shropshire – she was easily freaked.

'That's unfair, James,' said Margot.

'Is it unfair? Is it, Margot? Do you *really* think so? Listen! Danger is man's natural condition. If you remove danger from life – which is what has happened in the modern state – then man loses his momen-tum, his definition.'

'I think the nuclear bomb is danger enough for anyone,' said Lord Flamingfield. Lady Shropshire clutched frantically at the air while Flamingfield went on 'I think Thorne, it's more true to say man is designed for movement.'

'Poof!' announced Thorne and screwed up his nose. But because he was an honest philosopher he added 'I'll think about it, and get back to you, Mr Flamingfield.'

'And what do you think, Mr Manners?'

'Me? What do I think? I'll have to think about . . . what I think.'

They laughed and Guy realized he had made an amusing remark and felt for the first time that day a tiny pod of pleasure burst some-where inside him.

Margot said 'Right, all go upstairs and make room down here.' Flamingfield wheeled off in the chariot. She thought – Oh God, first faux pas of the evening. She took Guy's arm. 'Let's get some air. My head's spinning already. Trust the sodding publishers to get the date of his stupid book wrong! . . Where's my present, Guy?'

'Shit, I forgot.'

'What's the matter?' she asked as they wafted onto the balmy ter-race.

'Nothing's the matter.'

'I'm worried about you. You're tight as a drum. Look, you mustn't examine everything too closely. Or things start to fall apart. You lose the drift of life, its meaning.'

'Sure, Margot.'

'Do you know, I think we only start to grow up when we begin to realize just how damn stupid we are. Remember Penang?'

'Sure, Margot.'

'Oh you're impossible!'

But Guy's amusing remark had been a tonic for him – he didn't feel like making profound conversation about the meaning of life – that is exactly what he did *not* feel like.

'Charles Robinson's not coming to-night,' she said. 'He's meeting someone.'

'When did you speak to him?'

'A couple of days ago.'

'Well, I've got an amazing surprise for *you*. Charles has disappeared. This afternoon. And he swiped the Nineveh Codex on his way out of the office.'

'Good heavens, how very intriguing.'

'It's more than intriguing, Margot. It's a national treasure. He'll go to prison.'

'I mean intriguing in the sense of, well, intriguing. They haven't translated it fully or they've translated it but don't understand or—'

'I hear it's all about black magic, death, levitation, and unnatural vice,' said Lord Flamingfield who had rolled up silently behind them on rubber tyres. To-night's chariot was the electric chair, very quiet, for town and evening wear. The Earl was followed by Philosopher Thorne who had found Flamingfield's lack of respect for his, Thorne's, opinions singularly refreshing.

'Really?' leered Margot at the Earl – she adored anything like mysticism or weird intercourse and liked to cultivate a reputation for being enigmatic, when she remembered, to offset the cliché of riches. 'And did you know, Flamey, that Charles Robinson has disappeared with it?'

'Yes!' said the Earl, leaning forward in his chair. 'Henry spoke to me this evening. They'd been on to him to find out whether Robinson had gone up to Risingtower. Did you know Robinson particularly, Margot?'

'In a way, yes . . . in a way, no,' she replied.

– Jesus, thought Guy, here's the enigmatic bit coming out.

'And what does that mean, Margot?' enquired Thorne, curving forward with interest.

'As Voltaire wrote, James, le secret d'ennuyer est le tout dire,' said Margot and arched an eyebrow so extremely that she seemed to be suffering from neuralgia.

'Of what Voltaire wrote,' said Thorne, 'about 15 million words

31

have come down to us. Why you should pick on those I can't imagine. It's as useless as trying to support an argument with the Bible.'

– Oh *fuck* off, she thought.

'I'm going up to visit Henry soon,' said Guy.

'The boy needs more company,' said Flamingfield, a sweet look of concern seeping into his eau de nil eyes beneath twiggy grey eyebrows. 'He stays for hours in his room looking at a big map of the world. He's started to dance in front of mirrors. If it wasn't for his radio transmitter he'd hardly talk to a soul.'

Flashback: Lord Flamingfield, in his study answering a letter from the Society Against Premature Burial – 'Regrettably, I must decline your unusual suggestion . . . ' – had been disturbed by a thumping noise and went off to investigate. He wheeled into one of the collapsing drawing-rooms and said 'What's that ghastly row, Henry?'

'It's reggae, Pop.'

'Well, turn it up – let's hear it then.'

The Viscount turned it up loud and a rare collection of glass excavated from Pompeii and Santorini began to rattle horribly in a cabinet. The Earl cocked his head for a minute then said 'Rubbish! Shut it off, it's going the whole length of the house.'

'You have to move to it, Pop, to understand it.' And Henry, who was extraordinarily long and thin, made curious serpentlike movements in front of a cracked Chippendale mirror and was gone in the motion. Ta boom . . . ta ta boom . . . ta boom . . . A tear came into Lord Flamingfield's eye and he pushed himself out onto the terrace and vanished into the afternoon.

Blond bananas 'n' cream English charm smooth Adam Shatner, who wheeled and dealed among the rich, who often had cash to throw around though not *deep* cash, was not invited but came all the same. He would have been good on the Stock Exchange had he not despised his colleagues as pathetically limited; he would have been good in Advertising (where he went next) had he not regarded that whole crowd as unutterably common. He only felt interested among people much richer or more dangerous than himself.

'. . . Mah . . . goh . . . ' His approach was always unemphatic – nothing strident or specific which might cause a line to be drawn between himself and the opposite number.

'Mr Shatner, how is the world of coin?'

'I'm going to Brazil in a few weeks.'

Margot, who could not resist expressing her familiarity with the personalities of all continents, touched her glossy black chignon and said 'Give my love to Michael Horrabin if you see him.'

'Michael—?'

'Sir Michael Horrabin. Our man in Brasilia. But he's mostly in Rio.'

Adam made a mental note. Call on the British Ambassador and say Lady Ingot, no, Margot Ingot had told him to drop in. Already things were beginning to adhere to this Brazilian idea. Perhaps he'd go after all. Perhaps he'd arrange to meet that American guy there, someone called Beau Bute who'd phoned him out of the blue about a deal. How did this stranger Bute get his phone number? How did the American know that Shatner was dossing for the moment at Venetia Vane-Tempest-Wormold's place? Adam shifted lazily on down the room, silencing such questions, looking for openings.

Guy was initially attracted to Margot because her money smashed right into and pulverized such statements as bills produce anxiety, let's go to Penang for the week-end is a silly idea, 'caviar at the Connaught' is only 4 words. Flying to Penang, just for the week-end, had been amazing, just amazing . . . They'd met at the London flat of whacky American socialite Gloria van der Pumpernickel and taken it from there. In fact they'd grown very close until Guy met Kate, discovered what real closeness was, and ended it with Margot.

'Oh I see, a man of principle, can't have 2 women in his life at the same time,' said Margot playing with a platinum golf ball suspended on a hook through her ear.

'Not principle, Margot. Principles have nothing whatsoever to do with personal relationships.'

'I don't like Kate much but I do like you so it hurts. Are you going to marry her? I wish you would. It'd get you out of the way.' Margot lay back on the pillow and breathed deeply. 'Do you mind pouring?

I feel a bit – you know . . . ' They were doing what they often did, spending tea-time in bed.

Later she said 'I get horrid withdrawal symptoms from being in love. Oh well, piss off then. Let's get on with it . . . '

After he'd gone, she went to the little cream and pink bedside cabinet where she kept her Vitamin B_{12} shots. The B shots she pushed aside and lifted out a silver statuette of the Virgin Mary 6" high. She contemplated the figure for a long while.

– You poor cow, she thought, what have they done to you, Mary? Those horrible brutes depriving you of your womanhood . . .

Then she snapped back the silver head and poured onto the glass top to the cabinet a powder of 1 part amphetamine and 3 parts morphine, a mixture to which she had recourse on very special occasions.

Guy thought – I'm missing Kate at this thing – I don't know why I miss her – It's not my head or my heart that's missing her – It's an absence that hits the body directly, by-passing even such conscious functions as the will, romantic sentiment, or desire. Well, sometimes it is simply desire. Sometimes when she isn't there and enters my head, I get an erection like a solid piece of wood, zip! up it goes . . . Is this love? And sometimes I'm not thinking of anything like that, I'm absorbed in a task, and zip! up it goes – and then she enters my head. Is this love? And sometimes walking through the streets of London, I think of her, she isn't there – a panic comes over me. Is this the body demanding the presence of the other? And when I'm with her, it doesn't matter if we're fighting or contented or whatever – it feels right. It may feel bad, but it feels right. And when she isn't there, whether I'm up in an aeroplane or in the bath or in a hell of a good mood – it feels wrong. Is this love? Love before was always a constant irritation of the nerves, being insomniac, penniless, hung over. But now, although I feel all of that, basically I just feel . . . . . odd.

'This is a wonderful party,' said Señor Sergio del Fontana y Banjo.

'Oh, Ambassador,' said Margot, 'let me introduce you to somebody you'll love – a revolutionary poet!'

The revolutionary poet, Rudolfo da Silva, was in touch with everything that slid and scurried in grass and jungle in Latin America. He wore a beautiful dove-grey suit with a white shirt and had raven black shoulder length curls and looked like a very successful male model.

'Hullo, Sergio,' said Rudolfo.

'Don't Sergio me,' said Sergio, stretching every inch of his short height on high heels disguised by low-cut trousers. Da Silva had been at university with Sergio's daughter and was the reason the girl started chewing rugs and had to be put on tranquillizers for a term. The affair was over, but Sergio could not forgive. Not forgiving – it gave him something to do. The diplomatic life was so dull. Latin America was eventful – but dull. The women were slow and clinging and came, if at all, with an inexorable passionate orgasm that flowed on and on and on in curves and whorls and volutes of intrigue and desire for years and years. He had heard of lightning love, had yearned for the refreshment and splash of it. But always his liaisons had been: the slow build-up – the burgeoning emotion – then the breaking wave of passion – the fighting – more passion – that was perhaps the first year – then the slow slow wind-out – years of assault, recrimination, desperate whispers, sudden loud abuse at cocktail parties – why did Love have to be so serious? The dark furry vagina with the smell of decaying flowers – why did it always ruin one's plans? He'd rather given up on Love and instead went round not forgiving people various things. Nancy Canvas had been talking to the revolutionary poet and Sergio didn't forgive her her cough. She was pulling now the arm of a fair-haired man with a furrowed brow, doing her 'I'm Nancy Canvas/ Who are you?'

'Don't pull me like that,' said Guy. 'I hate being pulled.'

'You look as though you need a holiday from your hates. We have a house in Florida. It's on the beach. Go and stay in it.'

'Amazing. Thanks. You're quick.'

'Yeah, well, we'll all be dead next week, won't we?'

'I love the beach,' said Guy. 'It's so mindless, so peaceful.'

'It's mindless just about everywhere in Florida,' said Nancy. She had inherited a chunk of Ohio and come with it to Europe. She always felt braver, naughtier, more free, more consequential in Europe.

'Good,' said Guy. She stared at him with enormous, incredulous, watery thyroid eyes, coughed a great lungful of cigarette phlegm up into her upper throat, loosened it with another rolling cough, then swallowed it. The multiple pouches under each eye quivered as she spoke. Looking at her, Guy, who was already feeling pretty foul, felt much worse and steadied himself by staring at a small waterfall of diamonds pinned to the left side of Nancy's chest – her breasts had no separate definition and appeared to join up in one all-purpose wobbliness of bosom.

'You can bring someone if you like,' she said. 'I'm not after your dicky. You better tell me your name. Have you met the Spanish Ambassador?'

'Actually,' said Señor del Fontana y Banjo when Nancy had left them to it, which she immediately had done, 'I'm not the Spanish Ambassador. I am,' he said with a curl of his red fleshy lip beneath the black moustache, 'not even the Mexican Ambassador. What am I? I'm the Mexican stop-gap. They won't go ahead with accreditation in case they want to yank me back without fuss. They are looking for a new man, perhaps someone more corruptible.' He did a little shuffling fandango on his heels and touched Guy's arm. 'But this posting, it was a chance to get away. You've no idea – Mexico City can be so – full. Ah, thank-you.' Señor del Fontana y Banjo lightly lifted a glass from a tray of champagne that was cruising past on a white glove. 'You don't see so many white gloves any more. Black gloves have become much more common. And what do you do, Mr Manners?'

Kate, back at the flat, was depressed – Why am I so depressed for God's sake? . . . I feel so bad, so depressed . . . I'll watch television.

It was a programme about how to combat depression. It made Kate even more depressed to feel that she was to be associated with these crappy losers on the box. To be linked to them, through the great global community of the depressed, was worse than depressing, it was humiliating, sickening – oh God yes! she felt sick . . . sick . . . she was going to be sick . . . this was much better than feeling depressed because feeling sick was tangible and precise.

'Can this be the beginning of an upturn?' she enquired of the meaningless environment and in doing so she retriggered self-obsession – and began another descent, going down helplessly, going down as in a lift which you enter at the ground floor and discover that it goes down, down . . . down into dingy regions, descends past unhappiness, past claustrophobia, past anxiety, past even fear in the end because endless fear is intolerable, descends into the shapeless fathomless suffocating pit of nothingness . . . She wasn't that bad, not to-night anyway. To-night she was depressed as if 2 unpleasant-smelling hands were pressing on her eyes blotting out too much of the information she required to navigate successfully through ordinary life. Drink made it worse, drugs made it worse, and sex – sex with Guy at least – because briefly it made it better – made it biliously churningly worse, as of a beautiful possibility snatched away again.

Kate sat in the kitchen drinking coffee and smoking cigarettes – this of course made it worse. Inside she was all cut up with razorblades, half-ideas swooping at her and through her at jagged angles, but the pain of it all had been blunted by depression into a generalized foggy yuk, forever impending, forever preventing. Oh, the bliss of again feeling the clear sharp line of pain! The bliss of being again capable of focusing on an objective! She couldn't remember the last time she'd really focused on an objective. Happiness – what is happiness? Happiness is clarity, that is all . . . Kate wanted to cry but she couldn't. A hot wetness in the eyes was the best she could manage.

She checked the fish under the grill. It was revolting; curled up, burnt, and staring at her.

– This is rock bottom, she thought.

Then another thought occurred to her – The one good thing about getting to rock bottom is that something *else* has got to happen.

Another thought occurred to her – Like the rock starts to crumble?

Fear went through her in a horrible wave. She broke out in a cold sweat. She felt isolated and greatly agitated. But the fear contained adrenalin. The fog cleared. And in absolute terror she said 'I must go to the party!'

Rory McLulu, the McLulu of Tack and Fan, quite stupid-looking with his big nose and wet mouth, but unexpectedly tough in the face of life's dirty bucketful, had just been turned down as prospective Conservative Party candidate for South Banff, something which had never happened in his family before. He'd rung up his good friend Kate and splattered down the phone to her – it helped. The McLulu's people: after trying for generations to exact a decent existence from 8000 acres of rock in South Banff, they threw in the towel, sold to Americans, and moved to the South of France to think about what to do next. While thinking, maybe because of it, Rory's father had died, leaving his son what was ostentatiously described as 'everything': several old sticks of furniture and a mortgaged farmhouse in the Massif des Maures. (There was also an illegitimate son living in Vauxhall attending art college but he does not participate in these events.) Rory, stuck for a prospect, drove a motor car all the way back to South Banff – but had no luck. Rejection. An unwanted male. To-night the McLulu of Tack and Fan was feeling deeply wounded, very randy, disagreeably political and flushed with drink, all of this emphasized by his red hair sticking up in a brush.

'As for Communism, Ambassador,' said the McLulu through his wet nose and big mouth, 'it strikes me as very odd indeed that a system ostensibly based on comradeship should ban fraternizing.'

'Isn't it odd,' said Dmitri Tcherenkov.

'I suppose there's no explanation for it, Ambassador.'

'There are various explanations. And I'm not the Ambassador, just a miserable attaché at the Russian Embassy,' said Dmitri with a sigh. He was enjoying his spell in Britain and, as his use of the word 'miserable' suggests, had picked up on the local style of humour to develop a vein of irony he already possessed. 'Why has Russia always been afraid?' he continued. 'Boxed away in Northern Asia – who wants to go there? More to the point – who wants to stay there?'

'Can I quote you on that?' said Rory, taken aback by this reply. Coming from South Banff he had a tendency to feel boxed away himself.

'I'll deny it. I'm drunk.' Dmitri was practised at denial. For example, he had the best collection of Elvis Presley records in Russia and was always denying that.

'I met one of your fellows from the Russian Trade Delegation. He wasn't at all like you,' said Rory. 'He had very short hair and very thick legs.'

'Sounds like one of our intellectuals,' said Dmitri.

'Or was it thick head and short legs? He was in charge of wooden dolls and lacquer boxes, export of, but he knew a lot about weaponry, almost as much as my old man.'

Tcherenkov tried to glide away but the McLulu glided after him. The pair of them went gliding about the pillared room between groups of people. 'Do you like guns?' persisted Rory as they glided past the Venetian window opening into the garden. 'Did you know that the Echo of Simonetta near Milan will echo a pistol shot 30 times? I read it somewhere.'

'Guns leave me cold,' said Dmitri, stepping out onto the terrace.

'You're a knives man, are you? Quite like knives myself.'

Dmitri went down a few steps.

'Or is it balconies? Do you push people off balconies?' asked Rory, running a damp hand through his feverish red hair.

'Everybody does that, you fool,' rounded Dmitri. 'So personally I never go *near* a balcony.' He ventured a few paces irritably onto the lawn.

'Oh I see! It's poison!' blurted Rory, bubbles of disgust at the corners of his mouth. 'Blow darts, nasty little capsules, mercury in the orange, jabbing umbrellas!'

'If you must know, you Great British moron,' said Dmitri turning quickly round and speaking furiously under his breath, 'I specialize in microwaves! And if you don't, as you say, fuck off, I'll fry your fucking brains inside your skull – if it contains any – with this simple piece here.' He pulled out what normally passed as a tortoise-shell cigarette lighter and jammed it under Rory's palpitating nose.

'You people make me sick,' Rory murmured. He spotted the Duchess of Dollar and Stirling looking sulky and skinny in the open window and went in to her.

Dmitri sat on the steps for a while, reflecting. He breathed in the fragile perfumes of the garden and he released vapours of melancholy . . . O Melancholy! O Curse of the Slavs! Always so far from the Joyous Mediterranean! . . . A helicopter flapped above in the warmness of the night, flashing its lights and occasionally signalling with laser beams to others of its kind. Then it flapped away.

The Rt Hon. Timothy Quaintance, the Minister of Technology,

middle-aged, good-looking, with plenty of straight brown hair boyishly combed over to one side in a bang which was an essential part of his good-egg-6th-form prefect act, had recently arrived – minus Mrs Quaintance who was tying up lupins in Hampshire as usual.

'Hullo, Timothy, how are you?' asked Lord Shropshire.

'I'm afraid, Dingle, that's strictly confidential.'

They both laughed.

'There's Willywonky over there,' said Dingle. 'If I see any more earls I shall suspect a plot to make me invisible. The Willywonkies are very poor. Irish. They've been very poor ever since the 18th century.'

'It reminds me of that story,' said the Rt Hon. Timothy. 'Once upon a time there was a very poor family. The father was poor. The mother was poor. The 2 children were poor. Even the butler was poor.'

They both laughed, but Shropshire thought – These modern politicians, so heartless – Not quite out of the right drawer – Quaintance cannot be relied on.

Lord Willywonky, drunk, complained to the nearest ear 'But they want me to wear silver clothes and I don't want to wear silver clothes.'

'The BBC's just given him his own chat show,' said the Rt Hon. Timothy. 'The Earl of Willywonky Show.'

'Really?' said Shropshire who felt piqued that the show had not been offered to him first – not that it was remotely his line, but whenever he heard of the success of any of his contemporaries he always registered a soft imprecise twinge of resentment. 'My son Dominic's just been posted to Ireland. I didn't want him to go in the army but it was that or the dole,' he said to change the subject.

The discomfort of Guy's mind resolved into 2 options:

     1) I go
     2) I stay

'Perhaps I'll give Kate a ring and arrange to meet her at the Fountain of Youth,' he remarked to Adam Shatner.

– Perhaps I'll ask Sophie instead, he thought.

– . . . Or Anthea, he thought.
– Perhaps I'll go there now – alone, he thought.
– Perhaps I'll stay for a bit, he thought.

A jam at the bottom of the stairs.

'I wish you'd stop seeing my daughter. One abortion was enough,' said Violet Cartridge as, trying to get up to the first floor, she crashed with a young Cockney in black boots called Billy – he looked like a boy who'd stroke frogs to the point of orgasm. Billy had met Emma Cartridge with Sophie Shatner in the dole queue.

'I have stopped,' he said.

'He's going out with me,' said Anthea van den Clack but Violet had already gone up and away. Anthea's hair had been hacked out of shape, tied up in knots, hacked again, glued and sprayed prune, and she wore one breast exposed. 'Billy just had my knickers down in the loo,' she said to Adam, and Billy muttered 'She's very rich, Sarf African. Diamonds.'

'I heard that, you shit,' said Anthea, punching him quite hard. 'We're not, we're Dutch. Oh look, there's Kate over there. Is she still with Guy?'

'They're terribly in love,' said Adam. 'It was love at first fuck. Very passionate . . . but passion's no basis for a relationship.'

'I get worried about Henry,' said Lord Flamingfield to Lord Shropshire in the hall, fingering the Flamingfield wart on his brow. Henry, the first Flamingfield heir in 7 generations with a wartless brow. What could it mean?

Flamingfield had married again very quickly after Rapunzel's death, then divorced very quickly.

Viz:- 'Henry, your stepmother and I are getting a divorce.'

At the time, Henry had been in that funny stage just after leaving school, a stage he'd remained in ever since, and was having lunch with his father in the spidery gothick decrepitude of the dining-room. There was a large damp patch on the ceiling in the shape of Africa. Every now and again a drop of water fell from near the Cape of Good Hope.

41

Henry was thinking – Delicious decay – Dame Nature reasserting herself – Decadence is the return to nature – Soon there will be plants on the walls, vines among the pillars, goblins in the hall . . .

'The word stepmother's a bit of an exaggeration, isn't it, Pop?'

'Well, we are. Kitty means no harm but – these Puccini records before lunch! I can't take that din any more! . . . At the moment I don't see myself marrying again, but that might change. Don't you want to get married, Henry?'

'Of course I don't.'

'Don't you want children?'

'Oh God no,' drawled Henry at his most peevishly, expiringly epicene. 'Ugh, the monotony of procreation, the sheer tedium of making it all . . . happen again.'

'But I want an heir,' said Lord Flamingfield curtly. A drop went plop into the zinc bucket and he blinked.

'You've got an heir. Me.'

'I mean after you.'

'After me there's old what's-his-name in Devon.'

'I mean a real heir, direct male line and all that. You can't beat it for holding things together.'

'So let things fall apart, float about in the air for a generation or so.'

'Next thing you'll give up the title, I know it.'

'No. Responsibility is what bores me. I like the title. And – which is far more important – the bank likes the title.'

'Titles are fun, aren't they, Henry? Even life peerages can be fun – look at Poppy Treasure dancing round the Riviera with his. Can't understand why some chaps refuse to accept em, these ex-prime ministers and so on.'

'Didn't Winston Churchill refuse the title Duke of London?'

'I'm not surprised,' chortled Lord Flamingfield. 'That one sounds like a pub.'

'Oh Pop, they all sound like pubs!'

'I'll drink to that, Henry! Fetch up another claret!'

Kate saw Guy at the far end of the saloon on the first floor.

– He's looking wretched, she thought and this made her feel better.

– Let him come up to me first, she thought.

'Rory, I wish you wouldn't wear those dreadful pinstripe suits,' she said. Rory swallowed. 'And that hideous shirt. Is it made out of a deckchair? God, I hate stripes.' Rory swallowed again and wiped his mouth. He felt both insulted and titillated. He'd noticed Guy in the distance, looking cool and moody as usual, looking interesting as usual. 'This is Mary Yodel,' Kate went on, 'who's Fred Yodel's wife and she's writing her first novel.'

Mary went bright red under her orange face powder and said 'I've just begun it and it's very . . . ' Rory, keen to have someone else put on the spot, pressed her. Mrs Yodel giggled nervously. Sweat broke out through the face powder. The sweat would later dry, turning the powder into flakes. 'It's very passionate, it's about this brief wild romance in the Caribbean during a hurricane. It's called *Passing Wind*.'

Margot went out to the front porch to chat to the 2 policemen posted there. 'All quiet on the western front?' she asked, with a small jocular movement of her head. They smiled. She smiled. A warm breeze stirred in the plane trees. The perfume of honeysuckle, coming from somewhere, drifted across her face like a question.

– Policemen are so enormous these days, she thought on her way back in – Or perhaps it's me, perhaps I'm shrinking.

The Chief Superintendent was inside as one of the guests, an extra precaution. 'I'm turning a blind eye to some of the things I'm seeing to-night, Lady Ingot,' he said. 'There are several young people here clearly on drugs. And if I'm not mistaken 2 males have just had a relationship in one of your bedrooms which, though the door was locked, constitutes for their purposes a public place and is therefore prosecutable.'

'Don't worry so much about vice, Sam. Concentrate on crime.'

'If we've got to have a poor Britain, Lady Ingot, at least let's make it a clean Britain.' Margot felt a sense of unease. 'Don't worry, I'm turning a blind eye this once, but it's not my fault if some of my juniors pick up a few drunken drivers later on. Perhaps you'd warn the, er, obvious cases.'

'Sam, you're such a bear,' said Margot, laying her hand a trifle

43

twitchily on the Superintendent's shirtfront, 'but I tell you what – I'd be very grateful if you'd go and break up that fight over there between the Duchess of Dollar and Stirling and her husband. She's started on the glasses.'

A group of young men, following an ancient custom of the island, had all at once dropped their trousers and pushed their bare bottoms in the direction of the Duchess. The Duke burst into laughter, declaring it a fine display of what England had to offer, namely a row of arseholes – he was of course Scottish. She, Brenda Lagonda from Florida, was under the romantic misapprehension that the Duke should have defended her honour, and she'd hit him. Being a duke he didn't have the inhibitions of the lower ranks and he'd sloshed her back. She'd hit him back. It was still going on, slosh-slap-slap-slosh-boo-scream-slosh. Then Brenda had started on the glasses.

Dick Tring, who loved a good fight, was laughing under an arch while Violet Cartridge said to Kate 'This is Dick Tring, my favourite multimillionaire.'

'I expect its video and computers and stuff,' said Kate.

'That's right, Kate,' replied Dick beamishly.

'It's everything, dear,' said Vi conspiratorially. 'Electronics, insurance, property, oil, games, lots of games.'

'Mrs Cartridge, don't embarrass me,' said a grinning Dick. 'You know how it is, Kate, how everything involves everything else sooner or later. I started out with nothing and before I knew what'd happened I was being hit with philanthropy.'

'He gives so much away,' said Mrs Cartridge in a loud whisper. 'It must be deeply rewarding to do that.'

Tring's original winner was Toto Jelly. Manufactured from a secret formula, he had made an enormous fortune from it, especially in the Third World: Toto Jelly: Can do anything: Moisturizer, hair conditioner, suncream, inhalant chest rub, all-purpose cooking oil, temporary adhesive, great in the mornings on toast or at night as an anal lubricant: Go, go with Toto! Then Dick had made another small fortune out of an Arab compass that always points to Mecca.

The Rt Hon. Timothy Quaintance came up and said 'Dick, we must have lunch. And soon.' There was a brusqueness in the Minister's tone and since he was looking Tring right between the eyes, the beam momentarily went out on the millionaire's face. Then the Rt Hon. Timothy noticed Kate and stared at her in a milkier manner.

44

'Professor Yudkin tells us,' interposed Violet Cartridge, 'that to dispose of a good business lunch you must play squash for 8 hours.'

The Rt Hon. Timothy gave her the look of death. 'Let's go and get some food, Dick,' he said.

'I could do with some food too,' said Kate brightly. 'Have you noticed how all these caviar nibbles make everyone's breath stink of fish?'

'Actually, Dick, I was hoping to have a word with you in private,' said the Rt Hon. Timothy and turned a huge smile onto Kate which was like the slam of a hand in her face.

Through groups of extremely dressed people, Guy saw Kate. She wore a long close gown in gas blue silk. She looked like a blue staircase. She was talking to Rory with animated facial expressions which looked rather silly like television with the sound turned off. Kate was overdoing the animation – obviously she felt like shit inside. She's talking to Rory already. Why didn't she come up and say hi first? Rory's looking very smart and top-hole and – integrated . . .

Dreadful things were taking place in Guy's chest. Anger and tears battled there, bottled there. But this other thing, this horrible THING which gripped him hotly and gave off powerful shudders of love and hate and violence, this thing which made him feel dirty and choked and frantic, this grotesque thing which swooped down from nowhere and took him over like a virus, this thing called jealousy. . .

'Aren't you Dmitri Tcherenkov? I'm Sergio del Fontana y Banjo. We met at that dreadful party at the Cuban Embassy last month. Or was it at that Libyan party?'

'I didn't go to that – it was the day of the Elvis Presley auction at Sotheby's,' said Dmitri. 'Was it worse, the Libyan party?'

'All the women wore black elastoplast over their mouths. It's the law in some of those countries now.'

'You're the Mexican, er, chappie, aren't you?' continued Dmitri. 'The women of Mexico City, I recall, have developed magnificent chests from breathing at a high altitude. Mexico has the prettiest policewomen in the world. Do you know Moscow? No? I hardly know it either, though I've often lived there. The police – very ugly. Take my word for it.' Dmitri Tcherenkov in early middle-age had a manner both open and world weary. His face, fine-looking in the severe Russian way, with just a breath of the Orient about the eyes, had been softened and made agreeable by a fatigue that was wry rather than limp. He was not without a certain primitive vanity and was always fiddling with the arrangement of his hair which had been carefully trained over a hateful bald gap on the crown of his head. But this did not convey an impression of nervousness. His irreverent attitude to most things, including Russian things, and general sense of lacking ulterior motive, relaxed others and sometimes inspired useful confidences. His air of disillusionment made him appear intelligent.

'Got anything to swop?' asked Sergio.

'You're very bold, Mr Banjo – which is laudable – but swopping isn't my department. I did it once, received a roll of microfilm from a Cambridge graduate without knowing what it contained. This took place in the Gentleman's Lavatory at the Wallace Collection. And that's about the extent of my trading experience. Of course, one is here to observe the English way of life and, insofar as one is able, describe that remarkable phenomenon to the boys back home. Do you know it?' asked Dmitri with his sweet weary smile.

'I know English life a leetle . . . '

'No, the Gents at the Wallace Collection. It's quite wonderful. Magnificent tiles, very colourful. It's like,' and Dmitri searched for the right phrase, 'it's like pissing in a mosque.'

'Can you have dinner with me on Thursday?' said the Rt Hon. Timothy. It sounded like a command.

'No,' said Kate. 'Thursday's my self-defence class.'

'Cancel it.'

'Look, I might as well say it, I don't fancy dinner with you on Thursday or any other day.' Kate was feeling stronger, more centred, was glad she came.

'What?'

'I don't want to have dinner with—'

'Yes, yes, I heard what you said.' The Rt Hon. Timothy removed himself in a marked manner. It was such a problem being heterosexual in British politics, he thought – It was much safer to be impotent or even queer if you could make that look like impotence – Fucking little bitch . . . He didn't make love to his wife any more. That had ended after the second child – how could you screw the mother of your children? And in fact genuine desire for her had been killed stone dead by the very act of marriage – he'd spoken to a few chaps at the club about this and found the experience pretty common. Poor Shirley Quaintance, living out her days in the potting shed, tying up the lupins in Hampshire . . . Damn oh damn, why must I think of Shirley now? . . In the custard of the Rt Hon. Timothy's centrifugal affections, always the stoneless prune of sexual guilt! Mary Yodel, who had never taken any interest whatsoever in politics and didn't know who he was, said to the Minister 'Such a lovely crowd Margot's got in, a really lovely crowd.'

'Vomit puke chunder,' said Venetia Vane-Tempest-Wormold. 'Isn't that Ganglion Vapers?'

'Who?' asked the Rt Hon. Timothy, wondering if this girl would like to have dinner on Thursday. Thursday was the only day he could manage.

'Ganglion Fucking Vapers, the concert pianist,' said Venetia. 'Doesn't he look ultra sick. I'm going to talk to him.'

– Little bitch, thought Timothy.

The Greek concert pianist was rolling his hair around and saying to somebody's wife 'I love love, don't you?'

'You're so sick,' Venetia interposed swooningly, 'so – supersick.'

'Am I?' said Ganglion, somewhat deranged by this and interested. 'Do you love love too?'

'I detest love,' said Venetia pushing her chin under his chin and ogling him with her eyes. 'It brings out all my worst qualities. Deceit, paranoia, self-pity, jealousy, pettiness, grovelling – yeah grovelling – I hate grovelling! Love is for sadomasochists.'

'Yes, yes,' said Ganglion, excitedly popping his eyes, 'I love it like that too. Pain! Hurt! What do they know of love who only loving know? Pain is growth, pain is hope, pain is the future!'

47

Rory and Guy started fighting a bit then stopped.

Fran Coddle, the feminist radical, turned to a man in a dog collar (he was the Archbishop of the Indian Ocean) and said 'The Eucharist! Fucking cannibalism, mate! Fucking human sacrifice, mate! You? You're just a big fucking Aztec, that's what *you* are!'

The Archbishop, stunned, made a gallant attempt to keep his head above water by grasping at the straw of Einstein. He said 'Einstein thought the most, er, interesting question was: Did God have any choice in the creation of the Universe?'

'God so loved the world he gave his only begotten son blah blah,' continued Ms Coddle, sloshing her wine glass round in the air. 'God's got this big hang-up that love means death! I'm bloody glad I'm not God's son, that's all I can say.'

Brenda Dollar and Stirling came up sucking on a cigarette, wearing one breast exposed in the fashion of the time.

'You've got cigarette ash on your nipple, dearie,' said Ms Coddle. 'Do you know the bish ere? He's been resorting to Einstein.'

Brenda passed on without speaking. Religion depressed her.

'The only thing I have to say about God,' continued the feminist, 'is that with all these nuclear and biological weapons about, may God save us from strong men in power. I think it's a big step in the right direction that the Opposition Leader is changing his sex.'

'So do I,' said the Archbishop who didn't know his own mind.

'You agree!' said the feminist in fury. 'This is the liberal trap of repressive tolerance. Typical dirty establishment trick!' Then a dollop of brown stuff landed in her eye and both of them turned to watch Sophie and Billy smearing chocolate mousse down dove grey silk curtains.

'How terrifically sick!' wailed Venetia gaily.

Anthea van den Clack burst across their vision screaming 'No I haven't seen Charles Robinson! Would everybody stop asking me about Charles Robinson!' And she crumpled into a little weeping. Anthea had been wearing one breast exposed – now both were out in an excess of emotion.

'I met this Robinson once,' said Philosopher Thorne, 'when I had to visit the Museum in connection with an analysis I was making – it was in the old linguistic days – of the parallel texts on the Rosetta Stone. Though very helpful, he did strike me as having his chthonic side. But doesn't every man? Don't *you*, Mr Quaintance?'

'Ah . . . ' said the Rt Hon. Timothy and he slapped one of his cauterizing smiles over Thorne.

Thorne went on 'Professor Boggis of All Souls has indicated that devices like the Official Secrets Act are boy scout attempts to lend an aura of excitement and significance to otherwise utterly boring and inconsequential jobs. In my next book, *Secrecy*, I suggest however—'

Venetia ostentatiously patted her mouth in a simulated yawn-yawn and said 'Up my arse too.' Fran Coddle nodded violent agreement while the Archbishop mumbled something about Einstein – or was it Freud? – he couldn't quite recall.

'But will your next book give the man-in-the-street more of a chance?' enquired the Rt Hon. Timothy with a deep frown of synthetic concern.

'The Man-in-the-Street, Mr Average!' expostulated Thorne. 'Who is he? *What* is he? He is, I venture to declare, a nondescript mush streaked with prejudice!'

'Come now, you don't believe that,' protested the Rt Hon. Timothy.

'I don't. You're right. But *you* seem to, you certainly seem to, Mr Minister of Technology!' Thorne had suddenly developed his wild eye.

Glancing at them from afar, Rory McLulu thought – Intellectuals, politicians, and bishops make me sick – What did they ever give anybody? – Torture, concentration camps, inquisitions.

'Then again, you certainly don't, Minister of Technology,' said Thorne getting rigid in the neck, 'because the only things you *really* believe in are the techniques of control and manipulation. People are being beaten up in padded dungeons beneath Whitehall even as we speak! And the subtle movement from accusatory to inquisitorial methods in the treatment of minorities marks a retrogression in our society to a more superstitious, therefore more primitive phase.'

'Now, now,' said the Chief Superintendent, 'we may have lost our Empire but we haven't lost our sense of right and wrong. If we must have a poor Britain, at least let's make it a clean Britain.' Sweat on the Superintendent's chin gave off the odour of onions.

'Britain!' ridiculed Thorne. Saliva fell in strands from his writhing lips. 'Britain, an illusion merely! The internationalizing effect of technology, Minister, has turned all cultural distinctions into gim= micks for the tourist trade! To know and to plan are – ugh!' Philosopher Thorne, with his ideas splitting amoeba-like in endless ramifications, fell backwards into a chair, insensate.

'Is Thorne all right?' the Rt Hon. Timothy asked the Philosopher's wife when, considerately, he had tracked her down in the cathedral-like basement of the house discussing profiterole pastry with Mr Jean-Pierre Wilkinson.

'Has he passed out?' she asked, speaking through a thick slurry of confectioners' custard.

'Yes.'

'Yes, that's all right. I'll just come and get his wallet.'

Guy went up to Kate who was eating a large slice of gâteau as light and feathery as a cloud of baby's eyelashes. 'You look fantastic,' he said.

'I feel like death.' He looked at the gâteau. 'I always eat when I feel like death,' she said.

'I know,' he said. 'You look fantastic.'

'Shut up or I'll cry. Are we in love? I hate it.'

'Being in love is bloody hard work if you ask me,' he said, finishing off his drink and looking everywhere but at her. 'Um . . . can I get you another drink?'

'I'll be over there somewhere. I can't think of anything to say. Is there dancing?' she said.

'Sort of dancing. In Margot's gymnasium,' he said.

She was unhappy and restless. Her mood was all irony. She didn't mind being with Guy but she didn't feel like talking to him. The simplest remark carried an implication to something deeper, less pleasant, more hurtful. No matter what they talked of, it was always somehow a discussion about 'it'. Is there dancing? How mad it sounded. 'Aren't important people disgusting en masse,' she said.

'Anything's disgusting en masse,' said Guy.

Then Kate left the party with Rory McLulu. 'Meet us later at the Fountain,' she said.

50

'Fuck off,' said Guy.

When the lover goes away, the world drains of meaning and the mind loses focus, drifts in an acrid smog of tepid sulphuric vapours; tears jump unexpectedly into the eyes, quickly dry up; and the heart flaps like a bird with a broken wing irregularly about the floor. It makes sense to tie up the lover and lock the lover in a room until you return – but it is antisocial. People should give themselves wholly and freely to each other, but this seems to be extremely rare. One nearly always has to tie up the other, put a gag in the other mouth, plaster over it, until one returns. Love is such a problem.

'I don't believe in God,' said Venetia to the Archbishop.

'I do,' he replied, 'because life would be very boring for me if I didn't.'

At that moment a bomb exploded. *CCCRRRASH!!!!*

It was a large bomb and it exploded in the dining-room on the ground floor. The actual explosion seemed to take place in a tremendous silence, as if it had blasted a hole right through the phenomenal world of the senses. Everything went out of sync.

Margot the Hostess was framed in the Venetian window which opened onto the garden. She was frozen there in a silent scream, her lips pulled right back in a beastly baboon snarl. Her thin white arms were outstretched against the dark shape of the open window and the joints of her fingers were twisted like bright claws. This image seemed to shimmer in silence forever, until something at last began to move in the tableau. It was shit sliding down the legs of the hostess, sliding down below the hem of the black jewelled dress, sliding down treacly and orange. As if this were a signal, the ears were then deafened with noise and the eyes abruptly blinded by hot dust.

Many were killed, more were maimed. Ghastly black messes were plastered everywhere. Lots of ears were bleeding. The dining-room was destroyed and the explosion had ripped through part of the ceiling to the main saloon above. Dust and smoke filled the air. People span about hysterically like catherine wheels off their pins, screaming, shouting, crying, choking, whimpering . . .

51

Outside in Eaton Square all was quiet and normal for a bit. A hot brown moon hung in the navy blue sky. Nothing happened for a bit. The warm breeze stirred gently the leaves, and hidden honeysuckle squirted tiny rays of perfume into the night air. Cars shuttled back and forth in the distance as sets of traffic lights switched gay luminous colours. Over in Buckingham Palace the Sovereign's heart skipped a beat – but it seemed to be nothing.

The people were the first to arrive. A few individuals had already been hanging round the front door watching the guests come and go. Now a large pensive crowd began to be drawn instinctively and inexorably towards the site like cells towards a wound. Then the police came. Then the army and helicopters came immediately after. Followed at a greater interval by firemen. Followed by ambulances. Followed by newspaper reporters. Followed by television and radio. Followed by friends and relations. Followed by the foreign press.

Guy was shaking all over. That wasn't new in itself. But this was different. He didn't know he was shaking all over. He didn't know anything, except that he was lying on the floor conscious. Somebody passed him a cigarette.

'Take this . . . it'll ease you up . . . ' It was a heroin cigarette. It eased him up. Some more plaster crashed to the floor, sending up more clouds of dust. He took off his jacket, pulled his shirt out of his trousers, undid all the shirt buttons, and didn't do anything else . . . Far away in the distance, like a voice crackling on an old-fashioned radio, he heard Lord Flamingfield saying 'Don't move, anybody, unless you want to. Help is on the way, friends.' Though sounding immensely distant, the words were perfectly clear . . . People were stunned, weeping, confused. Brick and plaster continued to fall at irregular intervals. Who passed me that cigarette? Guy turned his head on the floor and saw Billy's face smudged with tears and carbon. Billy sat up and said 'I really want to get out of this place before it's cordoned off. I've got some stuff on me.'

'Give me another of those cigarettes, Billy. I'm going to find Kate. She left.' In the confusion Guy got away. He flowed along pavements. Eventually he stopped and found himself in the Fulham Road. He felt very whoozy and fell through the plate glass window of a car showroom, cutting himself all over. Some policemen arrived, kicked him with sullen expressions on their faces, threw him in the back of a van. He came to, in a cell. Someone had thrown a bucket of cold water over him, then gone away. There was a lavatory. He peed in it, then vomited into it a wavy ribbon of old booze. His throat burned and the veins burned in his eyes. With stomach cramps and sweating all over he slumped onto a prickly grey blanket. A high-watt ceiling light struck him like a hammer. His cuts had been crudely covered over, strips of sticky plaster laid straight onto them, with no lint. Later when they came to interrogate him on simple matters, they slowly pulled the plasters off the cuts and stuck some more back on. He screamed. 'Don't be such a baby. We're just assessing the damage.' He heard a heavy noise far away. It was himself hitting the pavement outside the police station. They didn't know he'd been at the bomb party. Just another drunk, they thought. They needed his cell for someone else. His money – oh God, where was it? Relief . . . They'd returned his money. Of course they'd returned his money, this was England. He feebly raised an arm and a taxi stopped. He got in and sank back into the luxury of its high padded haunches. As it purred off, he thought – Thank God I was no use to them, thank God I'm useless. And he took Billy's cigarette out of his shoe, lit it, and drew a long tape of opiated smoke into his lungs.

–3 –

The Disco

The Fountain of Youth was huge. A disused repair depot for the underground railway at the back of Waterloo Station had been turned into the most spectacular resort in London after midnight. You could arrive by land – or by water at the Festival Pier and take a stroll in chilly drizzle through the Jubilee Gardens (occasional stabbings), taking care not to get lost among the mighty glass/concrete palaces of art on the South Bank all settling jerkily together. These palaces were overgrown with ivy, surrounded by trees, and colourfully floodlit in unexpected ways. The whole had taken on a spectacular random beauty and now resembled a Mayan jungle city of the prehistoric future. The Fountain of Youth was just the other side of the South Bank and very successful. The art crowd went and so did the unemployed – these 2 groups go everywhere, being by nature extremely restless. The rich and famous went there to feel young or, if they were already young, in search of experience. At the Fountain nobody bothered the famous – so later in the night the famous would move on to somewhere more intimate and expensive, somewhere that made them feel famous again. The fashion and pop people went to display themselves in the latest modes, swop pills and keep-fit tips. The straight crowd went and sat at tables demanding waitress service. The bent crowd and the wild crowd went, circulating like a bloodstream round other groups which they would sometimes invade and dissolve. Even people who never went anywhere went there, though usually they didn't stay long. Mums and dads, metaphorically speaking, did not go there. The only rule on admissions was *No Animals* – a waitress had had her cheek ripped out by a cheetah at the opening night party – and *No Weapons*.

The reason for the Fountain's success was not its amazing space, lights, and music. It was not because this vast subterranean hangar, its great arches of brick and tile already covered with gantries, ladders, and catwalks, had recently acquired a swimming-pool of Olympic size lit with underwater laser lights. It wasn't the funicular railway which transported revellers across the roof in bright suspended carriages like Chinese lanterns. And it wasn't because it was cheap – because it wasn't. It was because – it was safe. No one was stabbed here. The police didn't raid it. The management kept it smooth. It sold more whisky, beer, and mineral water than any other establishment on the planet. Everyone was happy.

As Guy entered, the music was deafening and an enormous video screen was flashing up pink and turquoise images of malnutrition and despair in the Third World. He staggered up to a slowly rotating bar in the shape of a skull and asked for vodka. The girl with green hair behind the bar looked right through him.

'Vodka!' he yelled above noises. His cuts were stinging.

'Don't have to shout, I heard you the first time,' said the girl in a piercing tone. She was an expert lip-reader (as her great-grandmother had been in the Yorkshire cotton mill) and could eavesdrop as far as her eyes could see.

Overhead several naked people were swinging on trapezes among laser beams. Guy felt the oppression of clothes and checked in his jacket and shirt. He recognized a pop star in lizard tights talking to a sports star whose trousers had braces running between the legs, pulled up either side of the genitals to emphasize them, and on up over the shoulders – made from a soft tracksuit material, these were the new trousers this season (the braces were sometimes worn crossed over for a more pronounced effect). Guy sat on the back of a sofa with his feet on the seat and sipped vodka. Someone in a gold top hat sat on the seat against his legs and said 'My mum died from Legionnaire's Disease.'

'My mum's not dead yet,' said Guy, smoothing down one of his plasters.

'In Lloret de Mar it was. I like your outfit. The Casualty Ward Look,' said the gold top hat. Guy felt a mouselike hand pinching the hairs on his leg just above the ankle and said 'Not now thanks' . . .

He was at another bar, this one in the shape of a fist. He rested his chin on the shoulder of the person in front of him who turned his

55

head round and licked Guy's nose. Guy gave a pale smile and winked – or blinked – it tried to be one and ended up the other. He went up to a gallery and looked down on the dancefloor which was the size of an ice rink. All was vivid confusion for a minute. Then his attention homed in like a telephoto lens on a figure and the image locked: in the middle of the dancefloor was Rory McLulu in nothing but a kilt and pair of gym shoes. He was spinning wildly and the kilt, opening behind in a generous flare, disclosed small elegant buttocks like 2 ivory billiard balls. Guy's telephoto attention searched quirkily in the region of Rory. The image locked. Kate. She was rotating much more slowly than the McLulu, with a grim expression on her face and moving her arms as if wielding 2 tomahawks. Guy ran down staircases, along ramps. He reached the ground and waded into the swirl of dancing but they'd vanished. The music was overwhelming here. Guy started to move to it to avoid fainting.

Billy arrived, saw 2 friends, Trish 'n' Dave, propped against a wall rolling their eyes at the rest of the world. 'Am I glad to see you,' said Billy.

'What?' said Dave.

'He says – is he glad to see us,' said Trish.

'Oh,' said Dave.

'Why?' said Dave.

'What?' said Trish.

'WHY?' shouted Dave.

'Yeah, Bill – Dave wants to know why,' said Trish.

'Let's find somewhere quiet,' said Billy. He pulled them to a fairly quiet table in an alcove with a good view. 'Listen – I was nearly killed.' Billy's eyes were bright with adventure.

'Nearly killed?' said Trish 'n' Dave, almost interested – which was for them an extraordinary degree of curiosity.

'Yeah, at this flash party, government people, the lot there – it was fucking bombed wernit.'

'No,' said Trish 'n' Dave.

'Yesss,' said Billy emphasizing the final consonant. 'I'm lucky to be alive.'

'That's what I keep telling Dave. He's lucky to be alive. But he don't agree with me, do you, mate. Ever since he lost his job, he says it's a bunch of shit. But I say you're fucking lucky to be alive, don't I,' she said, playing with Dave's spiky blueblack hair.

'It was orrrrible,' said Billy. 'You don't believe me, do you?'

'We believe you,' they said.

Silence. Billy gazed into the flashing pit of sound and dance. Images of recent events crunched in his head like balls of thick paper. Then he saw Guy swerving about on the dancefloor. 'Hang about,' he said. 'There's a geezer I was with – he'll tell yer.'

'I feel much better having danced,' said Guy as Billy led him into the alcove.

'Call that dancing?' said Billy.

'. . . And now I feel much better having stopped dancing . . .' Guy added. In the relative quiet of the alcove his ears sang like baby jet engines. He rubbed his chest and nipples with satisfaction.

'This is Trish 'n' Dave. What happened to the others, Guy? Did they get stuck there?' Guy shrugged. 'Who'd do a fucking thing like that? Wernit orrible,' Billy continued. Dave nodded in agreement. Guy stared at the table. Billy examined Guy's plasters and said 'That's a pretty neat costume. The Thoroughly Damaged Look.'

'I don't want any pressure on them, not even a shirt. I fell through a window and got picked up by the police.'

'Seriously?'

'Seriously.'

'Not your fucking night is it.'

'I thought maybe you was in the medical profession, er,' said Trish, then mouthed silently at Billy 'What did you say his name was?'

'He's called Guy,' said Billy aloud, adding 'I used to be in the medical profession myself. Wheeling bodies about. Ambulances and stuff.'

'Until he got the sack,' said Trish to Guy, 'for passing a severed finger round in the canteen.'

'Leave it out, Trish, not now,' said Billy with an odd expression on his face. 2 red circles had flushed onto his cheeks like clown's make-up but in the red light of the alcove these circles looked black.

'Well, it's true. He pulled this finger out of his pocket, he'd picked it up off the pavement at a car crash. Oh look, there's Mitzi Smith. She's a sex-change. Funny innit. Dave's a test tube baby. Dave had a

57

job recently. Well, he lost it. He had a milk round.'

'Helping out on a milk round,' Dave corrected.

'How did you lose *your* job?' asked Guy, leering forward.

'Oh, he just lost it,' said Trish.

'Yeah, I just lost it,' said Dave. 'They called it – what did they call it, Trish?'

'Rationalization.'

'Yeah – I was rationalized.'

'Near drove him mad,' Trish said. 'For a few months I had a lot on my plate with Dave. Then the doctor gave him some pills which were a Godsend. He feels OK now.'

'I feel OK,' said Dave.

'And he's got all his vigour back,' said Trish, playing with Dave's spiky head.

'Vigour? Is that what Dave's got?' mumbled Guy.

'You should've seen him last winter,' said Billy. 'Like something a turd wouldn't touch.'

Trish waved at the sex-change who ignored her. She turned back to Guy and said 'Are you employed?'

'Oh yes,' said Billy, 'Guy's self-employed, Guy's one of the bosses.'

Guy contemplated a creeping nausea in his belly. Mitzi Smith sauntered over and fingered one of the plasters on his bare shoulder.

'Hullo, Mitzi love, you look great,' said Trish. Mitzi was wearing a sort of nurse's outfit in scarlet satin with leather and metal epaulettes. She brightened, bent down and whispered something in Guy's ear. He reddened slightly and she poured a little of her drink over his head. 'Seen anybody interesting?' said Mitzi to no one in particular. 'I haven't seen anybody interesting for weeks,' she continued, fiddling with Billy's ear-ring, 'and I prefer the Pink Swastika to this dump – it's more *intime*, more *simpatico*.'

'Fuck off to the Pink Swastika then,' said Billy. She slapped him with her gloves. 'Squirt,' she said and ambled away, blowing Guy a kiss over her shoulder.

'What did she whisper to you?' asked Billy.

'She said "Push your whanger up my dish",' said Guy.

'Trust you to get an offer, ya jammy cunt. She usually says "Get me a drink. A large one".'

'And I say let's have a large one too, and 2 fingers to life!' said

58

Trish, sticking up 2 fingers and blowing a raspberry.

'Yeah, 2 fingers to it,' echoed Dave, doing the same, and adding on his own behalf a long rolling fart of great resonance and no odour.

Larry and Wanda walked slowly across Waterloo Bridge arm in arm. They'd come from a late supper at the Savoy where they'd left the car and were feeling very peaceful. In the middle of the bridge they stopped and rested their elbows on the parapet towards St Paul's.

'One of the great sights of the world,' sighed Larry. 'Or it would be if they hadn't shut off the lights so early. And there,' he said, turning round to another impalpability, 'is another of the world's great sights. The Mother of Parliaments. Or would be if they'd kept the lights on.'

London is both grand and higgledy-piggledy. Though other capitals may be more beautiful or more shocking, here, in the middle of Waterloo Bridge, the great curve of the Thames, with buildings piled up on its banks in infinite and haphazard variety, creates a vision of solid urban might which has no equal; and because London has been bigger longer than any other metropolis, this vision contains evidence of the whole range of human enterprise from all periods of history: neither museum nor future city, it embraces both in a colossal living continuum.

'London town,' sighed Wanda.

Her mind went back to the early days in Soho. 'We Never Close' flashed in shocking pink neon outside the dive where she worked. But her heart never opened. She liked being a stripper but the one thing wrong with it was it got you into a way of thinking so that your heart never opened. Then she'd moved upmarket to a revuebar, Wanda Bonnebouche in *Pardon My French*. One night Larry came backstage. She couldn't get those tassels off her tits fast enough.

'Our city,' sighed Larry, belching up a vapour of Tournedos Rossini, 'and nobody has more right to own it than us, Wanda.'

Perhaps that is why they'd moved to Sussex and eventually given up the flat in Chelsea altogether, the better to own London, because one cannot possess something with which one is too involved. To possess something you have to be able to walk all round it – and let none of it walk round you.

'So why don't you make me Wanda Perkins?'

'. . . I'm still thinking about it.'

'Ya big toilet!' She bashed him affectionately. And they continued across the bridge towards the club. Behind them, at a discreet distance, followed Reg the bodyguard.

Adam, Venetia, Sophie showed up – met Billy and Guy – started crying, except Adam who said 'We got detained. Then Sophie got the shits in the taxi.'

Eventually the police had said 'Please, everyone, go home. Try to get some sleep. We'll be in touch with you in due course.'

'But they arrested Anthea,' said Venetia.

They were about to give Anthea one of the valium shots being routinely administered but she said 'You'd better not do that. I'm excessively calm already.'

'So they searched her,' said Sophie, 'and found a little plastic bag of pills up her . . . ' Sophie's voice trailed away.

'Up her what?' asked Guy with a wobble of his head.

'Up her snatch,' said Adam.

'Oh,' said Guy, getting a tingle in his groin.

'And they arrested Fran Coddle too,' said Adam. 'She started shouting about knowing her rights, being a free citizen of a free country – of course they arrested her immediately, on suspicion.'

'On suspicion of what?' asked Guy. He wanted the details of these things.

'They think of that afterwards,' said Billy. 'By the way this is Trish 'n' Dave.' But Trish 'n' Dave were chewing each other's faces and didn't want to be introduced.

'Now the police are looking for you,' said Venetia, fixing Guy with her gimlet eyes. 'Perhaps you know who did it, Guy, ya? I bloody resent being bombed!'

'I'll go and see them to-morrow, I couldn't face it to-night.'

'Are they looking for me?' asked Billy.

'Not yet, you weren't on the guest list, but they will be.'

'I threw my stuff away,' said Billy.

'Maybe I can get something here,' said Adam. He went across to a group of Imperial types one of whom he appeared to know. The

Imperials drank gin & tonics laced with tranquillizers to keep them smooth, way back from it all, way back when – they floated and sometimes smiled – occasionally one would tap out a rhythm on the table or one might applaud something – they never danced – they viewed the spectacle as from a warm verandah at sunset . . .

'Have you seen that new series on TV . . . ' began Sophie, wiping her red eyes, wanting to take her mind off things.

'Yes, I have,' said Trish and in order to say so she unfastened her teeth from Dave's nose. 'But it looked a real drag.'

'How can you say that?' said Sophie, offended.

'Because it's really you know . . . boring. We watch films on the video round Dave's mum's mostly. If we do anything,' said Trish.

Adam came back and said 'No luck' just as Lord Willywonky crashed into their table. He swayed and tried to focus on Dave's red raw face. 'Do you mind if I sit here?' he said with a slur, collapsing on the banquette next to Dave with the suddenness of something cut down from a gibbet.

'Be my guest,' said Dave who lifted up one of his thighs and plonked it back in the same place on top of Willywonky's.

'I'm Al,' said Willywonky, 'and I've had . . . a few.' He gave a burp which snapped his head back. 'And you . . . ' he said with a watery look towards Sophie, 'didn't we meet at Margot's divine – burp – party . . . ?'

Sophie burst into tears and Guy said 'Piss off, you old drunk.'

'Don't speak to my friend like that,' said Dave.

'Well, ask him when he left the bloody party then,' said Adam to Dave.

'I had to go and meet a television person,' said Willywonky. 'They want me to wear silver clothes – I don't want to.'

When the horror of the night was explained to him, Willywonky appeared not to take it in and said to Dave 'Can I have my leg back?' Then he uttered a macabre wail like a banshee being strangled. The music boom-boomed far away. He said 'Because I'm Irish you think I did it, you think I'm a terrorist, don't you? But I'm not! I'm on the side of people who don't like bombs going off.' He picked up someone's drink, swallowed it, and burst into tears.

Venetia stared into space and said 'Will it be in the papers? Was it too late for the papers? Are the papers out yet?'

'And there was something else interesting,' said Adam. Guy

looked up from the table. 'Dingle Shropshire was among the dead.'

'Were many killed?' asked Guy.

'Over 15, I think. So far. But that's not the point. This was different. Old Shropshire had been shot.'

The green people and the purple people and the orange and blue
people were crashing wildly with the lights, shuddering to the
music. The video screen flashed up a giant cartoon of the Prime
Minister and superimposed a pistol target on it. A great cheer and
whistling went up from the floor.

'I might go to Brazil,' said Adam, trying to shake off the mood.

'Can I come?' asked Sophie. 'Brazil sounds brilliant.'

'Go to bed like the policeman told you,' replied her brother.

'I don't want to go to bed! All my life people have been telling me
it's past my bedtime and I'm sick of it!' It was the most Sophie had
said all night and she sat back dizzy with a nasty fluttering in her
chest.

A man peed from one of the trapezes. The stream began falling on
the dancefloor but as the trapeze swung through its arc, it sloshed
onto the Imperials' table – but they hardly moved.

One of them said 'What was that? Was that something?'

Another said 'I believe it was something.'

An Indian girl with them said 'I believe it was urine.'

An Indian boy with them, who wasn't used to this style of
extreme phlegm, said in a Birmingham accent 'Are we gonna just sit
here all night?'

Re the urine: 2 bouncers lowered the offender at once and threw
him out. A notice by the trapeze ladder read *The Management respect-
fully reminds patrons that discharges from the trapezes are strictly forbidden.*

'Do you know anyone down Rio way?' asked Adam.

'I don't think I do,' said Guy.

'I know the Mexican Ambassador,' said Sophie. 'I met him at the
party, he invited me to stay in his glass pyramid in Acapulco.'

'Let's go and get some drinks, Guy,' said Adam.

On the way to the bar Guy said hullo to a man in dark glasses and
parachute silk shorts whom he recognized from somewhere.

'So how's business?' asked Adam.

'What a peculiar question . . . ' mumbled Guy.

'Kate's here somewhere,' said Guy. 'I should be tough and break with her. We only stay together because we can't bear the thought of no one there in the evenings. I think Charles Robinson came here to-night too – that's another whole number I can't handle right now.'

'Why don't you marry Sophie?' suggested Adam. 'She's got a bit of money if she gets married. Ever since our parents were killed I've sort of had to be daddy as well as brother. I wish she'd get married.'

'I heard that about your parents.'

'They were murdered by guerrillas in Africa. In their farmhouse. In their beds. Bwana and the Missus strangled with elephant cord. Let's go for a swim.'

Steam was rising from the surface of the swimming-pool and carrying with it a blue light. They saw Trevor. He had just launched himself off the top of the diving board. He noticed them half-way down and started to wave. The 2 ideas became hopelessly entangled and he entered the water with a stinging sideways slap.

'He's better than that usually,' said Guy to Adam.

Trevor swam up and climbed out like a Greek god who'd been given a funny rubbery face. 'I met you once,' he said to Adam.

'Where was that?' said Adam.

'Here.'

'Really?'

Trevor reclined on the side of the pool, flexing his elegant muscles. There was a big red mark along his torso that matched his strawberry swimming trunks. The other 2 shared a garden swing seat and told him about the bomb party. 'Nothing like that ever happens to me,' he said ruefully. Guy asked if Jill had shown up. Trevor shook his head and splashed unhappily away into a backstroke. Adam and Guy swung placidly to and fro.

'Would you do me a favour?' said Adam at last.

'Why should I?'

'I'll pay you.'

'Ah . . . '

'I'm supposed to pick up a package at the docks at half past 4 this morning, but I've got to shoot off somewhere else – could you pick it up for me?'

'Sounds very bent.'

'It's not drugs or anything, I promise. I don't want to go into details, I just want you to collect it.' Adam then named a sum which Guy found very useful, and was jotting down directions when Trevor swam up again.

'Not coming in?' said Trevor. 'Pansies. Right, I'm coming out.' He put on a white towel dressing-gown and slipped off his trunks.

'I don't suppose anyone's seen Kate?' Guy asked.

'I saw her somewhere with old McLulu,' said Adam.

'The cow,' said Guy.

'Perhaps you ain't been giving her enough donald,' said Trevor.

'She's just a cow,' said Guy.

'Your Kate's all right,' said Trevor.

– Where's Kate gone to? Rory thought, slumped and swooning drunk in a dark corner under an air vent blowing warmish cool. 'I don't feel very well,' he said aloud to nobody. He'd lost one of his gym shoes. A stranger kept fiddling between his legs under the kilt but Rory wasn't sufficiently interested to push the hand away. Some people in a jumble of leather jackets, boots, and zips crossed his vision. When somebody slipped a moistened finger up his arsehole he went 'ouch' but didn't otherwise complain. His eye studied a beam of deep red light which intermittently struck the wall. And when somebody put a sticky pair of lips over his, he thought – There's a sticky pair of lips on my lips. Rory slumped further and thought – And if I'm not mistaken that's a tongue doing ingratiating things to my tongue. The disco roar crashed against the wall above his head and poured down over him, hot and thick. He felt that something slimy and close had wrapped itself round his penis. He felt vaguely that his penis was in some gently pulsating socket, and he thought that maybe his penis therefore was involved in some sort of hard-on activity, or at least had swollen sufficiently for this warm squelching socket thing to have taken a slippery hold, but he couldn't be bothered to rouse himself from his drunken pleasantness/unpleasantness to investigate. His toes curled to the boom of the music. A tingle began to spread like satin sheets all over him and his back arched slightly. His whole body began to tremble and fizz and twitch, and all the twitchiness, all the nervous vibrations in the universe seemed to gather themselves into cords which wound into thicker cords and contracted and mounted and mounted until everything contracted into his centre and . . . whoosh! . . . shot effortlessly out through the centre and he was jettisoned into empyrean peace . . . . A sequined torso slumped against him. In a while someone whispered in his ear 'You're an amazing fuck.' Then a weight removed itself from his chest and he felt warmish cool air dropping softly on him. The voice sounded as though it could have been a girl's.

Mitzi broke away from 3 black boys with Cockney accents who were starting to disturb her clothes and came over to the table again with a black girl called Tania. 'Where's Guy?' she said. A group came on and played some death music on the other side of the dance arena. 'That's really sick,' said Venetia admiringly.

'Have you got their album *Give Me More Carrion*?' asked Trish, humming along in a guttural way.

Tania said nothing. The intelligent serenity of her face was wonderful to behold. Her body was supple and composed as if drifting a few inches off the ground – except for her left hand which played with a set of worry beads made from pieces of turquoise and baby teeth.

'This place has gone off,' said Mitzi.

'Let's dance,' said Billy to Sophie and they went.

'Yeah, let's dance,' said Trish to Dave.

'Na,' said Dave.

'Oh *you*!' said Trish, thumping him one. 'What would you do with him, Mitzi?'

Mitzi smirked and attempted to blow a bubble with her chewing-gum.

Tania said 'My brother was sectioned to-night. He got very depressed. He said it was like real life is happening on the other side of a pane of glass and he can't get through to it. Then he got violent. They took him away to-night, the police and men in white coats. My poor mum.'

'Come on, Tania, let's dance,' said Venetia and they went.

Billy and Sophie returned with Kate.

Kate said 'I've lost Rory. Where's Guy?'

'Trish. Dave. Mitzi. Kate,' said Billy.

'That's what I'd like to know,' said Mitzi giving Kate a big fruity smile. Kate was rather startled by it.

'I think that Guy's a bit funny,' said Trish.

'That's what I like about him,' said Kate curtly.

'Everso pardon,' said Trish. 'Where d'you meet a feller like that?'

'Can't remember,' said Kate. Yes she could. At a party – he'd asked her along to an exhibition of nuclear fallout shelters at Olympia and she'd said 'I'd love to'.

'Know where I met Dave?' said Trish. 'An all-nighter of horror films. 9 hours of bloody intestines and chopping up. My girlfriend walked out on me half-way through. Then I saw these 2 boots coming over the seat, this geezer nipping over from behind. He was in my bra like lightning. That was Dave.'

Billy told Kate about the bomb very quickly to get it over with. He was sick of the bomb. He was going to have nightmares about the bomb. Kate said 'I don't believe it,' but she believed it and was quiet. Guy and Adam arrived, followed by Trevor in his towel dressing-gown. Then Venetia and Tania came back.

'Sophie. Mitzi. Trish 'n' Dave. Kate. Adam. Guy. Er, sorry, mate, what's yer name? Trevor, this is Trevor. And Tania . . . and Venetia,' said Billy.

'I'll go and get some drinks,' said Guy.

'No, I'll get them,' said Trevor.

'We'll all get them,' said Kate.

'I'll come and help you,' said Mitzi.

For a shocking moment bright white lights went on throughout the immensity of the disco in a burning zzzzzzzzzzz! For a moment everybody's acne and lines and overdone make-up and general tattiness and desperation and guffawing laughter were hideously revealed in a merciless light. Then the lights went down again and all was glamorous again. There was a crush at the bar. They pushed in and waited. Eventually Trevor shouted to Mitzi above the music 'You've got your hand inside my dressing-gown!'

'Sorry, sugar,' said Mitzi with a twist of her mouth, 'I thought I was holding your arm.'

They plonked some drinks on the table. 'That'll have to do,' said Trevor. 'It's a madhouse back there.'

'I'd quite like to go home,' said Kate.

'I wouldn't mind making a move,' said Trevor. 'I'll take you back.' And he went off to put on his clothes.

Kate leaned across and shouted above a tremendous rage of music which had suddenly burst out in the alcove (Music Control would sometimes flush out tables in this way from a sheer sense of fun) 'Trevor's taking me back. If you see Rory—'

'Fuck Rory,' said Guy.

. . . . . Trevor and Kate didn't say anything in the car. They drove quietly in the night with their own thoughts.

As they approached Queensway, Trevor said 'Do you fancy a hamburger?' Kate realized she was starving. She said 'Yes' and he said 'Great'. They sat in the enveloping warmth of the car eating hamburgers under a sodium streetlamp whose faulty mechanism prevented it from casting a full yellow glare like the others. Instead, it flooded the car with the most delicate strawberry light. Rain began to fall on the roof of the car in large confident drops – inside was the noise of engrossed eating.

Back at the house, there were no lights on, Jill wasn't back. Trevor said 'I don't understand it. Come and have a nightcap.' They sipped glasses of black Spanish brandy in the kitchen, while outside the large raindrops, widely spaced, fell loosely and warmly to the ground. Kate went to the window – the wet street glittered. She'd never been alone with Trevor before. Trevor came up and put his arm round her. He was tense. He felt a tension in his leg muscles and at the point where the stomach disappears under the rib-cage. His arm moved a finger backwards and forwards across a small piece of her bare back. 'I'm not very happy . . . ' he said. 'Nor me . . . ' she said. He relaxed his whole weight against her, nuzzled her ear, felt a stiffness in her body. Then Kate let her body relax against his with a long outward motion of feeling like a breath and they held each other softly and quietly. They started to take off their clothes. Then they saw each other. Between his shirt-tails poked Trevor's foreskin in a twist like a Turkey gobble. – Oh, hell, it's not going to get hard, he thought. Kate's breasts hung down sheepishly and she felt her shoulders hunching forward with self- consciousness. – What if Trevor's got VD? she thought. Then they stopped seeing each other and made intense love in the nourishment of oblivion.

67

An aside. A flashback. One afternoon at the VD clinic a number of men in a variety of colours, classes, income groups, and moral viewpoints sat against a wall on a row of chairs in a long corridor opposite a row of coloured doors. They had all adopted different stratagems to outwit their sense of – what? Not guilt exactly. But their sense of having been caught, caught out in the game. One read a book, one stared at the ceiling, one kept a bright open it-don't-bother-me face which turned into a swagger when he was summoned and passed through one of the coloured doors – he was insecure, the swagger was overdone. One read the evening paper, a couple of flap-wristed queens swopped gossip (very much at home, they could have been in their favourite bar), others stared at nothing, and had the butch-legs-apart or nervous-legs-crossed, some the arms-folded-waiting head-down-on-chest legs-stretched-ahead ankles-crossed-over. But no one was utterly distressed because for no one was it actually a harrowing matter of life and death (the leukaemia virus and AIDS boys did not come here), and mixed with the unease is a sense of community and pride. We are all male! We are all sexual adventurers! We have all been caught with our pants down by the Green Drip or the Big Scratch or the Creepy Crawlies or the Waving Warts or Christ Not Syph! That we have been caught is evidence that we fuck. Because although for most men it is necessary to screw for peace of mind, equally important for one's peace of mind is that the rest of the world should know about this, know that yes you too are part of the great seething fucking mess of humanity. Plus of course the relief of finally being in a place where something was going to be done about one's Green Drip, Running Scab, whatever.

Guy's arms were folded and his head was on his chest with his legs extended and ankles crossed over. A man was called in through a red door. Another was called in through a green door – just a boy, don't they start early, why at his age I'd . . . Another was called through the green door. Now one went in through the red door, and another through the blue door. What was the blue door for? They processed people even *more* slowly behind the blue door. Time sluggishly passed. Red door, green door, green door, red – when the fuck was his number going to be called? Numbers. This was a world of identification by number. Names were never used in the VD clinic. The venereally diseased might not come if they thought their names were going to be sloshed up and down the corridors just any old how. Red

68

door, green door – wait a minute – I came in before that bloke, and before that one! They're calling people ahead of me! Guy got a bit panicky – people do if they think their number has been lost.

'Nurse, nurse!'

'Yes?'

Guy unfolded his arms. 'Will it be much longer?'

'You'll be called when it's your turn.'

Red door, green door. Guy felt the green stuff ooze into his pants.

'No. 123456, through the red door please.'

Thank-you. He went through the red door and closed it firmly behind him . . . . . An Indian doctor put on a pair of clear plastic gloves and asked him the most searching personal questions he'd ever been asked. No, he wasn't sure who gave it to him. Yes, of course it was a girl! The doctor asked Guy to pull his cock to encourage the discharge – more green stuff oozed out. The doctor picked up a tiny long-handled plastic spoon and pushed the little scoop into his urethra. He waggled it about in there, withdrew it, and smeared it across a glass slide. Guy went '. . ugh . . . ' It wasn't painful exactly – just the most disagreeable sensation he'd ever experienced. The doctor threw away the spoon.

'Do you have oral sex?'

'Well, er, yeah . . . '

'Open your throat.' The doctor pushed a spatula to the back of Guy's throat, withdrew it, smeared it across a glass, and threw the spatula away. Guy gagged horribly.

'Better look at your back passage,' said the doctor.

'Oh, that's all right. I've just got regular clap.'

'We can't be too careful.'

'Are you suggesting I – I – I let guys do it to me?'

'Back passage.'

'But doctor—'

'No. 123456, will you please get up on that couch and bend over. I have an examination to make. Then I'd like to go home. It's my daughter's birthday. Thank-you.'

The doctor expertly smeared some Vaseline onto a steel gun and pushed it into Guy's rectum. It felt cold and – strange – disagreeable again, oh yes, and made him sort of feel like shitting, except that he didn't feel like shitting. The doctor turned something inside the gun, withdrew it, and put the scrape on a glass. Guy felt – strange.

'Now go up the corridor where they'll take a blood sample. Then come back and wait outside until you're called again.' The doctor removed his clear plastic gloves and threw them into a bin full of same.

Guy went up the corridor and a syringe of blood was taken from his arm. The blood was dark red and important-looking. He returned to the row of chairs in front of the row of coloured doors and waited in agitation – what would it be? what hideous news? was his whole body turning to pus?

Eventually his number came up again. The doctor said, 'You've got gonorrhoea. Pull your trousers down.'

'What, again?'

'Yes, pull them down and lie tummy down on the couch.'

The doctor wiped something on his right buttock and jammed in a huge syringeful of penicillin-type drug. As the doctor slowly depressed the plunger a heavy grey ache, an extreme but diffused pain, spread agonizingly through his gluteus.

– Jesus . . wept . . . Guy thought.

'Come back in 2 weeks for the result of the blood test – that's for syphilis. And please tell your girlfriend to go for a check-up.'

'You've got a nerve!' said Kate when he told her.

'Look, I'm sorry. It must have been someone at a party.'

'Guy, sometimes you just get on my bloody nerves.'

'Yeah, well, I'm sorry. I went as soon as I noticed.'

Kate had her check-up but was clear. Guy hadn't screwed her for ages anyway. Wasn't it over 10 days now since he'd screwed her?

Dmitri looked irritably over the parapet and scrutinized the frenzied throng.

– So this is what it's about, he said to himself – This is what we Russians dream about behind our ice walls – This is the promised land, is it? – and damn, I'm late – I hope I haven't missed Charles Robinson.'

'Hullo, old chap,' said a penetrating voice behind.

Dmitri jumped. That slightly nasal, slightly burry voice – yes, it was the mad Scotsman in nothing but a skirt and one shoe.

Rory's body was smudged with dust like a coal miner's and his red hair stuck up in a brush. 'I didn't think this'd be your kind of place,' he said to the Russian, leaning on the parapet beside him and looking down through a gantry of lights.

'I had to meet somebody here,' said Dmitri, and as a great fatigue settled over his mixed feelings like a roof of pastry over a pie, he added 'That damn bomb delayed everything – then the police and their endless questions.'

– These poor Ruskies, thought Rory – Their heads always full of bombs and police.

'She certainly knows how to throw a party does Margot,' said Rory.

– This must be the famous British irony, thought Dmitri.

'She can cope with anything,' said Rory.

– This must be the famous British phlegm, thought Dmitri.

'I wouldn't mind a party like that every night!'

– And this must be that famous British death wish they tell us about in Moscow, thought Dmitri.

'Shame I had to leave so early. Girl trouble, you know,' said Rory.

– Ah! The penny dropped for Dmitri. So this loony Scotsman missed the bomb! I have before me an ignorant man.

And Dmitri metaphorically rubbed his hands and felt warm inside, for there is no more exquisite sensation for a man involved in power games than to find himself in the presence of ignorance. It makes him feel that life is full of possibilities. Dmitri smiled and said 'Let's have a drink.' He summoned a waitress – she was wearing a g-string and her head was zipped into a leather hood which completely covered the face. Dmitri stared at her glorious breasts and his fatigue wholly lifted.

'Well, well, well.'

It was Larry. Guy was on a staircase leaning against the wall, receiving some cool air as it was laundered down from the grubby streets above. His eyes were closed but those 'wells' were like 3 hammer blows knocking 3 legs off a tripod. He opened his eyes.

'Heard Beryl's new album yet?' Larry went on. 'It's majestic, mate. Fucking majestic. She's going solo.'

– Oh God, he's starting to talk business, Guy thought.

'I thought you were going north.'

'I am,' said Guy.

'You look terrible,' said Larry. Guy mentioned the bomb. 'So you were at that party, were you? Very . .' and Larry lifted his nose in the air to indicate snootiness but with no particular malice. 'One of the porters at the Savoy was full of it. Nasty business. That Ingot woman's a game old bird they say. Your Henry Mountsavage told me she tried to blow him in a box at Covent Garden. "Gobbling away in my lap like a great turkey with all these blue feathers sticking out of her shoulders. But Mozart makes me feel so chaste," he says all bright and innocent, you know like he is. Wanda shit herself laughing. She likes a good laugh, does Wanda. Hang about, she'll be back in a minute, she's gone to the Ladies.'

'That's a crappy thing to say about Margot,' said Guy. 'She wasn't killed anyway.'

'No, people like her don't get killed. They go on for ever. Er, I don't like to mention it on a night like this but, well, I've had to call in the money. Or rather Ernst of Teck called in the money.'

Guy's body went numb. Long needles might have been pushed right through it without his knowledge.

'Ernst wants to become a racing driver. He was looking very down at Gstaad this year. His doctor said he should boost himself by doing something, instead of drifting between hotels and villas. I can't really see Ernst behind the wheel. He's too fat! And too sleepy. And too stoned most of the time. But the money I lent you was part of the block he lent me and I've had to call in the whole thing, I'm sorry.'

'He only needs it to buy more damn horsebags of coke – he can't have it yet!'

'I'm afraid he can, Guy. We set it in motion to-day. I know your accountant tried to contact you at home but the phone was off the hook.' The accountant was the only full-time professional still working out of Guy's office. 'I'm sorry, mate, but I did warn you.'

Guy was white and shaking. 'I'm bust, you sod, bankrupt, broke,' and he threw his fist into the centre of Larry's face.

Now this kind of assault hadn't happened to Larry for a number of years, a fact which he regarded as evidence of his maturity. Guy's fist offended Larry's sense of what a man who has come to own a manor house in Sussex might reasonably expect. He lashed back at Guy but

72

being overweight and surprised by the fucking little runt's bottle, he missed. Then he called in Reg (who was a couple of bars away) on the walkie-talkie. Guy saw Reg coming towards him like a pulp machine and flitted off. Reg was a hitter but Guy was a runner and he shot through a door marked EXIT, turned sharp right, ran along a serpentine corridor, through another door, and found himself overlooking the swimming-pool. Reg followed through the door marked EXIT but being Reg, a man of merely logical efficiency, went on rolling until he'd actually discovered the Exit, and went through it, and thereby found himself on the calm deserted concourse of Waterloo Station some time after 3 a.m. Like a man accustomed to being in the wrong place at the right time, he immediately gave up the chase and took an early morning newspaper from the stand. A big black headline said

DEATH PARTY

That took most of the front page, but lower down in the right hand corner was 'Theft of Priceless Manuscript from British Museum – see page 3'.

Somewhere back inside, Larry was rubbing his face and whimpering to Wanda 'The bugger hit me. Just as I was going to suggest a way out of the problem, he hit me, the cunt.'

'Stop talking,' said Wanda, cleaning up Larry's bust lip with a white lace hankie. 'Don't know why you get mixed up with little farts like that. You don't need it, Larry. You've got problems of your own, lover.' It was true. Larry was a cash man, a barrow boy writ large, not a finance man. And so his fortune was not cleverly managed – he paid vast amounts of tax to the government for example – and outgoings of a labyrinthine splendour ringed it round. Larry was a great character but he had no glamour, he was a spectacle without the tragic dimension. And this was because he never led anywhere except back to Larry: no mystery, just money. If he crashed, no one, except perhaps Wanda, was going to feel that anything particularly unfortunate had happened. So when he had to call in a loan, he had to call it in. The ancient trustees of Ernst of Teck, operating with implacable courtesy and sang-froid from their offices in Zurich, would insist on it.

73

Guy fled past a huge video screen flashing up death statistics – the number of murders in the United Kingdom that week, the number of deaths on the road, the number of stillborn babies. Each new statistic was greeted with mighty applause and stamping of boots from the floor. Guy fled into the nearest Gents, into a closet, and threw the bolt across. His legs gave way, he sat down, put his head down, heart beating wildly, head in a swirl. A fruit machine was being played outside at the end of a row of washstands – he heard money falling, falling, falling . . .

To recap. Guy had money anxiety – the utter impossibility of getting X pounds by Y date, Z pounds by X date, always this problem week after month after year, no money, impossible, crash, the heart goes BANG! bang bang bang – agh! flutter . . . flutter . . . then zoom! panic! BANG! oh God I'm going to have a heart attack attackattackattack . . . ack . . . ack . . . ugh, what was that funny twitch in my chest, the floor gives way under me, ugh.

He had career anxiety. He should be doing things, going places, instead of this corrosive waiting, waiting, waiting for what? Waiting for the Big One of course but . . . his career – his career – kept slipping out of gear, I'm slipping out of gear, my tyres won't hold the road, out of control, losing my grip, skid-d-d-ding ugh panic! BANG! ack! ack! ack!

He had love anxiety. Why can't she let it be simple? It'd be so simple if only she'd do this do that, not do this not do that. Why *won't* she let it be simple? He'd have to finish it. Then he'd be alone. Alone at the bottom of the mountain. How could he start again with someone new? No energy to start again, alone, shivering . . . shivering in the great emptiness of the world, the echoing and predatory emptiness, ready to swallow you up, annihilate you. To be separated from her made him nervous. To be with her made him depressed. Unexpected crying, loneliness, despair with an aching head. Capricious fragments of memory would shoot into him like vindictive pieces of glass.

He had a constantly-on-the-verge-of-panic-behind-the-wheel-in-a-traffic-jam anxiety. How much longer could he hold out? Keep this great threatening thing from bursting through and engulfing him? The fine tissue which divides a balanced mind from insanity is – is dangerously distended! The slightest jolt might cause the first fatal tear in it. What's that funny feeling in my chest? That's not a normal twitch . . . oh hot/cold sweating in groin and feet. Very funny tingles like anxiety crystallizing in the muscles. With the uprush of adrenalin the knots start to appear, as if stomach, chest, heart and throat were being gripped and twisted by many invisible hands. For God's sake, why doesn't the traffic MOVE! I'll have a seizure! my head bursts! heart bursts! . . . bursts into tears, no, mustn't break down, mustn't, keep it stiff, mustn't cry, mustn't move an inch to left or right, must stay rigid BANG! ack! ack! ack! ack! ack!

Basically, Guy had anxiety.

Beneath it, demanding a cooler head, was that opponent which, unlike anxiety, requires man's noblest attention: the Fear. Anxiety, though terrible indeed, is really kid's stuff, a singular vanity thwarted and buckling back on itself. A man must so equip himself and arrange his affairs that he is in a position to take on: the Fear.

At this point in his perturbations, a large fleshy white penis nonchalantly presented itself through a hole in the partition on Guy's right. 'What the hell,' he whispered. The penis was semi-erect and wobbled there like a giant overfed termite. Guy was tempted to give it a decisive yank – but something held him back, an atavistic loyalty to the great community of cock owners perhaps, or maybe a plain unwillingness to touch a strange pisser – 'germs' a little voice said, rumbling up like a small bubble from the submarine grottoes of childhood. The thing still wobbled whitely there. Guy gripped it by the foreskin and pulled down hard. A sound of great distress arose from the other side of the partition, followed by a rapid withdrawal of the member. Then 'Don't be like that' complained a hurt military voice, 'when I didn't hear the sound of shitting, I assumed you wanted action.'

Now Guy realized, with an awesome sense of urgency, that indeed! yes! defecation! The matter was about to be taken out of his hands. Quickly he pushed down his trousers, plonked his bottom on the seat, just in time. All Jean-Pierre Wilkinson's buffet and a great deal else besides poured into the pan.

'Hi, dearest, I'm home. What sort of day have you had?'

'Not very nice, dearest. The postman slipped on the front doorstep this morning and broke his neck. Then I went to the hair-

75

dresser to try and forget about it and Florian, normally so wonderful with scissors, took a thin slice off my ear while giving me the latest look. Do you like it, by the way? You haven't said.'

'Sorry, petal, I was distracted by the bandage – yes, it's lovely, really suits you.'

'Florian was very apologetic, said his friend had just died from sexually transmitted leukaemia and he couldn't think straight this morning. I drove to Mother's for tea and sympathy and the clutch went on the motorway. When the Rescue arrived, he pulled over onto the hard shoulder, and was hit by a car going very fast in the slow lane. He isn't dead but they say he'll never think again. I was in a state and the police kindly took me for a cup of tea – at the other end of the Motorway Café a great commotion was caused by a man choking on a piece of meat, yes, choked to death. Dearest, when I have to go, I hope I don't go that way. By the way, Mother was well and sent you her love. When I got back the postman's wife rang to say he'd just died and she's suing us for manslaughter, so, no, not a nice day.'

'Poor petal. Well, you just put your feet up and I'll make us both a nice cup of tea.'

'Oh, ever-loving one, here's me going on about me and I haven't asked you about you. Did you have a nice day at the office?'

'Mr Manners has gone bankrupt,' said the accountant, 'so I've lost my job, petal. But I'll tell you about it later.'

One cannot stay forever within the temple. Eventually one has to face life. Guy came out of the closet, rinsed his hands, splashed his face, stared at himself in the mirror: a plastered mess. Over his shoulder he saw Mitzi come into the Gents with Tania, the black girl.

'The police are out there looking for you,' said Mitzi. For some reason Guy shook Tania's hand – perhaps it was Tania's elaborately beaded hairdo which made her look like an official representative of her race – or perhaps it was Guy's need to hold onto something.

'I was talking to a friend of yours to-night,' said the black girl, 'Charles Robinson.'

Guy's eyes emitted a strange light. 'You know Charles?'

'Known him ages.'

'How amazing. Where is he?'

76

'He's gone to America. Wish I was going to America.'

'How do *you* know Charles?'

'Don't be so rude,' said Tania with a giggle.

'The police have taken off Billy,' said Mitzi. 'Don't know about the others.'

'Where in America? Shit . . . . . I've got to go to the docks.' His face was contorted with distress.

Tania said 'Here take these' and dropped her worry beads into his hand.

Mitzi said 'Please say you'll make love to me one day, Guy, please say it, promise to make love to me one day, please.'

Guy fled.

'So you haven't seen Manners all night?' asked the Chief Superintendent, now smelling of peppermint mixed with onions.

'Absolutely not,' said Adam.

Sophie opened her mouth to speak but Adam kicked her under the table. She said tearfully 'I was only going to say, Adam, we haven't seen him since the party.'

'Spread out, men,' said the Super, 'I'm sure he's here.'

The men surveyed the vast arena packed with outlandish forms and one said 'What's he look like?'

'Light brown hair with plasters on – get on with it! And what about these 2?' asked the Super with a jerk of his head towards Trish 'n' Dave. Adam didn't at all like the way he seemed to be the main target for the Super's questions and decided to say nothing, merely lift his eyebrows.

'We aint done nothing, we never do nothing,' said Trish lacing up the front of her grey suedette bodice. The Super had a good look at her and knew she spoke the truth.

At this moment Rory turned up in a filthy state, kilt skew-whiff, no shoes. 'Hi, gang,' greeted the McLulu in a jocular tone.

'What is this – object?' enquired the Superintendent, sweating with contempt.

'Don't look at me in that churlish way, my good man. I am Rory McLulu, the McLulu of Tack and Fan, a title that has been in my family since the 16th century.'

'Are you a friend of one Guy Manners?'

'Indeed I'm not. Can't stand the bugger.'

'Get that down, he knows Manners. And were you at the Ingot party to-night?'

'Indeed, I was,' said Rory. 'Margot has been a dear friend for many—'

'Take him in, boys.'

'What are you doing!' protested Rory, 'and what about him?' pointing angrily at Dmitri.

'Good evening, Mr Tcherenkov,' said the Super. 'I didn't see you there.' Then glaring at Rory he said 'Mr Tcherenkov has already been more than co-operative. But you, sir, the Muck of whatever you are, are going to join a young feller called Billy in the back of our very cold van.' He emphasized Rory's state of undress with a withering look. 'Decent people were killed to-night,' he said, pushing his face up close with a horrible, almost lascivious curl of the lips.

Rory went awfully hot. He thought he was in the presence of a madman. 'I demand you leave me alone, you bloodthirsty maniac, I demand my solicitor, I demand—' He disappeared under escort, the Super high-stepping behind.

'Can I buy a round of drinks?' said Dmitri when they'd gone and hailed the waitress in g-string and hood.

'That's the girl who had her face ripped off by a cheetah,' said Adam.

Tania came back without Mitzi.

'Isn't this Manners a friend of Charles Robinson?' asked Dmitri.

'So is Tania,' said Venetia.

The hooded waitress brought the drinks. As she was putting them on the table Dmitri ran his finger up her thigh, over the buttock, and up to the right breast. His finger went round and round the rose-red nipple several times then onto the small tray where the rest of his fingers released a banknote of high denomination. 'Keep the change,' he drooled. He thought she smiled. He couldn't be sure. This was the intense aphrodisiac thrill of secrecy, of constriction.

Venetia said to Adam 'I couldn't fancy you in a million years. You're so in love with yourself. You keep ice cubes up your arse.'

'I believe you know Charles Robinson?' said Dmitri to Tania.

'I've never met a Russian before,' said Tania. 'You've got funny eyes.'

'Would you like to dance?'

As they moved towards the dancefloor one of the huge video screens was flashing up clips of a heart operation. Dmitri felt Tania open herself to him. His head was humming with activity – he'd never had a black girl before.

Guy looked at his watch (which was a very expensive present from Margot). He was early. The route to the old docks took him past Anthea van den Clack's Thames-side conversion, so he rang the buzzer. She was in. 'I'm in the bath,' she said over the intercom, 'come up.' He went up in a lift and came to another door and another buzzer and finally entered her enormous living space overlooking the river. All other rooms opened off it. It was full of winking electronic technology and must have contained over a dozen television sets, each tuned to a different channel and all with the sound turned off (on the roof terrace outside an aerial bowl scooped satellite programmes out of the night sky). In one corner a light sculpture was going through its routine. A young man was in the room playing chess with a computer, sipping black velvet. Guy said hullo and the young man raised his hand without taking his attention off the board.

'I'm round here,' said Anthea. Her bathroom was round a curved brick corner and the bathroom itself was round, as was the marble bath into which one stepped down 5 curved marble steps. Big square taps shot masses of hot pale blue water into the steaming foam.

'There's someone playing chess with a computer back there,' said Guy.

'Really?' said Anthea. 'I wonder who that is. He won't win – it was programmed by another computer so it's unbeatable . . . I'm soaking. I've been soaking for hours. I've had a lot of crummy lesbian policewomen pushing their hands up me all night. I don't mind lesbians but I hate them in uniforms. I was there for hours, and I've been here for hours, soaking, trying to get them *out* of me.'

'You seem OK,' said Guy. He glimpsed one of her crimson nipples through a bank of white foam.

'A friend of Venetia's came with me – then disappeared. Whatever happened to you?'

'It's a long story,' said Guy, smoothing down a small plaster curling off his chin.

'If you want to put some fresh stuff on your face, it's in that cabinet.'

He went across to an object like a guided missile fixed to silvery interior pipes, opened a panel in it and took out the First Aid. He bent over a washbasin which was a sculpture of half a grapefruit and dabbed his face with warm water. He washed away the dust. Then slowly and painfully he peeled off 2 large plasters and 2 smaller ones. He patted his face with more warm water, followed it with cold water, patted it dry, and applied to the cuts a quick-setting liquid called 'New Skin'. Then he did the same to his chest and to the cut on his arm. Then he looked coldly at himself in the mirror.

'I'm so glad you came,' Anthea was saying from her frothy redoubt. 'It's been one of the worst days of my life. First the bomb. Then the police station. I hope Daddy doesn't hear about it – the police station, I mean. It's the sort of thing those beasts would do, tell Daddy, isn't it.' Guy sat down on a blue plastic Chesterfield sofa and picked up an American magazine off the bathroom coffee table made from knots of steel and plexiglass. *Tired of feeling tired?* asked an advertisement in the magazine. *Sick of feeling sick? We can help YOU – with Super Colonic Lavage!* 'And as for Mummy, she'd go up the wall, no, perhaps she wouldn't go up the wall because for one thing she doesn't live with Daddy and she's a bit wild herself. She'd probably just slap my face and say no more, but Daddy would go up the wall and probably force me to go and live in Switzerland or somewhere hellish where I'd *die*. I don't even like skiing, and they might even stop my money, and ah no, they can't do that because it came from when Grandfather died but they might be able to stop some of it. I think they're going to charge me with illegal possession of some pills – I didn't know what they were. The police looked them up in a book and they have codeine in or something and I'm not supposed to have them without a prescription but they're not really terrible so . . . Guy? . . . . Guy . . . . . '

Anthea, having paused for breath, also stopped staring up into the white-painted iron vault of the ceiling, and turned her eyes towards Guy '. . . . . Oh Guy,' she said, 'you're crying, oh Guy, no, you're crying, don't, I can't bear it, don't . . . ' Anthea stepped out of the bath dripping bluish water and foam and went across and sat beside him and put her arms round Guy and covered him all over with water and foam and he fell against her and something slackened at last inside him and he cried and cried and cried and cried and cried and cried and cried.

The rain had stopped. The sky had cleared. Rows of warehouses and jagged rows of cranes were silhouetted a deeper black against black sky by the light of faint stars and a melon-slice of moon.

Once the crowded dynamic heart of an empire, the warehouses had long been empty, the cranes long been obsolete, the men who worked them had died, gone away. All had long been deserted and still. The developers had not arrived. There was an absence of sound as of all sound sucked out by an apprehensive intake of breath held there at the edge of exhalation.

Blacker than the sky, blacker than the warehouses and zig-zag cranes, was the great rectangle of water, a most sinister unrippled volume suffocatingly deep, black bricked box of water perfectly secret. Its surface was a smooth black lawn vanishing in eerie distances. No starlight or moonlight reflected off it. The hush was velvety deep like that of something successfully buried alive.

Then, for no apparent reason, a ripple moved across the surface like the stir of death in a tomb. This single ripple caught faintly the starlight . . . . . From round a black jetty a tiny boat came into view. It was made discernible by a single red light and motored quietly across the water towards Guy.

It was cold. He trembled in the black cold. He waited on the dockside as the boat approached. Guy made a motion with his arm by way of greeting. The moment he did this the motor was cut. The single red light went out. Silence. Nothing. A ripple. The ghost of the boat glided on. There was a small flash, followed immediately by a dull report. Another flash. Another dull report, like the sound of a golf ball whacking into a mattress or a fist into a belly. Wood splintered just above Guy's head. Complete confusion. By the time his perceptions had realigned themselves, he discovered that his body had spread out flat like a starfish against a vertical wall protected by an abutment of black brick. He thought he heard, with his left ear, the boat moving quietly away. His other ear was pressed hard against the damp brick wall and this emphasized the curious clicking noise made by his heart when it pounded violently, something it

81

now, last of all, began to do. He saw nothing, felt nothing, except the violent pounding of his heart which grew and grew in his consciousness until it was the only fact . . . . This centripetal fact of the pounding heart was breached and shattered by a tremendous screeching noise. Screeching of tyres! Blazing of headlights! White fire in the eyes and heart! Many headlights pinning him starfishlike against the wall! He turned in terror, back pressed to the cold wall, shielding his eyes. He could see nothing but a blaze of white light rolling towards him in a nauseating peristalsis.

A voice shouted 'Don't move, Manners. Just don't move. You're under arrest.'

Night overtook him in waves of hot dream, waves of clinging mud . . .

Part Two

– 4 –

The Beach

Phoebus, whose chariot was unbeatable at 11.50 a.m. local time, rode arrogantly above the beach and glared down in burning torrents of light. Mr Success! Soon after sun-up the heat had begun to descend in relentless throbs that went zing . . . zing . . . until about 11 a.m., after which the heat simply dropped through the atmosphere and onto the land like a lead weight. Bougainvillaea, clematis, and jasmine in gardens along the shore shrank into themselves and withered at their extremities in dead curls – and Phoebus smirked. Where paint blistered, burst, and flaked away, where motor cars became ovens wherein a poodle might be cooked alive, and tarry pavements turned spongy and sucked at the feet, Phoebus, in his hauteur, smiled a brilliant hard white glaring smile hundreds of miles wide.

Playful erstwhile upon the sand, now, at noon's approach, human beings begin to withdraw under porches and striped umbrellas to drink coolness through straws, or lie in long venetian-blinded saloons, or sink themselves into swimming-pools which erratically bead the coastline here with a string of tiny rectangles, circles and kidney volutes of supernatural blue. From the Gulf of Mexico the waves emerge quite small to-day and flop languidly onto the lion-coloured strand, throwing the thin foam ahead of them with a careless lack of purpose. The foam bubbles willy-nilly at the water's edge like the turmoil of saliva at the lip of a cataleptic.

Only 2 figures remain on the beach, adjacent to a small round dune from which dark green blades of grass sprout like hairs from a wart. One of the figures sits upright cross-legged in an orange sheet, smoking Turk cigarettes; the other is prone, almost naked, and

85

glossy with Toto Jelly.

The Swami leant across the girl's back and extracted a can of Coca Cola from the icebag, pulled a cold ring – phzzz . . . and slaked his thirst, making a funny face as he did so. The Swami had small, precise features drawn with a very fine nib.

'What's your fantasy to-day, Carol?' he asked.

She turned her head so that the side of it lay against the beach towel. 'My fantasy is . . . . I don't have one.'

Something sank slightly inside the Swami while, overhead, Phoebus like an enraged slave-master beat furiously her back with golden lashes, little knowing that this was her pleasure and caused her to purr soft downy purring noises and smell sweetly in secret places of suntan lotion mixed with young love. 'I've got a funny pain in my back,' she pretended. 'Will you rub it for me, Swami?'

'Must I?' appealed the Swami, waving his cigarette about in an expression of helplessness.

'Please . . . '

'I suppose I must.'

'What is reality, Swami? Tell me some more.'

The Swami had been meditating upon Carol's back for some time, and now, when he touched it, the golden thing possessed the demonic allure of a dream-come-true. He gasped discreetly. Little ripples of pain moved out from his heart and some of them worked their way through to his fingertips causing the hand to tremble as it traversed the young girl's back and hopped every now and then over the bikini strap. Beneath the orange sheet which he wore as the outward symbol of inner utterness, the Swami's small purple penis stuck up like a claret cork.

'Empty your mind,' he said.

The moment he said this, Carol's mind, which left to itself had a natural tendency to drain entirely away, began to buzz with random crooked pictures. The face of Beau Bute loomed large among these. In fact Beau started to swoop at her rather unpleasantly so she lifted up her head with eyes wide open, and shook her brown hair – it was brown like thick milk chocolate. Her eyes noticed a young couple with small child, walking onto the beach laden with towels and food. Far away but quite clearly could be heard the high-pitched prattle of the child who kept on saying 'My thingummy hurts, my thingummy hurts.' Carol's thoughts drifted to a stop.

'Reality, Carol,' said the Swami, his mind kept just this side of

86

ineffability by a deep gaze into Carol's bottom, 'Reality is a hot strawberry.'

'What?' said Carol, bewildered by the brilliant riddle.

'Reality is a finger in the nostril.'

Carol rolled onto her back and her breasts relaxed beneath the 2 dabs of purple polyester which comprised her upper garmet.

'Reality is . . a soft swing . . . ' he intoned, stealing from beneath his lowered eyelids tiny glances of the young meat so high-school and ready.

– He is a great man, Carol thought.

The Swami laughed tinnily and rearranged his drapes. 'Is there any popcorn left?' he asked.

Who is this coming up the beach? A male in blue swimming shorts is running along with a slow certainty as if the object of running were merely to run the run-in-itself. This is Dale Lauderdale, the best looking man in his year at Harvard. 'Naw . . . ' Oh yes. The beautiful body in addition to the wonderful face – it's unfair – and now this body is tanned a gold deeper than the gold of his hair by a holiday on the sands into its third week. The golden thighs and springy calves pound Earth and propel Dale towards the seated pair. He falls with a roll beside Carol, sweating copiously, soaking the golden fuzz of his body.

– The golden boy . . . she thought, opening one eye slightly to see who it was, which made her whole face twisted – Mr Beautiful – What a bore . . .

Dale looked blue-eyedly out across the blue sea. 'Nice day,' he said. It had been a nice day for the past 2 months.

'The Oneness . . . ' breathed the Swami, the subtle smile of his lips infusing by degrees his whole body with the odour of sanctity. More than one person present always turned into a congregation for him.

'I feel a lot of Twoness,' said Carol with a touch of huff. She sat up and fixed to her face a pair of sunglasses in the shape of 2 black hands with pink fingernails.

'Twoness precedes Oneness. If you experience Oneness without first having known Twoness then the chances are you're not very well. Either that – or immortal. But when one is immortal the nature of consciousness is not a problem.'

'Are you immortal, Swami?'

'You are too kind, Carol.'

'You said you were at one of Mom's parties.'

'Did I say precisely that?' wondered the Swami, picking a piece of popcorn out of his teeth.

'But you shouldn't smoke so much,' said Dale.

'Every man should cultivate one vice, Dale,' said the Swami with a tilt of the head. 'Vice separates us from the animals, the animals who are so good, so obedient to the intelligence of nature.'

Dale shyly rubbed the back of his neck which was as wide as his skull. 'I'd like to be immortal,' he said, and stretched out on the gruelling sand with his hands clasped behind his head.

'That's not the problem you might imagine,' said the Swami with a slow whisk of his eyelashes. 'But those who would be immortal must first understand one thing.'

'What's that?' asked Carol apprehensively.

'The fact that they will die.'

An electric current passed through the ropes of muscle which ran down the back of Dale's neck into his shoulders. Carol shuddered and said 'I'm going in.' She walked up the beach to the house, the softness of the sand causing her to waggle her bottom in an extravagant way that was entirely unconscious.

The house, which was separated from the beach by a small lawn of coarse grass, was much older than its glassy neighbours to left and right. It had been built in the era of servants by an unhappy film star. She had been famous for walking sideways with one hand on hip until – during the filming of *El Dorado* – an alligator had knocked her over with its tail and swum away with a grin, leaving her broken on the riverbank. The famous hip set badly and she was lamed for life, career finished. 'I shall never forget,' she declared and named her house 'El Dorado' so that the name blazed up first thing every morning when the mail was handed to her at breakfast by the faithful Hannah. She would spend the rest of the day ruminating on the nature of tragedy, reclining in a long chiffon gown through which her uneven hip bones poked, staring across the Gulf of Mexico from a shaded balcony. In the evening friends might arrive for drinks and she would relive the good times until midnight which always struck at her suddenly and drew her to the scented pillow and a sleeping pill . . . . After her death, El Dorado travelled over the years via remote cousins into the ample lap of Nancy Canvas. Nancy hadn't seen her hip bones since at the age of 15 she'd had a lightning interlude – about 6 months – between puppy fat and real fat.

The house had a suburban stylishness, with gables, balconies, a colonnade, and blue & white awnings facing the sea. The garden was full of bright flowers and green waxy leaves. Since the place was erratically occupied, the servants had given way to a part-time gardener and part-time cleaning woman shared with several other holiday houses on Tallulah Drive.

'Just throw yourself down and spread yourself out,' Nancy would say. One who had was her old friend Senator Bute, at present in the 'library', a room on the sunless side of the house which contained a writing desk, a Collected Mark Twain, a novel of the Great War called *A Farewell to Arms and Legs*, and a plant which looked dead but which caught and ate any small creatures straying into its vicinity. The Senator, in baggy shorts printed with a pattern of multicoloured ice-creams, was picking his nose at the writing desk. He reflected awhile beneath a full head of white wavy hair. Then wrote some more of his letter. It was to Brad, a US attaché in Brasilia.

> El Dorado,
> 222 Tallulah Drive
> Whitewater, Fla.

Dear Brad,
Thanks for yours of last week. Keep an eye on those Russian tourists on Amazon safari. You never know with tourists. Or Russians. If it hots up, let me know what you need – we're always willing to help a good cause. You probably heard – Dingle Shropshire got shot during a bombing incident in London – they kept this detail out of the papers. So don't take any chances. Am sending this via ordinary mail, diplomatic channels being what they are these days. Please destroy after reading. Love to Gale and the kids. Jolene sends hers.

PS. Give me a ring

The Senator re-read it. He left it unsigned. Then he tore the printed address off the top as an extra precaution. However he shifted uneasily in his seat. His piles were playing up slightly. Had they got wind of something? He usually listened to his piles – what was brewing down there? He lowered his shorts somewhat. The crotch seam was riding uncomfortably into his piles. At the same time the Senator's mind turned to sex. Wearing shorts frequently had this effect; something to do with fresh air on the backs of the legs.

– At my age I still like it, he thought – I wish Jolene was here.

Jolene was Curtis Bute's second wife. He often described her as a 'survivor', which was for him a great compliment. But endurance, though not a negligible virtue, is an extremely boring one. And mere endurance would never have satisfied Jolene. She didn't merely survive. She worked hard against the flow of time, and was currently at a scissor farm in the Sierra Nevada, 'getting myself the way Curtis likes me', having her second facelift, first bottomlift, third boob job, being pulled apart, reset, rubbed, scraped, hosed out and pinned up, starved starved starved, packed with vitamins and vitality juice and fibre, smeared with miracle custards, slapped, turned over, slapped again, exercised – hup! hup! hup! – gzuggh . . . . . 'Curtis better be damn waiting for me when I get outta this hellhole!' He thought of her now, on the slab, with scalpels sticking out of her arse, and he got hard for the first time that week.

Carol was sitting at the kitchen table, slicing the components of a salad to go with the barbecue that evening. 'The Swami was very sweet to-day, Mom,' she said. 'He called me an illusion.'

'You do go about in a dream, Carol,' said Nancy. 'I think I'll send you to Europe to get tightened up – a year in France, a year in England.'

'It's not only me. He said you're an illusion too, and this house is an illusion and America and everything is.'

'What about the last time he cleared me out of caviar, was that an illusion? If you ask me, Carol, it's an illusion that it's an illusion.'

'I left him on the beach with Dale,' said Carol vaguely.

Nancy thought of Dale's father, Mr Lauderdale Sr, who lived in Philadelphia and owned the beach house next door. She was attracted by the shyness of his smile and the uncomplicated newness of his money. He was Heritage Swimming-Pools – you can have a Greek swimming-pool, a Tudor swimming-pool, a pool to match the Hacienda, the Log Cabin, the Oriental Beach Pagoda. The Greek model was superbly restrained, a colonnade at each end, a string of clear plexiglass Venus de Milos complete with missing arms. The Tudor model comes with genuine Anne Hathaway Peekaboo Gazeboettes at each corner in bulletproof polystyrene and REAL TREATED WOOD. The Pool of the Future was completely transparent in all its parts and had rainbow-coloured water.

– What would my smart foreign friends think of Mr Lauderdale? thought Nancy – Not to mention Mrs Lauderdale, who likes to come down without her husband but isn't giving him away – Perhaps I should stop thinking that my future lies in some castle in Europe – the Canvas money comes from Ohio – good solid Ohio – but – but . . . . There were times when Ohio seemed desirably close to Nancy, and times when it seemed desirably far away. This was her basic problem, her relationship with Ohio.

'Fix me a bourbon, darling, it's time,' she said to her daughter. 'Do you and Dale, I mean, have you ever . . . ' Nancy's voice trailed away.

'Oh Dale,' Carol pouted. Every time she saw Dale's empty face she wanted to fill it up. Fill it up with anything. Pleasure, pain, diesel oil, old salad ends – anything, she thought, was better than that superbeautiful totally unused look.

Nancy pulled a stack of steaks out of the freezer and dumped them on a draining-board to thaw. Senator Bute came into the kitchen and said 'Be a good girl, Carol, and fix me a bourbon on the rocks. I've just dropped a line to Jolene, Nancy. I sent your love.'

'Oh good, Curtis.' Nancy, whose face had fallen many years ago and stayed down there despite a lively social schedule, thought Jolene a silly bitch.

'When is your English friend arriving?' asked the Senator, scratching the grizzled rug on his chest and winking at Carol. The Senator at 60 plus felt he was on the whole extremely attractive to all women and tended to dislike any other men who were, referring to them often within earshot as 'greaseballs'. 'Did I see Dale jogging along the beach? Fine boy, fine boy. You'd never guess he was studying anthropology at Harvard,' he said ambivalently. Senator Bute was an old-fashioned American with a suspicion of anything ending in

91

'logy'. Dale for some reason was not a greaseball.

Nancy replied with a mighty scouring cough and goggling of thyroid eyes. The phlegm rolled through her lungs like thunder, was hooped raggedly into the throat, then swallowed. 'I need another cigarette,' she said. 'Someone must meet Mrs Cartridge's plane at 5. What about you, Carol?'

'There's a very good-looking black man staying next door,' said Carol changing the subject. The Senator allowed his eyebrows to ascend. Blackness wasn't the strong suit on Tallulah Drive.

'With Dale?' asked Nancy.

'No, the other side. He wears canary yellow swimming trunks.'

'Well, I hope he remembers this is a family beach,' said the Senator. In Florida, beach shorts were the thing for a man to wear. Trunks which outlined the genitals were considered unseemly.

'I wonder if that means Archibald isn't coming down this year,' said Nancy with a sense of disappointment. She liked Archibald. Archibald helped to jack things up around here socially.

'Is Beau coming?' asked Carol.

'I never know,' said the Senator curtly.

Carol pushed the salad away, stepped into a pair of turquoise mules, and went out onto the terrace and flopped face downwards onto a lounger. She stared closely at the paving stones and saw that they were inhabited by minute red creaturelings. If you squeezed one a small dot of red dampened the finger.

– What are these red things called? thought Carol – I must look them up in a book. But she never did. She snoozed in the sun. The gardener, Jake, who was trimming back some honeysuckle, paused and gazed at her. How often he had dreamed in his narrow bed on the other side of town, dreamed to the point of pollution, of flicking the tip of his tongue rapidly back and forth across Carol's clitoris.

An aside. A flashback. Archibald, one of several pretenders to the throne of Montenegro, yet possessed of a Floridan mother, stepped out of the jacuzzi and into a cream satin dressing-gown which was cold and clung to his scrawny wet body. Then, as he usually did about this time, he fell asleep in the warm spring sunshine waiting for the telephone to ring.

After a fortnight or so of nothing whatsoever, he said 'I can't stand a whole summer of this! I've had enough!' He retreated indoors behind panels of glass and veils of silk and waded through deep cream pile into a large chamber of beamed concrete and hotel lamps where a television talked brightly to itself. A deodorant advert was in full swing – *Don't smell less than you are* . . . . . Many video cassettes were strewn carelessly about the floor.

'I'm going to let this place. I'm bored. I'm going to Bali. I've had enough of my' – he surveyed the brand new high-grade plastic interior tingling with electrostatic – 'roots!' he said with a sob.

In due course the house was let to a man called David Zoton for an indefinite period.

Despite the heat, Dale continued to urge his body along the sand at a jogging pace until he came to Poseidon's Ki-Ki Closet, a shack-style café at the point where the private beach went public. He fell through the flimsy door, staggered to the bar, and felt the air-conditioning settle on his shoulders like snow.

'Hi, Dale.'

His head was lowered in anguish and it was some time before he could say 'Hi, Louella' and ask for a pint of fresh orange juice. Pop music issued from a radio cassette player (of the David Midland type) behind the bar.

> Love
> Is just one big shove
> You screw me
> Then you look right through me
> Jealousy hurts
> Like nothing on earth

On the far side at a wooden table near the window the Swami was being fed rum & cokes by a couple of open-mouthed collegers. He was saying 'Of course you must understand that when change is the only constant, stability must be gyroscopic in character. As the *I Ching* says, amid all fellowship, the superior man retains his individuality. . .'

The gardener, Jake, moved up and sat beside Dale. He smelt of sweat and said 'Got anywhere with Carol yet?'

'Nah . . . '

> *Don't hang around*
> *Being shy with your wound*

'I'd give anything for a poke there,' said Jake who wore blue dusters with nothing underneath. He was a Kentucky boy, short and stocky. His upper body was flecked with tiny thorn scratches.

'Hi, Dale – where's Beau?' said others.

'Tell Beau I've got some business for him.'

'When's Beau arriving?'

'I like this one,' said Jake, clicking his fingers and rolling his tousled head from side to side.

> *A dream of love in savage places . . .*

'We must find you something to do with those muscles, Dale,' said Louella. Dale saw Louella lying naked and squirming on the bed in his bedroom at the beach house. But most of all he saw himself magnificently erect standing over her. He saw this in the surface of his orange juice.

> *Love destroys perfection*
> *Offends like malformation*

The Swami's voice passed across the room like a fine wire. 'The point about gyroscopic stability is however – if you're not careful it can stop you growing. To *do* anything throws the gyroscopic stability or GS off balance. To maintain both GS and growth is a subtle affair. To *do* anything, you must be prepared to look ridiculous. Gyroscopic stability therefore is not the same as being well-adjusted.' The Swami stopped here and sent up clouds of smoke.

'But psychiatry tells us—' began one of the collegers, a teenage male with long sweeping Veronica Lake hair.

At this point a handsome black man entered the café, wearing yellow swimming trunks which outlined his genitals. He sat on the bar stool recently vacated by Jake and a couple of heads turned.

'Hi,' said the stranger.

'Hi,' said Dale.

'It is most necessary to forget psychiatry in order to act,' said the

94

Swami and he began to rattle the ice-cubes in his empty glass in time to a brilliant burst of rock 'n' roll.

'Have you just come from England?' said a young girl with a smile.

'Yes, dear,' said Violet Cartridge smiling back.

'That's beautiful. Can I show you this beautiful recording by the Holy Dynamic Community? There's a book to go with it.'

'I'm Church of England,' said Violet coyly, trying to move on.

'That's so beautiful,' said the girl, upping her smile. 'We're into all religions. Can you spare a donation for our work? There's too much negativity in the world – we're working on that.'

'I have my own charity, dear.'

'I can see you're a truly caring person. A small donation would—'

'I really don't have any change, I—'

'What've you got? I can change it. And give you a receipt. All donations are tax-deductible.'

Violet tried to push her airport trolley past the girl who cringed in her path and smiled and said 'You don't realize it but you're full of tension and hostility. Our work intends to—'

'No, dear, I'm not full of hostility – despite that nasty man at immigration who wanted to know if I had any money.'

'Oh, I can see you're full of hostility, but don't be because life is such a miracle that—'

'Young lady, I've had a long flight, I am not hostile, but—'

'You are, you are, you mustn't be!' said the inane smile.

'How dare you address me like this! I don't know what the form is here, but in England it's considered very rude to go round insulting people. If you don't let me pass, I shall beat a path forward with this bottle of duty-free gin!'

The girl vanished instantly. Violet trolleyed forth in anger and guilt. Nancy and Carol came towards her with arms outstretched, Nancy wearing her semicircular iguana smile.

'Nancy, there's some sad creature back there trying to sell me religion. Do you think she's all right? Dear, the cigarettes are for you. Carol, how you've grown!'

First time in America! They sped over flyovers in the Buick station wagon, along palmy causeways, through jungle, past free-standing

95

liquor stores in the middle of nowhere. Nancy said 'Is Margot still in a coma?'

'She is, poor dear. It's all deeply upsetting. Oh, did you see that? What a pretty liquor store.' As they sped along, Violet thought the great thought – It's just like television.

In late afternoon, as Phoebus's chariot descended burningly towards the wide curve of the sea's horizon, Dale ran slowly back along the beach with the stately rhythm of a kangaroo. In the back garden of the Canvas house, coals began to glow in the barbecue. Senator Bute came out, tottering beneath an armload of steaks. The Swami sneered at the meat and said 'I shall have ginseng crushed in lemon juice for dinner.'

'Gin? Did I hear gin?' enquired Violet Cartridge from the depths of a swinging contraption with fringes in which she was cosseting her jet lag. 'A gin & tonic would be lovely. Would you be so kind, dear?' she said, addressing the Swami. 'I'm sure you know where everything is.'

'I can't touch alcohol,' he said.

'Can't you?' said Vi. 'Are you an alcoholic?'

'This'll soon put hairs on your chest, Mrs Cartridge,' declared the Senator, unwrapping several huge slabs of meat. 'Bute's Law: What goes in, must come out. If you're gonna take on life, have a steak first.'

'Go and ask Dale to eat with us,' said Nancy from inside a fridge. Carol shuffled off in her mules to the Lauderdale house where a tape of the sound of the sea was playing at high volume in the living-room and Dale was masturbating furiously (like all young men, he felt it of the utmost importance to reach orgasm as quickly as possible) over a copy of *Wetgirl*. He looked up, 'Oh Christ!', missed the towel, shot all over the sofa.

'If you want some food, Dale darling,' sniggered Carol as the boy mopped at the sofa with the towel in utter confusion, 'we're having some now.' She turned on a mule and left, humming *Breaking Down the Walls of Heartache*. Dale fell onto the sofa and stared at the ceiling, breathing heavily. He'd have to get a place of his own, away from all this, away . . . away . . . . .

96

Nancy came out of the house in her afternoon diamonds and an old frayed beachrobe in cornflower blue towelling, carrying a tray of Dairi-Fresh French Onion Chip 'n' Dip and Stella d'Oro Genuine Italian Style Sesame Breadsticks. 'The Reverend Big Jim Hotchkiss and his wife Beth are joining us,' she said.

'They better hurry up. The steak's doing nicely,' said the Senator, who was never happier than when rollicking by the barbecue with a beer in his paw. Hunks of animal flew into the air, flipped, and back down bang! splat! zzzzz. His hands were covered in blood.

The Swami said to Nancy 'What's your fantasy to-day?'

'Same as always, Swami. To get laid.'

'Are we having green vegetables?' asked Vi with a powdered frown of concern.

'Lima beans, squash, and greens with chopped turnip,' replied the Senator. 'And how's England?'

'Much the same,' said Vi, sipping gin.

'Much the same as what?' asked the Senator.

'Much the same as ever,' said Vi, turning bashfully away in search of the veg pot. 'Look, are you sure they're *green*?'

'We have 2 other guests from England arriving at the week-end,' said Nancy. 'Guy Manners and his girlfriend Kate. Do you know them?'

'Sort of,' said Vi faintly put out. 'But, Nancy, hasn't he been in rather a lot of trouble?'

The tide was out. Nancy spotted some interlopers on the water-line looking toards the house. 'Go away!' she yelled, 'this is a private beach!' which heaved up a lungful of phlegm. 'Now, Vi, I thought of doing my bedroom in powder pink & mustard. I wouldn't dream of doing it in Europe, but Brenda Lagonda had a bathroom in it over at Palm Beach and believe me, in Florida powder pink & mustard *works*.' Vi felt dizzy – the gin had suddenly hit her jet lag. 'Because I'm so *bored* with black & gold & indoor cactus. Oh darling,' continued Nancy, giving Vi a bearhug and a great iguana smile, 'it's so lovely having you here. We can play sisters.' Nancy had never had a sister. She'd had a brother but he'd died young. She'd had a husband – he'd left years ago. Ash dropped from the end of her cigarette into the dip and she said 'Damn.'

'I don't know much about cactus. I say, those people are getting closer,' declared Vi, gazing at a sozzled sea.

'Clear off!' yelled Nancy. But the 2 figures, a fat man in gaudy clothes and a thin woman in dowdy ones, continued to approach. 'Hey, you, scram! . . oh . . .' It was Beth and Big Jim Hotchkiss.

'Can I call you Big?' said Vi with a girlish laugh.

Overhead, white light hummed and fell in a perfect sheet. Nothing could escape. It stripped the protective surface from everyone and everything. All was nudity in the supermarket . . . Overhead, soft alpha wave music issued from speakers but it stayed up there circling against the ceiling. The purple lenses of closed-circuit television rotated vigilantly and from time to time a scream would be heard, followed by sobbing, as another victim was caught falling off the straight and narrow path. *We always prosecute thieves.* Air issued from polythene apertures, air rinsed and chilled, reconstituted and perfumed with synthetic lavender, air so abstractly pure and correct that its cold precision stung the membranes of the nose and irritated the eyes. No one talked in the supermarket. Coloured lines of products receded in exaggerated Uccello perspectives. Banks of upright refrigerators were packed with chilled beer, frozen foods, frozen juices, readymade sandwiches oozing excessive fillings which bulged in clingfilm like gargantuan larvae. Rows of bottles gleamed in battalions to various vanishing points. Masses of yellow this, heaps of blue that, were set up in eazigrab positions. The Soda Fountain discharged cardboard buckets of Coca Cola, bathtubs of icecream, pints of coffee, Kingsize cookies, goo, fizz, squelch, hiss 'n' hiccup, and superfat kids demand more and more in stentorian voices . . . Fish in boxes, meat in boxes, everything in lurid boxes and polythene bags printed over with chemical particulars and computer instructions in panels of black lines, vitamin/mineral/carbohydrate/ protein/fibre breakdown – freeze, heat, eat – tin, heat, eat – safe, convenient, no dirty fingers, no smelly pans, no waste, no lingering effusions, no stains or other ebullitions of vitality, no funny bits that resemble *ugh* intestines? rude organs? and no slimy unexpected juice which coagulates like an obscenity in the pan – and all because the supermarket was a palace of art, the art of hygiene and packaging.

David Zoton walked up and down the aisles of plenty, trying to connect. He couldn't decide what to eat. Boxes, bags and tins didn't stimulate his juices. He'd fancied some cheese – the assistant had pulled out a thing the size of a suitcase, vacuum-packed in polythene, and threatened to cut him off a slice.

'Cheese is supposed to come from cows,' said David.

'I don't think we stock that type,' said the assistant without a hint of irony. David trolleyed on. Tea. He needed tea. Lipton's, the Brisk Tea with the Flow-Thru bag – clunk! a big box of it hit the trolley on top of milk, ice-cream, 25 tubs of fruit yoghurt in one snapeazi frame. He came to the region of cleaning products, the biggest, most highly evolved department in the whole supermarket. He thought of the kitchen back at the house. The ad said a maid came with the rent but no maid had materialized. Now the kitchen was not simply untidy, it was taking on a life of its own, and insects and small reptiles were beginning to plan a future in there. Clunk. Clunk. Clunk. Plenty of hygiene hit the trolley. David then went down a line of fridges taking something from each one. 4 sixpacks of beer, a box of spinach. A Key Lime Pie in neon green – on the box illustration it looked like something that might land on your lawn from outer space. Clunk, clunk. He'd have 2 of those. Frozen prawns, readymade sandwiches – clunk, clunk, schluck . . . one of the sandwiches split open and its innards oozed across a box of Key Lime Pie. That was enough, he stopped – some saliva welled sweetly into his mouth – I'd love some cheese, he thought – No, they don't sell real cheese here, it's the smell, real cheese smells of . . . bodies, so none of that horrible stuff here thanks very much! When you eat cheese it's as if you've been putting your fingers in funny places and fiddling with naughty things and gone sniff sniff sniff, letting the nostrils hover and dilate above the fingertips, catching that odour . . . David found himself with an erection pressed against the handlebar of the trolley. All his nerve endings had come alive like fine uncurling hairs tingling in the rarefied atmosphere. He found himself in front of a long shelf of petfood, boeuf bourgignon for dogs, chicken à la king for cats, and his erection subsided. He thought – Fancy petfood is the unsexiest thing in the world.

Back at the house, David made himself a pot of tea, cut a slice of lime pie, and turned on the television. An alcoholic rehabilitation programme based on caring non-judgmental conversation. Click. John Wayne in a Western. Click. An advertisement for a germicidal mouthspray: *Don't let love turn into a scab. Spray before you kiss.* Click.

Lucille Ball shouting at someone. Click – off. He found a stack of videos left behind by Archibald of Montenegro. One of the titles caught his eye and he picked it out. *Headless I Love You*. Clunk, click, click, the video began to play . . . David settled into the armchair for a pornrub . . . . On the screen there was elaborate and light-hearted sadomasochistic foreplay which, with its stylized flourishing of whips and handcuffs and chains, rather resembled dancing. He giggled and wasn't particularly excited by it. Then, without preparation, as if quite separate footage had been rudely cut into the film, the face of an American Indian girl fills the screen. She is clearly out of her mind with terror. Next shot: the Indian girl, alive and screaming, is held down face upwards on a table by 4 men. The men are naked except for domino masks. A very fat woman, also masked, and trussed in leather straps held together by steel rings (trussed so tightly that her flesh bulges through the interstices like hot cross buns), this woman is sawing the girl's head off with an ordinary woodsaw. David does not believe what he is seeing. Then an acute anxiety strikes him, a fit of violent trembling, because he cannot establish whether the event is authentic or simulated. When the head has been removed the men take it in turns to insert their tumescent penises into the channel of the throat where blood pumps out in warm spasms. They work their haunches until orgasm is achieved, buttocks wobbling as they do so. The woman stands to one side rather oddly, as if she doesn't know what role to play now. The video ends . . . . . David was sweating. He looked down at his trousers. He'd ejaculated. He felt unbelievably ghastly, ran out onto the back lawn and vomited an arc of green Key Lime Pie high into the air.

4 elderly Americans – Nancy, Curtis Bute, the Rev. Big Jim and his wife Beth Hotchkiss – were sitting on garden chairs eating in the warm evening sun. None was talking, each was looking in a different direction, and chomping on steak. They looked like 4 contented cows. The Swami, Carol and Dale sat on the grass. Vi was compelled to break the silence: 'In a lifetime the average Englishman eats 10 cattle, 38 sheep, 29 pigs, and 530 poultry. I read it in a Christmas cracker. What does the average American eat?'

'At least twice that,' said Nancy. 'Plus hamburgers.'

'What about India, Swami?' asked Vi. 'A handful of old shoelaces, I should think.'

The Swami, who'd been staring at Carol on her back, said 'Reality is . . . a smelly melon.'

Big Jim smiled indulgently and said 'We had a great time in Calcutta. We went to look at the poverty.'

'Incredible poverty,' echoed Beth.

(Big Jim and his wife had once sat in a coach in a Calcutta traffic jam having a conversation on poverty with other tourists. 'Look at the poverty.'

'Yes, it's worse than Mexico City.'

'They say Cairo is pretty bad, from the poverty point of view.'

'I'd love to go to Egypt.'

'The worst poverty I ever saw was in Glasgow, Scotland. D'you know what was so awful? It was *cold* poverty.'

'Beth, we going to say a special prayer to-night.' The traffic lights changed and the tourist coach with blue tinted windows inched on a block or so. The fierce Bengal heat was filled with laughter and shouts and the hooting of decrepit carhorns.)

Nancy sat imperiously in her chair like a manitee. Poverty talk made her uneasy. 'Vi, have another drink,' she said.

'In a minute, dear . . . ' said Vi with a tremor in her voice. Vi was feeling distinctly hot and bothered. She had just seen some funny sloppy green stuff fly up into the air next door, on the other side of the garden fence. Had gin and sun on top of jet lag been a terrible mistake? What on earth could it be? Was it an emanation of ectoplasm perhaps? It certainly resembled what her fancy imagined ectoplasm to look like ever since she (and she alone!) had failed to see any bobbing about at a séance in Belgrave Square.

('But, Vi, you *must* have seen the ectoplasm,' Margot had said.

'Nope. Didn't see a thing, dear. Just heard a lot of breathing. Did you notice that smell?'

'No . . . ' said Margot opening her eyes very wide.

'Deodorant failing on the job.'

'Ah – the odour of apprehension,' said Margot conspiratorially.

'It just smelt unhygienic to me,' said Vi as they climbed into a cab.)

'Have a beer, Beth,' rollicked the Senator – like Nancy, he couldn't stand wallflowers, boozewise.

101

'Juice is fine, Senator,' said Beth with an upfront smile that looked trained. She had known lushdom. She had been cured not by caring non-judgmental conversation but by some heavy humiliation from her husband. 'Does the Lord want you lying on the floor stinking of rum with your knickers down and lipstick all over your face!' he bellowed triumphantly. Loosened by massive amounts of booze, Beth had for weeks been making wild love with the black man who delivered groceries – until Big Jim surprised them on the living-room floor one day when he got back early from church. The grocery man fled. Beth just lay there, white come dripping sluggishly from between her legs. She wept. Then Big Jim had done something extraordinary – he'd forgiven her! But he never made love to her again. Love-making? Pshaw – with his huge belly and tiny penis he'd never actually been able to do more than tickle her anyway – and Big Jim wasn't mentally the kind of man capable of allowing a woman to get on top. Such an arrangement would have struck him as blasphemous. But he'd forgiven her! She could hardly believe it – crippled inside, she'd been writhing at his feet ever since. No one knew this story. It was known only that years back Beth had gone through a bad patch.

'Talking of juice,' said Vi, 'did you know that the average human mouth produces 3 pints of saliva per day?'

'You seem to pull a lot of Christmas crackers, Mrs Cartridge,' said the Reverend Big Jim.

Nancy leaned forward into an enormous guffaw full of phlegm. The veins engorged in her eyes, her beach-robe opened, and one of her dugs swung happily into the late sunshine.

'How is Brenda Lagonda doing in your country?' continued the Reverend. He had spent many delightful afternoons at Brenda Lagonda's paradise with gold taps in Palm Beach, trying to cure her of sin. She'd seemed so well adjusted to sin – a husband, a lover, a dog, 2 Persian cats with their claws removed and balls off, and the outrageous, amusing, cultured, faggy Jimmy de Goldstein next door. Suddenly she went off with the Duke of Dollar and Stirling. Big Jim never understood why. His understanding had limits.

'I think the Duke lets her fuck around,' said Vi and she at once put her hand to her mouth, astonished that she'd used that word. America had gotten to her so fast! The Swami let out a great cackle.

'Call me old-fashioned,' said Beth Hotchkiss, 'but I think sex out-

102

side marriage makes God unhappy,' and she touched her bun (into which red hibiscus had been tucked to show she was no killjoy).

'Love and hate are more interesting than that,' said the Swami. 'For example, if you make the sentence "Love hate", it reads as an injunction to hate, i.e. please love hate. Now if you make it the opposite, "Hate love", it comes out the same, or at least something equally bad, an injunction to despise love. Now – let's try sentences not using opposites but using the same, viz. "Love love". This emerges as a request to love. Likewise "Hate hate". So – however one manipulates opposites, the result is always negative. Whereas when the quantities are the same, no matter that they may be negative in themselves, the result is always positive. I find this interesting.'

'I find it incomprehensible,' said Big Jim huffily.

'Oh well,' said the Swami brightly, 'the advantage of the incomprehensible is that it never loses its freshness.'

'Why do you wear that orange thing?' rounded the Reverend.

'Have another beer, Jim,' interjected the Senator.

The Swami fully extended his arm and scrutinized his fingernails.

'You guru types come over here, filling our kids with rubbish!'

'Calm yourself, Jim,' said Beth, twitching at the mouth. It wasn't often that she sought to contain her husband. He glared at her with contempt.

'Quiet, woman! These purveyors of bullshit—'

'Dale, take the Reverend for a game of tennis,' said Nancy.

'Too much red meat,' mused the Swami philosophically.

'Would you give me a game of tennis, sir?' Dale asked Big Jim.

'Yes, I would!' thundered the Reverend.

In a remote fastness in Mexico, a lizard climbed slowly up the wall, across stained patches and cracks in the adobe, stopped in a blade of sunlight. Then it waggled rapidly up into a long cool shadow under the beams of the ceiling. Below, 4 people – 2 men, 2 women – were discussing the next course of action. One of the men said 'Maybe we should move all operations down to Brazil now.'

One of the girls said 'But we know we're safe here. And it's convenient for Los Angeles.'

The other girl said 'I had a bad time in Brazil once.' She was feeding a desert rat, which sat tamely on her shoulder, with crusts of bread soaked in Coca Cola.

'It's so fucking hot in this desert . . . '

'Things are beginning to happen now down in that Brazilian jungle,' said the first man.

'If we went down there, it would be the end of our movies, wouldn't it?' said the first girl.

'We can make one more before we go – if you can find the kids,' said the first man.

'What will we find in Brazil?'

'You'll find all the others there for a start,' said the first man. 'It's time we joined them. It's starting to happen down there now. This present phase has come to an end. One more movie – then we go. Is that agreed?'

The man who hadn't spoken yet, whose hair was in small pigtails and who wore a waistcoat of Tzigane character, walked to the door of the hut, sipping from a tin of beer. He looked out across the parched desert. 'I'm sick of this place,' he said. The other 3 turned and stared at him. 'And I've got some unfinished business in Florida.'

Carol came out of the house bearing in her arms the weight of a Chocolate and Coconut Chiffon Pie.

'I've got to watch my figure,' said Nancy, her bulk vibrating with pleasure.

'Is it just me or was the Reverend in a temper?' asked Vi whoozily.

'As the wizard says,' said the Swami, 'when you hear the sound of marching in the tops of the mulberry trees, you must become alert and take care.'

'I jolly well think you should,' said Vi. 'In fact I think you should see a doctor.' She burped.

At this point, David Zoton, who had continued to feel most disturbed, who craved 'normalcy' and someone to talk to, came unsteadily round the beach end of the garden fence and said 'I've rented the house next door. Can I borrow a cup of milk?'

The Senator, his knife pausing above the surface of the chocolate pie, called out 'Sir! Try some of this!' The knife plunged down, did its work, and the Senator advanced on David with a plateload of pie whose inner goo glittered incontinently in the twilight. David took one look and ran towards the sea holding his mouth. They all blinked deeply.

A violent noise burst above the house. A tremendous roar grazed the roof. Beau in flying goggles was waving from the air and throwing out handfuls of flowers as he swept back and forth in his little plane. He swung up in a great curve, appeared to hang in the sky for a few moments, then shot towards the house with a sickening rush, just missed it and landed on the not very wide concourse of Tallulah Drive and taxied quietly onto Nancy's front lawn (gouging it up).

'Don't you *ever* do that again,' said Nancy hugging him.

'I almost crashed into a tree this morning,' said Beau, 'watching a pair of alligators fucking in the Everglades. Say, what goes in hard and dry and comes out soft and wet?'

'Oh dear,' muttered Beth.

'Chewing gum!' said Beau and Carol's breasts tautened.

'I'm going for a paddle,' said Beth and she skipped off towards the water. Everyone relaxed. Dale and a dangerously flushed Big Jim returned from tennis. And after a while Beth returned too – with David Zoton. Big Jim's lip curled with disgust. David shook hands.

'I met him by the water,' said Beth weirdly. Her eyes shot all over the place. She snatched at herself and fumbled in the air. At last Beth managed to retrieve the wide upfront smile and began to stretch it endlessly back from her shining white teeth. As she did so, Big Jim stared, moved closer, stared again. His eyes bulged like 2 hot tomatoes fit to burst. He gave a profound grunt, of the kind made by a man on a lavatory seat attempting to overcome the reluctance of a constipated bowel, clutched at his heart, and collapsed – for he had been flabbergasted to discover between his wife's 2 front teeth, curling round and round in a whorl, a very crisp, very black pubic hair. And the great ball of the sun, which had been sinking and bleeding into the sea, now at last went snap below the horizon with a green flash.

– 5 –

July 4th

Lord Flamingfield sat in the chariot under a linden tree, fingering the wart on his brow and reading a book by one of his ancestors, *Cockerell's Letters Home*.

. . . . . *We went up the Irrawaddy a considerable way*, it read, *then afterwards came down the Irrawaddy, with nothing to detain us in either direction but immensities of mud. Shot a few unrecognizable things. A poor bag included one native fisherman who turned out not to be dead after all and made off with our money during the night. Morality, properly understood, does not obtain in the East* . . . . . Colonel 'Bunty' Cockerell, after service in the Indian Army, had taken to travelling into many outlandish parts of the globe . . . *Wales is fine enough, but not for the whole weekend* . . . Cockerell's letters to his cousin, the 11th Lord Flamingfield, had been edited into a companionable volume by Samson Parsley, the witty Student of Christ Church . . . . . *Dear Hyacinth* [for such was the 11th Lord Flamingfield's Christian name], *I find myself in Laos after a long journey in a cart with a sprained ankle. They call it the Kingdom of the Seven Umbrellas and I must say it hasn't stopped raining since I arrived. There are a number of lethargic French around in some sort of administrative capacity, but they usually do what one tells them, having no contrary notions of their own, so that's all right. Laos is the only landlocked country I know which manages to convey the impression of being submarine. This is the result of a great deal of rain and a great deal of opium. The latter stuff has proved extremely kind to my ankle which in consequence is almost fit again.* . . . . . The cache of original letters, a dozen or so yellowing bundles tied up with faded green ribbons, was still in one of the attics at Risingtower whither they had been reposited by Mr Parsley. Another university man, Tom Kite of Harvard, had not long ago flown over to try and buy the letters. 'It would plug a lacuna in our collection,' said Professor Kite. But the Earl had not really liked the idea of having family correspondence fingered by people to whom he'd not been introduced. Kite, unperturbed, had then spent a lot of time with Henry.

Anne Coddle, Risingtower's housekeeper/cook/etc. and mother of the feminist Fran Coddle, came trundling across the lawn while his Lordship was engrossed in a passage on France . . . *Arrived at Lourdes late afternoon. Overcast and warm. A charming town but with a high incidence of disease. The railway station was jammed with malformities . . .*

'The Prince and Princess have just been on telly,' said Anne.

'Do you think if I asked nicely, they'd come for the week-end?' said Lord Flamingfield.

'No, I don't,' said Anne.

'Neither do I!' and his hand shot up her skirt and grabbed a bunch of cami-knickers.

'Help!' squealed Anne to Henry who came dawdling across the lawn, his head like something suspended in water with arms and legs all trailing after.

– Humph, thought Lord Flamingfield, I hope Henry washes his privates properly – A single man mustn't fall down on personal hygiene – The ladies notice.

'We'll have tea in the Japanese Garden, Anne,' said Henry. 'Tell Guy to join us. What's that you're reading, Pop?'

'*Cockerell's Letters Home*, m'boy.'

'Is it fun?' asked Henry and yawned.

'Fun?' replied Flamingfield. 'Cockerell is our ancestor and a hero.' Bunty Cockerell's heroism was authentic – he had once been cast adrift in the Bay of Bengal by Arab pirates and had kept alive by absorbing a mixture of urine and seawater through his anus.

'Come on, Pop, I'll wheel you. You mustn't sit under the linden tree – linden trees are poisonous.'

'I can wheel myself.' Flamingfield preferred the manual chariot for normal country use because of the exercise it afforded.

'Don't argue,' said Henry, wheeling his father into a couple of spine-shattering potholes. Flamingfield groaned. 'And please leave Anne's knickers alone.' The Earl looked straight ahead with a tightly closed mouth. He hated being treated like a cripple. He'd done it

107

once, a fund-raising thing. *Enjoy a Day Out with the Disabled and Meet Lord Flamingfield*. It was one of many offers which had pursued him since his gallantry at the Bomb Party. But he'd hated it and had felt humiliated. 'I had to try it once,' he said later, 'but it wasn't my sort of thing. I don't mind people having no arms and all that but all in a gang it doesn't seem natural.'

'Look at the view, Henry. Isn't it marvellous? Daddy made it. He was your grandfather.'

'I know who Daddy was, Pop.'

The pastels of the approaching Japanese Garden were backed by green hills and woodland. It had stopped raining and the air was very clear. Big clouds like the wigs of judges moved individually across the blue sky.

Guy lay like a mackerel on a long sofa in a pale 18th century gothick room. A 19th century novel, one he had always been meaning to read, lay inert in his lap. On the floor beside him was a silver bell. He picked it up and shook it and produced an unexpectedly penetrating racket. In due course the pointed door opened and a bowed head said 'Yes, sir?'

'Glover, could I trouble you for some tea?'

'And some biscuits, sir?'

'No, just tea.'

'Very well, sir.' Glover withdrew and had just closed the door when – tinkle tinkle . . .

'Yes, sir?'

'Actually, Glover, sorry – would you make that coffee.' Guy thought he needed more reviving than tea was capable of.

Glover withdrew again and took a few steps along the corridor when – tinkle tinkle!

'. . . . . yes, sir?'

'Sorry, Glover, to be a pest, but are there any chocolate biscuits actually?'

'I believe so, sir.'

'I think I'd like some chocolate biscuits.'

'Right.'

Glover withdrew, walked down the corridor the distance of 3 window bays. Meanwhile Guy remembered that coffee can sometimes make one jittery, and jitters were things he wished to avoid at all costs. Tinkle tinkle. Glover made a lemon-sucking face and returned.

'Sir rang?'

'Yes. I was thinking – better make that tea, not coffee. Tea's better.'

'Are you sure now, Mr Guy?'

'Yes, I'm sure. And if you haven't any chocolate biscuits, any old biscuits'll do.'

'I believe there are some chocolate ones left over from Christmas. His Lordship occasionally has one, last thing at night, with his Ovaltine.'

'You've got Ovaltine? Then I should – no, no, no, stick to tea. One can't go wrong with tea. A cup of tea would be smashing. And a biscuit.'

'Thank-you, Mr Guy.' Glover withdrew, closed the door behind him, waited a few moments looking up at the ceiling, heard only a deep sigh within the room, and so began his long journey to the kitchens.

The morning sunshine fell along the beach like new money. It crashed and shouted in a hard young voice 'To-day is not yesterday!' The air was frictionless, outlines were sharp. Nancy walked onto the back lawn with a cup of coffee and breathed 2 good lungsful of ozone. Her lungs immediately contracted in a rasping expectoration of phlegm which, after glancing to left and right, she spat onto the coarse grass.

– No hangover this morning, she thought – No thickness in the brains – That's a relief.

She placed her coffee on a wrought iron table rusted from the salt air and did a brief jog-on-the-spot, lifting up her thighs as high as she could, which wasn't very high. She had a rest, wheezing rather, and examined her cellulite. Same old cellulite. Afterwards she walked across the gently warming sand to where the waves foamed like cold lemonade and went for her morning dip.

When Glover, after travelling in sheepskin slippers down corridor after corridor, which took him from the late 18th to the mid 18th century region of the pile, at last reached the ancient kitchens – which were mediaeval and of monastic origin – he found Anne standing there in front of the television, holding a large lacquer tray laden with tea things, absorbing a soap opera.

On the television screen a middle-aged man with wavy hair touched up grey at the sides – or more likely touched up black on the top – stood stiffly opposite a middle-aged woman and said 'I can't live without you, Pam.' The woman, who had chrome yellow hair teased out and lacquered into a big bonnet, picked up an Adam-style cigarette lighter and lit a cigarette. She sat down pertly on a fake Georgian settee upholstered in green nylon, blew out some smoke, and said 'Well, Martin, you'll just have to.'

'His Royal Highness wants tea in the Lavender Drawing-Room,' said Glover, interrupting.

'Tell the malingering little sod he's joining the others in the Japanese Garden,' and Anne swept with the tray out of the kitchen.

Guy wasn't unduly upset when the dreadful news of tea outside was conveyed to him – the 19th century novel had slid onto the floor – he'd managed almost a paragraph between Glover's visitations, an extensive 19th century paragraph – I could do with a holiday, he thought as he creakily desofa-ed himself.

Although he had been lolling about Risingtower for over a month, it hadn't exactly been a holiday. For one thing, he was convinced Anne Coddle had it in for him: there had been large amounts of steamed chocolate pudding lately when Guy had made it plain right from the beginning that steamed chocolate pudding was one of his major horrors foodwise. And then again, yes, he'd been through a bad time. Rollo McLulu, Rory's cousin and a solicitor, had helped him battle the police who had been watching Anthea's flat for undesirables. ('Girls like that are often attracted to criminal types,' said the Superintendent, 'or to blacks.') After a terrible week in prison bail had eventually been granted and none of the major charges had stuck, but in the unsticking Guy had suffered – and he knew the police continued to watch him because of Charles Robinson. Fuck Charles. . . . The business went under. He broke with Kate, reunited, broke, reunited. His days fell apart, he drank. It can't go on! It goes on. He'd had insomnia, nervous attacks, palpitations, sweats both hot and cold, the horrors. I JUST CAN'T TAKE ANY MORE!!!!!!! He jumped into a taxi and trembled violently in the back of it bound for a doctor in Harley Street while life swirled queasily outside the window. 'Am I going mad, doctor?' The doctor gave him some pills which helped. Henry kindly offered him the run of the house and the peace of the countryside where, Guy hoped, no one would shoot guns at him, etcetera.

'It was a nasty business,' said Lord Flamingfield biting into one of Anne's Viennese Whirls. They were sitting beneath a broken Japanese arch which had long ago been painted red. 'Poor poor old Shropshire. He once borrowed my logarithms at school. They came back smelling of Chanel. I was impressed. It's extraordinary how magnificently Jan has taken it.'

'Isn't it extraordinary how Jan's come out,' said Henry. Jan had gone from strength to strength and now considered herself a hostess to rival Margot, something made easier by the coma from which Margot had yet to emerge.

Guy felt like getting away from it all. He thought of Charles Robinson again. Charles had got away. Gone to America? Gone West? Guy wanted to go too, maybe find Charles, break out, a wider world, new things . . .

'Do you know an American called Nancy Canvas?' asked Guy.

'No,' said Lord Flamingfield.

'I think I almost know her,' said Henry.

'She invited me to Florida,' said Guy. 'I'm going to go.'

Between tea and dinner, the Viscount Mountsavage retired to his quarters in the Burning Tower. These had been Henry's quarters since leaving the nursery and there was something puerile about them. Plastic aeroplanes dangled from the ceiling. There was a large map of the world with masses of pink on it to designate the territories of the British Empire. American comics, music tapes and empty boxes of chocolates are piled on chairs. The floor is covered with clothes. There is a view of the Temple of the 4 Winds from the window.

Henry is in the dressing-room with his back to the door and facing a wall of ultramodern radio equipment. Dials, switches and coloured

111

lights respond to Henry's adroit fingering. A swooping whistle issues from the speaker as he works the tuner.

'Hullo, hullo, anyone there?' he says into a microphone. 'Hullo? Oh, there you are, is PLX 041 there? Why not? Well, when he gets back tell him to call me *immediately* pronto toot-sweet, very urgent, mucho urgento. You understand? You understand English?' Henry cranks out something he hopes is Portuguese – it isn't, it's his all-purpose 'continental'. He switches a few tabs, adjusts a couple of dials, and shuffles into the bedroom in old carpet slippers. He throws himself onto the bed, flicks the pages of a photograph book of Sudanese tribesmen wearing costumes of paint and nothing else, closes it. Henry plays with a curl of hair in the nape of his neck, thinking, while he waits for this very important radio call from the New World.

For Violet Cartridge there were 3 huge flies in the ointment of beach life: the sun, the sea, and the sand.

The sun. It caused the surface of her skin to boil like milk.

The sea, the sea. The problem here – sharks, the conviction that they must be lurking down there somewhere round her ankles (she never went in above her ankles when abroad). Paddling was a terror – any second now – clunk!

The sand. She preferred pebbles as at Eastbourne or Nice. Sand always got in one's mouth; at least it always got in hers. Those sudden crunches in the egg sandwiches she remembered from Torquay as a girl. And somehow sand always found its way into redoubts even more intimate than the mouth, causing the kind of irritation associated with violent honeymooning. And it made the cheeks of her bottom itch. After half an hour or so on the beach she was seized by an irresistible desire to scratch away like hell at her buttocks with both sets of fingernails – bliss, agony . . . this brought her to what was perhaps a fourth fly, *sex*. The beach made her feel sexy and though by no means against this in principle – she wasn't one of those sad types – she found it the opposite of relaxing . . . .

All of this is why she was now indoors drinking tea in the kitchen, working through a pile of newspapers and magazines. Everyone else was out. She caught the drone of the vacuum cleaner in the living-

112

room where the Puerto Rican maid was getting into her stride. Vi picked up *Harper's Bazaar* and read 'Can Orgasm Give You A Headache?' . . .

A glossy black face came round the kitchen door and said with a giggle 'All alone are we?'

Violet jumped, went red, flicked to another page.

'Coming for a dip?' asked David in his canary trunks.

'I'm reading,' she said.

He came and looked over her shoulder and read *Death Begins in the Colon! Colonic Detox Combined with the Chlorophyll Flush.* 'Sounds interesting,' he said.

'Have you seen Carol, dear?' asked Vi, getting up and doing something unnecessary with the teapot.

'Yes, she's lying on my back lawn,' said David. Vi blushed again, redness invading redness.

Guy and Kate landed at Tampa Airport in a great splash of unreality whose ripples were to travel outwards for ever, causing unexpected and fundamental changes in their lives. Strange how the unreal can become real.

'What's that building?' asked Kate as Dale drove them past a structure like a space station in the Aztec style.

'That's the town hospital,' he said. 'Oh look, there's Nancy.'

That afternoon she'd had her colonic lavage, then gone sick visiting. She was standing at the top of the hospital steps in a billowing beach dress, beaming about her with an air of tremendous vitality. After the colonic she was always at her happiest – and it was Nancy's misfortune to look her most grotesque when at her happiest. There was something about that iguana smile of pure happiness which caused strangers to shudder. She got in the car and hugged her guests as best she could in the confined space.

'You look wonderful,' said Guy.

'I can be very ordinary here,' she said. 'Dale, I've just been visiting Big Jim. He's recovering.'

Beau had flown Big Jim onto the hospital front lawn just in time. Beth saw her husband through the crisis, then said 'Jim, I'm leaving you now.' She kissed him tenderly and he blinked like a stranded whale. 'Jim, I can't be what you say I must be. I'm going to roam the South.' Beth's smile was tinged with an emotion that contained sadness but not unhappiness.

'Hullo, this is me,' said a pretty face, lifting herself half out of the water so that her 2 applelike breasts rested on the edge of the swimming-pool. 'Who are you?'

'Guy,' he said, lifting up his sunglasses.

'I'm Carol. Come on in.'

'OK.'

Some days later on the beach.

'I'm going to walk up the beach, darling,' said Kate. 'Coming?'

'OK, darling,' said Guy.

'Shall we go this way?' said Kate.

'I went this way yesterday, darling.'

'Well, all right, darling, let's go that way.'

They were calling each other darling a lot, a bad sign.

'I don't mind going this way again,' said Guy.

'But I think that way looks interesting too, and if you've already been up this way, darling—

'But I thought you wanted to go this way,' said Guy. He gave her a smile, a really vicious one.

'I don't mind – because I haven't been either way,' said Kate.

'All right, let's go that way then,' said Guy.

'Sure, OK, but it looks a bit stony that way, hang on, I'll get my espadrilles. Has anybody seen my espadrilles?'

From prone positions, several lumps groaned at various pitches which Kate took to be negatives.

'Carol, did you see me bring my espadrilles down? Where the hell . . oh here they are, oh fuck it,' she muttered quietly, 'this Hawaiian oil's got all over them . . . ' (Her espadrilles, bought especially for this holiday from Sloeman Grunnidge of Knightsbridge). She wiped them with a towel. 'Look at this bloody mess, Guy. I'll rinse them in the sea. I don't suppose the colours will run. They were bloody expensive. Guy? . . . Where are you? . . . '

114

Guy wasn't there. Kate looked in both directions with shielded eyes. No sign of him. At her feet flesh cooked. Scattered people paddled at the water's edge, a few pranced in the waves. A lump came into Kate's throat and a twinge of dissociation tensed her breast.

– Isn't it funny, she thought, how on the beach people either look fantastically good or really terrible – There seems to be nobody in between – I belong to the grotty set.

For some reason she wasn't getting off on this holiday. She walked down to the sea, corkscrewing her feet into the soft sand and balancing the spine on the small of her back. She could feel her haunches working and she imagined she was a native woman carrying on her head a pitcher of water from the well to the elegant hut thatched with banana leaves. At the water's edge she bent down and rinsed her espadrilles. Her eyes became watery with pent-up emotion. She was no longer a native woman but an ungainly lost creature with red skin, frighteningly insignificant, somehow excluded from the rhythms of life. She had felt terribly alone in the London flat. And now she felt terribly alone on the rim of the Gulf of Mexico.

'Time to get pregnant,' whispered a voice inside her. The air was hot and very still. A white motor launch out at sea zipped in a circle round a becalmed yacht, then zipped away.

'This is the time *not* to get pregnant,' whispered a different voice inside her. She looked down at the espadrilles dripping in her hand. The colours had run.

Frustrated and maddened, riding in a becalmed yacht, Dmitri Tcherenkov swept the shore with his binoculars. Yes, the Englishman Manners had arrived! How annoying. End of holiday break. Just as it was getting relaxing. Nonetheless Dmitri proceeded with his duty and made a note in the little black book which lay in his head: 'Manners's rapprochement with Charles Robinson expected any day now.'

'Can't you get this fucking thing to move?' asked Dmitri in Russian. The 2 crewmen stared at him emptily. He repeated the question in Spanish, adding under his breath 'Bloody Cubans – the myth of Communist efficiency . . .'

'Chinga tu madre . . .' slurried one of the Cubans.

The motor had broken down and the sails when unfurled had failed to catch anything at all. Dmitri felt totally vulnerable, a sensation which sickened him. And he didn't like the way that motor boat had just circled them, taken a good look, then zipped off without so much as a wave. His crew of 2 were drinking beer on the poop and playing some weird Latin American game with old bottle tops which Dmitri felt culturally excluded from.

– I bet they can't even *spell* totalitarianism, he thought.

Dmitri was becoming every minute more conscious of drifting aimlessly about on one of the most sensitive membranes between the Communist and Capitalist worlds. It produced in him a fine mental anguish. He recalled a story from his childhood in Lvov, *The Ant and the Jackboot* (the ant was Russia and the jackboot was everybody else). He sighed, flicked his eyes about the deck, and fiddled with the hair trained over his bald patch which no sea breezes had threatened to expose.

At the end of El Dorado, on the first floor, was a large balcony facing the sea. There were potted plants out here and white lattices through which the prickly arms of bougainvillaea had been encouraged to indulge their slow devious passion for adventure. Overhead a blue and white awning blocked the sun. This had been the film star's favoured platform. Now the Swami sat there, fanning the occasional fly from his face with a copy of the *Whitewater Trumpet*, eating chocolate. Below he could make out a conversation between Vi and Nancy.

'What did you have?' asked Vi. 'The Colonic Detox with the Chlorophyll Flush?'

'No, I had the Steam Detox with the Niacin Flush. But I've had both,' replied Nancy.

He heard them shuffle off and this was followed by a long period of nothing, something which the Swami thoroughly enjoyed. He breathed up one nostril and down the other, then reversed the process. He thought – I must eat my rag – I haven't done the rag for ages and ages. (The rag was a 45 feet long strip of cotton which the advanced yogi swallowed and pulled through the alimentary canal and out of the anus, to promote inner cleanliness.) The Swami heard the clunk of the outdoor fridge below and a tin of beer being opened phzzzzzzz . . . He heard Kate say 'It's so close. Will there be a storm?'

'Sure there'll be a storm,' said Beau Bute. 'Do you have hurricanes in England?'

'Not really,' said Kate.

'Do you know an English guy called Adam Shatner?' asked Beau.

'Yes. How very strange you should mention him.'

'I've never met him. I've only spoken to him on the phone. What's he like?'

'Well, he's – not my type – he's—'

Someone switched on pop music radio and the Swami lost the rest of the conversation. A jet plane bound for Miami Airport throbbed overhead for an endless time then peace . . . peace . . . more peace . . . until Guy came onto the balcony and sat in the other chair and they got talking.

'Yes, I had a small record company,' said Guy. 'Tried to branch into video. It went bust. But I put out some interesting stuff.'

'I see you are a frustrated artist, my friend,' said the Swami.

'Do you think so?' replied Guy, who found this a more attractive proposition than failed businessman.

'Of course. These days everyone in the West is a frustrated artist.'

'Or an artist of course.'

The Swami humphed. 'Well, yes. But most artists are frustrated artists too. With your technology, you Westerners have made work obsolete as an idea – so now you want to move up a step, where the machine cannot follow, to the realm of creativity. However, your obsession with things remains – you want to produce artistic things. The West will choke to death on bad art.'

'Or on bad religion,' said Guy.

'Ha, the age-old conflict between the Eastern respect for the interval and the Western respect for the object.'

'I thought the age-old conflict was between symbiosis and individualism,' said Guy.

– Argumentative little bugger, thought the Swami, and he gave Guy the cold eye.

'I'm not sure what my own conflict is,' continued Guy. 'I just feel so strange all the time.'

'Most people, my friend, feel strange most of the time. We couldn't have found ourselves in a stranger place than this universe

of ours. Once you accept that, you won't find it so strange. One of
your English thinkers, James Thorne—'

'Him?'

'Do you know him?' enquired the Swami with real interest.

'Not any more, he was killed by a bomb.'

'He wrote a marvellous book – *The Moaning of Meaning*, wasn't it?
– which rescued your philosophy, I feel, from the impasse of post-
existential post-linguistic relativism. Believe me, my friend—'

'Can't you call me Guy? "My friend" gives me the creeps.'

The Swami said 'I'm going inside to wash myself,' and left with a
certain tightness.

Guy dozed fretfully.

By and by he heard Dale and Beau talking below. Dale was talking
about an anthropology professor at Harvard, Tom Kite . . . the name
rang bells for Guy, Tom Kite, Tom Kite . . . Yes! Charles Robinson
used to bang on about Tom Kite, the great Tom Kite of Harvard,
anthropologist, psychologist, neurologist, famous for his golden
eyes. And hadn't Kite paid a visit to Risingtower last year? Why? For
some oddball reason . . .

Beau was saying 'I hear Kite has now moved into black magic and
the paranormal.'

'All I know,' said Dale, 'is that he's vanished and nobody knows
where to.'

'Take me, take me . . . ' gurgled Carol.

'. . help me, help me . . . ' swooned David. They were moving
with such jerky alacrity that he kept slipping out of her. Eventually
they hit the rhythm.

'. . . Beau, oh Beau . . . . ' schlupped Carol.

David stopped, raised himself up on his hands, and looked at her.
'Beau? What do you mean Beau? . . . ' Then he carried on.

Beau, stoned, with parched tongue, and dragging his feet like a
refugee, made it across burning sands to Poseidon's Ki-Ki Closet.
David Zoton, sharp, bright-eyed, sat at the bar. He gave Beau a nod
and said 'Can I buy you a beer?'

'Thanks,' said Beau blowing a kiss to Louella. 'You know, you're the first black, er, resident on Tallulah Drive.'

'What's the difference between a black man and a bicycle?' asked David.

Beau felt around in his head. It was numb. He hadn't been expecting intellectual stuff. There was no way he could begin to construct an intelligent response. That Colombian grass – phew! He shrugged pathetically.

David gave his cute twisty smile and said 'You can put a chain on a bicycle and it won't sing "Ol' Man River".'

Beau shrieked. It was like a rat being skewered. David giggled. He was a giggler. Beau fell off the stool, holding his sides, went out onto the porch, howled and shrieked and bent double, beat his fists against one of the posts, swung up and down, threw his head back, roared, spluttered. Laughter passed through him like jets of gas through liquid, turning him to a helpless fizz. David giggled and looked at Louella whose tits were shaking with silent laughter. Out on the porch Beau was stamping his feet and slapping his thighs. Tears poured down his face. Eventually he gave out a long expiring wail and it appeared that the seizure had passed and he came back inside.

'It wasn't that good,' said David.

Beau had to go outside again.

When he came back in his face was all moist and red, loosened up and relaxed, and he said 'It can be pretty dull down here.'

'That's why I came,' said David. Then he made his first move. 'But I was very surprised by some of the videos lying about the place.'

'What?' said Beau tensing.

'*Headless I Love You.*'

Beau was furious that Archibald of Montenegro had been so careless, leaving stuff like that for just anybody to find – but he stayed cool . . . 'You, er, like that kinda stuff do you?' asked Beau, moving closer.

'Maybe.'

'You'd be surprised some of the things I can get.'

David felt a tiny spurt of adrenalin hop into his bloodstream. Beau could be useful – very – perhaps . . . 'Your father is Senator Bute, isn't he?'

119

'That's m'Dad, yes siree.'

'How long's he staying for?'

'A few weeks I guess.'

'Where's home?'

'New England.'

'Does he have any friends down here?'

'Not particularly.'

'Will he—' David found himself being overinterrogative and checked it. He had noticed that a small space had cleared in the cloudy penumbra of Beau's mind and a thin beam of something akin to vigilance was now projecting through Beau's green eyes.

Someone came up to him and said 'Hi, man, can we do some business?'

'Not now, man.'

'I wouldn't mind some grass,' said David.

Beau gave him a look, relaxed a little. 'Maybe I can find someone to help you out.'

'Carol's a pretty girl,' said David, continuing to swim away from suspicion. 'Is she your girlfriend?' He stood up and stretched to clear the closed-in feeling.

'Carol? No.'

'Oh, I thought she was.' David giggled.

'I was her first screw, that's all. I had her in the Palombos' greenhouse surrounded by Venus flytraps and bromeliads.'

The door opened and Guy came into the bar. His shoulders were rather red. He and David looked at each other with awkward curiosity and Beau introduced them.

'Oh yes, you're living in the house next door,' said Guy. 'You sound a bit English.'

'I am English,' said David. 'Born in London. Didn't stay there.'

'You can tell he's not American,' said Beau, 'because he cracks anti-black jokes.'

'So where's home?' asked Guy. He often asked himself the same question.

'I'm not an expatriate,' said David, 'just a rover. I've got a flat in London behind Harrods.'

120

It was a hot close night in the American bedroom. Guy and Kate tossed separately in their single beds.

'Are you awake?' asked Kate.

'Yes.'

'What are you thinking about?'

'I was thinking,' said Guy, 'about the first time I slipped my hand in your knickers. I couldn't believe that you'd let me.'

'Why didn't you go on? I'd've let you go on.'

'I came in my pants.'

'Oh ya.' Short silence. 'Next thing I had to have an abortion.'

'Don't say it like that, Kate.'

Silence. The atmosphere sat heavily on the earth like a beast drugged in itchy reverie . . . The beasts of night lay across their path, blocking them off from rest.

'Did you know that Beau Bute knows Adam Shatner?'

'Really?'

'Well, they've spoken on the phone.'

'Really . . . tell me about it . . . '

'That's all, I think. . . '

A long silence. The sea, which had been forgotten, now swished into their ears.

'Do you want to do anything, Guy?'

After a long silence he said 'What did you say? . . . . '

The sea swished. . .

'It was a mistake, my coming . . . ' she said. 'I think I'll leave. Not back to London. I'd like to go on a Greyhound bus. I think I'd like to go down to Mexico. . . '

Eventually, on cool pads, sleep tip-toed towards the 2 forms elongated in solitude.

2 days later Kate got herself waved off on the Greyhound bus, bound for Mexico.

Vi Cartridge sat upright at one end of the sofa, her hair in electric rollers, reading a novel called *A Right Ol' Business*, page after page of intelligent mush laid down like pastry by a friend of hers, 250 pages and not one memorable line. Perfect. Mrs Cartridge had lost the taste for memorable lines one warm afternoon in Somerset – some-

121

one had said 'lovely weather' and at the age of 51 she had realized that the simple statements, the simple questions were best.

Guy came in and sat down and raised his eyebrows at her. 'Any good?' he said after an interval. He was ready to go out for dinner.

'Very,' said Vi and allowed herself to be immediately reabsorbed by the text. She wasn't absolutely wild about other English on foreign holidays – it made her feel slightly cheated actually.

Beau, unobserved behind a newspaper at the far end of the room, gave out a wild whoop. 'We've invaded some new place it says here,' he said to the other 2. The wild whoop was the only thing Beau had learnt from his one embarrassing term at West Point. It was a mixture of the swagger of privilege and a murder yell. It said 'I am a US boy with money and class and I know 17 different ways of snapping your spine without even loosening my tie'. But Beau was kicked out of West Point for constitutional loutishness. The Senator was mystified by his son. And when was Beau going to take a Southern woman unto him? Though Northerners, all the Butes took Southern women. The Senator's father, Virgil Bute III, had taken unto him 4 Southern women in rapid succession – Curtis's mother was number 3. There was something about Southern women – they knew the score, they didn't lose class when they went down on a fellah.

Carol came in, also ready to go, and said 'Is the Swami coming out with us?'

'Does that man teach you anything, dear?' asked Vi, suspicious of religion on American soil.

'He says I've got to empty my mind.'

'You shouldn't find that too much of a problem,' said Beau.

Carol poked her tongue at him and went all hot. 'And he says that his urine contains holy secretions and that one day, if I'm good, I can drink some of it.'

Vi was so shocked that 3 rollers fell out of her hair and she covered her confusion by fumbling about on the floor for them.

Guy said 'I think he's overplaying the urine card.'

'It's OK and everything,' said Carol. 'He showed me a book with it all in. It can be an important part of it apparently. He sometimes drinks my urine which he says is full of young things.'

Vi, on all fours, pulled her head round and said 'Does your mother know about this?'

'She's not interested in religion,' said Carol.

122

Guy affected wide eyes and said to her 'So what do I do to be happy?'

'Be into what you are,' replied the girl with confidence.

'But I'm a mess.'

'Oh . . . ' said Carol frowning.

The Senator stomped in and said 'Everybody ready?'

'No!' squealed Vi and disappeared to do her hair.

'What about Dale, Carol?'

'He's studying anthropology to-night.'

'What about Nancy?' asked Guy.

'Oh she's coming. She goes everywhere and does everything,' said the Senator. 'She's a survivor is Nancy.'

'I could be a survivor on 20 million dollars,' said Beau.

'You,' said the Senator glowering at his son, 'you could have been anything you wanted to be – if you'd wanted to. And I hope you're not coming to the Palombos dressed like that.'

'No, I'm not,' replied Beau. 'In fact I'm not coming to the Palombos at all. There's some exceptionally trashy stuff I wanna watch on TV.' He undid his shirt and flopped down. Printed across his sunburnt chest with sunblocker was the word FUCK.

The Senator felt very sad and said 'You look lovely' to Nancy as she entered looking what was perhaps her most hideous that month. She wore a green and purple frock decked out with heavy pewter jewellery set with rubies. A cigarette dangled on her lower lip. 'Fix me a quickie, Curtis. Vodka on the rocks.'

'Should we take 2 cars?' said the Senator.

'No, no, let me go on top!' beseeched Carol. Ever since she was a little girl she'd loved to go on top.

Nancy picked up the phone and punched out a number. 'Come on over, David, we're ready to go.'

Nancy, Vi, Guy, David and the Senator got into the car and with Carol face upwards strapped to the roofrack, the twilight whizzing above her, they sped along the highway for dinner with the Palombos.

It was the 4th of July and Merriel and Tonio Palombo were not entertaining in their beautiful gingerbread house up on Decent

123

Bluffs. They had been going to entertain. Tonio had driven into St Petersburg to buy the biggest fireworks he could find. Merriel had even steeled herself to draw up a menu (food was distasteful to her). But they'd had a row after the first phone call (which had been to Nancy) and Merriel said 'If I can't have *my* friends, I'm not going to have *your* goddam awful friends!' Tonio had hit Merriel. 'Not hard, I never hit her hard, she's my darling.' He'd been feeling pretty off lately, acidulous, stabbing pains in the belly – was it an ulcer? Merriel then phoned Nancy again saying 'It's awful, I love him, and he hits me . . .'

'We'll come over anyway,' said Nancy. 'Are you eating enough, Merriel?'

The only other person to be present was Sally Grootenjoy, Florida's most boring heiress, Tonio's goddaughter who was staying with them while her parents went on safari in darkest Sicily.

The house was a mile inland with a sensational view across the Gulf. During the day it glared, as if someone had pressed a button and caused this white fantasy of verandahs, pepperpot turrets and frilly gables to rise up into the sun on a platform. But in the evening it began to take on a sublunary mystique and became gently incandescent in the pastels of twilight. Heavenly aromas lifted from tropical gardens filled with plants of peculiar shape, and Nature rose up around the house to claim it like a lover with an embrace that was both soft and incontrovertible. No mosquitoes harassed the flesh of revellers at Decent Bluffs (Tonio had fixed up killer lamps to draw them off) and all who came here found that the cares of the world slid off from them as easily as a scarf, with a sigh, and that they went forward lighter, luckier, with a sense of effortless consequence.

To-night however something was wrong . . . Merriel greeted them on the verandah. She was painfully thin and her cheeks bore the traces of tears recently patted away. Probably her eyes did too but these were hidden behind catlike sunglasses in black frames. Her hair was fine, dead straight, canary yellow, and hung down almost to her waist. Whenever she moved it floated about her head like the ghostliest gossamer. She wore a black pleated skirt drawn tightly in at the waist to emphasize her thinness, and a cream silk blouse which gave no evidence of breasts.

'Isn't it a horribly sticky evening?' she said by way of welcome. 'Tonio is just putting Tyrone to bed. This is Sally Grootenjoy.'

Florida's most boring heiress smiled and her smile was like a vacuum opening up in a place where previously there had been only emptiness.

'Are you English?' said Merriel to Guy. He nodded enthusiastically. 'I love the English, all that tartan and stuff' she said. 'Do you like Florida? I'm not mad about it. Here's Gerry with the drinks.'

The Senator put his arm round Merriel's waist – there was a lot of arm left over. 'Pretty as ever.'

'Oh Curtis . .' But Merriel, who lived off compliments the way others live off meat, would need a lot more than this before she'd count the evening even tolerable. She was currently having trouble with her thighs – she couldn't get any more off them. When once in a blue moon Merriel visited the beach, a large triangle of air showed between her legs.

Tonio entered, belching painfully. He went up to Carol and touched her face. 'You're getting far too beautiful, sweetheart,' he said with a Brooklyn accent.

Gerry, the black butler with grey hair, served Mint Juleps in frozen silver goblets from a silver tray. When he came to David he almost raised an eyebrow but crushed it just in time – a niggah among the guestsah! – it wasn't exactly normal. Back in the kitchen for refills he said 'It's one of her funny nights' to Esther the half black/half Polish maid.

'May I show Mrs Cartridge the bromeliads, Tonio?' requested the Senator.

'Show her anything you want,' said Tonio with a liverish snarl, massaging his painful belly.

'I like your house,' said Guy.

'So do we,' said Tonio. 'We prefer this side of the state. Too much crime on the Miami side. No place to bring up a kid. Guns, murders, drugs. We like to live nice over this side. Have you been to New York yet?'

'Nope.'

'Guns, murders, drugs – but it's a great city,' said Tonio. 'Go straight to the centre of town, then after you've been mugged, relax and cruise around. You'll find what you're looking for.'

Meanwhile Carol said to Sally 'Seen any good films lately?'

And Sally replied 'I don't take drugs or anything like that. And do you know something? I don't even want to.'

125

'I don't want to either,' said Carol, 'but I take them anyway. My boyfriend gives them to me.' She lied. She didn't have a boyfriend and if she meant Beau, the only thing he'd ever given her was some internal bruising.

Sally said 'You see them all puffing on grass at the drive-in movies. Do you like bourbon? I don't like bourbon.'

'I'm into religion right now,' said Carol.

'Oh, yeah! I don't know where I'd be without Jesus,' said Sally.

'The Swami told me Jesus was a homosexual,' said Carol.

David sat on a whicker chair at the far end of a verandah where night-blooming jasmine discharged a delicate perfume over him. Guy went up to him and said 'I'm starving, aren't you? If I see another breadstick I'll die.' Then he added 'So what brings you down to Florida?'

'Same as you presumably,' said David.

Guy sat down with a sigh and said 'I don't know why I'm here . . . Maybe I'll bump into a friend of mine, Charles Robinson. Did you read about that business with the Nineveh Codex?'

'Didn't everybody?' said David.

Guy leaned forward and pushed back his sunbleached hair. 'Well, I picked up a very interesting lead from Dale Lauderdale . . . '

David wondered – Who the hell is this Guy Manners? Apart from a geographical identity which says England, straw hats, real ale, soft green hills, a large garden to play in, a civility and a tension in that civility. Come to that, who is David? Blackboy in whiteboy world? Blackboy in whiteboy business to be precise – what a perfect cover, they said, handing him a wad of banknotes. I was born in London, father came from St Lucia. He was a newsagent. That was pretty original for a start. All the other newsagents were Indians and Pakistanis. Why is that? Why don't the blacks wake up and *do* something? Brother, don't moan so much! Be constructive! Tighten up those brains! My daddy was the only nignog newsagent in town so he wanted *everything* for his boy; school, university, the works, old boy; and I was young and handsome with a cute smile pulling white girls, white girls, creamy cunts, pink, pink juice, pink love, white heat, crème de la crème, hard as ivory, cold as marble, pale as clouds, soft as come – how white my come is! I always noticed that, wanking as a boy, slurry of gleaming white on my black belly, so wonderfully white as if rinsed by a superbiological detergent. You don't have to be black to be a misfit but I was a misfit too – in the middle of a crowd I'd get the plunging feeling which is similar to self-pity but is not self-pity. It's just feeling out of it and trying not to let it show, keeping up the front. There was a couple of other nigger boys at my quite posh school but we avoided each other in case it looked like clubbing together out of weakness. And Mr Manners, you look a bit shell-shocked too because that big white world which was supposed to be a sweet sweet orange for you to suck in your own good time, it proved to be nastier, more dangerous, more intractable, so much harder to fuck than you *ever* imagined! You sustained injury. It made you more attractive. Now maybe you know something of what I feel, David, black David – actually I'm fairly light brown and don't have that bumpkin tribal quality with grooves cut in my cheeks dressing ju-ju style etcetera – yes, I'm a black man in a multicoloured world, with a living to scratch.

But listen, I don't want to be a great dancer all the time, I don't always want to smile, forgive me if I don't, and I don't want to be a great fuck all the time – coz sometimes I'm really not interested – and I don't want to be Mr Carnival playing reggae nonstop nonstop reggae reggae nonstop I like reggae but I don't want to be limited to reggae, I don't want people lifting their eyebrows with patronizing surprise, oh how agreeably surprised, just because I play Mahler records. Therefore I play Mahler when no one else is around, that way no one gets upset, just me and Mahler sobbing and screaming and swooning and shouting and laughing and whispering into each other's soul.

– So, David, what do you want? asks David.
– Yeah, brother, *don't moan so much*, says David.
– I want to make some money!
– Possessions, man, that's nowhere, says David.
– I don't want possessions, David replied, I want money because MONEY IS FREEDOM FROM BULLSHIT.

Ah, freedom, freedom, the freedom in which all these Davids can happily coexist, in which these divergent impulses cease to be mutually exclusive, and expressively interlace in the fullness of an evolved personality. . .

Guy continued: 'Well, I asked Dale about this anthropology professor at Harvard called Tom Kite. He's quite an amazing character and he's been on television a lot apparently. He was also a friend or an acquaintance or something of Charles Robinson – and now they've both vanished – why? And another thing, Kite visited England last year, ostensibly to buy some old letters from Lord Flamingfield which were supposed to be of anthropological interest, early travellers' eye-witness reports and so on. But it seems his real interest was in Flamingfield's son – that's Henry Mountsavage who was in business with me for a bit. What on earth would he want with Henry?'

'I don't know,' said David. 'Was Robinson a good friend of yours?'

'Not so much lately but . . yes, he was. The Codex is very curious, you know. It is only partly translated. That is to say, it's only partly understood. They know most of the words or glyphs but they don't grasp what it's on about – it's in a priestly idiom, you see, for the initiated. Charles always thought it included an analysis of brain functions – hence his correspondence with Kite whose main interest these days is neurology. Also it refers a lot to death. All those old things do of course, but this isn't about dying, it's about deliberate killing. There's a parallel with the Tower of Babel story to which the Codex is related in some way. Way back in old Babylon a lot of people got slaughtered for some reason.'

A breeze shifted moodily in the palm and eucalyptus trees, the frangipani and acacia. Where the sun had set there glowed a half-circle of peachy red on the sea's horizon, deepening to crimson and seeping upwards by degrees into a great fan of mauve. Several of the brightest stars glimmered in a field of darkening blue. David and Guy stared into the balmy murk of the garden. The languid putt-putt of a sprinkler was suddenly switched off and a few lights came on concealed in bushes. Merriel came up in her sunglasses, although it was now fairly dark. 'Do you chaps like food?' she said, affecting a little Englishness.

'We like food,' said David.

'That's a very healthy appetite to have,' she said. 'My favourite food is laxatives.'

Guy laughed – Merriel looked at him strangely.

Esther and Gerry, having set up a lobster buffet in the rose dining-room which opened onto another verandah, had then retired to the kitchen for steak, chips and television. Gerry hummed a little tune through his steak-filled mouth.

Every day I get the blues
Like I'm walking around in a dead man's shoes. . .

On television was an advert for menstrual inserts. A gaggle of young girls was jumping about in a gymnasium, bright as bottletops, sweatless as alpine flowers. No bloodrops embarrassed their sporty costumes or their firm golden thighs. Even their hair, glossy and thick, seemed to have benefited from this product. It was followed by an advert for haemorrhoids – 'Kiss your piles good-bye with Heaven Below!' Then there was a local newsflash: *A man's body was to-day recovered off the coast of St Petersburg, Pinellas County, having been accidentally discovered underwater by a scuba diver. The police have so far not been able to identify it, and at first could not even determine the sex because of all the lampreys that came up with it. The corpse had been mutilated by the removal of hands, feet, arms and genitals. Certain items of clothing suggest he was not an American. Now back to* The World of Wicked Wally.

'Nasty,' said Esther, genteelly inserting a chip lengthwise into her capacious mouth. 'Nasty using a word like that. Geni . . genitolios. They shouldn't use words like that. Children might be watching.'

Merriel stared at the buffet and wondered whether she could stomach a little lettuce. Tonio had just eaten a great deal and was looking green; he'd thought it would make him feel better but it made him feel much worse.

Sally Grootenjoy was thinking about Jesus the Homosexual. ——

——————————————————————

——————————————————————

——————————————————————, thought Florida's most boring heiress.

Vi, who'd had too much Mint Juleps (she hadn't realized that it was just a pretty name for neat bourbon), was eating well, feeling flushed. As her head span, she thought of her husband Ivor Cartridge, who at this very moment was probably trudging round the farm or organizing the distribution of 100,000 eggs to the profound contentment of his soul. What a lovely man her husband was. Dull but . . . Her head went round. No, not dull, she didn't mean dull, really she didn't. She meant, er, what did she mean actually? On the way back from the bromeliads the Senator had said gruffly 'Vi, you carry yourself well.' It was enough! She knew what it meant. She'd never been unfaithful to Ivor but she was all of a tizzy down below

and her head went round – ooo – Vi, remember you were born a
Winstanley-Stanley – there were times when Vi found it enormously
steadying to remember her origins – the Winstanley-Stanleys,
though merely county folk, merely provincial, had certain preten-
sions to glamour and should have been capable of taking a spot of
infidelity in their stride – ooo – naughty – Vi's head went round and
round – she thought she saw the Senator leering at her across the garden but it turned out to be a large cactus illuminated purple . . .

The Senator was in fact saying to David Zoton 'Have you seen the
bromeliads?'

David looked up surprised. It was the first friendly thing the
Senator had said to him all evening. 'The Palombos' greenhouse is
quite something,' said the Senator in a jolly mood, 'though no doubt
all paid for with dirty money.' Curtis felt he'd been indiscreet and
tried to cover himself. 'Just my joke.' Then went in deeper. 'Tonio's
no nun of course. He'd tell you that himself. Knows Miami like the
back of his hand. Some say he is Miami, but that's probably an
exaggeration – you know how folks talk. But I think Merriel goes
through hell on the quiet.'

'She doesn't seem that quiet about it,' said David.

'There's a lot we don't see.' And the Senator called over to Sally
Grootenjoy who had been telling Carol about her desire to visit
Scandinavia one day. Sally was really hooked on the idea of Oslo in
March. 'Sally, why don't you show our friend Mr Zoton the
bromeliads?'

'Can I do that?' asked Sally.

'Of course, he's English, he doesn't know anything about
bromeliads.'

'Bromeliads seem to be quite the thing down here,' said David.

'Oh . . ' said Sally whose blankness had, extraordinarily, acquired
a tinge. David steered her off the verandah as if steering her onto
a dancefloor which was something Sally could cope with very
well; she was born to be escorted; without an escort Sally simply
stopped.

'You got a girl?' said Tonio to Guy.

'She's gone to Mexico.'

'Shitty country,' said Tonio. Merriel's nose quivered with distress. This was the sort of thing she loathed/adored in her husband,

130

the use of words like shitty – did he have to in public? couldn't he wait until they were in bed?

'She speaks elementary Russian and makes very good ice-cream,' said Guy.

'Aaaargh!!' burst out Tonio.

'Tonio,' said Merriel with unusual concern though this may not have been obvious because of her sunglasses and because a note of concern was often in her voice. Tonio had gone bright red and had an enormous rictus. He was sweating copiously. Tremendous belches rolled up from the pit of his guts making a loud evil noise like the creaking of heavy church doors. Farts popped from his bottom and came rattling out between the buttocks.

Merriel looked desperately about and made a grab for high-tone normalcy. 'There's a concert coming up at the Alligator Bowl,' she fluted, 'Ravel, Chopin, a Greek pianist, Ganglion Vapers.'

Nancy, who'd been dozing on a divan, revived at this and said 'I know him. We must go. We don't get much culture down here since Jimmy de Goldstein left for Italy.'

Tonio was mute with pain.

Merriel said 'Let Gerry get the fireworks, it's time for those, let Esther get Tyrone down, get the others – where are Sally and David?'

'They went to look at the bromeliads,' said the Senator.

Sally and David were in the greenhouse.

'Your hair smells so lovely,' said David.

'Oh . . ' said Sally, 'I've never smelled it.' Which was true – she'd never been able to reach her pubic hair with her nose. David's tongue flickered in and out of her like a small flame. This flame went flickering all over her. 'You seem to be entirely covered in a chemical prophylactic,' he said, pausing for breath.

'I spray something just about every place,' said Sally under the impression that he'd paid her a compliment. 'What's that?'

'It's my penis.'

'It's my teddy-bear,' she said, hugging it.

David squirmed – 'Let me make you a woman – quick!'

'Don't tell my parents,' said Sally.

She gasped with pleasure/pain as her hymen went the way of all hymens; and David ejaculated deep within Sally's bloody orifice as

131

a shell burst in the sky overhead like a pink chrysanthemum. It refracted oddly through the glass. Sally whimpered and was worried by the blood. She had flashing images of Mummy and Daddy with tomahawks sticking in them. A variety of liquids, most of them strange to her, smeared her clothes as she and David unglued at the groin.

Little Tyrone clapped his hands with glee at the fireworks and jumped up and down. 'Son . . . ' Tonio mooned tearfully over the boy. Tyrone, another only child (his younger sister had poked her head out between Merriel's legs, taken one look at the world, and promptly expired), was wearing a one-piece warm-up suit in lemon polyester suedette elasticated at the waist with zippers at the front – the guggums! who's gonna be a sports star den? Tyrone stopped jumping up and down with glee, swayed thoughtfully for a moment, and brought up something creamy which dribbled down his chin.

Tonio, despite his agony of flatulence, bent down and wiped it off with his loosened tie, saying 'There there. . . ' Tyrone looked up at Da Da with absolute devotion. At this point Tonio's face went rigid and he gripped his stomach and his whole posture froze. The boy sensed something, became very afraid, burst into tears.

Huge roman candles cannoned balls of spangled colour high into the air and at their zenith these balls exploded with a brilliant flash and a stunning loudness which crashed against the house and echoed through the trees in hard pulsations. Further down the garden, Gerry was letting off shells. Phut! Head over heels they'd go, spinning up secretly into the night – moments later the shell would explode – a sudden unexpected spectacle in the sky – releasing its pent-up glories in dazzling supernovae of fulfilment. Phut! And another would begin its secret ascent to glory. Gerry let off some green and red sky flares which dropped curtains of smoke and lurid illumination across the scene, and in this visibility it now became obvious that Tonio was having real trouble. He was staggering backwards, howling, exploding at his outlets. His eyes rolled back in his head – the whites showed horribly – and with violent jerks a sludge that looked to be dark green began pumping out of his mouth. Everyone fell back aghast. A most disgusting discharge now replaced the green sludge, as if he were vomiting up small pieces of flesh bristling with needles. The explosion of fireworks died away

132

but the flares continued to shed their awful silent light upon the suffering man, a man disgorging his own entrails, a man who continued to claw onto the life being torn out of him – he scraped frantically at his chest and belly so that the flesh bled, ripped and came away in his hands. With a final convulsion and a dreadful roar, Tonio corkscrewed up on his toes, went completely stiff, and fell dead at the feet of his son, his wife, and his guests.

– 6 –

The Hurricane

Prelude. Guy leaned over and sneaked a look between white venetian blinds without getting out of bed. 'Another wonderful day . . . ' he groaned and flopped back.

'Who are you?' he said, looking down at the curly head he'd leaned over.

2 eyes slowly winched open in an immobile face. 'I feel a hundred,' she said. 'What year is it?' She was young.

'It's another wonderful day,' said Guy. 'I don't think I can take another wonderful day . . . I've forgotten your name.'

'Me too,' she mumbled. 'Where's your waist? That's better . . . '

Over breakfast, 3 orgasms later (2 for her, 1 for him), they swapped names.

'I hope you haven't got any nasty diseases,' she said.

'So do I,' he said, 'because I didn't have any yesterday.'

'This coffee's not doing the trick,' she said. 'I'm going for a swim.'

Guy never saw her again or ever forgot her name, which was Fudge, goddess of dawn . . . . .

The Senator clutching his head came onto the back lawn where morning coffee was to be had. He too felt a hundred. The sun banged nastily against his eyes and there was an ugly tautness in the heat. Among shouting photons, he made out Vi's face, so obviously a happy and integrated thing to-day.

'Coffee, Curtis?' she said with the geniality of one who's got out on the right side of the bed. Curtis's bed. They hadn't done much, just flopped together after too much drink, but during the night she'd played with Curtis's genitals, she'd actually *played* with a man's genitals for the first time ever, and Vi felt a whole new amusement park of life had opened up for her.

'Yes please,' said Curtis sheepishly. He knew he hadn't screwed her, knew he hadn't come, she had, oh yes, she'd been *there* all right, but he'd just lain on his back being used and finally – he hadn't come . . .

'Coffee, Jake?' said Vi. The gardener was sweeping up some dead stuff. 'Curtis . . . '

'Yes, Vi?' The Senator cowered. Was she going to say something about 'it'?

'Jake's a fine looking boy,' she said.

Fine looking boy? Was she implying that Curtis Bute was less than breathtakingly fine and virile himself? Did she think his penis wasn't big enough or was a funny shape or something? He'd always wanted a bigger penis – 5 inches was below average whichever book you read . . . He also wanted to be rugged and successful and rich, yes, and rich. Old Virgil Bute III had left them nothing except a sense of their own importance. Big deal! Politics – you didn't make money in politics, not exactly, but the man who comes out of politics poorer than he went in is a fool. Curtis was no fool, no siree.

Vi thought – Am I right in thinking Curtis is deeply offended by something? Has he got toothache?

Nancy came sluggishly onto the lawn in the faded blue beach wrap. 'There's a parcel for you, Curtis, and a couple of letters. I've been thinking, Vi. I'm going ahead on the pink & mustard bedroom.'

'Oh yes,' said Vi. 'Take the plunge, what the hell.'

Nancy drew her head back and narrowed her eyes on Vi. She handed Curtis his mail and went for her morning dip. The parcel was maddeningly taped up, but eventually he got inside to a box with a flip-top lid. Vi sipped her tea, she always stuck out for tea first thing, and watched the line of Jake's body as he plied the broom.

As Curtis lifted the flip-top his face, which up to now had been rouches of flab, tightened miraculously onto the bones. The eyes, puffy and red, now drained of blood and the whites went grey. There on his lap, nestling in the tissues of the box like a pair of lovers, were 2 ears. On the inside of the lid had been scrawled *These may help*

135

you to listen to our warning. A quavering grunt remained trapped in the Senator's throat like recalcitrant phlegm. He pushed the things off his lap, stood up, and took 3 steps back – all in one movement. Vi did not understand at first when he started to stammer 'Ears . . . horrible great dead ears, don't want em, don't need em . . . horrible dead ears . . '

It was Jake the gardener, an expert on unusual plant life, who diagnosed the cause of Tonio's death: the deadly Minever plant, which originates in Amazonia. The seeds, when administered in food, attach themselves to the walls of the stomach. 3 months later the body is infested with a growth of needles which it is impossible to kill or excise without killing the host. Death follows anyway. Seeds of the Minever are the perfect long distance poison. The murderer has several months to get away and when the act is discovered, it is always too late for the victim. Jake read them the appropriate reference in Pammel's *Poisonous Plants*.

So Tonio had been murdered. But by whom? And why? Merriel took her husband's death badly – much to everyone's surprise. She clung desperately to Tyrone until some people from the Board of Education came and pulled him off her, saying it was time he started school. In due course she founded the Tonio Palombo Award in Botanic Sciences at St Petersburg University – the first award went to a student who developed a defoliation bomb which destroys all vegetation but leaves humans, animals and buildings merely stunned.

Senator Bute said he always knew Tonio was big in the underworld and that this proved it. The Senator had however been unnerved, given up eating vegetables altogether, concentrating on steak, cake and pills, and in this condition the ears had come as a major shock.

Nancy went briefly into a depression from which she was roused by vigorous colonic irrigation every day for a week. 'Nasty stuff – let's swill it out – swill it away – let's lift you up high and bright and clean as a soap bubble – up – up – up!' said the irrigator, working the hose and taps and jets like a maestro at his instrument.

Where Tonio had touched Carol's face, the cheek broke out in boils some days later. 'He must have been pure poison by the end,' said Vi who, having lived another day herself, was in an excellent frame of mind. 'It's no good blaming the plant,' she said. Death always had the effect of switching her onto life. Decidedly she got a buzz from funerals. Most of her visits to London from the country were alone (Ivor never liked to get closer to the metropolis than Windsor) and were for memorial services. If she wanted to go to Harrods or the theatre or an exhibition, she'd usually chime it in with a memorial service. Usually they were for people she hadn't particularly known when they were alive, but once you start on the memorial service circuit, well, for a start you meet very interesting people, and you often get listed on the Court page of *The Times* so that people get to know you're still about. 'Such a shame,' Vi would say to somebody, 'so undeserved. Why him? Why then? Why in that extraordinary way?' And on the train from Paddington back to Mandalay-on-Wallop, her heart would sing out 'It's so good to be alive!' and she'd be filled with a rich balmy kindness for her neighbour.

On the night of Tonio's death, Guy and David went back to David's for a nightcap on the terrace. There was no moon and the sea was hidden in blackness.

'Do you think he was into anything weird?' wondered David.

'Almost certainly,' said Guy. His leg was over the arm of his chair and he got a sudden cramp.

'Stand on it,' said David. 'Put pressure on it. You're not putting pressure on it. What sort of weird?'

Guy looked at David with a face which seemed frozen in the act of sucking a boiled sweet.

'Stand on it for heaven's sake! Look, come inside, I want to show you something.' Guy hobbled after David who went up to the video and slotted a film into it. 'It's called *Headless I Love You.*'

After some minutes Guy said 'I'm not enjoying this.' David switched it off at the point where the head was connected to the body only by a few thinning threads of gore. 'Why did you switch it off?' said Guy.

'I only wanted to give you the idea. There are a couple more tucked back there. Are they for real?'

'Seems so,' said Guy. 'I came across one in London. Same style. What happens next?'

'The head comes off and they all screw her in the neck. Now you know the story you don't have to see the film.' They went outside again for fresh air.

'What are you going to do?' asked Guy. 'Give them to the police?'

'No,' said David.

'Good.'

'Why good?'

'Mine came from Charles Robinson.'

The whites of David's eyes flashed in the gloom of the terrace and he let out a lot of breath. 'If I come clean with you, will you come clean with me?' he said.

'Is that a proposal of marriage?'

'Oh hell,' said David and went in to get a couple more drinks. Guy looked out into darkness, to where the sea lovingly, invisibly massaged the black beach with swishings and suckings.

Guy lay on his bed sweating out a session of the horrors, too much drink, twitched up, vertiginous. A black hole had designs on him. From its core came a powerful magnetic force, a great suck, the suck towards chaos. And he was a frail flicker of tormented light, no more than that. But Guy didn't move, he just lay there, all violence turning within, coiling back on itself. The stability which is gyroscopic – well, the problem here is self-enclosure. If the gyroscope should decide to overspin, overheat, then the only thing which can stop it is exhaustion. Or violence. Violence is self-enclosure giving way. Guy's thoughts went back to prison, back to the canteen eating slops of gristle – he'd overheard a man say 'Something just snapped inside me and I found myself gouging out her eyes with an apple-corer.' The man who said this was a mouse of a fellow who worked for the Inland Revenue. This 'something snapped inside' need not be very bad – sometimes it can be very good – but always it involves major change in an individual's life. Guy had had a few snaps. Small-ish snaps. Not the Big Snap. What happened when the big snap came? Or what would happen if the Big Snap never came?

The word Kate rose and fell and drifted in his consciousness like a rubbery water-filled balloon, heavy with equivocal reverberations of complex meaning – Kate . . . then unexpectedly the anxiousness

138

fell away as a fog may abruptly clear, and he found himself concentrated with an intense erection. He turned on the small bedside lamp. Blueish veins started out of the shaft of his member and the knob was swollen tight like a fat purple plum and the tiny lips of the urethral opening whispered crazy secrets to him from an ancient world. Guy stared at this large proboscis, its very singularity a metaphor of loneliness and endeavour, sticking up from the base of his belly like a shout from the holy universe of pure fact . . . Kate is a black girl, an African with big lips and sweltering crotch – she's white again – creamy thighs bitten and bloodied – David is white, no black – particoloured body of blackandwhite female/male – David is – Guy touched the member and something began to roll and tingle, began . . . That contact between fact and act which we call reality, and that contact between fact and discovery which we call purpose, and that contact between reality and purpose which we call truth – contact was made. The penis spat into the vacant air quanta of white gunk which flew around in strings and globules as the convulsion rolled through him in a magnificent mindless wave—

Poseidon's Ki-Ki Closet looked its best at 10 a.m. because it was still relatively free from human defilement. Louella's younger brother, who took the morning shift, was stacking soft drinks in a fridge. In one corner the Swami was smoking and drinking decaffeinated coffee. He felt exceptionally well this morning, having yesterday had a session with the rag – he must do it again soon.

The door opened and a stranger entered. He was tall and swarthy and despite the warmth wore grey suede boots, baggy blue trousers that were not jeans, and a shirt and waistcoat of Tzigane character. His black hair was done up in pigtails. The face was attractive, weather beaten, with a crooked smile that knew no dentistry and the brown eyes had a purring humour in them which immediately found the rather similar eyes of the Swami. He smiled a smile not to trust (this was the reason for its charm) and said to Louella's brother 'A large vodka with orange, and a cognac on the side.'

'That's some breakfast,' said the boy. 'We do ham and eggs as well.'

'Noon is time enough to start contemplating solids.' The stranger

139

turned to the Swami and said 'Good morning, your Holiness. How's the weather up there?'

'Same as down here,' said the Swami. 'Join me for a cigarette?'

'No, but I'll come over and watch you die. What brings a man like you to a backwater like this?'

'Have you been to Calcutta, my home town?'

'No, I haven't.'

'If you had you wouldn't be asking why I'm here. The modern world is divided not into the rich and poor but into the fixed and unfixed. Those who must remain in one place, no matter what place and be it ever so important, are what we understand in the modern world by the word "provincial". I move, according to my wishes.'

'I'm a mover too,' said the stranger. 'I just moved up from Mexico. The desert. Couldn't stand it any more. My half sister lives up at Decent Bluffs. Merriel Palombo?'

'Oh yes. Her husband was poisoned to death recently.'

'Ah . . . ' said the stranger whose eyes danced with an unexpected zest, and there was silence for a while.

'And what were you doing in the desert, my friend?' asked the Swami.

'Working on a film.'

The Swami had noticed that in America the usual way of giving oneself cachet without revealing anything was to say 'Working on a film', just as in London men said 'Something in the City'.

'Avant-garde stuff . . . ' added the stranger oddly.

– Boring, thought the Swami, all those arty experiments, all that foreplay, never coming. Art is self-expression! they declare, whereas art is often the complete opposite of self-expression . . . the inside of Carol's leg . . . 'I like it here,' said the Swami. 'There aren't many tourists, it's ordinary and middle-class and clean.'

'Does Beau Bute still hang out down here?' asked the stranger.

'Yes, well, there are exceptions in every locality,' said the Swami. 'I believe he tries to shock me with his outrageous exploits.'

'Humph!' said the stranger and his furrowed brow was indicative of interior monologue – or interior dialogue actually. 'I'm going to have another couple of vodkas. Can I get your Holiness anything?'

'A Coca Cola would be lovely,' said the Swami, 'and some more cigarettes.'

The stranger's eye showed sudden anger. 'You can pay for your own death,' he said and went to the bar.

Carol, full of morning brio, was sitting on the end of David's bed saying 'No'.

David looked tense. He'd abandoned all attempts to be nonchalant about it. 'For God's sake please, come on.'

'No, I don't feel like it at the moment.'

'I'll make you feel like it.'

'No, I only dropped by to say good morning and be neighbourly.'

'Oh come on, it's nothing—'

'If it's nothing then – no,' said Carol.

'I don't mean it's *nothing*, I mean – oh come on, don't be mean.'

'Ask Sally.'

'So it's Sally, is it?'

'It's nothing to do with Sally,' said Carol. 'I just don't want to.'

'Carol, come on, please, look, look here.'

'Put it away. I'm not interested.'

'Yes, come on, FOR GOD'S SAKE stop teasing, come on, oh—'

'No!' she said like a little prat, like a clever little tight arse, like a pert little prude, like a shitty little madam. He lunged desperately at her across the sheets, his tool bobbing up ahead of him, an inconvenience, disproportionate, a mistake in the design. She danced off the end of the bed like a butterfly disturbed on a flower and shimmered down the hall to the kitchen. 'I'm going to get you a fruit juice,' she said. He padded after her, begging, abject, hunched, tumescent, wheedling, whining, but too proud to rape her – that is – 'Then I'm going to rape you!' He jumped forward but with a laugh like a shower of tiny golden bells she was gone through the glass doors. He felt sickened, picked up the fruit juice and drank mechanically. 'Bloody cock-teaser,' he said aloud. It was awful – he adored it . . . he went into the living-room and flicked on some bracing metallic pop music . . . A lizard hurried across the stone of the terrace, a shadow flitted across the corner of the plate glass window which was half open. David smiled his cute smile. 'OK, you can come back in now. My thing's gone down.' There was a soft noise out there. He

141

went onto the terrace and looked left and right. To his right a mass of greenery came up to the window in thick folds. And to the left – David turned quickly back to the right – THUNK! . . . .
. . . .

Next he remembered Carol's face in triplicate – the face zoomed slowly in and out. It was dark. No, it was light, very light. He swung his head to both sides to try and get his eyes out of the light. Carol was holding something cold and from time to time she touched him with it.

Carol disappeared.

David lay there rocking in the heat to the jungle drums of his heart.

Carol's face appeared above him again – this time 2 men were with her – no, a man.

'This is turning into quite a holiday,' said Guy. 'Help me get him inside.' On the sofa Carol placed a cold flannel across David's brow. 'Who slugged you?' asked Guy.

– The world and its fucking questions already, thought David.

By degrees normal perception reasserted itself. 'You may be suffering from concussion,' said Carol, drawing on her wide TV knowledge of such events. 'I'll order a doctor,' and she scuttled to the phone, buttocks a-wobble.

David said nothing for a while. Then something occurred to him. 'Those videos – are they still there?' Guy looked. They'd been swiped!

For the rest of the day nobody did much.

The Senator found that the physical symptoms of not having orgasm came on after about a week or so of abstinence (when he was young it was after 24 hours and he'd be obliged to masturbate each day he didn't have a girl – none of this 'let's save it up for the big moment' stuff). These symptoms were: twitching, hypersensitivity of the skin, preoccupation, and especially itchy legs. 'Itchy legs' was a very annoying nervous tickle in the muscles of the legs – it is fairly common among men having insufficient sex activity. The touching and cuddling and orgasm which the body would like, and does not get, is folded back and distributed through the limbs in sprays of twinges.

But to-night the Senator, relieved to be in bed alone, did not get itchy legs. Nor had he taken one of his pink pills which he sometimes did if he had a lot to do the next day and couldn't stop thinking about it. Vi, who had made a covert appeal which consisted of stretching out her arm which he had nimbly avoided (but it was a near thing – the extremities of her fingers had grazed his cheek), Vi had been tucked up in bed by Nancy.

'What do you think of Curtis, dear?'

'He's selfish,' said Nancy. 'That is, he's more selfish than he need be to be a man.'

The Senator was propped up in bed reading *How to Stay on Top without Being Nasty*, while sleep with a coy hand tugged at each eyelid. '"People are much more likely to obey if they don't realize they are being commanded,"' he read . . . '"You cannot control people, but you can infect them"'. . . .

The Senator had 8 hours' sleep and upon waking went round banging up everyone else. 'Come on, we're going deep-sea fishing, who's coming?' Guy, David and Dale were coming. Beau said he was flying down to the Swamp for a couple of days, and he slunk off. Vi, Nancy and Carol weren't coming. The Senator was pleased by this division of the sexes. The Senator wanted to catch shark, to do battle with something with teeth, and felt more single-minded in this if women weren't present. 'We have to be at the harbour by 11,' he said.

'It's almost that now,' said Guy whose mornings had a habit of draining away before he was quite with it.

Dale turned himself the right way up and went to get his bag (he'd been standing on his head on the lawn; this was the Swami's influence – 'Use gravity to massage your internal organs, Dale' – Dale was very pleased to learn this because his brow had often puckered over the problem of how to handle oneself inside).

Harbours are always full of activity, the clang and whirr of arrivals and departures, the buzz of motorboats, the throb of engines, shouts between land and water. But in this harbour there was no activity at all, just an old-timer sitting on the jetty staring inland. The water slurped up and down in the basin like warm saliva and on its surface a slimy scum curled in rainbow spirals of oil.

Eventually the Senator located the boat, the *Jolly Junky*, made from shining white plastic with an elaborate crown of futuristic

143

radar and radio contraptions on top of the bridge. The crew of 3 was missing and eventually spotted getting drunk in a nearby bar. The Captain, a hippy with long dirty hair and long dirty fingernails hardened and chipped by work, said 'You got the bread?' The Senator handed him a roll of notes. The Captain took half and divided the remainder between the other 2 who grunted (in due course one of these 2 would replace the old-timer on the jetty and become the new old-timer).

. . . . . Sharp white plastic bows cut through the dead flat sea while the crown of radar rotated above. Further out the sea took on a silky undulation but the only surf was that which foamed back from the prow. The water was clear and deep. The boat motored out . . . and out . . . and out . . . .

Darkness fell suddenly on this night like a hatchet. The boat shone brightly in a small sphere of white light upon the vast dark disc of the sea. O fragile light in the blackness forever impending! What is that thing which lies always in wait for you? Like the sound of alien breathing on an unlit staircase. We push our hands out blindly before us, the sooner to make contact with whatever ghastly thing it is –

'Oh it's you!'

'And thank God it's you! I thought I heard something on the stairs.'

'So did I. It must have been you.'

'Yes, and it must have been you.'

'It must have been us.'

Laughter. They return reassured to their separate bedrooms and close the doors and snuggle back under the covers and sleep until morning calls them. But in the night the thing which aroused them and drew them out along the landing, it still breathes there. In their passion for comfort they stopped hearing it and embraced each other – but it is still there, waiting on the staircase, lonely and predatory, breathing . . .

The Senator was smoking on deck in a chair while Dale performed his evening press-ups some distance away.

'Have you got a girlfriend?' the Senator said.

– Silly old fart, thought Dale. What business is it of his? He'll ask

144

about my fucking Dad next – fucking Dad!

But David came out on deck and the Senator turned his questions to him. 'Are you married, David? I've just been discussing women with young Dale here.'

'I was,' said David.

'I've married twice,' said the Senator, 'and I do recommend it for focusing a man's designs on the world.'

'Senator,' said David, 'why do you think someone slugged me yesterday?'

'Depends,' said the Senator, refilling his pipe (which he smoked on water; on land he smoked cigars).

'Depends on what?'

'On what you've been up to.'

Mmm – David's attempt to discover something without giving anything away wasn't working very well – it never does. It's a myth that 'closed' people know a lot. They endure just as much ignorance as they cause.

'And for that matter, Senator, why should someone send you a couple of ears in the post, eh?'

The Senator shuddered and sighed. 'Mr Zoton, we were all very upset by that. This country of mine, which I love so much, is nonetheless inhabited by a certain number of geeks. Remind me to show you the rest of my crank mail some day. We worship freedom in America. Inevitably this has its side effects.'

At that moment there was a high drone above, which sounded like a small aircraft. The boat, which shone like the ship of knowledge, was not inconspicuous from the air. But from the deck they could see nothing in the blackness. Next there was a godalmighty crash. Dale was knocked to the ground howling. A crate about a yard square had fallen out of the sky and clipped him. It tumbled over and smashed to a halt against a cabin wall. They looked at it. Sawdust and guns showed in the rupture. Dale continued to howl. His arm was broken. The sound of the aircraft faded away.

The others came on deck. The Captain said 'Jesus, man, guns from heaven.'

The Senator said 'What's going on here? I demand to know what's going on!'

They all stared at each other in the artificial light. They all accused each other. It got them nowhere and, riddled with doubt, they had to

145

go to bed, after examining the guns, stowing them below, and deciding to return to Whitewater first thing in the morning so Dale could get his arm fixed.

'Has anyone ever tried to kill you, Guy?' asked David from the bunk underneath. They were sharing a cabin. It was hot and airless and although the porthole was open, nothing moved through, as if outside and inside were in the same room.

'I was at the docks once in London,' said Guy from above. 'Someone took a pot shot at me. It was a guy called Adam Shatner landed me in it. He pissed off abroad. . . . . . . Does death frighten you, David?'

'Like crazy.'

'I don't know if it frightens me.'

'And it makes me feel randy,' said David.

There was a long pensive silence. From time to time one would make a noise or turn in his bunk to which the other would respond with another noise or movement. And at the end of a sequence of subtle widely-spaced noises, which was another kind of conversation, they fell asleep.

Dawn broke suddenly like a bucketful of orange juice tossed in a single splash up the sky, broke with alacrity, like a businessman locked out of his office, angrily twirling his moustaches, impatient to proceed with the affairs of the day. Then the blinding ball of the sun appeared magnificently above the horizon, touching the coolness of the sea with a liverish heat unnatural at this hour. The dark slippery wriggly things of the ocean which had risen up in the night to approach that magical interface where the upper surface of the sea and the lower surface of the air are conjoined in a nightlong rippling kiss, now descended again into more tenebrous regions, away from all the hoo-hah. Lifting in the east, the orange light began to push across the hemisphere of the sky, and night was forced back and down onto its knees until it crawled away in defeat. At roughly the half-way point in this transition, one of the crew knocked loudly on the Captain's door.

'Fuck off . . . ' growled the Captain, putting a pillow over his head. But the crewman persisted. With a greeting of 'What the hell!' the

Captain yanked open the door and exposed his sleep-creased face to the astringent rebuke of morning air. The Captain's locks were all awry and greasily mashed together. His eyes wobbled like 2 blobs of green mucus in a ditch. Crusts of sleep adhered to his blinking eyelashes and a foul odour, originating in the stomach and rolling out across the furred tongue, composed of stale alcohol and cigarettes, decomposed food, and plain old-fashioned bodily decay, issued almost visibly from between brown unbrushed teeth. In the absence of any breeze, the odour survived intact a good 4 feet into the open air.

'Captain, I think you should know, the barometer's dropping fast, very fast, I've never seen anything like it, it's dropping like a stone, I'd be glad if you'd come and look.'

The Captain retreated back into his lair to find some clothes and in due course appeared on the bridge in shorts and a t-shirt which bore the slogan *Life Is Hard* across the back. He looked at the barometer, tapped it. 'Shit . . . Willy, keep an eye on it. I'm going to grab another hour's sleep.'

Willy sat on the bridge while the boat slept beneath his feet in the early morning. He lit a joint of marijuana and dozed off himself . . . . . He was aroused not by any noise but by some minute alteration in the sensations on the surface of his skin, some absolutely silent gearshift in the atmosphere. His eyes opened, he looked dozily about, then he saw it in the east. He stood there for quite a long time, enthralled. Then went to the Captain's cabin.

'It's coming, Captain,' he called through the door.

'Ah . . . ' said the Captain. 'Wake them up then.' He crawled off his bed, went over to the washbasin and splashed his face.

At 8 a.m., the Senator, Guy, David, Dale, the Captain, Willy, and the other crewman, who was called Sam, stood along the portside rail looking at the eastern horizon. Dale, who'd had the worst night of his life, adjusted his arm painfully in a makeshift sling. The sky was a wholesome, defiant blue but at the foot of it, like Indian ink soaking into blotting paper, black stormclouds appeared in a turbulent line. It was as if night, by a macabre reversal of natural laws, was about to reclaim the world.

'Radio for weather, Sam,' said the Captain.

The man at the other end of the radio said 'Hurricane in your area. Best of luck, boys. By the way, she's called Juno.'

The stormclouds, tumbling and boiling, advanced into the blue like many overlapping explosions. On reaching the sun they recoiled, gathered their strength, pounced and eliminated it. The world went dark.

'It's still a way off. We may be able to outrun it,' said the Captain. The atmosphere was extremely strange. In such an atmosphere pterodactyls might have flown. The silence was complete, the stillness suffocatingly profound. And yet a tremendous violence was demolishing the sky. The effects seemed to contradict each other and this created great tension which made every nerve fibre erect. Then out of the grotesque stillness and prodigious silence, like a long thin cruel curling whiplash, came the first flick of wind.

Deep in the Amazonian rain forest it was dry for a change. The sun was shining in the sky as fresh as breakfast and in a forest glade slender prisms of sunlight, solid and contained in the way that laser beams are, pierced the canopy of leaves at various angles and shot into the earth like golden assegais. This canopy, forming jigsawlike almost a continuous membrane extending over 1000 miles in every direction, had in addition the property of translucence and allowed to drift down a soft green aquarium light, generally diffused, that had none of the characteristics of gloom. From time to time the irritated squawk of a rare hidden bird would echo in the glade; or high up in the branches there would be a scuttle along a bough and a scream, as something caught and killed something else. And in the clearing below, where a few shafts of sunlight shot at angles into a comparatively lawnlike levelness, a line of men and women in Western clothes stood quietly. They were facing a circle of naked Indians who were seated on the plush ground. Nothing was happening.

'How much longer do we have to wait?' whispered a woman to a tall blond Englishman with violet eyes.

The Englishman was motionless for a while. Then he slid his eyes off the Indians and turned them full on her. 'Shsh . . . be patient,' he said with a twinkle.

Click-clack, click-clack, down a corridor in the London Clinic whose walls gleamed like the shiny moist surface of an internal organ, walked 2 figures, one short, the other tall. The short one was a lady's companion called Joyce. It was the day of the week when she visited her mistress and usually she managed to inveigle someone into giving up their lunchtime to accompany her. On this particular day she had co-opted the arm of Rory McLulu. Behind them at a steadily increasing distance, comatose for months, on a life support system whose capillaries streamed out of her body into white steel boxes that flashed with lights, fluttered with dials, bleeped with monitors, being fed by the slow persistent drip of juices into her arm, lay Margot Ingot. She lay in Room 27 on her back with eyes closed, legs straight out, arms at her side, motionless, immured among technology like the consort of a futuristic pharaoh.

Joyce and Rory descended in the lift. 'I'm taking you for a snack at the Ritz,' he said as they swung through the doors and out to the world of light and human affairs.

'OK,' said Joyce matter-of-factly.

They got into a taxi in the Marylebone Road and Rory closed the door with a clunk! At this moment Margot's eyes happened to flick open.

With his mouth hanging open, Sir Glorian Jones was slowly turning the pages of *Discourse on Pure Ridicule* by James Thorne, a posthumous work, which had lately arrived by surface mail from Blackwell's of Oxford. Sir Glorian was short and tubby with a cloud of wuzzy white hair scooped out tonsurelike on top. He was reclining in creamy clothes in the *salone* of his exquisite villa, waiting for his coffee, having lunched alone. From their plinths, stone and bronze statues stared right through him. Outside too a string of them along the parapet of the terrace, variously bending a leg, sporting a fig-leaf, raising an arm in acknowledgement of the muse or a bunch of grapes to salute Dionysus, or simply standing there entirely naked in Apollonian composure, maintained a heartless scrutiny of the Tuscan hills, careless of the afternoon sun which scorched their naked stone shoulders spotted with yellow lichen.

40 minutes away by motor car and a dangerously swinging road

which had this year already 3 deaths to its credit, sat Florence in its depression, veiled thinly in a lemonish chiffon of polluted air, its narrow stone streets constipated with tourists and vehicles, baking beneath a thick crust of art and culture, too cautious freely to sweat, simply suffering, enduring, waiting for the high summer to roll over and die.

But through 3 tall windows with semicircular tops, draped in heavy brocade which swept the floor with old gold fringes, Sir Glorian was aware only of Nature and Man in a loose Arcadian embrace. True, an invasion of squat pylons across the hills to the left had given pain. They had gone up 10 years ago as a result of some holiday development mercifully (but only just) out of sight. Sir Glorian had however learned to live with the fact that not even he could cast life into a perfect dream – somewhere the bugs always got in.

– Where was Benedetto? Late with the coffee as usual . . . Sir Glorian limply turned a page. Ronny, a Shi' Tsu dog, ran into the room and sat down with intelligent activity in his eyes, waiting for his master to emerge from self-absorption.

– Where was Petr? Still in Florence? Looking at shirts and leather goods in the shops . . . Was it wise to have given Petr that credit card?

He rose from his seat in the shape of a seashell (an eccentric piece of furniture he'd grown very fond of), walked across to a long maroon velvet tape and yanked the tassel on the end of it. Nothing sounded in the room, but he hoped that far away in the place where bells rang someone would have the decency to respond.

At the end of El Dorado, in his garden room, where the walls of glass were covered with tendrils of black wrought iron and an upward flow of living creepers, the Swami was slowly feeding foot after foot of white cotton strip into his mouth, while his eyes rested on the needlepoint within. 3 days' fasting and pints of warm water had helped, and sitting cross-legged, he'd begun to swallow the rag at dawn, after urination and a very minor stool. With a gently rocking peristalsis, that moment must soon come when he would be able to complete the exercise by plucking one end of the rag out of his anus. He would then fold both ends, one emerging from the mouth, the

150

other from the anus, across the palm of his left hand and, by stopping the universe, enjoy an interval of perfect equilibrium.

A young waiter, mobile of hips and impassive of face, with a patchy stubble on his chin which would never flourish into a proper beard, came out of the café and set a jug of bad coffee and a plate of small breakfast cakes on a table under the porch. He wiped his hands on greasy white ducks, hovered as if a question stirred in his brain, then went back in without saying anything.

A dog stared abjectly from the dusty roadway but fearful of kicks did not approach. 2 black-eyed children hopped past shouting at each other. They stopped, detained by the head of gringo hair, and both the children simultaneously extended the palms of their hands as taught to do by their mother whenever gringo hair was encountered. Kate put a coin on each of the warm surfaces and the children ran away without a word.

– Little shits, they might have said thanks or hullo, she thought.

She sipped the coffee and ate a coil of currant pastry dusted with fine sugar. Another cake she threw for the dog which moved forward and swallowed it in one gulp and then returned to exactly the same position it had occupied before without the slightest gesture of pleasure, the cur . . . Kate was enjoying her adventure very much. Something cruel and indifferent, yet aware, in the psyche of Mexico had given her the mental space to organize her thoughts and resettle some of her emotions. She looked at her watch. The bus south was very late.

The Viscount Mountsavage was furious. Another crucial radio call was overdue. With clenched fists he stood in the window of his bedroom as, below, his father and the Duke of Dollar and Stirling, who was passing through the district *sans duchesse*, took a stroll before lunch.

'Why don't you rebuild that north east wing, Flamingfield?' said the Duke.

151

'But my father took great pains to demolish it into a picturesque ruin.'

'So what? I'm adding a new wing to Dollar Castle. Brenda promised me 2 turrets for my birthday but there was nothing to hang them on, so we're making additions to the castle according to plans originally drawn up in the 18th century. Why aren't there any statues down by your lake?'

Anne interrupted them by shouting across the lawn 'Come and get it!'

The Duke blinked and said 'Is that a servant of yours?'

'She's a bit more than a servant,' said Lord Flamingfield, flustered.

The Viscount slammed his window shut in irritation and the 2 men looked up. Henry crossed the carpet, picked up a cricket bat and whacked one of the model aircraft off the ceiling. It whizzed into a wall of faded William Morris wallpaper and shattered. 'For God's sake call damn you!'

The towerblock in Tower Hamlets had thrilling views across London, obscene graffiti in the broken lifts, piss on the staircases, and muggers in the corridors. 2 of its external flanks were pure concrete and rose straight up from the ground like vertical runways. The other 2 flanks were composed of windows and small interlocking balconies of orange plastic. Jill's mother's flat was near the top. It looked westward and in the middle of her view was the swelling of St Paul's Cathedral like a massive boil filled with black pus.

Trevor was kneeling on a nylon carpet the colours of boiled sweets. His hands covered his face and his muscular back was curved over and shaking. He was sobbing his heart out.

Jill's mother tried to comfort the young man, though worried stiff herself these past terrible months. Why hadn't the girl left a note? Why didn't she phone? Both knew somehow that Jill was still alive but the telephone just sat there like a dark self-satisfied toad, withholding the answer, never breaking silence on this subject.

'I'll make a cuppa tea, Trevor darlin . . . ' said Mum. She pushed her feet into fluffy nylon slippers, stood up and smoothed down her nylon housecoat and shuffled off to the kitchenette where she also began to prepare ham sandwiches with pickles. From her kitchenette window the view stretched across the heart of London. World-famous landmarks teetered on the tip of her nose in swirls of mist, sunlight and motor exhaust. But she wasn't interested.

Vi was woken up by a violent onslaught of rain on the roof over her bedroom and thunder hitting the walls with the concussive weight of dynamite. She sat bolt upright. The noise was horrific and made the house seem no more than a construction of cardboard and sticks. Lightning attacked the sea and thunder broke immediately after, sending vivid pictures of the Bomb Party skidding across her brain like ugly Tarot cards. A pair of windows burst open. With a nasty screech the venetian blinds were mashed together and destroyed. 2 curtains flew up hysterically, knocking everything off the dressing-table, snapping with the noise of firecrackers, and the wind supported them horizontally like 2 blue beseeching arms. The din was frightful. It was dark but the bedside clock illuminated 9 o'clock in the morning. Vi clambered desperately out of bed, pulled on a dressing-gown, and managed to jam shut the windows again. She was soaked. Going onto the landing she saw Nancy coming towards her with a valium in one hand and a bourbon in the other. 'Have these,' said Nancy. 'It's gonna be the real thing. It's too late to close the shutters, damnit.'

The lightning lit up their faces in gothic sharpness.

'I don't think I want those, dear,' said Vi.

'What about the men?' said Nancy.

'I know,' said Vi in a colourless voice.

Carol came up behind Nancy and said 'I'll have those, Mom.'

The scale of the storm had taken them completely by surprise and, as human beings often are by the great phenomena of nature, they found themselves reduced to a nursery state, even adopting that short-stepped glug-glug shuffling gait of young children. In this way 3 shaky girls went downstairs, as if walking were still a kind of novelty, and into the living-room. With a reflex action Nancy turned on the television to link them up with the rest of the tribe.

'Shouldn't we turn the box off, unplug it, and sit under a table?' asked Vi. 'That's what we do in England.'

'But you don't have hurricanes in England,' said Nancy.

Every few moments the TV picture was lost to a razzle of lightning, but in intervals of clarity a soap opera was under way, the life and times of an ordinary farming family in the Midwest. [Ma, that is Maw, was shouting at Young Billy who stood with a hung head and tears on his cheeks and a broken-necked goose hanging by its feet from his hand. Blood dripped off the end of its beak. Young Billy's favourite dog Muff, the goose killer, whimpered shamefacedly behind a tree. Maw said that Paw (Pa) was going to deal with both of them when he got back in the evening, thus condemning Young Billy to a whole day of anguish during which he would seriously consider running away, and would run away, would hop a ride on the railway train – mournful atmospheric sound of American train sirens like the faraway hoots of heaven – and end up confused in the sinful fleshpots of Lincoln City after dark. Here obscenely painted prostitutes and mincing male perverts, hitherto unknown in Lincoln City, would attempt to elicit Young Billy's manhood, but the police would pick him up and return him to the farm and forgiving hugs. (There is however a true version of this story in which Billy is repeatedly strapped by his father and locked up with the Bible – once after he'd been discovered with a magazine of naked girls under his bed – so that he'd learn the meaning of SHAME. You gotta have *shame!* Billy came to be paralysed by shame, walking about with round shoulders and a pain in his groin – until one day, due to be strapped again, something snapped inside and he picked up his father's shotgun and shot both his parents dead and took off into the night with all their cash. He got clean away and this is the first time his story has been told).]

Along the bottom of the TV screen ran a repeating message in neon red. *Severe hurricane in your area – waterspouts at sea – tornadoes on land – please take precautions to protect your life.*

'I'll make a cup of tea,' said Vi and the moment she said it she attained composure and knew she'd be able to handle the storm no matter what it threw at her – but it didn't quite happen that way.

Carol said 'This is exciting' and gritted her teeth, wondering when the valium would hit (it never did).

The living-room had a long wall of windows from waist-high to ceiling, facing the sea. Nancy said 'If we can't close the shutters we might as well see what's going on', and pulled up all the venetian blinds. Black clouds exploded with lightning. Waves pounded up the beach in walls of foam 30 feet high. Rain blew against the win-

154

dows in angry gusts and there were continuous booming noises. Then the television went dead. There was no warning. The sound went and the picture shrank to a dot and vanished. That was that. In all her years on this earth Nancy had never had a television set go dead on her. It was a traumatic event. She experienced a sense of shock followed by a creep of fear through her entire body which was the horror of isolation. She was cut off. The storm was breaking up the tribe, to pick them off one by one. In a cold sweat she moved across to the telephone and picked it up. The telephone was dead. She felt a weird spasm in her chest as the muscles clenched there. Her throat was tight and something was tight above her eyes impairing vision. She poured a stiff bourbon. Then all the lights went.

'Will we be washed away?' asked Carol.

'Don't be silly,' said Nancy as her throat closed in a swallow.

Vi entered regally with a tray of tea things and sandwiches. 'It's not very hot, the kettle went on me. Come along, dears, we haven't had any breakfast yet – ooo – what's that funny thing out there?'

The 3 of them strained their eyes at the window. Out at sea was a hanging strip of comparative paleness, a tower of foam swaying as if dancing to a Brazilian band, attenuated towards its middle but spreading funnellike below and above where it disappeared into clouds. This was a waterspout, monstrous offspring of the union between sea and sky. The waterspout seemed to be travelling closer to the house but weaving about like a drunkard with a horrible will-it-won't-it uncertainty of direction. Making an odd noise, almost a hum, it lurched onto the beach. It wobbled there among crashing waves like a pale giant going for a paddle. It seemed to notice the 3 women and to contemplate them groggily. They looked very small transfixed in that window, clutching at their breasts. There was a moment of unbearable tension. All hearts stopped. Then it zipped at high speed off to the right, cutting through the Lauderdale property – part of that house appeared to explode in a shatter of plate glass and water. The waterspout ran on inland, shedding water and sucking up debris which slowly darkened its trunk as it assumed the markings of a tornado.

The tea lay untouched on the table. Vi now proceeded to pour. A curler fell out of her hair onto the tray with a clatter. She said 'damn' and her hand began to tremble as she poured out the milk.

'I think we should go down to the nuclear shelter,' said Nancy.

'So do I,' said Vi.

155

At the bottom of the stairs, Carol said 'The Swami . . . where is he? We must find him.'

Until that moment he hadn't crossed their minds. They set out for the garden room along the ground-floor corridor – wind and water whistled down there and soaked their slippers – and pushed open the glass door at the end.

At first they didn't know what to make of it. Lots of glass had gone, half the room had been wrecked and was open to the storm. In the flashes of lightning they saw him. The Swami was swinging from one of the ceiling girders. He was trussed up like a turkey by a long rag which appeared to pass right through him. He must have died from choking or suffocation or internal haemorrhages. A long clot of blood hung from his nose, and another from the side of his mouth. His eyes and tongue started out in a parody of terror. In the lightning, the death grimace seemed to be a funny face the Swami was pulling for their amusement.

Carol moved forward, there was a crunch of glass underfoot. Nancy pulled her back. The storm howled into their awareness, rain stung their faces, a pane of glass shot across the room to smash into one of the iron uprights – another flipped across and smashed – panes of glass began to fly across the collapsing room as if under their own propulsion . . . . The 3 girls found the shelter and crept into it. They held each other while the storm mounted above, not knowing what it was they had seen or were involved in.

Over land and sea the mighty Hurricane Juno rotated in a dervish dance of sublime self-obsession. The men had failed to outrun her and Juno hit them . . . It was the worst experience of their lives. Worst? This is a trite word to use of something so fundamentally beyond the niceties of good and evil. Experience? This word is inexact if it implies something in which the individual participates. The mighty engines of the Universal Will had spat them out and reduced them to points of meagre awareness pinned to the turning wall of time. Their humiliation was so profound that it carried them to the threshold of truth itself – except that their apprehension of this proximity shrank a good deal when, later on, ordinary psychological life called them forward again to pay their household bills, make

156

an appointment with the dentist, or resume the search for lovers. In fact afterwards they hurried back into their old personalities as into friendly old dressing-gowns, which might strike one as the height of naïveté until one pauses to consider that this had the effect of making each one 'more' himself.

Their torment in the hurricane had lasted over 30 hours during which the eye of the storm had been a place of astonishing magic, filled with a divine light and a hush such as there must have been at the dawn of creation. And at the end of the ordeal they did not believe themselves alive in the normal way, but thought that the world of cohesion and sequence was an exception to the norm, a small cavern of consciousness created bubblelike in the eternity of Chaos. People when they encountered them seemed curiously flimsy, lacking both corporeality and a crucial dimension of understanding. People when they met them seemed to follow only their noses. Because they did meet people again – and quite soon –

– because, minus all the delicate superstructure of the boat, minus the dinghies and indeed minus virtually everything which wasn't moulded to the hull, including part of the bridge itself, they had been blown to Havana. Or at least sufficiently close to Havana for 2 small gunboats like 2 grey terriers to take great pleasure in yapping at them and towing them into the harbour of the Cuban capital.

Officials with beautiful Afro-European faces came on board in crisp white suits and searched the boat. They were followed up the gangplank by a slightly more dishevelled figure of almost true European appearance, though there was something barbaric in his features, something that hadn't known Ancient Greece and Rome. 'Well, well, well,' said Dmitri Tcherenkov, 'we meet at last, Mr Manners.'

Guy was dumbfounded. At the very least the men of the *Jolly Junky* had expected to find themselves blown to an alien shore populated by strange beings with transparent flesh and curling purple tongues. And yet here was someone who knew his name.

'Don't worry,' said Dmitri, failing to repress a yawn, 'I'll sort all this business out for you. Then we can go for a drink and a chat, yes?'

At this point one of the officials howled as if he'd trodden on a nail. It was the bureaucratic howl of triumph. He had found the guns.

'Oh damn,' said Dmitri, obviously annoyed, 'this makes things much more complicated.'

157

'I demand the American consul!' protested the Senator when they arrested him and the others.

'At least I can get my arm set,' said Dale stoically.

'Very comfortable,' said Dmitri as, chewing a toffee, he entered the Senator's cell. 'As a rule you will find the prisons very advanced in Communist countries.' So saying he took the toffee out of his mouth and stuck it over a microphone bug concealed in the wall, adding with a wink 'But the Cubans still have a lot to learn.'

'Why won't they let me see an American?' asked the Senator.

'They will. He's probably on his way,' said Dmitri licking his fingers.

'But a US senator in a Cuban gaol! It's a major incident!'

'Yes, it is I'm afraid. And if it isn't, the Cubans will make it so. A US senator gun-running in the Caribbean – it's not every day they get a chance like that.'

'But I'm not a gun-runner, it's a mistake!' Curtis sat down with a thump of despair and winced – his piles had come up flagrantly overnight.

A guard brought in some coffee and said that a message had arrived from the Americans saying they couldn't get anyone round until to-morrow.

'He's lying!' Curtis appealed to Dmitri.

'I don't think so,' said the Russian.

Curtis wailed with self-pity, he imagined all the Americans too busy playing tennis to bother with him, but the truth of the matter was that the mission had been so shocked by what had happened that they had to ring Washington and just about every other major capital and have a big pow-wow before daring to make a move in any direction. Then the Senator growled 'I thought you said you could control these Cubans.'

'Now, Senator, that's an error you Westerners always make about us. No one can control people. The best we can do is . . infect them.' Dmitri must have been reading the same book. 'But I didn't know you had *guns* on board, did I?'

'They just fell out of the sky!'

'So you keep saying and we'd all like to believe you but . . . '

For one spine-chilling moment the Senator thought he was going to cry. He managed to fight it back by a series of perverse muscular contractions which he could feel crushing the very life out of his soul. As a result he immediately felt tired and depressed. He started to tell things, personal things . . .

'Ears? Did you say *ears*, Senator?'

'Yes, pickled . . they didn't smell too bad . . . '

When Dmitri had recovered from the jolt, a tremendous feeling of relief passed through him. He stared the Senator squarely in the eyes and said in a low voice '. . . I received a hand.' The moment the words were out he looked jumpily over his shoulder as if the entire Politburo might be glaring at his back, and while he did this the Senator experienced an equivalent relief – they had both found someone to confide in.

Dmitri came up closer to the Senator. 'Ears are ears,' he said with no great profundity, 'but to receive in post a hand is not nice, pickled or otherwise. A detached hand has power which is terrifying, as if at any moment it might leap up and grab you by the throat! And in post the following day I received a foot . . . After the hand, the arrival of the foot was not the trauma it might have been but even so, I've hardly slept since. Somebody's up to something, Senator, and I believe we can help each other.'

'Let me think about all this,' murmured the Senator, fading into dismay.

Dmitri gave the nod of understanding and made to leave. He plucked the sweet off the bug and put it back in his mouth. 'Delicious toffees – English,' he said, and disappeared, while the Senator, over-loaded, fell asleep under a brilliant light.

The evening is very straight in Havana. The Cuban Führer likes it that way (like all Führers, he tortures homosexuals and poets). You can sit in a café and watch the ironing walk by – and that's about it – because anything more real is off-limits for visitors. That's what Dmitri, David and Guy were doing. The Cubans had decided to concentrate on the Senator and get rid of the rest. Dmitri had man-aged to negotiate an hour out of custody for David and Guy before they were forcibly flown back to the USA. (Dale, because he was American, waited under guard at the airport. These events had brought out a sober strength in Dale. The hurricane had taught him

159

that the only place in this life to live and stay sane is in the eye of the storm. You had to accept the storm, the rage of the universe, the terror of fate. But there was the eye. You could inhabit it and know peace – without being ignorant. And with one arm out of action, the thing that Dale had accomplished in his cell had been work on his buttocks. His buttock muscles were now so hard that he could crack walnuts with them.)

Guy said 'I heard once that a plane dropped half a ton of cannabis on the wrong boat off Florida. It was night and they mistook the signal.' He added, turning to David, 'Beau told me that.'

'Well, if the Senator's innocent, then someone wanted to get him into trouble, that's what I think,' said Dmitri.

'You heard about the ears?' said Guy.

'Yes, I heard about them.' But Dmitri didn't mention his own mail. 'Did you know, Mr Manners, that there was a working connection between the Senator and Lord Shropshire?' He fiddled with the hair over his bald patch.

'No, I didn't know.'

'Neither did I until this morning,' said Dmitri. 'A wire came through.'

'Can you tell us who shot Shropshire?' asked David. 'Or who planted the bomb at the party?'

'They say the Irish terrorists phoned up to claim responsibility,' said Dmitri, 'but they often say that when they don't know what else to say. But it wasn't an Irish job. I have good reason to discount the Irish. But, Mr Manners, my superiors in Moscow have asked me to find Charles Robinson – I think I can tell you that. They feel he would be extremely helpful in sorting this thing out.'

'Yeah, well, if I see him I'll ask him to give you a buzz,' said Guy irritably.

A spasm, which might have been a smile, briefly afflicted Dmitri's mouth. He wasn't normally so stiff but to-day he had a headache and he slowly rubbed his temples in small circles with the tips of his index fingers. Tension – again – perhaps if he'd had a more straightforward job his hair would've stayed in longer. If he wasn't repressing a yawn, he was repressing a twitch, nursing a knot in his stomach, and sometimes he felt the acid flow in his belly which in a few years would presumably graduate to an ulcer, which is why he carried antacid tablets. What was the cause of it? Conscience? Dissatisfaction? None of the top boys in the KGB chewed antacid tablets. They were the real thing, men who knew not inner conflict. Or was he the real thing, the real human thing? Half-way up the KGB, with a bag of antacid tablets. 'It's so hot in the Caribbean,' he said. 'Er, tell me, Mr Manners, does that nice girl Jill still live underneath you? She had breasts of the most agreeable consistency.'

Guy choked on his drink. David slapped his back. Adjacent café-dwellers turned to look and looked away. Guy's fair hair had made him of sufficient interest for most of the Havana *bon ton*, whose rendezvous this was, to feel obliged not to look at him.

'Who's Jill?' said David to Guy. 'You never tell me anything.'

'There's nothing to tell.'

'So who is she?' David persisted.

'What's the matter? Just some girl who lived underneath me in London. Listen, Tcherenkov—'

'So why should *he* know her?' continued David, jabbing a finger at the Russian.

'Just shut your mouth, David, will you? Give me a moment.'

'I hate your shitty side,' said David and went silent.

Dmitri was surprised by the intimacy of their exchange.

'Now listen, Tcherenkov,' said Guy, 'when did you last see her?'

'I heard she disappeared,' said Dmitri. 'But I last saw her some time before that.'

Guy was confused. Further interrogation, however, was prevented by a loud bleep at the table. Dmitri took out a tortoiseshell cigarette lighter, fiddled with it, held it to his ear, and received a message; then he got up, crossed the road and had a brief word with 2 greasy thugs in drooping sunglasses leaning against a lamppost. When he came back he said 'They really don't want you to miss your plane. Isn't that thoughtful?' Guards appeared out of nowhere. They were young and muscular and beyond reason like guards everywhere. They took possession of David and Guy rather roughly.

'But you haven't said about Jill yet,' said Guy.

'Another time,' said Dmitri. 'I'm going to have a cake and some coffee. Good-bye, friends, good-bye.'

From the back of the police van David and Guy saw Dmitri, all alone at the table, recede into the past as if down a tunnel.

−7 −

The Swamp

In a suburb of Rio de Janeiro a young girl practised her scales on the piano with a sense of decreasing vigour until she stopped and stared at her mother . . . . . A boy of 15 secreted himself in his ground-floor bedroom on a ranch not far from Melbourne and silently opened a volume of the Marquis de Sade . . . . . And in a cabin infested with cockroaches and mosquitoes, hidden deeply among the suppurating bogs of the Everglades, Beau Bute stubbed out a joint of marijuana in the lid of a jam jar and thought – Why did they arrest the silly old bugger? . . . Beau had been doing some drinking and thinking lately. The Swami's death started him on it, then he'd gone to visit Big Jim Hotchkiss in hospital, and now this Cuba business . . . . . Beyond the open window, made somewhat dim by the fine grille of a mosquito net, the swamp bubbled and clicked. Curls of steamy gas formed above stagnant pools thick with microactivity, and wound lazily up through leaves of diamond, spear and oval shapes. The whiff of vegetable decay came through the grille in irregular waves. There was a rustle and a splash as an alligator roused itself to investigate a disturbance on the opposite bank which might be a meal. Yes, it was very beautiful. And very boring. And Beau hated this time of day: the horrible virtuous morning. He longed for the night always. He switched on the radio and moved the tuner, searching for the latest news of his father.

The storm had transformed Poseidon's Ki-Ki Closet into several wooden stumps sticking out of the sand and a rectangle of discoloured concrete. Louella collected the insurance – she had insured for everything including acts of God and hostile visitations from outer space – and went to New Orleans where she opened Louella's Unfit Wardrobe. Nancy moved to a friend's vacant apartment further down the coast while she prepared to leave for the seething antiquity of Europe (that rather unreal expatriate Europe where she could be anonymous and flattered and a somebody all at once). The apartment was in a condominium 24 storeys high, was the penthouse in fact with views and a pool up there and astroturf. Dale moved with them. He had to share a bedroom with Carol. She was not the one Dale chose to give all his love to (this person would appear later in his life, with disastrous consequences). He sort of loved Carol but that gnawing fretfulness of passionate love, always eating at one's flesh and bones like sprays of acid, that wasn't there. And Carol for her part spent many hours on the balcony wondering if a man with an unshaven chin would fly past in a small plane and pluck her off and take her to heaven. But Dale and Carol did get on, and Dale did get Carol pregnant. She was to be impossible during her pregnancy, refusing to have an abortion, refusing to get married, and considering the whole swollen-up business a terrific humiliation. When the child was born she was happy because the responsibility for being herself dissolved away and into the identity of another. Besides, Carol's spirit was not often waterlogged by circumstances; she had the gift of buoyancy. But in the tintinnabulation of her girlish heart there was always to sound one strange note, producing a distant discord which did not usually distract her but when it did would do so unexpectedly, with a sudden sensation of loss or emptiness or the consciousness of a life incomplete, that one inescapable note of darkness which seemed deeper and sadder and more wonderful and true than all the other notes and which sounded there forever because she could not have the man she really loved.

Vi stayed on to help Nancy tidy up the Whitewater property. She also seduced Jake the gardener. Her brief skirmish with Curtis had loosened her up. Jake was sweet, with a concentrated seriousness which attracted her. She wondered if Ivor could find him a place on the farm. 'That's playing with fire – and he's just a boy,' said Nancy, shocked and piqued by it all.

Jake it was who cut down the Swami with secateurs.

'Perhaps we should phone the police first,' dithered Nancy.

'You can't leave him swinging there like that,' Vi had replied. 'He was your guest, dear.'

The Swami fell onto the tiled floor with a hard noise. They all expected a soft flop but it was a hard rich noise like an expensive suitcase falling off a trolley. Jake, Vi and Nancy stood under a blue innocent sky staring at the stiff hummock of the Swami's form. Death the Great Rebuker which can activate big pistons in the living soul – such a terrible discrepancy usually between the grandiose fact of death and the tawdry appearance of it . . . Jake had never seen a corpse before and had a reaction similar to Dale's with the hurricane – he experienced it without commenting on it because he felt both reduced and liberated.

'We must *do* more from now on,' said Nancy. 'Go to the movies, go to concerts, explore the wildlife, some applied shopping.'

Eventually the police arrived, and surrounding the Swami's death they found much evidence of foul play.

Back in the USA, Guy and David underwent a CIA debriefing session and were then told they could go but not to leave the States just yet. Nancy and Vi wanted them to stay for the duration of Curtis's ordeal – they went on and on about how they should all be together at a time like this so that Guy and David could think of nothing nicer than a thorough change of air.

Some remarks on men and women. Men want to move, women want to stay. Women want to trap men in circles; it's their function, to hold men, to kill in men the expression of adventure. And having done so, women then accuse their men of being dull! Women love men to be adventurous, they are aroused by this aspect of maleness, and yet wherever they find it women always seek to kill it – because men must return to the nest each evening with the booty of their adventurousness. Men must be tamed; but a tame man is boring and useless: this is the impossibility of men for women. Women want 2 conflicting characteristics in men: tameness and wildness. If men understood this, women would cease to perplex them. And what do men want? To break out, to break in: room for expression. They want someone to have and to cherish and to be comforted by, when they return from adventure, because adventure is tough. And they want to return – whenever they feel like it. Because a man mustn't have his style cramped. Then men want to go off again. Is this why men and women hardly ever do what they want to do?

Guy and David sprang into a rented red Chevrolet and hit the road. Freedom! That's what men want! They drove at high speed through Mustang County (motto: Follow Your Restless Dream) with the sun and wind cleaning them. They ate junk food behind the wheel on the wing flashing through coastal towns – stopped – on again – on and on – lovely junk food, as obscene as nursery rhymes, as nourishing as dreams—

'As nourishing as dreams!' shouted Guy with the wind in his hair.

'Dreams aren't very nourishing!' David shouted back.

'I thought you blacks believed in the power of dreams.'

'Not me. Dreams – it's the dustbin of the mind.'

'But if you're deprived of dream sleep,' shouted Guy, 'terrible things happen to you.'

'I know all about that,' David shouted back. 'It's like shitting. If you don't shit you get into a very bad way – but only a loony wants to hang on to his turds.'

They drove on, with the percolating gunge of the swamp on one side and the gently heaving surface of the sea on the other. It was that time in late afternoon when after a scorcher the sun lays warm hands on the shoulders and seems to say 'We've both been out all day. Now why don't we put up our feet and relax a bit?'

'That looks all right. The Mockingbird Motel,' said Guy.

'That? No.' David was in the mood to drive forever – he didn't want to hang about. This was post-hurricane freedom, man!

'Yes.' Which was post-hurricane decisiveness. And since Guy was now driving, he pulled over and pulled up.

'It looks silly,' said David, and went into one of his silences.

The motel was built in powder pink adobe, covered with purple and shocking pink bougainvillaea, and it surrounded on 3 sides a kidney-shaped pool of clear blue water edged with royal blue astroturf. A very fat man with crewcut and criminal face sat filing his fingernails behind the reception desk. He wore cut-off jeans and a black leather waistcoat and was covered in tattoos. His naked hairy belly gave off whiffs of A Gentleman's Cologne by Chanel.

'Welcome to the Mockingbird Motel,' he said.

'Welcome to the Mockingbird Hotel,' said a mynah bird in a white cage.

'My name's Culver,' said the man.

'My name's Culver,' echoed the bird.

'Jesus . . .' groaned David.

'It's all right, honey,' said Culver, pushing a couple of heavy bangles up his arm, 'that exhausts his repertoire.'

'My name's Culver,' said the bird.

'We're all booked up,' said Culver, 'except the Honeymoon Suite. That sleeps 4. How many are you?'

'2. We'll take it,' said Guy, and he said to David 'Won't we, darling?'

'Idiot,' giggled David.

'Welcome to the Mockingbird Motel,' said the bird.

Culver cocked his head on one side and smiled sweetly like a never-ending drip of treacle from a spoon. He loved letting the Honeymoon Suite. It was in powder blue with pink bits, contained a large bed and 2 single beds for choice, and smelled of freshly washed plastic. They went to the supermarket to stock the fridge and when they got back Guy phoned Nancy with their number – she was all excited, she said she'd discovered a whole new set of people who were really quite interesting, some of them were anyway. They went for a swim and a wander round – for a booked-up place it was pretty deserted – a fat American couple were sucking up cherry red cocktails on loungers under pink lights by the pool – they said, 'hi' – it was a hot night so they swam again and went indoors – 2 pairs of swimming shorts dropped onto the floor, 2 puddles on the carpet – they wrapped themselves in towels – David poured 2 stiff tequilas – Guy flicked on the TV – *Listen. Your body is speaking to you. Our blood tests will indicate your gland and organ functions, vitamin and mineral levels, uncovering hidden food allergies, digestive and immune disorders, the source of depressions, headaches, and much else. Visit the Wiseguy Lab – there's a branch near you!* – Guy finished off a torpedo sandwich (meatballs and green peppers) – David dozed – they brushed their teeth, took off their towels, and both climbed into the big bed.

Next morning Culver woke them up in bright sunshine by announcing over the intercom 'It's nearly noon – will you be staying over?'

'Yeah . . .'

166

'It's cheaper the more you stay,' said Culver. 'Shall I bring you coffee? That's part of the service on the Honeymoon Suite.'

'Yeah . . . '

A few minutes later Culver waddled in in white mules and one diamante ear-ring, carrying a tray of coffee and steak sandwiches. David got out of bed naked and went into the bathroom. 'I guess I'll leave you,' said Culver and waddled out with a sigh.

'Appalling coffee,' shouted Guy. He lay back and stared at the ceiling, listening to the sound of David defecating in the bathroom, a comfortable sound. As David came back in, drying his hands on a pink towel with small blue horses on it, Beau Bute telephoned.

The desk bell made an unpleasant grating noise. Culver was in the back-room flicking through the pages of *Social Cancer*, a new weirdo magazine with fantastic artwork. He'd just jotted down a product ad on his shopping list: *Bio-King After-Sex Genital Body Wash for the Disease Conscious Male – from Bio-King International*. Again the desk bell grated out an appeal. 'Goddamit!' Culver had paused at a page of photo-bestiality, but he lifted his fat legs off the sofa, tidied up his erection, and went out.

'We're all booked up except – oh – no, sure, we got rooms, we got plenty of rooms.' Culver liked the unkempt look of Beau who was alone.

'What makes you think I wanna stay in this dump?' said Beau.

'No need to be nasty,' said Culver.

'My name's Culver,' said the mynah bird.

'I'm looking for 2 men, one black, one white, they're expecting me,' said Beau.

'You with those foreign boys?' asked Culver.

'My name's Culver,' said the bird.

'You ever feel like shooting that thing?' asked Beau, thumbing in the direction of the mynah. Culver looked wounded.

'Welcome to the Mockingbird Hotel,' said the bird.

'Where are they?' said Beau.

'My name's Culver,' said the bird.

Beau slammed the cage sharply with the flat of his hand. The mynah bird was knocked off its perch, hit its head on the side of the cage, suffered brief concussion with its 2 feet sticking in the air. Then it fluttered upright and stamped about the cage blinking its eyes fast.

'You pig,' said Culver.

Beau blew Culver a kiss and Culver found he was very aroused. 'You wanna drink in the back-room?' he heard himself asking mechanically.

'After I've seen my friends.' Beau winked.

Culver's mouth went dry and had the metal taste of excruciating sex anticipation. 'They're in the Honeymoon Suite the other side of the p-pool,' he managed to say, making a clicking noise because his tongue was all glued up in his mouth. Beau left and Culver went into the back-room and gripped the sofa with eyes closed. He opened them and looked down at the magazine. *Stay healthy – fuck with dogs – the only thing THEY give you is Love.* Culver came.

The foreign boys weren't in the Honeymoon Suite but sucking up long blue drinks poolside. They'd been talking to the male half of the fat American couple and the man was saying to Guy 'Well, isn't that something, you knowing Dick Tring himself. My wife works for the Dick Tring Organization in New York, but just in the office.'

'I don't actually know him,' said Guy.

'But you were there when it happened.'

'Ya . . . ' said Guy making a funny face.

'What was it like?'

'Not very nice.'

'Really?'

'Really not very nice.'

'Hey, Roxanne.' He called his wife who at that moment wobbled out of their room in a bikini, eating a doughnut. Her skin, new to the sun, was the full pink. 'This guy knows Mr Tring and was there when it happened.'

'What what happened?' said Roxanne.

'When the bomb went off at that party where Mr Tring was.'

'We don't see much of Mr Tring in New York,' said Roxanne. 'In fact I think he's become a recluse. Nobody's seen him for a long time now.'

'But this gentleman was there when it happened – isn't that something?'

Champagne, blood, diamonds, terrorism, shit, sex, death: time had made of the party a most glamorous occasion. Not everyone had been there when it happened.

'Say, Fred,' said Roxanne, 'I wanna go to the supermarket. We're running out.'

Beau walked onto the blue astroturf wearking no shirt, FUCK printed across his chest with sunblocker. 'What's with this place?' he said. 'I just made a date with the fruit at the desk.'

Culver, who with his windows open in the back-room could make out much of what was said poolside, winced with an ambiguous sense of resentment.

'Should I let him suck me?' said Beau cutely. Culver clutched himself.

'We'll be going to the supermarket now,' said Fred and Roxanne. 'Happy meetin ya.' They moved away in ripples of flesh, nice regular people with a proper sense of disgust.

When they'd gone Beau threw something down on the table. 'Ever seen any of this?'

'It looks like seeds,' said Guy examining the clear polythene packet.

'It is seeds,' said Beau. 'It's Tonio's last supper.'

'Amazing . . . ' said Guy slowly.

'It's turning up in some strange places,' said Beau. 'Coming out of Brazil. And connected with those video people. You know something about it?'

'You're the one in the video business,' said David.

'Don't get smart,' said Beau. 'I do a bit of distribution, that's all. But I don't make em! Selling a few on the side, it's a lot less harmful than gun-running which you big boys go in for. Yeah, don't think I don't know about *you*.'

'What's the moron talking about?' said David to Guy.

'I'm no fucking moron! These snuff movies,' said Beau, angrily sweating, 'open any history book – it's chicken feed to what's gone on. A few snuff movies – terrible entertainment – it's nothing to what the Roman Catholic Church has amused itself with in its time. It's nothing to what the Islams get up to! The only difference is that human bestiality was never captured on film before. Not like this. The real shock about all this is having to face facts about what we do and always have done. Do you know why I distribute these films?

169

Not to make money. The money doesn't cover the petrol. It's to say "Look, you bastards that's what you do! This one's on film, this is Belsen, Gulag, Cambodia, this is Amin, Caligula, Stalin, Torquemada, the Ayatollah, the works!" And remember as I'm talking now, people are having their eyes gouged out or their nails split open or their balls prised off or are being shot up with drugs to make them talk, to make them not talk, to make them mad, to kill them. But the world leaves this so-called necessary work to government thugs. "I say Brad, how about a round of golf?" and they walk away from that subterranean corridor lit at intervals with a yellow light because very soon it will be noisy with screams. "How's Samantha?" – "She's fine. And Alice?" – "Alice is pregnant." – "Oh, congratulations". And beneath their feet the screams echo down that corridor, screams, weeping, torture – always the torture . . . Well, fuck them, let's get it above ground, let's all have a look at what *people* can do.'

There was a silence, then David said 'Do those who actually make the films also have a moral motive like you?'

'Maybe,' murmured Beau.

'Anyway you've suggested that the snuffers and poisoners are linked,' said Guy.

David said to Guy, 'Presumably they use the films to flush out the really brutal types. Then they bump them off.'

'It may not be that simple,' said Beau. 'That would work for Tonio but not for the Swami. I thought maybe you 2 knew something . . . Look, I'm doing a pick-up down in the Swamp in a couple of days. Do you wanna come along? See if we can find out some more? Good. I'll leave you for the time being.'

'Where are you going?' said Guy.

'To have that aperitif with Mr Culver.'

Guy and David sucked at their long blue drinks.

Beau's aeroplane was an ingenious toy, the very latest in home flying, bought with an inheritance from his grandmother. The flight down to the Swamp was exhilarating and the 3 of them landed in the evening on a remote lake whose surface was misty with mosquitoes. The aeroplane putted to a landing stage and they made a dash for the cabin through a gauntlet of these ghastly bloodsuckers. Inside, the

170

cabin was full of mosquitoes *and* cockroaches. There was no air-conditioning and the humidity was overwhelming. Guy thought it the most unpleasant place he'd ever visited and said 'I can't take this.'

'It's all fine natural stuff,' said Beau.

'So was the Bubonic Plague fine natural stuff. I want to go back.'

'You namby-pamby English—'

'Fuck you!' burst out Guy. 'I've just been through the worst fuck-ing hurricane in fucking God knows—'

'Don't talk about God like that,' said Beau in a serious tone.

'Ugh?' said Guy.

'I said don't talk about God like that.'

– Oh Christ, thought Guy, is religious mania to be added to the list of Beau's great qualities?

'Beau, have you got any mosquito sprays?' interposed David, 'and I'd love a beer.'

'There's a supermarket down the road.'

Beau got out a pick-up and they drove 6 miles in the clammy dusk, a dusk which was only a gathering dimness bringing with it a sense of ennui – because sundown hereabouts was the thing which put an end to the hope that something more interesting might happen to-day.

Then this brilliantly lit box appeared like an outpost of heaven in the palpitating shades of a nether world. Flashing on and off above it in scarlet neon was 'Alligator Supermart' surrounded by ice white neon stars. 3 or 4 cars were parked outside, driven from God knew where.

'The mosquito sprays are down the back there past the surgicals,' said the checkout girl, cheerful under a blonde backcombed hair-do. She wore a black and yellow check party frock scooped out at the front to air her pale bosom, with a large black bow across the lower cleavage. Near the top of her left breast a roseate mosquito bite shone like a small misplaced nipple. Mosquitoes clung to Guy's exposed parts, especially his face (the scramble between pick-up and super-market was enough time for them), but they hated the delicious chill of the interior and fell dying to the floor.

'Those won't be much use to you,' said a deep rich voice behind Guy. He span round to find himself facing a middle-aged sheriff in drooping sunglasses. Given that it was night-time, this was doubly shocking. Was he to be arrested? Guilt, lying very close to the surface

171

of his skin these past months, erupted in a rash of goose pimples, and he felt his bowels liquefy. Caught already! But had they committed any crime yet? Rapidly he scanned his recent conduct – scrutinizing himself for the source of guilt he came up with loads of stuff – which? what charge? who? where? why? Guy heard himself say 'Why, but why?'

'Because,' said the deep voice, 'the little buggers mutate so fast. The manufacturers can't keep up with it.'

'I'll try these,' said Guy, scooping an armful and rushing to the checkout. He saw some plain gauze headscarves and grabbed one and tied it over his head.

'Have a nice night,' said the girl, touching with a set of scarlet nailed fingertips a black bow in her hair-do.

He turned back at the door. 'My 2 friends – have you seen them?'

'They're in Jennifer Julep's Neon Lounge,' she said with a smile. 'That's round the back.'

Culver was horizontal, looking up at the sky through wraparound sunglasses with turquoise frames. He drifted backwards a few feet every minute or so, the dome of his belly rising above the surface of the pool like a pudding on a plate, and the water, neither warm nor cool, slid under him and soothed him with the natural support of an old friend. From time to time his 2 hands twirled in the water on each side and in this manner he propelled himself round the pool, making several circuits in conformity with its asymmetrical shape.

– Why did he hit me? I'm not a nasty person. Why did he kick me?

Beneath the wraparounds a swollen bruise the colour of midnight over the Bay of Naples filled the socket between cheekbone and brow, forcing the lids together which had then been sealed by a gummy discharge. The other eye was OK but there was a bad graze on the other cheek and some blotchy bruising of a random kind, presently submarine, across the shoulders. Beau had been nasty.

– I suck him off and he beats me up. Why? What did I do wrong? Doesn't he like being sucked off? He seemed to like it a lot. He came on so nice to begin with and then . . .

Culver drifted to the side like a loaded barge, clambered out and put on a towel dressing-gown as thick and white as snow.

172

'Come eat with us later,' said Roxanne as he went by. She'd been sweet, held a raw steak over his eye.

In the back-room Culver poured himself a beer and started work on his accounts. Soon his head was jazzed with numbers. The bell rang at the front desk, a new bell which went pinggggggggg! Culver went out and saw 2 mysterious figures in dark glasses, a man with a complexity of pigtails and a girl with a crewcut. Both were dressed in black ultra high-fashion commando dress.

'We're looking for a friend of ours,' said the man in an utterly unfriendly tone. 'Here's a picture of him.' It was Beau poking his head round a bunch of bananas and putting on a silly grin.

'Never seen him before,' said Culver, adjusting his sunglasses – his nose was slippery with sweat.

'That's funny – because he was here,' said the girl. Her lip developed a cruel curve like a Saracen blade.

'Him? No, never seen him before.'

'We-think-you're-lying,' they both said together in a sing-song way.

'No, really I'm not,' said Culver but his voice cracked half-way through the sentence.

'Since he's lying,' said the man with pigtails looking at the girl, 'what should we do with him?'

'I think we should um . . . ' began the girl slowly.

At this point there was a cackle behind them and the mynah bird said 'My name's Beau! My name's Beau!' Violence had imprinted its memory! Everyone gasped. And the man with pigtails started to smile. The smile grew and grew and when it seemed it couldn't get any wider without slicing his head in half like a grapefruit, he said 'Intelligent bird you got there. Now where'd Beau go? We're in a hurry.' Something pushed out the leather among the stylish flaps and rouches of the man's chic top. Culver realized it was a gun. He was close to tears and stammered out 'He said the S-s-swamp.'

'Anyone with him?'

'2 foreigners. English boys.'

'That Beau is a complete fool,' said the girl, playing with one of the many metal-tipped cords which emerged from her blouson battle jacket.

'A complete and utter fool,' confirmed her partner. 'What he wanna bring strangers in on this for? What sort of – English boys?'

173

Culver actually gave it some thought. 'Well, I mean, men, they're 2 men. I couldn't quite work them out to be honest. One of them's black.'

'Come on,' said the man to the girl.

As they turned to leave Culver said – because despite everything he simply had to know – 'Excuse me, I hope you don't mind, but, well, where did you get those fabulous clothes?'

'It's French flying gear,' said the man.

'No, it's not, it's Italian,' said the girl.

The man with pigtails glared at her and said 'Don't be so damn argumentative all the time – it's French.'

'Have it your way,' huffed the girl who turned to Culver and said 'but it's Italian.'

'Look, you big fucking know-all, I *know* it's French see.'

'Italian!'

They jumped lightly onto their motorbikes, fixed helmets covered in black silk – still arguing. There were 2 roars which merged and they were gone in a single cloud of dust.

Jennifer Julep's Neon Lounge.

'What brings you to the USA?' Beau asked David as they leant back against a vast wall of plexiglass on the other side of which strange trees, strung with Spanish moss, writhed out of water and were floodlit hideous colours.

'Fresh air,' said David. Gas rose from the fetid water and settled in dense plateaux at a certain height. These layers of mist absorbed spongelike the floodlight colours, creating a theatrical vision of hell. 'I always travel light,' said David. 'In a sense I was born that way – being black . . . ' He chuckled at his own joke.

'We fly down to-night. Like Guy says, no sense sitting around getting bitten,' said Beau. 'You any good in a fight?'

'Not that good.'

'Neither am I. I'm not expecting trouble but . . . I'm thinking of getting out of all this and going to India.' Beau lit a cigarette. 'They say Jesus went to India.'

'Do they now.'

'Are you sure you're not involved with my father?'

'I told you – the guns fell out of the sky.'

174

'I must be mad bringing you 2 with me. Still, the way I read it, you're implicated so—'

'Listen, Beau, I could walk out of here an innocent man right now.'

'Believe me, man, you're covered with fingerprints.' Beau drank and wiped his upper lip smiling. David shifted nervously and Guy came in.

'What the hell are you wearing?' asked David.

Guy untied the scarf and peeped out. 'It works. That's all I care about. There's a very sexy girl on the checkout. Sort of eccentric sexy.'

'I've had her,' said Beau. 'She's called Mary-Jane. Her pussy tastes of menthol.'

The aeroplane was clever and could take off on a short runway of swampwater. It hopped into the air like a mosquito. The 3 of them were sitting one behind the other under a bubble of fibreglass. It was a clear night.

'Amazing little number this,' shouted Guy through the intercom. 'I thought you said you could barely cover your petrol.'

'I do plenty of other things,' Beau shouted back, 'and anyway my Granny bought it for me.' It amused him that his grandmother, who had been a Bible Belt teetotaller, had been responsible for it.

The heavy air of the Caribbean vibrated all around them like an immense, transparent blancmange. A radar monitor above Beau's lap said they were flying towards the Keys but were still over land. At this late hour the scattered lights of houses and boats below made the position of the shoreline uncertain. These lights became more and more scarce until they disappeared altogether. The aeroplane droned on through the whistling dark and gradually a sense of remoteness began to make itself felt. And then the disturbing breath of directionlessness . . .

'You know where we are?' shouted David.

'The Keys should be coming up soon,' shouted Beau.

'Have you noticed anything?' shouted Guy.

'No, nothing at all,' shouted David.

'Exactly,' shouted Guy.

'What's that supposed to mean?' shouted Beau angrily.

175

'What I mean is – there are no stars.'

'Things get clouded over,' shouted Beau.

'But there is a moon,' shouted Guy.

Yes, there was a moon. It seemed peculiarly placed, ahead of them and below, a little to the left, hanging there like half an apricot with the straight side rather indecisive and on a tilt. There was a corona about it brighter than its surface. The moon cast no reflections on any clouds or water. It was just them and the moon flying together through the night. Some time later the moon vanished. And it was just them.

'Must've gone behind a mountain,' shouted Beau.

'There aren't any mountains in this part of the world,' shouted David.

And on they droned through the void.

On and on . . . . .

All of a sudden they were struck by a powerful beam of acid yellow light from the righthand side. It was so strong that it made their own headlights almost invisible. It came out of the nose of some other craft which appeared to be approaching them at high velocity. The craft, striped and shaped like a wasp, shot across their bow, sailed up in a long curve, red and yellow lights flashing at its extremities, hung for a moment at the apex of its trajectory, then curled back and bore down on them again with its horrible beam.

'We're being pipped!' shouted Beau as a small missile shaved their fuselage in a laser track. Beau abruptly accelerated. This almost produced a collision and all 3 looked over their shoulders to where the other craft, surprised by the turn of events, seemed to have applied its brakes and skidded to a halt in mid-air. Beau flew his plane up in a wide arc – rise above it! This was the essential task. The little plane laboured into higher realms and a more rarefied air. The other craft waited a while, blinking its beam, then shot straight upwards in a line of light and hung above them, poised, taking its ease, contemplating among several options the next effortless manoeuvre.

'That's some incredible machine!' shouted Beau. 'We can't beat it. I'll try and take us down.'

'Down to what?' asked Guy.

'How the hell should I know!' yelled Beau.

176

Beau turned the plane into a descent and it began a plunge, but as it did so the other craft came alongside and formed some kind of lock on them which kept it abreast at a distance of about 100 feet. Green and lilac ripples of electricity like a St Elmo's Fire now ran back along its body and vanished into the tenebrae behind. They couldn't make out the figures in the cockpit. Then there was a pink flash and a crack, a splintering of fibreglass.

'For fuck's sake, they're shooting at us!'

Another pink flash, magnesium white at its core, another crack. Beau was hit – he felt greatly stunned as if his head had suddenly been immersed in thick lambswool. He felt a dribble run down the side of his cheek and a drop fall off his chin – and again and again. He touched it, licked it. He thought – That's blood. He thought it very quietly and slowly as if he were looking at a picture of himself on a television screen with blood running down the side of his face. But it didn't taste like . . . it tasted tinny, tasted of old tin cans. There was a muffled booming in his ears and the faint sound of laughter. Beau raised his hand and passed it slowly backwards and forwards across the controls in the cockpit with a sense of detached curiosity and unlimited time. The lights, dials, radar and digital readouts were still operating but there was a long interval between each new set of readings. Normally the flight panel was a mass of flickering activity, but the alterations came slowly now, giving one p-l-e-n-t-y of time. The booming came and went like the booming of mountainous waves. Beau saw his hands passing across the controls. They seemed to be searching for something with a calm assurance. He felt quite uninvolved with these hands. He felt he could unscrew them at the wrist if he wanted to. Then indeed, without any special fuss, the hands floated free of him. He watched them as they floated up and moved independently like 2 amatory doves in pursuit of their simple task, moving elegantly among the controls, passing a subtle comment of whisper on this odd state of affairs.

Then Beau's vision split into 4.

– It must have got chilly, he thought, because I'm shivering.

Then his vision split into 8. Then into 16. And continued to multiply in this fashion for some time, giving him a terrific headache – but it returned to 4 again which, after the previous multiplications, passed as a tolerable clarity. 8 hands moved whisperingly about the cockpit. 8 beams from his own headlights stretched out ahead, fanlike, to infinity.

177

Breath emerged from Beau's mouth in a ribbon. With every exhalation more of the ribbon emerged. It was ribbon of a specific length. How infuriating – this ribbon breath – that one has only a certain amount of it, and when that's been breathed out, well, that's that: end of ribbon, end of breath . . death . . . Beau could feel the ribbon unwinding in the mysterious pit of his stomach. The last dozen or so turns of it. He sort of smiled and breathed very slowly . . . . . very very faintly . . . . very . . . . going . . . . yes – going . . . . going . . . . . . he felt the tail of it flick off the mysterious spool in his stomach, flutter up his windpipe, and – poof! . . . out of his mouth . . . . . . gone . . . . the tail of ribbon fluttered forward into eternity and as it did so he shot violently backwards and the universe seemed to split open along a fissure of lightning with a mighty scream! A confused gusting of wild winds!

– Oh yes, this was it. She remembered with a passionate grace which grew as the heart grew, as the heart grew too large for its confinement within the ribcage and caused bizarre pressures in throat and chest, and these pressures in turn gave rise to others, to a tingling in the hands, to a watery fullness in the eyes, and a slight careening swoon of perception which was neither pleasant nor unpleasant but simply the effect of memory coming in from afar, coming in from the side, and pushing away awareness of the present, memory which now had her walking with a lilt along a curved street of houses and into a stone square on a night sultry with the aroma of jasmine and mimosa. The village square in Provence was lit with pinkish lamps and in one corner of it a boy was packing up the tables and chairs of a café. 2 men slouched smoking against a motor car. A fountain issued from between the lips of a satyr whose large friendly head was 4 feet across and embedded in a wall of crumbling honey-coloured stone. Water had issued from this mouth and fallen with a warm clatter into the scallop basin for hundreds of years, so that the lower part of the satyr's face was covered with a bright slime the colour of green baize on a new billiard table. A church bell struck 1 in the morning. It struck the hour twice with an interval of a minute or so between. To the right of the square stood a fine shuttered house with a beautifully carved door. The wall of its back garden formed part of the

178

square and was overhung with the loose hair of creepers. A cat zipped along the wall and disappeared. A window was open on the first floor and gentle lamplight, which also lit up a ring of the ceiling, flowed out of it and mingled with the stars, the glow of cigarettes, and the small hard single light bulb buried deep within the café where Madame was locking up her metal money box at the end of an ordinary day. And piano music came out of the first-floor window too, and it touched one's whole being in a moment of passionate grace suspended between sadness and happiness, tears and exaltation.

'This is called *Gaspard de la Nuit*,' he said, brushing his lips across her cheek.

'Can't it go on for ever?' she said.

'You know it can't,' he said. 'I leave to-morrow. I leave for always.'

'I know . . . ' she said softly. Tears brimmed in her eyes and fell down her cheeks with a wondrous economy and intensity – just a few precious individual tears like the ultimate distillation of all their time together. It was love. It had happened. And somehow it went on for ever. She felt it now. This was it, *Gaspard de la Nuit* . . . up there, coming from the stage.

'Oh dear,' said Nancy dabbing her eyes with a hankie from her bag. 'I'm a silly old thing. I first heard this in France. When I was young.' She held Carol's hand on her right, as soft as a baby's; and she took up Dale's brown hand on her left, warm and huge; and she felt very happy that on this particular occasion, at the Ganglion Vapers concert at the Alligator Bowl, she found herself sitting between these 2 particular people.

– So this is death, Beau thought.

– Very unusual, Beau thought.

– But mmm, perhaps not quite as unusual as one might have expected, Beau thought.

Beau thought?

– Beau's thinking, Beau thought.

– That means . . . . 'So I'm not dead yet!' he yelled. 'I'm not dead, I'm alive, alive, alive!'

'What? What!' yelled David.

'I'm alive, I'm alive!'

The lights on the controls suddenly speeded up and were now flashing hysterically with all kinds of appalling news. There was another pink flash and a much larger blue one. A crash and the whole aircraft shuddered.

'We're gonna have to bail out!' yelled Beau, blood pouring down the side of his face. 'I'm pressing the ejectors now – see you later – bon voyage!'

It all happened so fast that Guy and David had no time to worry, which was just as well since for both it was their first experience of falling from a very great height. The fibreglass bubble flipped off into darkness, followed by the ejection of Guy, David and Beau like 3 champagne corks. Up, up! . . . Then they started

falling –

falling –

falling –

in what they hoped (for it was by no means certain) was the direction of the earth.

Nancy added 'I wish Vi were here.' Dale, Carol and Nancy had seen Vi off at the airport and driven further inland to the Alligator Bowl, a concert platform floating on the lake with an audience of 5000 floating in front of it. A phial of citronella to keep the bugs off came free with the programme but Nancy always wore her one-piece zip-front warm-up suit in lime polyester suedette on these Alligator occasions, elasticated at wrists and ankles, and if it were especially bad, wore also a heavy veil and hired earphones for a microphone relay from the platform. But to-night wasn't especially bad – and Ganglion Vapers was playing. How mysterious it was to drive into a swamp and find a man in a white tie playing Ravel on the piano in a gigantic blue-lit shell floating on a lake – stars and spotlights – the bristling silhouette of trees against a starry sky – insinuation, plongeurs, silence, ecstasy, itch – that piece of Ravel from way back when . . . Nancy had wanted to hold that music, to caress it, roll it between her hands, run her fingers over it, press her lips to it again

180

and again, but this was not possible because one can only do this to a disc, a tape, a score, the repositories of music – music itself is free and lives in waves upon the air – it always escapes – where has it gone? But the memory of it continues to resonate in the human heart like heat in a meat stew. Ah the notes . . . yes, this was it . . .

But what was that?

A great parachute of silvery pink swayed slowly out of the darkness above the lake. One of the lighting men decided to swing a spotlight off the stage and onto what was now clearly seen to be a black man in a silver suit descending on a parachute sensuously distended by the heavy air. At first the audience gasped. Then they started to whistle and applaud, shout, cheer, laugh and yell their appreciation as David with an acutely worried expression fell plosh into the black water. Ganglion Vapers, frozen by astonishment, stopped playing. Then he could be seen (but not heard) tearing up sheet music and anything else he could lay his hands on, including his own hair and nearby hair. And a second silver suit appeared out of the dark sky, swaying slowly down, followed by a parachute in lemon and silver stripes. It was Guy. A spotlight tracked him and he grinned like a big stupid 5 year old at his own birthday party. The hooting and applause redoubled, but while Guy was falling with inane inexorability towards the turdish surface of the lake, a fight broke out on stage between Ganglion Vapers and someone who resented having his hair torn out. Blood splashed from Ganglion's nose and this was the cue for fights to break out everywhere. To their surprise Guy and David found they could stand on the floor of the lake without being sucked under. Certainly it was sloppy but after sinking to mid-calf in mud, they came to a halt, with the water – and the foul lumps of ambivalent stuff which floated on it – no higher than belly-button level. They disengaged from their harnesses and stared up at the sky, waiting for Beau to appear. But Beau didn't.

On the assumption that if she wasn't back home in London yet she soon would be, Guy had sent Kate a big Florida postcard with a *very important question* on it, express.

'The hurricane, Cuba, the Swami's death – and Tonio's – it's put it all in perspective for me,' cooed Guy to David. 'I've got my priorities right once more. And I feel better than I've felt in ages.'

David didn't say anything. He was having one of his silences.

Guy, carrying a cup of coffee with a fudge brownie in the saucer, walked to the edge of Nancy's borrowed penthouse. Only an iron railing of stark design separated him from extinction upon the sandy shore. He didn't understand how people could suicide off buildings. It was hot. He gazed across the Gulf of Mexico – and thought of England. The English countryside. A log fire on a late summer evening, smoke rising from an old chimney among trees – a stone casement glimpsed through branches whose leaves were beginning to golden – a deer in the foreground – jackdaws . . . 'The English countryside is the most beautiful in the world,' said Guy.

Dale, naked but holding a towel in front of his genitals, popped onto the terrace and said David was wanted on the phone. David returned a couple of minutes later screwing up his nose. 'I'm being recalled to London. They want a full report. They don't want me straying too far.'

'Do they not? Is that what they don't want?' said Guy almost petulantly. 'White-bloody-hall, pip, pip, Zoton! At least you're dropping the pretence at last.'

In a little while Guy said 'I've been thinking . . .'

'Everybody's thinking. It's like some stupid virus,' said David.

'I've been thinking it's time for me to go home too, that's all.'

'You're not going to stay on and find Beau?'

Search parties had failed – what could Guy do? 'Besides I want to give Kate a surprise. I asked her to marry me.'

David gave Guy a serious look. 'When?'

'On a postcard. It'll get there to-morrow.'

'Jesus. Isn't it time you 2 called it a day?'

'Look, mate, I want to turn up in my suntan and go with Kate for an Indian meal somewhere – see what it feels like. So we might just as well fly back together, OK?'

David said nothing.

'Oh for fuck's sake, David, liven up! What on earth's the matter with you?'

'Haven't you learnt *any*thing?' exclaimed David.

48 hours later.

'It's amazing the junk one collects,' said Guy, stuffing into a corner of his bulging suitcase several pairs of lurex underpants with mottoes printed on the front pouch, *Florida Juice, Feel the Goods*, etc. 'We never did get to Disneyworld.'

'Were we going?' asked David.

'We could've gone.'

'You want this?' David held up a t-shirt with *Yes, if you ask nicely* on the back. 'Or this?' He proffered one of the small plastic telescopes sold on the public beach for getting a closer look. David could never understand why with all this titillation his canary swimming trunks had been considered so remarkable (so much so that he'd been psyched out of them and into swimming shorts). 'Or these?' asked David holding up some worry beads.

'Hey – they're my worry beads – I've been looking for those.'

'What's the time?'

They were late.

At the airport Nancy embraced and wept and felt horribly left behind. But she said she'd see them in Europe when everything had been sorted out. Dale gave firm handshakes and a firm smile. Carol gave lovely baby kisses and hugettes in skintight bluejeans and shirt knotted at the front. David winked at her. Dale clicked in his mouth at Guy. Sweaty and wired up with lateness, they fell into their seats at the last possible moment. 2 jet engines rose to a thin scream and the plane moved onto the runway . . . .

. . . . It was a connecting flight. At Miami they picked up the big one for Heathrow. There was no room to lie down and hardly any to stretch one's legs. The lights went down for the in-flight film. Soothed by the purr of the engines, Guy and David leant against each other and fell fast asleep.

Part Three

– 8 –

The Dinner

A summer afternoon in Tuscany.

Petr Tytarský was seated cross-legged in a window, a bang of straight black hair falling over one eye, trying to come to grips with *Discourse on Pure Ridicule* – and drinking too much wine.

'I don't understand this,' he said petulantly, flinging the book aside. 'Haven't you got anything else?'

'Something more morose you mean?' asked Sir Glorian from his comfy seashell.

'Something more serious, more political.'

'Go down into the town and fix yourself a girl or something.'

'I have no sexual needs,' said Petr with a sense of longing. 'Sex is a complete waste of time. Is there any more of this, er, almost excellent wine?'

'Oh Jesus,' sighed Sir Glorian. 'Why are you East European refugees always so pretentious? Except, of course, the Jews . . .'

Petr thought, and said 'Perhaps we are conscious of our barbarism, and in trying to disguise it, we over-compensate.'

Sir Glorian stared at the boy who stared back with a curious look.

– Extraordinary, thought Sir Glorian – He's never said anything like that before. Is he perhaps growing up? Sir Glorian looked again, askance – Or can he possibly have the gift of irony?

Tytarský drained his glass and burst into tears. Sir Glorian kissed his head. Would the boy always be unhappy? He was 18 and had escaped to the West from Czechoslovakia where his parents were in prison for being both weird and vocal. Sir Glorian handed him a silk hankie with a purple monogram in one corner. The boy emptied his nostrils into it with a hefty blow.

187

'I feel such a failure . . . ' said Tytarský.

– At 18 by Jove! 'That's not so bad,' said Sir Glorian. 'Failure is interesting. Success is rather dull, don't you think? The terrible allure of failure, the complexity of it – how simple-minded is success!'

Tytarský looked up. Sir Glorian's eyes twinkled. The boy gave a blubbery laugh and held out his glass for more wine.

The evening of the same day.

Alfredo the Butler, whose magnificent physique bulged out of the black trousers, white string vest, red bandana and open white jacket which were his uniform, called Sir Glorian to the telephone.

'Yes?'

'Oh hullo, is that Sir Glorian Jones?'

'Yes.'

'I'm Guy Manners.'

'Yes.'

'Oh, you were expecting my call?'

'No.'

'Oh. It was just the way you said yes.'

'I see, yes.'

Guy hated making this butt-in phone call. The days of the letter of introduction were much more comfortable. You presented yourself and handed over the unsealed envelope and waited to be accorded hospitality. Guy had the feeling that Sir Glorian got rather a lot of these hullo-you-don't-know-me-but calls from passing English – and from passing Welsh for that matter. Guy felt that to himself no quality of distinction adhered which might commend his intrusion. And he felt that to phrase it so was putting it mildly. Yes, yes, yes, the old knight showed as much interest as if it were the Gas Board ringing up.

'Er, Margot Ingot said if ever I'm in Florence be sure to ring Glorian Jones.'

'Yes, she's a very generous woman.'

'Margot sends her love.'

'She does? Oh wonderful. She's better then?'

'Oh, I see, well, no, but she would've said "Give Sir Glorian my

188

love" if she'd been able.'

'That's very sweet of you. Did she lose anything in that terrible incident?'

'Apart from her consciousness you mean – well, only her emeralds. No limbs or anything. Someone swiped the emeralds from round her neck in all the confusion. Her maid noticed it the next day.'

'I'm glad she wasn't *disfigured*. How appalling about the emeralds. Some people have no standards. Where are you staying?'

'At the Pensione Esperanza.'

'Don't know it.'

'It's in the Via dell' Inferno.'

'Are you under 60?'

'Yes.'

'Good. I find there are so many *old* people up and about. What brings you to Florence?'

'I'm here quite by accident. My plane was hi-jacked.'

'What?'

'Hi-jacked.'

'Good God, you weren't actually on *that* plane were you, the one at Pisa?'

'Yes.'

'You *must* come over and tell me all about it. Do you know where I am? Have you got a car?'

'Yes, we rented one.'

'We?'

'I'm travelling with a friend.'

'Oh – well, you come over first, my boy, and if that's OK, you can both come over for dinner.'

Guy came for a drink. Ronny, the Shih tsu, peed against his leg. 'He does that sometimes if he likes people. Down, Ronny, down,' said Sir Glorian. Guy explained about the hi-jack, how over the middle of the Atlantic they'd all been woken up in the half-lit gloom of the cabin by 3 crazies with guns screaming about ALF (the Amazonia Liberation Front) devoted to the Evoluzione of the Nuovo Uomo in the Quinto Mondo – they're called the Quintomondisti in the press – but they were heroin addicts and got the shakes really badly and forced the plane down at Pisa because they knew where to get heroin there and the whole pie-in-the-sky business had collapsed in shivers,

189

horrors, terrible shitties and weepies – dirty hands smearing anguished faces – the plane was easily overrun by the Italian army. David had then telephoned London (Guy didn't tell Jones this bit) and London asked him to stay on for a few days, to liaise with the British Consul in Florence for funds, and determine whether the hijackers were involved in anything more important than their own personal tragedies.

'What they should've done of course,' said Tytarský with a supercilious expression of contempt which he imagined connoted noble blood, 'was plunge the plane and its contents into the very heart of the Colosseum – that's the way to attract attention to a cause.'

– Ugh? thought Guy.

Sir Glorian tutted and said 'Can you, Guy, and your friend – Mr Zoton was it? – a curious name – I don't believe I've come across it before – I'll look it up in the book – would you spell it for me – I see – can you both come to dinner on Saturday evening at 8 o'clock? I'm having some friends in.'

On Saturday evening Sir Glorian came out from behind Alfredo onto the front steps of the villa by way of greeting. He was wearing tartan trousers and a cream silk shirt with discreet silver cufflinks and no tie. His thinning hair was fluffed out in a soft grey cloud the colour of morning mist on the River Wye. His shoes were black leather slip-ons, cut low to reveal cream socks, and his plump insteps pushed up out of them like rising brioche. He looked as tubby as before but had a dancing-master agility that was unexpected.

'Who do you know in London, Mr Zoton?' he enquired, taking David's elbow, as avid as every expatriate for gossip from home.

'I don't know anybody,' said David with a cute Clark Gable frown.

'Oh good – someone *new*.' Then he said turning to Guy 'Is that what they're wearing in London now?' Guy was in a pair of curiously shaped trews, black, showing deep crimson pocket linings.

'I don't know. I can't seem to get back there to find out,' said Guy.

Some days later Sir Glorian said to Nicholas Knightly 'Neither of them was quite what I expected.'

As they entered the *salone* the knight said 'Let me introduce you to um Nicholas Knightly – he's working on a study of Carlo Dolci, aren't you, Nicholas.'

'Trying to, Glorian. I'm in a caecum however,' said young Mr Knightly looking at David, 'a caecum most decidedly.' Mr Knightly was of medium height, thin, with an outstanding Adam's apple. His eyes were snot-green, his chin was covered with shaving cuts and small red dots. His clothes seemed English in inspiration, but looked locally made, with an Italian enhancement of detail that was both stylish and rather common. His voice demonstrated an affected precision and was formed at the very front of the mouth, not at all in the nose or throat. He was thought to be 'very randy on the quiet' and a pair of spectacles in chic grey frames sat half-way down his slim nose.

'Do you like Carlo Dolci?' Mr Knightly asked David.

'Never met him,' said David in a jocular manner.

'He's dead.' David had suspected as much. 'He's the worst painter who ever was,' went on Nicholas, hovering above his seat, not quite sure whether introductions were over and he could sit down again. 'Too appalling.' He resat – plop. The seat was low. His knees stuck up, his thin ankles on display.

'Mr and Mrs Hatchett-Smith. The first "H" is silent – unlike Jack himself,' said Sir Glorian.

'We've already met,' said Guy.

'That Pisa business – could've been nasty,' said Jack Hatchett-Smith, the British Consul in Florence. Several drops of watered malt whisky clung to his moustache.

'Couldn't it just,' said David knowingly.

Jack's wife Iris beamed a smile of square-cut teeth to welcome the 2 boys – its frigidity was refreshing in the Florentine heat (for it was a hot night). Ronny trotted in and peed against David's leg.

'Don't worry, it's a good sign, it means he likes you,' explained Sir Glorian. 'He won't go *near* Nicholas.'

'No, he won't come *near* me,' said Nicholas.

Alfredo came massively up in silence bearing on a silver tray several glasses of a dark cocktail and a plate of cheese straws drawn freshly from the oven.

'Will you have a Negroni?'

'Are they in honour of me?' asked David.

'That's a good one!' said Sir Glorian, showing all his plastic teeth

191

in a wide smile of interracial ease. 'But I'm afraid it was invented at the Café Giacosa by Count Negroni long before you were born.'

'The Principessa Giulietta is coming,' said Nicholas Knightly, enunciating the 2 Italian words in an involuntary parody of the accent. 'Do you know her?'

'I don't think I know any princesses,' said Guy.

Knightly's eyes protruded in a slow gawk of amazement. 'None at all?'

'But I know a prince. Ernst of Teck. Do you know him?'

'Oh, those German things, no, no, no,' gobbled Knightly. 'But you must get to know a few princesses. It's so useful when you wake up depressed and it's raining – you telephone a princess and everything is delightful again. She's awfully bright is the Princess Giulietta. And very beautiful. Her smile is very, very er . . . '

'Sphingine,' interposed Sir Glorian with a manual gesture.

'Yes, exactly so, thank-you. Sphingine,' said Nicholas. 'That is to say . . . Giaconda-esque.'

'Signor Didier Marque,' announced Alfredo.

A man even smaller than Sir Glorian, and much more compact, entered like a clockwork toy. He had slicked-back hair and perfect hands and feet. His feet were visible because he wore sandals. Apart from the sandals his dress was formal: grey suit, white shirt, black & white tie. But the tie was in his hand. 'I took my tie off in the taxi, Glorian. It's too hot to play the bourgeois.'

Iris laughed. It was like a jet of cold water pinging into a saucepan. Jack drank deeply from his whisky, wanting to pack in another before dinner. On arrival he'd been offered a Negroni but had said 'I loathe all that sort of muck, as well you know, Glorian.'

'Mershoor Marque lives in Florence,' said Nicholas.

'That's right,' Monsieur Marque concurred, 'because Paris is so im*poss*ible these days. I'm writing a thesis on the neurology of plants. Are you staying with Glorian?'

'No,' said Guy, with one of his slightly vicious smiles.

'I stayed here once. There are scorpions in the bedrooms.' Monsieur Marque turned to his host and raised his voice. 'Glorian, you have scorpions in your bedrooms!'

'We aim to please,' said Sir Glorian and he sucked in one cheek.

'The Principessa Giulietta,' announced Alfredo.

All heads turned. She was very beautiful, dark-haired and pale-faced, not at all Sphingine but grinning like a cowgirl, her hair flung carelessly – perfectly – about her head. She wore a dress of emerald green beads which swished divinely about her calves drawing attention to those elegant muscles and the light which flashed between them. A little holster fixed to a narrow belt carried an exquisite pearl-handled pistol which worked. A look of slobbery excitement came over Nicholas's face – he hovered, snickered, sweated in palms and groin. His spots glowed.

'Giulietta darling . . . ' beamed Sir Glorian.

'I have a present for you, Glorian,' she said in a smooth voice and handed him a walnut with a tiny gold clasp on one side and a gold hinge on the other. He opened it and took out a roll of something which unwound like grey slime. There were 2 – what on earth were they?

'You never guess, Glorian,' she said with a smile which flowed all over her. 'They're gloves made from byssus silk. They fit you.' (Otherwise known as *lanapesce*, byssus silk is spun from the fine silky threads by which the large Mediterranean mussel, Pinna Nobilis, attaches itself to rocks.) 'They are made for the Archbishop of Taranto at the end of the 18th century,' she added.

'Oh, oh,' gurgled Glorian, 'and for what do you do me this honour, Giulietta?'

The Princess looked at him enigmatically.

'What a wonderful garden,' exclaimed David. He was standing in the open French windows as the sun sank voluptuously in the west. The garden was breezeless and purred like a cat. David stepped out with a crunch of gravel and sauntered to the balustrade. Overhung by stone deities, he took a deep breath. Pine, herbs, scented flowers. There was another crunch of gravel as Jack Hatchett-Smith came insouciantly to his side.

'Lovely, isn't it,' said Jack. 'There's a very good book called *Tuscany: the Second Berkshire* by Mrs Carew Hunt. Do you know Berkshire? That's where we're from. Jolly nice to meet you socially like this. Makes things so much easier I always think, don't you?'

'Yes,' said David, 'so much less . . . grating.' He was inclined to giggle but didn't.

'Well – are you getting any comeback?'

'Yes. And no,' said David. He undid another shirt button and absent-mindedly rubbed his left nipple. It was warm indoors but it was much warmer out.

'They're getting worried in Whitehall,' said Jack. Espionage wasn't really Jack's ticket. To be honest he felt a bit of a chump doing it – and at the same time uncertain, excited and appalled by a sensation of sinking out of his depth (in this it rather resembled Jack's experience of sex). Consequently his diplomatic career had not been a *cru classé*. His file had been marked CFOO – a deadly designation which stood for 'cold feet on occasions'. As HM's minister in Katmandu he'd failed properly to monitor the passage of information between China and India. Then he'd had an affair with a temple dancer, which was allowed – but had chosen a dancer supposedly reserved for the King. It had got out. But not right out. It had been hushed up. He was offered the consulate at Florence. Iris insisted he accept. Anything to get out of Asia, she thought. Those randy little Gurkhas hanging round *her*, ugh. It was all she could do to employ them. The idea of touching one was . . . Now it was mostly repatriating art students who'd run out of money.

'I'm not surprised they're worried, with MPs changing sex and everything,' said David. 'Anyway, it's their job to be worried. Their worry is what glues the whole show together.'

'Yes, well, has there been any sort of *approchement*?' enquired Jack lifting a shaggy eyebrow.

'Don't think so. And I've stuck fairly close.'

'The blighter's a cool one. Nobody of course was taken in by his I've-got-to-get-away act. They're pretty convinced that Manners and Robinson are in this together – they're school chums, you know. And having taken a look at Manners – he's obviously cleverer than he seems. This sort of languid, sort of irreverent . . . I suppose it's a good cover to drift around like he does. He's got a police record, you know. A not very nice one.' Jack waited. David said nothing. Jack continued 'A little bird tells me that you bumped into Dmitri Tcherenkov in Cuba.'

'We did. But it didn't get us anywhere and I don't believe it got Tcherenkov anywhere.'

'I believe you. Thousands wouldn't. And in fact they don't. They say you couldn't've got off scot free without having traded something.'

'They think that?' said David with a frown.

'They do. And I must say, if you didn't give the swine anything, why should he bother to help you?'

'Perhaps he felt he'd get nowhere with Guy locked up in Cuba.'

'Aha, so that just about confirms it then, doesn't it? That Manners and Robinson *are* up to something,' said Jack with a bulging eye, polishing off the remains of his whisky from the glass he was holding. 'In which case we'll expect something more from you.'

'I really can't play more than a waiting game at the moment. But I am looking into this Quintomondist thing meantime.'

'Can't see that that's going to get anyone anywhere,' said Jack. 'But I have my orders – which are to liaise if necessary. On the Pisan hi-jack front we have one lead. One of the buggers had a note in his back pocket. It looked as though it'd been through the laundry a few times – you know what these dagos are for their laundry – but they managed to make it out – it said "If you run out of the hard stuff ring this number" followed by an English phone number.'

'Did they trace it?'

'Of course. It's a place called Risingtower. Belongs to Lord Flamingfield. What do you make of *that* then?'

David said 'I don't make anything of it,' but many things started to spin in his head.

'Neither do I. Lord Flamingfield is beyond reproach.'

Alfredo appeared at the French windows and called 'Dinner iss served!'

Before they went back in, Jack said 'By the way, I've got your money – in sterling. Pick it up soon; just come during normal office hours.'

Guy went to the loo. He went as directed out of the saloon and into an antechamber, down a corridor, took a wrong turning, found himself in another corridor, went down it, an open door, a brightly lit room, radio playing quietly, a woman in blue housecoat surrounded by enormous piles of ironing and working the iron backwards and forwards – she looked up and said 'Buona sera, signor' and carried on ironing. Guy retraced his steps and started again, down a different corridor, another antechamber, and then through a door heavily carved with flowers into what was definitely a chamber. It was vaulted and the size of a chapel (which is what it originally had been) and had a rose window at the far end glazed in rose-coloured glass. There were several life-size statues in the room, a number of plants, an 18th century sofa. In a special niche, lit like a star turn, was a broken bronze of a boy – at least it looked like a boy, though nothing survived of it above the naval or below the thighs. To the left of it was a marble basin with brass taps polished a brilliant tough gold. Bottles of toilet water and moisturizer filled marble shelves, with plump white towels hanging beneath. On the other side similar shelves supported books and magazines. Suspended from the centre of the vault, and already switched on, was a massive crystal chandelier fringed with triangular prisms which threw a thousand rainbows over everything. Guy paused to let his eye wander among the books . . . *Letters on Od and Magnetism* by Baron von Reichenbach, *Les Vex* – the latest Prix Goncourt winner, *All The Way* – the autobiography of Viscount Cecil of Chelwood, Sir Glorian Jones's own autobiography *To The Sound of Trumpets*, several issues of *The Connoisseur* including one opened and folded back at an essay by Nicholas Knightly: 'The Neo-Plasticist Revival' . . . at which point Guy's bowels gave a squirm – slightly green appleish gut pain, but not unpleasant – suggestive of a satisfying defecation to come – and this in turn drew his attention to what looked like an episcopal throne placed centrally beneath the rose window. He approached, kneeled, and examined it. The back was straight, triangular at the apex, and carved with ecclesiastical insignia. The arms stuck out at right angles from the back; they were padded and supported on small gryphons. The seat was boxed: front and side panels displayed woodcarvings of episodes from the lives of the Saints, slightly chipped here and there. A square brocade cushion occupied the seat. Guy was bewildered. He looked about. There was a cupboard against the wall; he opened its 2 doors; the top lifted as well: it was a bidet. There was no obvious device for crapping – the throne must be it. He returned for a closer examination – the cushion was fixed to a seat on a hinge – he lifted it – a brown wooden lavatory seat came into view – 3 cheers . . .

Guy lowered himself and before long the faeces began to slip effortlessly out. He noticed a copy of *The Times* beneath some magazines – he leaned across and took it. Last week's copy. He flap-

ped open the pages. Rainbows splashed across them. He browsed –
plop! . . . browsed . . . . . plop, plop! . . . plop . . . . . He was about to
close up the paper and wipe when a small item caught his eye. *Briton
Arrested in Swamp. Mr Adam Shatner, 31, of West Kensington, a finan-
cier known to move in society circles, was yestrday arrested in the Everglades
along with Mr Beau Bute, sin of the ill-starred Senator Curtis Bute, of
Shucks Farm, Vermont, and Miss Sally Grootenjoy, Bute's fiancée and
heiress to the Grootenjoy Meat Company. The Florida Palice Department
has stated that althogh drugs are involved more serious charges are to be
braught. Senator Bute is still awayting trial in Havana accused of spying and
illicit trade in small arms. Washington maintains that the charges against the
Senator are completely false but that it does not intend to intervene at this
stage.* It was a small item among a number of small items. It could
have been a biggish item – there was enough human interest there.
But someone had decided that for the time being this one should be
played small. Guy looked up at the fragment of boy in the niche,
swallowed, and read the item again. Phew . . . . . He wiped his bottom, hobbled over to the bidet with his trousers round his ankles,
thoroughly bidet-ed himself, dried off, buttoned up, washed hands,
looked for a way of flushing the loo, all the while thinking of that
cunt Shatner, so that it was some time before he realized that he'd
been looking for a chain to pull or a handle to turn or a pedal to
depress as in aeroplanes – for some time. How on earth did you flush
this loo? He went hot and cold. How embarrassing . . . He couldn't
simply leave the whole panful on display, the whole – what would
the collective noun for turds be? clutch? – the whole *clutch* of turds
floating there. So bloody typical of this Jones fruit to have no way of
flushing the loo! . . . He decided that the only thing was to go and ask
the woman doing the ironing for help. So he opened the door and
went out. In the corridor, seated on the stone floor and wearing
nothing but a pair of loose blue satin shorts, was an urchin of 14 years
or so with short black curly hair and a rich suntan. His magnificent
eyes lifted up to Guy and he said 'You feeneesh?' Guy nodded. The
boy got to his feet, showing purple gums and sharp white teeth in a
grin, and pulled a ring in the wall. Guy heard flushing within.

Sir Glorian, with the Principessa Giulietta on one arm and Iris

Hatchett-Smith on the other, ambled with self-conscious complacency towards the dining-room, followed by Didier Marque, Jack Hatchett-Smith, Guy biting his lower lip, David rather euphoric, and Nicholas Knightly. As they entered, Mr Knightly looked aloft at the nymphs and satyrs, gods and goddesses gambolling among clouds, orchards and ruined temples. 'Heaven . . .' he drooled, and turning to David said in a more positive tone 'I always find food tastes so much better under a painted ceiling, don't you?'

Sir Glorian said 'My cook ran away to open a restaurant in Venice. Very thoughtless of him. And my new one, I really don't trust her with anything more taxing than potatoes. Now, if you'll excuse me, ladies, I'm going to make our hi-jack heroes the guests of honour. So, Mr Zoton, if you'll kindly sit on my right. And Mr Manners, on my left and – ' He arranged the others cleverly.

'Isn't the Bohemian boy joining us?' asked Didier Marque – the round porphyry table at which they sat came almost up to his chin and he couldn't quite touch the floor with his toes.

SIR GLORIAN JONES: He's been called. Apparently not. I don't worry him – he writes, I think, when no one is looking. He writes to a friend in Poland.

JACK HATCHETT-SMITH: Poland resembles Ireland, a poor peasant culture choked by religion.

DIDIER MARQUE: Certainly the coming of Christianity plunged Europe into the Dark Ages from which it only began to emerge in the Renaissance.

SIR GLORIAN: But witch-burning was at its height in the 17th century.

DIDIER: Humph! (*Uncomfortably – he was another who suffered from piles – and his piles were playing up.*)

NICHOLAS KNIGHTLY: I think I'd become a Roman Catholic if it weren't for the cult of the virgin goddess. Can't swallow that.

THE PRINCIPESSA GIULIETTA: I think the cult derives from the father's jealousy of the son.

SIR GLORIAN: Didn't it all begin in Athens? 'Parthenon' means 'shrine of the virgin'.

DIDIER: You slander the Greeks, mon chevalier, if you imply that they extended the concept of virginity into parthenogenesis. A

198

woman fertilized by the angel of the Lord? This is the sort of thing we laugh at in an African witch doctor.

DAVID ZOTON: Hear, hear!

DIDIER: And thanks to the Church, the West has believed for 2000 years that an occluded sexuality is a commendable thing – a spiritual deformity becomes a virtue! Except of course between man and wife, when any form of occlusion is held to be a sin. The irresponsibility of the Roman Catholic Church in respect of over-population confirms that the Pope is nothing more than a voodoo relic from the Dark Ages. I find it astonishing that people don't realize this.

GUY: Don't worry, they will.

SIR GLORIAN: I still go to church occasionally. I suppose it's comforting – like a rich old auntie. It helps the fight against loneliness.

IRIS HATCHETT-SMITH: You old silly. There are always so many people here.

SIR GLORIAN (*his eyes accusing Iris of diminishing his feelings*): I am not married, I have no children, I have a few relations apparently in Wales but I don't know them or wish to get to know them. There's just me. And when I go there'll be an empty space. And the house will be sold to strangers. Sometimes this makes me sad. What was America like? (*Sir Glorian darts this at David to prevent the conversation from getting stuck in a negative loneliness groove. Alfredo goes round the table pouring out Torricella wine.*)

DAVID: We had the er loungiest time.

GUY (*drawlingly*): Yeah, amazing. America's such a . . . lounge.

DIDIER: America is juvenile. That is to say – puerile.

NICHOLAS: Oh no, Didier, you're wrong. Youth doesn't last a minute – even in nations.

SIR GLORIAN: Indeed (*with a fine rubato*) one is hardly born before putrefaction sets in!

DIDIER: As Flaubert observed.

THE PRINCIPESSA: As they *all* observed, Signor Marque.

NICHOLAS: Baudelaire, one gathers, suffered from piles.

JACK: Not one of my problems.

SIR GLORIAN: At last, the artichokes! (*Alfredo presents each guest with a hot artichoke and Benedetto follows with silver bowls of (a) hollandaise sauce and (b) water for the fingers.*)

GUY: I see you take *The Times*, Sir Glorian.

SIR GLORIAN: I used to. Now I only see it occasionally. Sometimes Alfredo brings it in from Florence – he likes the competitions. And then I'll read it because, well, it's quite nice to remind oneself from time to time that one is no longer involved with all that, you know, British shit.

JACK: Come, come, Glorian.

SIR GLORIAN: No, Jack – it all seems desperately piddling from here.

JACK: But I'm sure if you were reading an Italian paper in England, *that* would all seem desperately piddling too.

SIR GLORIAN: I'm certain it would. But (*he beams*) I'm not in that unfortunate position. It seems, when I read these English newspapers, that people in England are always being arrested in public lavatories. Why is that, Jack, why?

JACK: Don't know, Glorian. Public lavatories aren't really my line.

DIDIER (*mockingly*): But the English – so polite, so civilized. You have more zoos per head of population than any other nation on earth.

SIR GLORIAN: Do they? I mean, do we? Oh yes, well, bestiality, that's always permissible. I remember as a young boy in Wales, the young farmers, the sheep, it was considered a lark.

DIDIER: The English are the world's most sexually perverse race.

NICHOLAS: I find the French terribly overrated sexually. They're too fastidious.

SIR GLORIAN: Nicholas, you're wrong. You only know about pictures. And, Guy, are the Americans as literary in bed as we're led to believe?

GUY (*blushing with irritation*): Can't remember.

DAVID: The wives of American clergymen are wild.

THE PRINCIPESSA: Oh tell me more! I love the religious angle!

DAVID: Not during the artichokes, Princess.

SIR GLORIAN: There's an American coming for a drink after dinner. Jimmy de Goldstein. Is he someone you've met, Guy?

JACK: Ugh!

DIDIER: Ah . . .

THE PRINCIPESSA: He's not so bad.

GUY: I haven't met him. I've heard of him.

IRIS: He's—

NICHOLAS: He's got a Titian in his drawing-room.

IRIS: That's what I was going to say.

SIR GLORIAN: It slides back to expose an organ which he plays to the

200

distress of guests. But I don't believe there's malice there. Some say there's malice – but I don't believe it myself.

NICHOLAS (*to Guy*): He lives half his time in Florence and winters in New York where he uses an ultraviolet lamp to maintain his suntan.

IRIS: Is that why his face is that funny orange colour?

NICHOLAS: His face is the colour of – diarrhoea!

SIR GLORIAN (*appreciatively*): Why, so it is.

NICHOLAS: Oh decidedly! Diarrhoea decidedly!

IRIS: And didn't you say, Glorian, that a frightfully important painter was coming too?

SIR GLORIAN: Ah! The mighty Tonto. Sorry, yes, no, he couldn't. He had to go to Vienna.

NICHOLAS: Vienna? Why Vienna?

SIR GLORIAN: How do I know? Some people go to Vienna. Don't be irritating, Nicholas.

NICHOLAS: Tonto is the only 100% certifiable genius I've ever met. The pictures of his Cake Period are among the most extraordinary visual phenomena of our time. Or any other time! This was the period (*to David*) when he painted nothing but cakes. And legend has it, ate nothing but cakes too.

SIR GLORIAN: Some of the canvases from the Cake Period, yes, I have to admit, they bear the clawmarks of genius. But his recent work – mostly hands and feet – I'm not so sure. This maybe is the influence of Vienna. I believe he goes there to take mescalin with a ladyfriend.

NICHOLAS: Sir Glorian, please, they are *not* hands and feet.

SIR GLORIAN: Tonto himself assured me at this very table that all his recent work is founded upon a prolonged contemplation of the hands and feet, especially the feet, of his ladyfriend.

DIDIER: He is a great painter. But flawed.

JACK: Very flawed, if you ask me. Isn't he that fellow, Glorian, who always tries to kill himself when there are other people about?

THE PRINCIPESSA: Rather bad manners, old chap.

NICHOLAS: Yes, flawed greatness! Flawed greatness decidedly! All truly great greatness has to be flawed! Has to be, *has* to be!

SIR GLORIAN: Steady on the wine, Nicholas, there's a good boy.

DAVID: Are you an art lover, Princess?

THE PRINCIPESSA: Pictures – I hate pictures – my family nothing but

201

old pictures pictures pictures – I like moving pictures – I was actress before.

SIR GLORIAN: That was before she became a barrister.

THE PRINCIPESSA: I hated being actress – publicity publicity – no private parts – I'm much happier now – I go to cinema like everyone else.

SIR GLORIAN (*in the fine rubato*): The public, that oven of love!

THE PRINCIPESSA (*to David*): You understand? I seem silly to you?

DAVID: Not at all, Princess, not at all . . .

David looked into the deep opulent eyes of the Princess Giulietta, then up at the gloriously painted ceiling and he thought – If my old Dad could see me now . . . . 'Cheers, Principessa!' he said. 'Cheers, Sir Glorian, cheers everybody!' He was having a wonderful time.

Guy wasn't. He was preoccupied by the newspaper report and bloody Shatner. Sir Glorian rubbed Guy's thigh and said 'I feel we are in some inexplicable way kindred spirits.'

'I think it's all smashing,' said Guy. Sir Glorian gave him a questioning glance. Next – Benedetto springs out unsteadily from behind the screen, laughing and bearing up an immense bowl of fettucine with cream and chunks of lobster and herbs. Sir Glorian gave him a look too, as much as to say 'Don't you dare drop it.' The boy's eyes shone with pleasure, and in his concentration on serving the guests correctly the tip of his tongue emerged a little way from between his closed purple lips. There was a pop! behind the screen and Alfredo came out cockily with champagne – opening champagne always gave him a bit of a lift.

'Krug sounds German, doesn't it?' said Iris as Alfredo filled her glass, pressing his leg against her arm. She wasn't at all embarrassed because she knew she was still an attractive woman, then she suddenly got embarrassed because she realized one wasn't supposed to examine the wine labels at other people's tables. Everyone did of course, but one wasn't supposed to let on. She'd gaffed.

– Silly old Riss, she thought, I've gaffed.

Alfredo however, who was watching her for signs of embarrassment, thought it due to his magnificent physical presence and subtly increased the pressure of his leg. At this point in his calculations champagne overflowed the glass and Sir Glorian thumped 'Alfredo!'

Nicholas, who was all messed up with fettucine while Benedetto stood patiently beside him holding the heavy bowl, said 'Sorry, it's because I'm left-handed. I always get in a frightful tangle serving myself.'

DIDIER: If you were left *wing* as well, you wouldn't care so much.

NICHOLAS: How do you know I'm *not* left wing?

THE PRINCIPESSA: Either wing, I'm afraid there's not much reason around these days.

SIR GLORIAN: Was there ever much reason about? When?

JACK: I think there was more of it when I was a boy.

SIR GLORIAN: And when was that, Jack? During some *hideous* war . . .

NICHOLAS: The world of reason ended in 1789 with the French Revolution.

DIDIER: Wrong. It ended earlier, in 1755 with the Great Lisbon Earthquake.

NICHOLAS: Can't one have both? The Apollonian and the Dionysian? Surely the appeal of Palladian architecture is that it is rational and romantic at the same time.

DIDIER: That is the English view. Palladio himself didn't think he was being at *all* romantic.

NICHOLAS: Certainly the greatest expression of this simultaneous effect is the Palladian country house in its English park.

DIDIER: Oh, the English! They always want the best of both worlds. And what is the result? At best compromise. At worst, dither dither dither.

JACK: But we *are* capable of defending ourselves – unlike the French.

SIR GLORIAN: And I think, Didier, that you are mistaking English style for English essence – which is a very French mistake.

IRIS: Oh absolutely. Look at all the countries we've created. That's hardly dithering. America, Canada, Australia for example.

DIDIER (*an expression of sublime distaste informing his features*): Is this something to celebrate?

IRIS: Well, no one else has done that. (*She swallows a chunk of champagne – she really doesn't like getting into arguments – they really aren't her strong suit.*)

DAVID: Spain has.

JACK: You mean all that nonsense called South America?

THE PRINCIPESSA: I hear the future lies in South America.

DIDIER: Quel fatras, Princesse! The future lies everywhere. It is like a
shower of precious stones. To be picked up if you can find them.

Iris swallowed more champagne. She felt her guts flinch. Had she
eaten a dicky piece of lobster? Iris liked abroad but her problem was
hair-trigger bowels. Anything remotely buglike or nerve-racking
and she was opened.

'But the future depends on what you're looking for and what
you're looking for depends on what you want and what you want
depends on where you've come from and that's the past,' said David
very fast.

'Not at all,' replied Didier impatiently. 'New opportunities present themselves daily. We're just too zoological to realize it.'

'I see,' said Sir Glorian. It was part of his charm to be sometimes
out of his depth at his own table and he surfaced by passing the buck.
'And what do *you* want, Guy?'

Guy groaned inwardly; but taking heart, he plunged forward into
the verbal universe. He looked at them with large simple eyes and
mumbled 'Happiness.' He mumbled it as though it were a shameful
confession – and his posture was terrible.

There was an explosion of laughter round the table; during it Petr
Tytarský came smilelessly into the room.

'Happiness,' intoned Sir Glorian in his hammiest voice. 'It sounds
like the soul sitting in a deckchair on a monthly pension.'

'Happiness is always somewhat vulgar,' mooned the Czech.

'Oh you,' said Sir Glorian, 'you're just a big misery.' Petr
twitched. A watery smile seeped into his face and seeped out of it
again. He walked over to the window, standing there a moment for
the guests to observe the grandeur of his feelings. 'Oh don't sulk, I'm
sorry, come along, my boy, you must have something to eat.' Petr
came back and found a place between Jack and Nicholas. General
contrition overcame the knight and he said to Guy 'I didn't mean to
be rude about happiness.' His fingers skuttled rapidly across Guy's
lap and back again like a white tarantula.

'The problem with all East European countries,' said Jack, 'is that they are peasant cultures trying to pose as modern ones.' It was something he'd read. Like all diplomats, experience per se was not something he was comfortable drawing on.

'You call me peasant,' Petr was on his feet and preparing to leave the table immediately – after all, he felt that had history been utterly different over the past 500 years he might possibly have been the King of Bohemia, or some sort of prince at any rate.

SIR GLORIAN (*a touch whoozily – the wine had suddenly hit him*): What's he doing now?

JACK: Oh, did I say something wrong? Petr, do you know any good jokes?

PETR TYTARSKÝ: What's 2 miles long and eats cabbage?

JACK: Don't know.

PETR: The Moscow meat queue. Ho, ho, ho!

JACK: That's quite funny.

IRIS: Will you excuse me? I simply must go.

JACK: You see, what you European chappies don't understand is the wider world. (*It was obvious why Nepal had been the high point of his diplomatic career*) Now we English—

'I think,' interjected Sir Glorian, 'that the relationship between England and Europe is an immensely rich subject for cogitation,' and he promptly fell asleep. The extinguishing of Sir Glorian's consciousness was the cue for some much-needed relaxed têtes-à-têtes. Iris returned and Guy who was sitting next to her said 'Isn't that the most incredible loo?'

'I covet the sofa,' said Iris. 'Glorian tells me that it came from Harold Acton's. It's the one Gertrude Stein urinated on. She was laughing so much at one of Diaghilev's jokes about D.H. Lawrence that she broke water. You'd think there'd be a stain but it's faded quite away.'

Sir Glorian threw up his head with eyes closed and drawled 'Rather like Gertie herself' and his head dropped down again.

205

'Did you see the Donatello?' whispered Iris. 'It's that boy's er . . waist. It's only a fragment but I mean, a Donatello in the loo's a bit, you know, I mean, *frightfully* grand. Isn't Glorian interesting? But you have to be a *bit* careful. My sister's husband has a ranch in Australia and their son Giles came to stay with us here to, you know, get a bit of Europe. And Giles had a birthday during his visit – we had a fabulous party – and Glorian gave him a volume of the Marquis de Sade as a birthday present. I was livid. It was only the boy's 12th birthday. This, you see, is Glorian's idea of being clever. I was absolutely livid.'

'But you still come to his dinner parties?'

Iris's brow creased quizzically. 'Of course we do. We adore him. So did Giles. What do you think is the *right* age for a boy to read the Marquis de Sade? I say, they're terrific trousers you've got on. I noticed them earlier. Is that what they're wearing in London these days?'

'Oh yes.'

'Do you enjoy . . . the grunge of groin and all that?' said Iris, snickering. 'I expect you do.'

'The what?'

'The grunge of groin. That's what Jack and I call it.' Iris was leaning towards him with a gushy, hushed, debby frankness. He smelt the milky perfume of her and continued to wind the last of his fettucine onto his fork while thinking of how to reply. Iris, no doubt emboldened by champagne, grew more insistent. 'Hey, did you hear what I said? I said do you enjoy the *grunge* of groin.'

Inspiration struck and he said in an undertone 'No, I hate it. I can't stand anybody even *touching* me.'

'But I distinctly saw Glorian playing with your leg.'

'Ya, I know. Isn't it awful? The idea of a groin simply makes me vomit. Even kissing is . . . I mean, somebody's mouth in your mouth – it's revolting.'

'Really?' she said, opening her eyes almost as wide as Nicholas Knightly was opening his to some other enormity on the opposite side of the table.

'Really, ya.'

'Really and truly and really?'

'Yes, really and truly. The idea of a sexual relationship with anything er animate – it gives me eczema.'

'Really . . . Isn't that extraordinary,' she said, 'that's just like me. I've gone *right* off it. Not that one was frightfully on it in the first place – but one forces oneself, doesn't one, one doesn't want to be a wet blanket, but I thought I was the only one who really, but, well, yes, now there's you as well, and, look, can you come over to-morrow? Jack's off fishing and we could go through it in detail. In my case I *think* it was because Mummy murdered my stepfather. I don't normally tell people that first meeting, but funny I've taken to you. My stepfather was a Horrabin and not nice. It was during the school holidays and I was there. Mummy was naked. They both were. It was a rifle. She telephoned the police herself. She hugged me very tightly while she waited for them to arrive. I can smell that funny animal smell of a murderess on her, I can smell it to this day.'

Sir Glorian started walking round and round the table to freshen himself up. His guests twisted their necks to look at him until he told them to stand up and do the same, that stretching one's legs in the middle of dinner is very wise. They all started walking round the table at different speeds. 'Do you know, gang,' said Sir Glorian, 'as I get older, life gets more not less mysterious. When you are young—' At this point, for emphasis, Sir Glorian stopped and put his hands lightly on Guy's hips which were in front of him. A couple of people stumbled into his back and they all stopped. 'When you are young, everything is relatively straightforward. Things don't have life-or-death consequences. An infinite number of chances stretches ahead, so as a youngster one is not defined by one's mistakes. Even unhappiness is a simple affair – it is simply that one isn't happy. This is what makes the opinions of young people so specific and refreshing.' Sir Glorian removed his hands from Guy's waist, leaving Guy feeling very old, and they all shuffled on again. 'Such youthful opinions are unclouded by knowledge, unbruised by the test. But now, being older, I am wrapped around with an ever burgeoning mystery. Luminous it is, with an indefinable significance both horrific and wonderful and—' Sir Glorian's voice, which had slipped into his declamatory eisteddfod manner, was interrupted by Iris.

'You should've married, Glorian,' she said. 'Grandchildren are very down-to-earth-bringing, very sanity-making.' She had recently been made a grandmother and was full of its therapeutic qualities as a bulwark against the fact that it also made one feel acutely redundant (such shocks as grandmotherhood, inflicted by time, revive one's appetite for life, as the much-bitten soul struggles to reassert itself before the lowering presence of extinction).

Sir Glorian looked at Iris as if she'd just blown in from a remote galaxy. 'Women, Iris my dear, are affirmed by marriage. But men are castrated by it. As the blighted pair leaves the altar, the woman looks radiant, happy, futuristic! But the man, oh the man –' The vibrato came on strongly here. 'The m ~ a ~ n, ah, he looks a buffoon, grinning helplessly as he drowns before the whole world – gutted, finished.'

Inspired by the sound of his own voice, Sir Glorian speeded up and overtook the Principessa in the circumtabular perambulation. The Principessa preferred to amble slowly round, placing the long fingers of her left hand (they were going anticlockwise) on the backs of the chairs, occasionally pushing herself off from them as a punt from a bank, moving first one hip bone forward then the other. This method of locomotion enabled her to lasso anybody of interest en passant.

But there was nobody of interest just yet.

She knocked into Didier and said dreamily 'The things one has to do. . . .'

He gave her an exceedingly twisted look. His attention was entirely in his piles – this surprise jaunt had done them no good at all.

They kept on walking. Petr pouted and sulked. 'I want to sit *down*, Glorian,' he said, biting at the words as they came out.

'Let's all sit down – *now!*' said Sir Glorian, coming abruptly to a halt so that most of the guests stumbled into the back of him creating a pile-up. A lifesize statue of St Paul, up on a plinth beside the fireplace, looked down at them irascibly out of one eye – the other eye was still obscured by a clot of soufflé which Tonto the painter had flicked at it with his fork in an expressionist moment some weeks ago. Nicholas squealed – Jack had trodden on his foot. More importantly – Jack had trodden on his shoe, his soft handmade extremely expensive brand new Italian shoe. Horrible clumsy great consul! In his horrible Great British brogues!

They all sat down in places different from before, according to 18th century custom.

– Damn, thought David who was no longer adjacent to the Principessa.

– Good, thought Petr who found himself next to Didier Marque, I can now have some proper intelligent conversation on important subjects.

– Hell, thought Didier, the Czech will try to talk philosophy at me.

Alfredo, who'd been watching the carousel from against the wall, occasionally plucking at his fly buttons but otherwise impassive, now went behind the screen and in due course reappeared with a huge leg of lamb.

'Carve it up, Alfredo!' blustered Sir Glorian. 'Bring on the red, Benedetto!'

Benedetto, holding 2 bottles aloft, one in each hand, came forward in a kind of Red Indian dance, his head thrown back, his young throat palpitating like a bullfrog's. 'Si, si, si, si, si, si, si!' he chanted. 'Si' was his favourite word.

'I can vouch for the potatoes,' said Sir Glorian. 'And I can vouch for the mint sauce – because I made it myself. And I can vouch for the claret. It's Château Montrose, Iris. But I can't vouch for anything else.'

'But the lamb looks heavenly,' said Iris.

'Do relax, Glorian,' said Jack. He beamed round the table and added 'Nature has ordained all things for the best.'

'You're quite wrong there,' said Didier. 'In fact – Nature is a bitch. Nature's always trying to kill us! It's her idea of a challenge.'

Jack ignored Didier opposite and turned to David and said 'He says that – but there's not a decent regiment in the whole of France. I recall the story of the Frenchman who disturbed an English regimental dinner by going out for a pee instead of pissing under the table into a wine bottle in the proper manner. Were you in a regiment?'

'Briefly,' said David. 'I got thrown out for screwing the General's daughter.'

'I see . . .' said Jack, bouleversed, having a distracting sniff of his claret. Because of David's statement (which was a lie), too many of Jack's prejudices were clashing for him to be capable of an adroit follow-through.

'What are you doing sitting over there, Guy?' called Sir Glorian across the table.

'The mint sauce is heavenly,' said Guy back.

'Isn't it,' said Iris. 'I was about to say so myself.'

'Such a frightful treat,' said Nicholas.

'I don't like this mint sauce,' said Petr.

'Petr, change places with Guy,' said Sir Glorian. 'Guy, come over here next to me. Petr is going to change places with you.'

Guy quickly involved himself in some eager talk with the Principessa beside him. Piqued, Sir Glorian inserted a boiled potato in his mouth and chewed. Petr ignored them both and waved his empty wine glass at Benedetto who was leaning against the wall with a hand tucked into his waistband, beside a genre picture *Saul at Play*. He was still in his blue satin shorts but now wore a black jacket as well. Glorian forbad nipples at dinner.

'Schopenhauer was in Florence, you know,' Sir Glorian said somewhat drunkenly through potato to no one in particular. Iris was the only one paying any attention and for her pains a piece of potato hit her on the neck. The knight swallowed and clacked his teeth which cleared the brain a bit, and said 'Did you know, Mr Zoton, that both Schopenhauer and D.H. Lawrence thought a white skin unnatural to man?'

'As a matter of fact – yes.' David had done a lot of racial reading in his youth as a result of his identity crisis. 'But I think it's codswallop.'

'I'm so glad you said that,' said Iris. 'Too much sun, skin cancer, all that sort of thing. Er, will you excuse me?' She scraped her chair and walked briskly out, head held high. One thing everyone understood, she felt, was funny tum.

David leaned over to Jack and drawled quietly out of the corner of his mouth 'Rather non-U, old boy. You think she'd have the savvy to shit into her finger bowl under the table, wouldn't you?'

Jack went purple. Was he going to laugh? Or bop this nignog on the nose? He didn't know. He got stuck in the purple dilemma.

'Why *was* Schopenhauer in Florence, Principessa?' asked Nicholas.

'God knows!' she replied. 'Hateful man. Wrote horrid stuff. By the way, I've finally got round to starting *Tristram Shandy*.'

'*Tristram Shandy* in a hot climate,' said Nicholas, 'the height of irritation!'

'Didier, what *are* you doing?' wondered Sir Glorian.

210

Didier was sitting on his hand, squirming, in a half-hearted attempt to push his piles back in, but not wishing to leave the table because (a) Mrs Hatchett-Smith was in there and (b) he might miss something out here. 'To be quite frank, Glorian, my piles . . .'

'How disgusting,' said Petr loudly. 'I know what piles are.'

'What about your piles?' asked Sir Glorian (a) because he was interested and (b) because he wanted to annoy Petr. So did Didier. They both enjoyed shocking the young. *Épater la jeunesse!*

'The cause of your piles,' muttered Jack, 'is your tight French arse.'

Didier tried to wither Jack with a look and pulled a piece of paper out of his jacket pocket. 'May I, Sir Glorian?'

'Yes, you may. And afterwards I shall read a newly discovered fragment of Swinburne.'

'Humph,' went Jack.

'What fun, a reading,' said Iris who had quietly returned in the interim. A reading – her mind went back to Mildew Mill, the house of her childhood, before Daddy died and Mummy married again, those autumn Sundays with the smell of burning leaves in the garden and the soft rush of water from the stream . . . crumpets with oodles of butter in front of the fire, Daddy reading to them from Beatrix Potter at teatime, oodles of teatime . . .

'On the subject of piles,' announced Didier, 'J. Alexander-Williams wrote in your *British Medical Journal* as follows: '*Few who reach middle age can claim never to have had any symptoms related to the anus—*'

At this point Jack put down his knife and fork with a crash. 'Lord Strewth, steady on, I'm still eating.' He looked round the table for support but found none. All had finished except he who'd had seconds – and thirds. Iris gave him a haughty pout which meant 'Be quiet, Jack.' She was interested. She was vested-interested. Her own anus was baboonlike with hot sluicings.

Jack thought – My God, the types one's got to eat with on this job, a bunch of fairies and perverts and nignogs and commies and smart alec sodding French philosophers. And that Manners chap is obviously *on* something – he's hardly said a word.

Didier continued '*Thomson has shown elegantly, if not originally, that what many regard as piles are normal vascular cushions. We all have them, and they are as natural as the vascular cushions at the upper end of the alimentary tract that we call lips. We are prepared to accept a wide variety of*

211

lips: thin lips, pouting lips, petulant lips, wet lips, and even hot lips. Similarly, variations in the vascular cushions at the anus should possibly be regarded as signs of character rather than disease.'

Didier took a deep breath and said 'Are your British doctors mad? I am in acute pain. Am I to be told that acute pain is part of my character?!'

Jack unfurled his lips from yellowish teeth set at jaunty angles and gave a slow full honk-honk of amusement.

The Principessa said 'Glorian, I must have a cigarette' and lit up.

'If anybody wishes to smoke now, before the ice-cream *bombe*' – Sir Glorian fell upon the word *bombe* as if it were a rugby ball – 'they may.'

David, Jack, Guy and the Principessa who were ranged *en bloc* opposite their host, mounted at once a united front of smokeblast. Petr coughed ostentatiously.

'And how do you like Florence?' the Principessa asked Guy who was politely holding his cigarette away from her so that it smoked up under Jack's chin. Jack was leaning back with a spluttery expression trying to avoid it and in the process he singed David's ear.

'Oh God, I'm frightfully sorry, frightfully sorry, *frightfully*—'

'OK OK OK,' said David hotly.

– Stupid clumsy Great Brit, thought Nicholas. Grotty Brits – he'd gone right off them – ever since a policeman had made sexual advances to him in a public lavatory in London and then, when he accepted, arrested him. That did it for Nicholas, Britwise. The incident, he felt, was so typical of all the sadness and sickness in the tight little island. He'd go back for visits but never again to live in his own wet country of shadows and regrets and longing looks into a receding majestic past: fuck 'em!

A rumble of thunder vibrated the stones of the old house. Through the dining-room windows, the long cypress drive was lit up by lightning. Ronny came trotting into the dining-room and placed his bottom between Sir Glorian's feet. Alfredo brought in the *bombe* and Benedetto followed with pink champagne.

'You were a friend of this Charles Robinson, weren't you?' Jack said to Guy.

'Yes, I was actually.' All eyes turned on him.

'*Were* you?' said Sir Glorian. 'How thrilling. You must tell us all about it.' His face was flushed with pleasure. He always felt his table was intended to be the centre of major events.

'Tom Kite has written a very interesting gloss on the Nineveh Codex,' said Didier Marque. 'He is extremely interesting on the Tower of Babel and the Song of Gilgamesh and the Great Flood. I've incorporated some of his conclusions into my own thesis, especially the effect of the Great Flood on the evolution of plant life.'

'But I want to hear about Charles Robinson,' bleated Sir Glorian. 'I don't want to hear anything about manuscripts. I've got one upstairs hanging over me like the sword of Damocles.' This was the knight's next volume of autobiography. He still had much work to do on those passages which seemed insufficiently spontaneous. Nor had he been encouraged by the reviews of his previous book, a biography of Sabrina Wallop, the gadabout dizzy thing & poetess & champion of black rights & cabaret artiste & opium addict, the daughter of Lord Vespasian – she was dead for 3 weeks in a barn in Herefordshire before anyone knew. The best review had said: 'Sir Glorian has gained weight but lost none of his lightness'. The rest were very cruel. 'Coffee, liqueurs, and all that jazz, in the *salone,*' said Glorian.

'I believe Mr Manners also knows a great deal about – pop music,' said Didier archly.

'Oh pop music, let's have some pop music!' trilled Sir Glorian. He crossed to the record player which was housed in a Venetian commode and soon sounds began to issue from 4 speakers the size of golf balls, one in each corner – mysterious electronic chords and schlupping noises as if a dinosaur stirred in a bog. There was a rumble-tumble of acoustic instrumentation, clearly influenced by Japanese temple music, and an angular falsetto voice sang:

> *After tea and cakes and ices*
> *We practised all the latest vices*
> *And in the evening drove quite far*
> *To listen to an operah*
> *To listen, to listen, to listen tooooo –*
> *An operah!*

Sir Glorian and the Principessa whirled about, arm in arm, with serious applied faces. Considering the difference in their heights they made a charming couple. The Persian carpet on the stone floor became covered with little twists. In the course of the dance she whispered to him 'I'm pregnant. It's yours.' They stopped, looked at each other, continued.

Jack and Iris had a go and found unexpectedly that they too were able to catch the odd rhythm of the piece. Benedetto sat on his haunches by the door, knees wide apart, clapping lightly.

Sir Glorian flopped into his seashell, throwing out his legs and puffing and saying 'What wonderful news, what wonderful marvellous wonderful news!' The Principessa swished and laughed coquettishly, ready for another dance. Alfredo announced Jimmy de Goldstein and withdrew.

Jimmy entered in a silver leather parachute suit unzipped to the waist and nothing underneath. Like Glorian he was getting on a bit, but the fact that he'd never see 60 again wasn't going to kill his wardrobe. He wore several precious rings, a gold collar, a diamond pin in the device of an express train, and a diamond stud in one ear. His abundant grey hair was rolled back in artful waves; the heavy orange face was wide open in a rubbery smile. He looked like a person you could be yourself with, take a problem to, and this was the secret of his appeal. A handsome young man was with him.

'Glorian babe! Ronny sugar!'

Ronny growled.

'Jimmy – Jimmy – I didn't say decorations would be worn.'

'Oh Glorian, I just threw on a few – trinkets!' Jimmy coughed; he'd been smoking drugs. 'This is Giorgio – I just met him on the Ponte Vecchio.' Sir Glorian gave his silver boxes a glance as the very handsome, quiet young man stepped forward and gave a small bow like a god on the steps of his own temple. Petr, who resented any kind of competition among the under 25s, glared. 'Giorgio's tired,' said Jimmy. Giorgio went and fell asleep on a sofa at the other end of the room.

'I've just got back from a cruise,' said Jimmy.

'Obviously,' said Sir Glorian.

'No – I mean, to the Galapagos and back.'

'You're the most – wonderful colour!' opined Nicholas archly. 'But where's Bruno?' (Bruno was Jimmy's bodyguard and driver.)

'He's gone into the village to see a girl.'

214

'Let me introduce you to everyone,' said Sir Glorian.

'Yes,' said Jimmy, not hearing properly because he was getting a bit deaf, 'it was on Johnny Lavenham's yacht the *I'm All Right Jack*. Johnny Lavenham's wild! He's got a Rembrandt in the galley covered in chip fat! I sent you a postcard.' Nicholas threw his eyes up to the ceiling; Jimmy sometimes sent him postcards addressed to Knickerless Nightly. 'My, who's this?' said Jimmy, approaching David and shaking hands. 'Once, on LSD, I was surrounded by black women with knives between their teeth and teeth between their legs. What do you think it meant? I bought this book *You and Your Dreams* but that one wasn't in it.' Ogle ogle, nudge nudge. He pecked Iris. 'Iris babe, what's that hunky scent behind your ears?'

'It's called *Désespoir*. I found it in the Great Loo.'

'I like it, I like it,' said Jimmy. 'Now tell me, Iris – what should a woman put behind her ears to make herself attractive to a man?'

'I don't know, Jimmy.'

Jimmy took a deep breath and said 'Her feet!' He roared and slapped his silver thighs. Giorgio raised himself up on one elbow at the other end of the room and stared at the Principessa as if to say 'What on earth's going on?' David and Guy went onto the terrace for some air. Jack said 'Iris and I better be going.' And Didier said 'Will you excuse me too, Glorian? I must go and find my suppositories.'

'Why are you leaving?' Sir Glorian asked the English couple.

'We have to be up early,' said Jack.

'We always have to be up early, isn't it a bore?' said Iris. But she was looking dove grey. The ice-cream had gone straight through her, unimpeded by anything.

'Now, Glorian,' said Jimmy, 'how about getting one of your boys to give me a nice fat vodka on the rocks – and I'll see what I've got in my travelling bag.'

Guy and David stood on the terrace, leaning over the balustrade. 4 pairs of French windows were at their back, brightly lit, glittering in the night. Summer lightning, hidden among clouds, flickered like a dodgy lightbulb, a continuous sky-wide flicker of ice blue light which illuminated the heavens and the earth below in ghostly detail.

215

Thunder prowled ceaselessly, rolling from left to right and back, backwards and forwards and at tangents, prowling without rest.

'Beau Bute has been arrested in Florida,' said Guy. 'With Sally Grootenjoy. And Adam Shatner.'

A jet of air passed out between David's lips and turned into a faint whistle. 'Poor old Sally. How do you know?'

'I was having a crap in the Great Loo. It was in *The Times*. Here, I tore it out.'

'Shatner's that bloke who nearly got you killed, right? . . . That's both Butes inside. Look, I discovered something too. One of the Quintomondisti had a phone number on him. They traced it. You'll never guess where to. Your precious Risingtower.'

'I don't believe it.'

'I met Henry Mountsavage once at a party at the Ghanaian High Commission in London. They suspect some heroin business – but did you know he did a gun-run to Namibia once? Maybe he went from drug-dealing to gun-running. If so, he'll be involved with this Latin American thing. Did he do anything to make you suspicious?'

'Not really. He always seemed so incompetent.'

'Incompetence is the best cover you can have,' said David. 'My guess is that the arrest of Bute and Shatner is no accident, that they are being sacrificed.' They wandered further into the garden and sat on a stone chair whose ends were hippogryphs.

'Sacrificed by whom?' said Guy.

'Don't know yet,' said David with a frown, then added 'Do you?'

'Me?'

'Yes, you, Guy,' said David melodramatically. 'Look . . . my brief was to ingratiate with you and track down Charles Robinson before the Americans or Russians or anybody else got to him.' Silence.

'. . . . . And what were you supposed to get out of Charles?' asked Guy in a thin hard voice.

'They didn't tell me that. I was just to find him. They never tell you the whole thing. It's safer that way. According to the book, everything is a conspiracy, and the drama of life is reduced to a fear of falling into traps. Well, I like that, it gives a buzz to things. Besides, in the modern world espionage and intelligence are absolutely vital and should be applauded; nothing is more dangerous between nations than mutual ignorance. But really, I shouldn't be talking like

216

this to you. According to the textbook one must conduct oneself *always* with an ulterior motive.'

'Sounds like religion.'

'It is a bit.' Silence.

'. . . . That Principessa is pretty amazing-looking,' said Guy.

'Decidedly fuckable,' said David. 'Fuckable decidedly!'

Summer lightning played magically in the atmosphere. David turned to go in and Guy followed. As they entered the house they were greeted by the noise of shouting. Glorian and Jimmy were having a terrible row.

With a razorblade Jimmy de Goldstein had carefully drawn out a dozen lines of cocaine on the marble top of a Florentine wall table, sniffed one up each nostril with a rolled Italian banknote, stood up, closed his eyes, and relished the tinsel entering his blood. Walking over to a mirror to play with his hair he said 'If anybody wants a line, it's on that thing.'

'Oh goodee, whacky dust,' said Sir Glorian. 'I haven't had any since you last came over, Jimmy.'

Jimmy didn't hear. He was staring at himself in the mirror which was huge and had a gilt wooden frame carved with musical instruments, fruits and birds. 'God, my face is the pits. Should I have it lifted? Anyone got a crane?' he said, gently tightening his face by pushing back at the ears with the palms of his hands. Nicholas went and had a sniff. The Principessa sipped elegantly at her coffee. Guy and Otis were somewhere in the garden.

SIR GLORIAN: They've discovered a new fragment of Swinburne. It was written when he was a schoolboy. I've got it here somewhere. Where did I put it?

THE PRINCIPESSA: Should I have a line?

JIMMY DE GOLDSTEIN: Have anything you want, Princess.

THE PRINCIPESSA: I'd like to have a boy too, a young one.

JIMMY: I had a 13 year old boy 2 weeks ago. His arse smelt just how a boy's arse should smell.

NICHOLAS: And how is that, pray?

JIMMY: Unpleasant!

(*Petr Tytarský pulls a face of utter revulsion.*)

THE PRINCIPESSA (*bending over the marble top with the rolled banknote*): Is that corruption, Jimmy?

JIMMY: You must be joking! I've never had a boy yet who didn't teach me something.

THE PRINCIPESSA: Nicholas, have you ever had a woman?

NICHOLAS: Not really, no.

THE PRINCIPESSA: What does that mean?

NICHOLAS: Well, she had me, but I didn't have her.

JIMMY: I've had a woman. But it's all a bit, if you'll pardon me, Princess, all a bit soft.

SIR GLORIAN: Ah! With boys it's buttockry, the art of buttockry! Girls have fesses. It's a different art, fessing around. The fully developed man of course has both male and female lovers – not necessarily at the same time. And I – me – I am – oh I'm going to tell them, Princhy – I'm going to be a daddy. With the Principessa! (*The Principessa, flushed, curtseys and bows. The rest applaud and refill their glasses. A toast, a toast! Benedetto asks what's happening. Glorian explains, and the boy does a little dance on the spot.*)

SIR GLORIAN: You can be godfather, Benedetto! Oh everybody, Benedetto is almost a son to me – I first slept with him when he was 10. His mother forced him on me. Already he was remarkably passionate – yet innocent too. You know, everybody, let me tell you, those who lose their innocence early in life, never lose it entirely.

NICHOLAS: Isn't it a mistake to sleep with one's servants?

SIR GLORIAN: Oh I'm sure. I've slept with *all* mine.

THE PRINCIPESSA: Ha! (*She starts to swoop up and down the long length of the salone in her emerald green dress, leaving red stains in the air behind her.*)

SIR GLORIAN: Where the hell did I put that fragment? I'll find it in a minute.

NICHOLAS: Benedetto isn't a Florentine. He comes from the Abruzzi. The Florentines are very cautious.

JIMMY: The Neapolitan boys are very randy. They stand about twanging their dicks against their bellies!

PETR: Nasty.

218

SIR GLORIAN: Oh for God's sake, have a line, Petr. Where did I put that thing?

PETR: I've already sniffed. Quite boring. (*In fact he'd only pretended to sniff; he'd been too nervous; but being greedy, he now goes and sniffs properly.*)

NICHOLAS: I've got loose! (*He removes his spectacles and drops them into a T'ang vase for safe-keeping.*)

PETR (*having sniffed properly*): I feel dizzy.

THE PRINCIPESSA: You need love. You know nothing of love.

PETR: I feel dizzy.

THE PRINCIPESSA: You need—

JIMMY: So when's this Carlo Dolci job coming out, Nicholas?

NICHOLAS: Oh *screw* Carlo Dolci! I'm happy! Up up up! I think I only ever feel really truly happy and up in the country houses of titled homosexuals.

SIR GLORIAN: I'm going to be a daddy, Nicholas. Do remember that. Now I know I tore it out of the paper and put it under something.

PETR: I've stopped feeling dizzy.

JIMMY: Glorian, are you going to find this fucking fragment or not?

PETR: He said your face is the colour of diarrhoea.

JIMMY: Say that again?

PETR: He said – Nicholas there said – your face is the colour of diarrhoea. What's diarrhoea? It's a new word for me. It is very interesting for me to come across a new word.

JIMMY: You cunt, Nicholas! I'm going to hit you (*smacks*). No hard feelings now. Face the colour of diarrhoea . . . same colour as your tongue!

NICHOLAS: OK, no hard feelings, Jimmy. You said. I let you hit me.

JIMMY: Let me hit you again to make sure!

SIR GLORIAN: Stop it, Jimmy! Look, you've made Nicholas cry. He sometimes says things. Oh shut up, Nicholas. Shut up, everybody. I've found it, the fragment of Swinburne, here it is . . . . (*in dulcet vibrato tones*) . . .

> The wan white wanton wasteland where we whanked –
> You looked at me. I spat! And then was spanked . . . .

JIMMY: Is that it?

SIR GLORIAN: It's only a fragment.

JIMMY: I don't think that was worth waiting for at all.

SIR GLORIAN: It's a very early fragment, when he was at Eton.

PETR: What does wanked mean?

JIMMY: Oh sod off, you silly prat, we've had enough of you!

THE PRINCIPESSA (*pricked for Petr*): Come, boy! (*She takes Petr by the hand and they run up and down the salone together for a while. Ronny joins them, barking at their heels. With a neat manoeuvre, she sweeps Petr out through the windows onto the terrace.*)

SIR GLORIAN: Swinburne was considered very wicked in his day. He mentioned things like lips and . . . wrists. Everybody in England thinks *me* very wicked too.

JIMMY: Oh it's the same for me in the States.

SIR GLORIAN (*nettled*): But America's so big, Jimmy, I'm surprised they think of you at all.

JIMMY: Have I got a funny smell to-night or something? The Italians think I'm wicked too. I like people to think I'm wicked. It saves time.

SIR GLORIAN: The Italians don't think me wicked. You miss a lot, Jimmy, because the Italians think you're wicked.

JIMMY: Of course I do, you silly pudding. We all miss a lot of something. It's called being human, having character.

SIR GLORIAN: No, you miss important things, because the people round here don't trust you. They trust me. Maybe it's something to do with my voice.

JIMMY: Don't make me laugh. You speak Italian like a cow.

SIR GLORIAN (*rising to his feet*): I speak Italian with great pleasure and with great clarity!

JIMMY: Well (*he stands up and puts his fists on his hips*) that's the first anyone's heard of it. And clarity of speech in one who talks a bunch of shit is no advantage! Daddy!

SIR GLORIAN: Don't you slander my son-to-be! You rat!

JIMMY: Well, if it's a boy that dumps out I'll chew my arse!

SIR GLORIAN (*jumping up and down with fury*): You – you – silly great Christmas tree!

NICHOLAS: Boys, boys! Please!

Meanwhile on the terrace, the Principessa was fumbling at Petr's fly. He was making choked noises. She pulled out his little penis while the boy stared rigidly off to the right, terrified of moving, of even

220

breathing. His member was as cold as a twist of bacon fat left in the fridge. She jiggled it and said 'Don't worry that I'm having Glorian's child. That was an accident – a happy accident – but not more.' Petr made a funny noise, part whimper, part squawk. The Principessa discharged a tear from her left eye while the right one remained dry. 'You like boys?' she said. Silence. Carefully she replaced his penis like one returning a piece of rare porcelain to its cabinet. 'One day you'll make someone very happy . . .' she said, then immediately felt a fool for having said it, because the idea of Petr making anyone happy, of his own volition, was distinctly remote.

With penis back under wraps, Petr emerged from the seizure. He was about to say 'How dare you' when they were both distracted by shouting in the salone.

'So how *did* you get your fucking knighthood then?' screamed Jimmy. 'Whose arsehole did you crawl up for *that!*'

'Stop screaming, Jimmy,' screamed Nicholas, which started Ronny barking again.

'If you *must* know, and oh how you've got to know *everything* oh yes! If you *must* know, you great Jewish tart, I was—'

'Don't call me a Jewish tart! You snotty Welsh—'

'Great Jewish tart is putting it kindly, believe me!' and a high-pitched wail emerged from Sir Glorian's purple head – it was supposed to be the laugh of effortless superiority but sounded more hysterical than that, as if steam were escaping at high pressure from a hole in his skull. 'If you *must* know, I was given my knighthood because the Prince and Princess came to stay when they were visiting Florence. The Princess tripped on the front steps and grazed her elbow. Alfredo very sweetly bandaged it for her. *That's* why!!!' Sir Glorian, utterly worked up, was screaming like a jet engine. Even Giorgio on the sofa woke up and rubbed his eyes.

– I think I'm going to get a regular job, thought Giorgio.

'You phoney shithead! Given a title for something your servant did!' howled Jimmy. 'So fucking British—'

At this point Petr fled into the room from the terrace, stopped in his tracks and screamed 'You horrible horrible homosexuals!' and fled out of the room. Giorgio went back to sleep.

The Principessa flew in from the terrace too, holding a hand up to her mouth. Glorian, Jimmy and Nicholas were in a ring screaming at each other. The dog was barking wildly. Now Guy and David

221

returned from the garden and as they did so, blood jumped out of Sir Glorian's nose. 'Oh oh oh oh,' he wailed, 'what's that? what's happening? what's that red stuff? oh oh oh!'

'Can't even take a bit of coke up it!' howled Jimmy.

'Oh oh oh,' wailed Sir Glorian. 'Petr, come back, come back! I'm sorry, I'm sorry!' And blood streaming through his fingers, head thrown back as far as was compatible with continuing to see where he was going, Sir Glorian ran tubbily out of the room after the Bohemian.

. . . . . Jimmy fell exhausted into an armchair, half laughing, half crying. Eventually he noticed Guy and David. 'You boys want any coke?' he said. 'It's on that thing over there . . . . . He's quite special, isn't he.'

'Sir Glorian is?' asked Guy. 'Oh yes, certainly.'

'No, not that old sack . . . I mean Giorgio.'

Alfredo announced Lord Treasure who entered blind drunk with a girl on each arm, smoky Italian beauties dressed simply in clinging cotton shifts held up by slender straps, and high heels. The girls looked about the room and laughed, exposing their throats. Lord Treasure's sweet eyes flickered over the Principessa. His fleshy mouth smiled waterishly and he said in a voice hushed with emotion 'Giulietta . . .'

The Principessa let out a mighty bellow, with a vocal depth which shocked and upset David. She slapped Lord Treasure's face really hard. He tottered half a dozen steps sideways, and the Principessa marched out. Heels echoed across the hall and before long her sports car was heard revving heavily against the stone façade of the house. It left in a burst of rubber on gravel and then there was silence. Ronny sat and waited.

. . . . . . Eventually Poppy Treasure went over to the drinks tray, poured 3 cognacs and sploshed soda into 2 of them. More silence . . . Jimmy groaned on the sofa. Nicholas broke the atmosphere with 'Before going into his study, Robert de Montesquiou would say to his servants "If you hear me groaning, it means I'm writing poetry and mustn't be disturbed".'

'Oh shut up, diarrhoea mouth,' said Jimmy.

Alfredo went to bed, Benedetto wandered about.

JIMMY (*eventually*): So where've you 2 come from anyway?

LORD TREASURE: Do I want any cocaine?

GUY: We've come from Florida.

JIMMY: Oh my God. Don't remind me. Yes, remind me. Which bit?

DAVID: Whitewater.

JIMMY: Did you meet Merriel Palombo? Married to a shit called Tonio.

GUY: She's a widow. Tonio was killed.

JIMMY: Killed? What happened? No, not now, some other time. Glorian tells me you were at the Bomb Party. Brenda Dollar and Stirling told me it was the most incredible party.

GUY: Well, a bomb went off if that's what she meant.

JIMMY: My head's killing me. Giorgio! Come over here and massage my temples . . . OK, don't then, go back and stand on your fucking bridge . . . .

LORD TREASURE: Have we arrived at a bad moment? Glorian said come for a drink after dinner. Where is he?

NICHOLAS: He's somewhere.

JIMMY (*to David*): Come and sit next to me for a moment.

DAVID: I'm OK here.

JIMMY: Don't be uptight, just for a moment, I need some human warmth, come on, just for a second . . . right, that's better, that's nice, see? You're still alive, I'm not poisonous . . . . . Now tell me – how big is it?

DAVID: Big enough.

JIMMY: Knew a black guy once with a dick *so* big . . he was inclined, upon erection, to pass out through loss of blood to the brain. He didn't have that much fun.

DAVID: Mine's not that big. I'm inclined to stay awake.

JIMMY: Come on, tell me what you and Guy do together?

DAVID: What?

JIMMY: Come on, front up. Tell me what you do with – Guy.

DAVID: Leave it out.

JIMMY: Shy shy shy . . .

DAVID: Let's have some music. I wanna dance.

223

NICHOLAS (*chortingly*): I expect you want funky rhythms! Will you teach me to dance funky?

JIMMY: Yes, something funky!

EVERYBODY INCLUDING BENEDETTO, GIORGIO AND THE GIRLS: Something funky! Something funky!

JIMMY: Let's all have some more cocaine!

LORD TREASURE: And some more to drink! Come here, girls! (*Giorgio was tickling one; the other was examining Guy's fair hair with the thoroughness of a housewife contemplating the purchase of an expensive handbag.*)

JIMMY: I've got something to get us *all* going in *every* direction! Giorgio, get my travelling bag from that seat, stop moaning, go and get it.

Giorgio came up waggling his tongue at Jimmy and handed him the bag. Jimmy pulled a black rectangle out of it. 'Now if you'll all follow me to the library – which is *much* more comfortable than it sounds – and where Daddy Glorian keeps his TV and all that behind a panel of false books – Glorian's part of that vulgar generation that thinks electronic machines are vulgar' – for some reason he shot this last observation at Nicholas.

They trooped into the library conga-fashion with Poppy Treasure leading with a loud boom-boom-boom-boom-booooom-paaaah! boom-boom-boom-boom-booooom-paaaah! and collapsed on top of each other among several huge English-style comfy sofas in front of a wall of old books. Guy's eye caught one title – *The Open Kimono* by Seymour Hare – before they all slid back to reveal a large screen and lots of switches. Jimmy slotted in the video. Benedetto turned out the lights.

At first, through the blur of alcohol and because everyone was giggling and lolling on each other, it was difficult to make out what was on the screen where shadowy limbs moved in bad colour. When the camera pulled back it revealed a number of naked people on a bed.

'Good idea,' said Nicholas being uncharacteristically forward and pushing down his trousers so that they concertina-ed round his ankles. His exposed middle parts were available while he fixed his

224

eyes uncertainly on the film – he'd forgotten where he'd put his spectacles. Hands began to rove among bodies.

On the screen there was no soundtrack of voices, just a swishing of the sea and clicking of cicadas. A face held up a fretsaw and grimaced. Another face held up a syringe and poked his tongue at the viewers. A girl was dragged to a trestle table by several males whose oiled genitals were strapped tightly into twists of leather. The man with the fretsaw wore a clown's hat and did a rumba, waving the saw in the air. Cut to a variety of objects being inserted into the orifices of males and females. Cut to the girl on the table who'd been gagged. The man placed the fretsaw on her arm – her eyes showed terror but her body seemed incapable of struggle. Perhaps she'd been injected with the syringe so she had to watch too. Benedetto said 'Me no like' and left the room. There was a quick close-up of the girl's face, a flash, a taste of her unspeakable agony, and a wave of horror shot out from the screen and struck Guy between the eyes. The fretsaw moved – on the arm – blood spurted from the arm – males and females came and licked the blood which fell (strangely the effect of this was effete and amateurish) – another close-up of the girl's face. Guy was rigid but his heart stamped wildly –

NO! NO! NO!

Guy kicked in the television set. Hit out at people indiscriminately. Went completely crazy screaming 'No no no no!!' David leaped at him. Guy fell to the floor sobbing and writhing. David fell on him and hugged him. The others quickly left the room while on the screen Kate was having her arm sawn off.

Jimmy gave some sleeping pills to David who administered them to Guy. Combining with the alcohol they knocked Guy into a morbidly vivid sleep – heavy resonant images came up from the depths of his subconscious like old bottles of wine coming up from the cellar to be smashed . . . . . so that when he awoke next day, exhausted, it was as if he entered a thinner, less real world. Sir Glorian was very upset by what had happened and his sensitive heart, only somewhat obscured by vanity, caused him to suffer a sympathetic pain.

The first thing Guy did was phone the flat in London.

225

'Who's that?'

'Kate.'

'Kate . . .'

'Yes, Guy, it's me.'

'But I thought . . .'

'What did you think?'

'I thought you were dead. I thought they killed you . . .'

'Killed me? No.'

'But I thought that.'

'Guy . . .'

'Yes?'

'Why didn't you phone before?'

'I don't know, I . . . . . it's like an awful dream.'

'Yes. It was.'

'I don't understand.'

'No . . .'

'But how?'

'How what?'

'What happened?'

'I went to Mexico and . . .'

'But I saw them killing you . . .'

'They didn't because . . .' Her voice trailed away.

'Kate.'

'Where are you, Guy?'

'Tuscany.'

'Trevor moved out downstairs you know. Emma Cartridge and Billy are taking it over. The mother's buying it for them . . . I'm glad you've phoned.'

'Kate.'

'Yes?'

'Did you get my postcard?'

'Yes.'

'Well?'

'I—'

'The question. Will you marry me then?'

'Guy.'

'Yes?'

'Rory and I got married 10 days ago.'

' . . . Ya?' said Guy weakly.

226

'Yes.'

'Big wet mouth.' A whole floor gave way inside Guy and crashed through to the floor below. Externally he appeared unchanged, but the damage within was major.

'He was here. He was marvellous.'

'Oh.'

'It was just a registry office . . .'

'Oh.'

'So . . .'

'I wish you hadn't.'

'I . . .'

'But I still wish you hadn't. Anyway, I . . .'

They were both blocked.

At last she said 'We'll sort the flat out when you get back. Who's paying for this call by the way?'

'Glorian Jones.'

'I see . . .'

'You don't see. Listen, I—'

'Don't say anything, don't. Don't say ANYTHING . . . . . And look, there's something else. There's a telegram here for you. I opened it. It's from Charles.'

'What does it say?'

'It says *Meet me 25th this month* – it came last week – *Manaos Railway Station 5 p.m. Sub Rosa Love Charles.*'

'Where?'

'Manaos. I looked it up. It's in the middle of the Amazon jungle. Presumably it's Charles Robinson. What are you going to do?'

'Read it again.'

Kate read it again.

'Can you read it again?'

Kate read it again.

A crystal precipitated out of a cloudy liquid and Guy said 'I kiss you. Burn the telegram. I'm going there.'

Part Four

– 9 –

Into the Jungle

Beneath Guy all was water

In a suburb of Rio de Janeiro a young girl practised her scales on the piano with a sense of decreasing vigour until she stopped and stared at her mother on the other side of the room . . . The mother walked across to the piano, her steps muffled by thick carpet, and held the child's head in her arms and kissed her on top of the head, leaving a slight moisture of tears in the blueblack hair.

'Where'd Daddy gone?' asked the girl.

The General had disappeared slowly up the drive in one of 2 long black cars while the gardener of mixed Negro, Indian and German blood leant on his rake staring. In the other car were 2 American generals.

2 weeks before, the same girl and mother had watched from the window as Rudolfo da Silva disappeared up the drive on a motorbike with 2 others. His father, the General, was not at home that day. Rudolfo had kissed his mother and sister good-bye, his face creased with tension.

'So what's the position now?'

'The Americans and Russians are both trying to find the Indian camp. If they succeed, I don't know what will happen. The Indians know what's going on but it doesn't bother them – it doesn't *appear* to.'

'Christ, the air is heavy, Charles. I can hardly breathe.'

'Get's worse, you know.'

'I'm thirsty, Charles, terribly thirsty.'

'Have a good drink of water,' he said.

On his return to London, David submitted his report. He was glad he hadn't followed Guy. He was glad he hadn't known the end. It avoided the sickening decision of whose side he wanted to be on. He'd had enough of sides. But the alternative? To keep all your options open? There comes a time when keeping all your options open is tantamount to paralysis of the will – and you betray everybody into the bargain.

David felt a great sense of loss that was hurtful and moving and

not entirely separated from happiness since both connoted the fullness, the drama of life – that extraordinary things are possible, that
everything can change at any moment, that one isn't prisoner in the
shell of routine. But he felt himself falling towards a sluggish melancholy because he felt out in the cold and party no more to crucial
events. He had called Kate several times. He was curious. More than
that, he wanted to stay involved. He wanted to recapture that sense
of his life, its daily moments and most banal actions, being bound up
with the lives of others. He was lonely.

After landing at Heathrow, David went straight to the front door
of his flat behind Harrods, put the key in the lock, took a deep breath
and opened the door. He paused on the threshold, took in the small
hall, the open door at the end of it and the sitting-room beyond.

There were no plants, no flowers. No fish stirred the waters of an
aquarium. No pets registered alarm (he had 2 cats, Lamont and
Glynis, but they were with foster parents). Nobody jumped up and
extended a greeting. No living thing moved in that flat, nothing was
disturbed by his arrival. Not even a tap dripped or a clock ticked –
David's clocks were electric. There was only the smell of wax on furniture. The char lady had left it spotless. He went through to the
kitchen and put on the kettle. The fridge was humming gently. He
opened it. There were a few long-life products inside: tins, a wax
carton of indestructible milk, some slices of processed cheese like
linoleum wrapped in cellophane. He threw the packet into the
wastebin, picked up a crayon and wrote on a board 'cheese'. The
char had left a note on the table.

Had that tap fixed in the bathroom. Hope you had a nice trip.
I'm visiting my brother in Scarborough for a week but expect
to be back before you!

Mrs A

Oh, she'd be back by now – how long had he been gone? How many
weeks, how many months? Time wheezed in and out like an old
concertina.

David put on a record and the moment it started to play he stopped
it. He was not yet ready to be emotionally dictated to. He opened the
sitting-room windows, double-glazed, to let in air and plugged in
the computer system. The blood of electricity circulated within the
capillaries of the computer and a panel blushed red. Something went

233

click and an artificial voice said 'Welcome home, David. Your telephone messages are ready when you are.'

'Not yet, thanks . . .' He walked over and turned off the system. Colour faded from its breast. English voices came in through the window, borne up from the street on a gust of cold air. David closed the windows, sat down and closed his eyes.

He had visited Kate. Rory wasn't there. She had an artificial arm. A sense of embarrassment and conspiracy had oppressed them making conversation difficult. The room settled into a silence. They stared out at the rain, pensive, but at length curiously comfortable, having accepted the silence, both wondering where Guy was, seeing flashes of his face, picking up far echoes of him.

Some weeks later David was taking himself to bed when he caught his face in the mirror. He was shocked by this involuntary glimpse of himself. He went over to it. No, not very impressive at all that face. He stared at it for some time.

– D'you know, I think I need a shot of Africa, he thought. Yes, that's what I need, a good long shot of Africa. You haven't been to Africa for ages, you silly bugger, you handsome fool . . . and when I come back I think I'll go into politics. The House of Commons needs someone like me. And a smile – not his cutesy knowing smile, but the Great David Smile, which on a good day was something phenomenal with the power of affecting distant sensibilities like a sweet contagion, so that profoundly intelligent men with tortured views of life capered once more in their hearts, so that the frigid began to secrete, the happy began to sing, and singers began to dance, and trees and flowers would turn to each other and say 'It's not such a bad old place, this world!' – *this* smile happened, which was dangerous because it was so genuine.

234

Appendix

Documents

II

The Times reported briefly on an inside page that *Charles Robinson the runaway Communist agent who vanished with the priceles Nineveh Codex from his post at the British Museum, was killed with sevral others 2 days ago in an incident with the Brazilian police in the Amazon jungle. The Brazilan authorities have said that Robinson and his colleagues, resisting arrest, opened fire and they had no alternative but to defend themselves. Robinson was holding hostage Professor Tom Kite of Harvard University who also regretfully lost his life the Brazilian authorities stated to-day. There is no extradition treaty with Brazil but the goverment wished to arrest Robinson for illegal entry into the country. The US Government has lodged a formal protest over the death of Professor Kite. Robinson is survived by a mother in Brighton and a sister in Australia.*

II

Margot awoke; and she took herself home where a day nurse and night nurse attended her permanently. Joyce, who'd started drinking in the empty drawing-room with only dust sheets for company, said 'I'm so glad' and stopped drinking. However Margot never regained her old self (or her emeralds) and spent most of the time in bed. On her birthday a few years after the Bomb Party, she gave a small soirée in her bedroom. When Tristram Shropshire, opening a bottle of champagne and leading the guests in a chorus of 'Happy Birthday to You', happened to spill the booze all over her bed, Margot was electrocuted to death by her electric blanket. In her will, after generous annuities to Joyce, Solon the bodyguard, and several remote relations, she left her fortune to a trust which was established to research into techniques of immortality.

III
David Zoton's Interim Report

Main objective: Who planted the bomb at the Ingot house? See below.

Main objective: Contact Charles Robinson. Negative result. No evidence of liaison between Robinson and Manners. Russians had same objective; result also negative.

Secondary objective: Investigate Quintomondisti. Verdict: incompetent offshoot of the Snuffers. No threat (heroin addicts).

Senator Curtis Bute: Currently in Cuban gaol, probably going to be swopped, despite Cuban sabre-rattling and US show of indifference. Bute's communiqués should be considered trustworthy – suspicion that Bute a double agent founded on spurious connection with his son. The Senator's a bit of an old fool however. Suggest Americans put him out to grass, if they haven't already.

Beau Bute: No evidence of connection between activities of father and son. BB started out flying drugs into Florida, mostly cocaine and marijuana of Colombian origin. Graduated to distribution of snuff videos etc. Recently arrested with Adam Shatner. Both peripheral to the Snuffers – and the girl arrested with them would be advised to plead diminished responsibility.

The Snuffers: Underground political organization whose political tool is selective murder. They are skilful at this and prefer to avoid frontal confrontation with authorities. Originated in the commerce of filming illegal events e.g. murders and tortures. Escalated to an ideology. Their customers are presumed to be either brutals or inadequates. If men of power or standing they are classified as brutals and eliminated to help purify the psychic genes for a healthier world future. Almost certainly responsible for Tonio Palombo's death and the Swami's. Possibly planted the London bomb too, although the radial splat (as opposed to the needle in the target) would mark a new departure for them and imply a loss

238

of control at the centre (as the phenomenon of the Quintomondisti already does). Headquarters: was Mexico. Probably now
transferred to Brazil.

Tonio Palombo: Trying to muscle in on the contraband video mar-
ket. Attracted by the bad smell – like all his type.

Dick Tring: Tring Pocket Video not involved.

The Swami: Knew too much.

Henry Mountsavage: Gun-running activities continue but, as
before, only to Government-approved destinations. Professional
connection with Manners ended with winding-up of record business. But DO pursue at your end this curious link with the Quintomondisti. Suspect it is NOT heroin.

Dmitri Tcherenkov: Co-ordinating the Russian presence in the
Caribbean. His connection with Charles Robinson – no actual
evidence of it, but strong suspicion. Pursue as opportune.
Tcherenkov is a first-rate operator, completely untrustworthy.

IV

A great many years later, long after all these events, 20 or so people
walked away from a damp country churchyard on the border of
Oxfordshire. It was early spring and a softness had entered into the
rain which bathed the swaying curves of the hills with considerate
wetness. The trees were in bud and daffodils hit the landscape like
splashes of lemon curd.

'Thank-you, Vicar,' said Andrew Manners. 'Do come back for
something to eat and drink.'

'Thank-you, I will,' said the Reverend Hyde, pushing back a
shock of imaginary hair – he was very bald.

Without haste they walked under a scattering of black umbrellas
towards the large gabled Victorian vicarage which had long ceased
to be a property of the church and had become a desirable residence
of mouldering stones. Some cars were parked in the drive, including
a couple of electric ones with transparent bodies said to be
crashproof. Andrew pushed open the studded front door and said
'We should've used the back entrance, traipsing all this muck in . . .'
His wife Rosemary said she was starving and untied her headscarf
and took off her gloves. She sat down on the bottom step of a wide

239

curving staircase. Above her a number of stuffed eagles climbed up the staircase wall. 'I'm surprised he wasn't cremated. He was the crematorium sort,' she said.

'The will made a specific point of it. Not to be cremated.'

'I'm going to be cremated. The worms, the worms! What lovely flowers over there – who sent them?'

'Some people called Lauderdale. Americans. Don't know them.'

The others straggled in, took off their wet things, and made for the dining-room where sherry, sandwiches and cake had been laid out in a dusty atmosphere of stuffed animals, old books and eccentric junk. The old boy's housekeeper, Mrs Greene, had gone in through the scullery and was making pots of tea. She said to Rosemary 'I'm sorry, dear, I haven't done the house for a week, what with everything.'

Andrew sat in a chair looking out through the window at the brightening metallic sky. The lawn was a vivid green. Shrubs and hedges were unclipped, as always. On the terrace where moss and weeds broke through the thin remains of gravel, 3 magnolia trees grew against the house.

'Could you live here, Rosemary?'

'I don't know,' she said. 'It's rather, you know – is creepy the word? I suppose one could do it up.'

'Let's stay here to-night at least.'

'Oh God, absolutely. I couldn't go back to London now. My feet are killing me. Besides I think Mrs Green would like it if we stayed.'

'But she always sleeps in the village.'

'I know but, well, we have to show an interest.'

Rosemary went to circulate among the others. A half-caste black boy came up to Andrew and handed him a slice of Madeira cake on a plate. 'Thanks, Tony,' said Andrew. Later when all the people had gone and the curtains had been drawn against the night and they were putting their feet up in front of a fire of roaring logs, Rosemary said 'Tony Mountsavage is so grown up already. It seems only yesterday we went to the christening.'

A tall clock ticked authoritatively in the hall as if saying 'OK OK OK everything's OK OK OK'.

'So that's the end of Grandfather Guy. I never felt I really knew Grandfather, you know,' said Andrew.

'You knew him better than your father did.'

240

'Oh yes. It's sometimes like that. Intimacy skipping a generation. Sometimes it does that. And when Father was killed, naturally Grandfather became . . . . I loved him, but I didn't know him, in a way.'

'Are you coming up?' said Rosemary.

'Not yet. You go ahead.'

Tired and wide awake, Andrew wished to persist in this state which a death can often effect, an unusual composure balanced between the inner and outer worlds. No great dreams of a life beyond this ruptured the fabric of consciousness. No preposterous ambitions and no frustrations were entertained. Mundane irritations ceased to impinge and yet one had the feeling of living to the full the ordinary fundamental life. Logs in the fireplace slipped, sparked, flamed again. He threw on another. At some point he'd have to go through his grandfather's papers. He wondered how long he himself would live. Another 40 years? Grandfather had a long life. Father a short one. It sometimes happens. Andrew Manners: almost 40 years old: how long to go?

He went into the study. There was a bunch of keys on the desk. He picked them up, felt curious, collected a torch from the scullery, and slowly climbed the stairs past the eagles who observed him with unblinking ire. On the landing he stopped and looked back down into the hall as if something had shuffled there. Then he walked past the bedrooms, careful not to rouse his wife, and made for a door at the end of the corridor which led into the servants' part of the house. This had long been shut up. He found the key, unlocked the door, and went through.

The odour of decay hit him at once, the odour of damp forgotten rooms, dead moths and rank air. He found a light. It didn't work. He flashed the torch into one of the rooms. The windows were blank with dust. The last people to live here had been a group of students from a nearby college but they hadn't stayed long – that was maybe 20 years ago. A number of beer tins on a window ledge betrayed their passage. Andrew climbed another staircase – this one was narrow and carpetless, showing bare wood down the centre and a band of old brown paint on either side. It led to the attic floor. The torch flashed a beam of parchment-yellow light ahead of him. He passed doors sealed by oblivion, servants' bedrooms long abandoned, and reached the door of an attic room at the far end where the locked

241

trunks were kept. He turned the round brown Bakelite doorhandle. The door squeaked. He went in.

The room, cut into by the slope of the roof, was a collection of angular shapes and shadowy with cobwebs. He shone the torch along the wall and located a light switch in brown Bakelite spotted with old yellow emulsion. He pushed the switch down and, miraculous to relate, a dust-covered bulb suspended from a slanting beam came on and filled the room with a pus-coloured light. He heard a faint click. It made him pause. He heard laughter, saw sunshine – it was as if a single bubble of champagne had somehow managed to survive intact from a neglected corner of an Edwardian afternoon and now burst under his very nose with a faint click, dispersing the final, the absolutely last molecules of living essence from that era. He broke free of this fancy and, careful to avoid striking his head against low beams, walked across to a brassbound trunk which sat among other cases and boxes. Its leather surfaces were cracked and very dusty. It hadn't been opened for a long time. Andrew fiddled with keys, more keys, he thought he'd never find the right key. In the dingy light he examined without success the fawn card labels tied onto groups of keys with string, their indications rubbed into illegibility. Then, as he was on the point of giving up, fatigued by the compress of forgotten things which at this late hour choked the air and the resolve alike with an excess of grime and wormy associations, he felt the heavy centre lock give slightly, as of a will influenced by a distant star. He continued to switch the key with subtle movements of his wrist, searching for the knack, until hey presto it surrendered. The lock turned stiffly. He flipped the catches and slowly raised the lid . . . . .

A cloud of disturbed time shifted about the trunk in misty undulations . . . . . the aroma of Spanish Leather cologne surged vaguely from the dark maw of the trunk, lifting like echoes of forgotten laughter, flickering out, flickering out, fading, fading, fading in the inexorable ebb of Memory through Time.

Andrew shone the torch inside the trunk. Papers. And more papers. Some bound in discoloured ribbons, some bunched in elastic bands which snapped with age at a touch. Bundles falling apart, papers unbound, bursting cardboard files of papers, a great stewy soup of papers in a bathtub of a trunk. He plunged his arms in up to the elbows, moving them slowly among the papers of increment and

242

expenditure, blocks of receipts with pins through them, demands, invoices, deeds, entitlements of dubious value, defunct bonds and covenants. Andrew was mesmerized by the exactitude of the documentary past, as exact as a flight of birds through clouds.

Then from the stew of rippling creams, browns, ivories and mushroomy fawns, up bobbed a black notebook. It was about the size of a school exercise book, bound in cloth boards, and for some reason had a seashell in a polythene bag sellotaped to the front cover. Among all those legal and financial registrations it had a distinctly foreign look, a thing with heart and significance. Andrew fished it out and with grey eyes dustily filmed over, he looked inside. It was written with a fountain pen. The first 2 pages were clean – fresh and white – age had not entered. The next facing page declared 'To Whom It May Concern'. Over to the next facing page. 'My Meeting with Charles Robinson and What Transpired by Guy Manners.' A text followed.

The notebook rested in Andrew's hands. The trapdoors of his memory flipped open and numerous unanswered questions poured through, making him alert. He closed the trunk, turned off the light and took the book downstairs. On the landing he paused outside a bedroom, and heard Rosemary sleeping soundly, and went on down to the kitchen to make some coffee. He took it into the drawing-room and poured himself a generous measure of cognac as well. The fire was low. He replenished it. He found his cigarettes and settled into the big snug armchair beside the blazing fire. He adjusted the lamp, drew in a long breath and began to read.

★　★　★

'My Meeting with Charles Robinson and What Transpired'
by
Guy Manners

I can hardly believe it now, looking back on it, *his grandfather began, speaking to him directly it seemed, but not over a great interval of time so much as across a great distance*, and although I come to write something of it, just for the record as they say, and because something serious in me insists the truth be known, I can never publish these words, nor indeed do I wish to pass them on privately while I'm alive. He who troubles himself with my remains will be the first to read this testament – ha! what a grand word for a trembling hand! – and the first to know of these events. Because these events are not known. It was all hurried from sight, burned away, edited out of the picture by human ingenuity and determination, and covered over with layers of earth and planted and soon it was as if nothing had ever happened, because plants grow thick and fast in tropical climates. I know that a record is not the primary matter, that a record is secondary to an event. But an event unrecorded passes into ignorance. Its weight is lost. Its brilliant flash of spontaneity appears – and vanishes. Always the great blackness is sucking at our deeds. But I am a witness. I must make my statement somehow, so that deceit does not have it entirely. The blackness of deceit is twin to the blackness of ignorance.

Right now I'm sipping a glass of red wine in the study of this old vicarage which I've bought with a windfall, an almost forgotten investment, gamble, which came good – to my great surprise since throughout an untidy life this was never the usual thing. I'm not getting any younger and I'm lucky to have somewhere to park myself when it rains, somewhere with more space than I need so that I can still wander. This is home now. The study I've grown very fond of. It's not one of your smart studies, in fact it's always in the most awful mess, but there's plenty of foraging matter and a rather good collection of recent books. Someone's just sent me a short memoir of Mary Yodel. She was always in the best seller list years ago and one would see her about at parties but she's long been dead and is quite forgotten now. I suppose they're trying to revive her as a period piece but it's embarrassing stuff. I always wanted to write a book. Could never sit in one place for more than 10 minutes however.

I write now, so many years after the event, because I want the story outside of me, so I can rest up without that awful weight upon the breast of an obligation avoided, which is similar to but not identical with the anxious pressure of a desire frustrated. Most of my desires have been frustrated. That's something I'm learning to accept. Frustration keeps one going.

And why must I keep these notes a secret? The answer's obvious – because they didn't know I was there. That is to say, I'm not supposed to know. If it got *out*, I should be murdered. There is not the slightest doubt about that.

Andrew looked up, shivered slightly. A wind moaned in the high trees about the house. The clock in the hall struck 1 a.m., the fire burned, he read on.

Not supposed to know – in case one tells – and one mustn't tell because knowledge changes people. And if it doesn't, then it's not knowledge but merely information. The knowledge certainly changed me. It simplified my life enormously, clearing the deck of all manner of distracting rubbish, and at the same time a specific tension entered my life which this present exercise is designed to assuage in part. The remaining fear, that at any moment my secret will be discovered and murderers burst in and shoot me dead, that I can never be rid of – but I worry about it less and less because I see how it has greatly increased my appreciation of each day. But the obligation, it took me a long time to discover quite what it was. I suppose I was too busy running. What is it in us symbiotic humans that we can keep nothing to ourselves? Someone has to be told our twisted individual truths, even if only through the intercession of a piece of writing paper. In this it resembles the impulse to love. The thing about love is that one wants to be seen, wants to stand revealed to the other person completely, and in this way ease the burden of life and free oneself from the personality.

Who is reading this? My son? No. He was killed in a car crash. And that event released another cache of knowledge which had to be swallowed and reacted to. The death of a son leaves a permanent, gaping hole in the material of the father's universe, as of a natural law aborted. It gives one a lopsided feeling for the rest of one's days – but people have to live lopsided very often, for all sorts of reasons. This relentless hankering after symmetry, perfection, the gratification of all appetites, the soothing of all vanities – it's asking for trouble.

Of course I came back a changed man. When eventually I saw Kate again, I felt there was something cheated in her demeanour. She said 'I think you were much nicer when you had problems, Guy.' Just like a woman. But one has to try and get on top of life a bit. One can't forever be flinching under the lash of it. It's not that one develops a thick skin or a cynical outlook, just that one begins to know more of what one really wants and the price it exacts. But it was thoughtless of her to imagine I no longer had problems simply because she had ceased being the greatest of them. I never got over Kate in the way she imagined. She was always there under the skin, capable of wounding me. But I had the rest of my life to live. Was I less nice, less interesting because the bleeding was less apparent? There was another phrase she used to hurt. 'You used to be so interesting. Now you're just a drifter . . .' This was on one of those few and fascinating occasions when we bumped into each other in later life, more or less by accident. It was a stupid remark. Interesting. It's a terrible word used by voyeuristic people who want you to be a spectacle to liven up their boring life – they want to see you throwing plates and drinking too much and raising mayhem and being interesting for them! But behind the spectacle is the pain, someone who was interesting this evening going through hell alone in the small hours . . . Mind you, a lot of people go through hell without doing anything at all interesting, just for the hell of it as it were, which strikes me as an absurd surrender . . . All this pain talk. You cannot avoid pain unless you are prepared not to live. And having said that, it occurs to me that living actually reduces pain and that the most painful thing of all is to be unused, to be suffocated alive with all your talents blocked within you, all the opportunities untaken. I shall do this when that has happened, and when so-and-so has been arranged for me then I'll be able to do the whatsit, but at the moment I cannot do this because the you-know-what is not quite so, and when that other thing has been fixed up, then I'll be able to— Death comes down like a guillotine across these meagre intentions and nothing has been done. Another one failed to hoist his flag . . . and the beast wins. The beast is stronger than the man. There is great violence in nature. There is great cruelty in the world. The cruelty of man is a spectacular phenomenon, like the violence of a supernova.

On the 25th of that month, the train pulled into Manaos Railway Station just after 3 p.m. I don't remember the details of how I got there. I was borne up on emotion and carried along by it and the actual tiresome business of having injections, changing money, squeezing myself onto last minute stand-by flights, tracking down obscure booking offices and the representatives of strange travel companies, making desperate taxi connections across one town then another, all these things had a way of taking care of themselves. I did it without thinking because my mind was concentrated upon an intention, upon a circumstance beyond the immediate problem. And therefore I did it rather efficiently. My train pulled into Manaos Central, with me in a First Class carriage and a gunman at either end of it, with not quite 2 hours to spare.

For the first time in years I felt composed, centred, away, outside the scrutiny and judgment of the world, and free. The First Class carriage I'd booked on a whim, a piece of extravagance I could ill-afford but stimulated by a fanciful notion of how the traditional British traveller launches himself on the jungle. I surmised, correctly, that this would be the last piece of civilized comfort I'd know in a long while. I'd sold certain possessions – gold watch, camera, travelling microcomputer – to boost dwindling funds. It was a reasonable assumption that if I didn't sell them they'd be stolen anyway in that wild land. The gold watch, flogged to classy jewellers in Rio, brought in a large amount. It had been a present from Margot and had all the platinum and diamond trimmings. Regret was followed by a sense of nakedness. I felt divested on several counts. These artefacts had been extensions of the human sensorium and their loss affected my perception, made me indeed rather more anxious than my actual prospect did. From now on I'd have to rely on my own head! But the brain is a marvellous, self-correcting instrument, when not too much interfered with, and the subsequent mental adjustment added significantly, I believe, to my sense of liberty and strength.

I stepped down onto the platform with one black leather grip and looked about me. What a shambles. The rail link with the coast wasn't many years old but it looked as though it had been there for centuries. The air was hot and sticky – extremely so – always so – there are no seasons in Manaos. The station steamed. Steam jetted from the railway engines and rose in thick clouds about their curvaceous oily flanks. A few electric trains slid in and out like electric eels, with a certain hauteur which kept them from being considered part of the main event – only blank people seemed to get in and out of them. It had rained not long ago and an evaporation wobbled up drunkenly from the platforms of cracked concrete. The whole of Manaos was windless and immersed in a heat haze. Even the railway station, normally so vibrant a place in towns, partook of this lassitude and train departures were followed by the inevitable collapse back into inertia. I saw a rat attack a cat and made my way to a coffee canteen. Silent forms in ragged clothing squatted everywhere. I felt I was the only wakeful man in a land of dreamers.

The coffee was of course excellent, though not as strong as I'd have liked. So I had 2 cups. At some point along the way I'd picked up a copy of *The Times*. Since I was a little uneasy, I thought I'd glance at it. But on holding up the newspaper before me, the sheets demonstrated an unreality far greater than my surroundings. The centre pages were an ignoble cacophony of priggish posturing prose, abetted here and there by photographs of pained or bewildered faces. I stared at it in astonishment. Was this my tribe? This vehement rabble? A muscle tightened beneath my ribs. It was responding to the caffeine of course. But it was also a symptom of distaste. I folded the paper and jammed it into a dustbin overflowing in one corner, then hurried back to where, like a fool, I'd left my bag unattended. Among such lethargic people one's vigilance may so relax that when, under cover of the general narcosis, a long arm darts out, takes something precious from you, and is reabsorbed by a bundle of rags, you notice nothing at all. On the other side of the canteen there was a pretty Indian girl standing in headscarf and bowler hat. She must still have been in her teens but already there was a hawkishness immanent in the features foretelling the toothless crone, drunk and irascible, which she would become in a few years' time.

A little after 4 another train comes in. Life splutters among the rags. I go outside onto the platform with numerous others. An old man makes a heartless grab at me with a gesture that is half begging appeal and half direct attempt to pick my pocket. But the only thing to pass between us is a momentary glance of mutual indifference. A group of soldiers alights from the train. A harsh American voice cuts the air. 'Da Silva's arriving to-morrow. They're always the last to arrive, the damn Latins. You can bet the Russians will have been waiting for us for weeks.' The man who says this is not in uniform but looks as though he is. His companion says 'Cool it, Brad'. It turns out that this da Silva is actually waiting for them by the Exit – he's a big, vigorous-looking man with general's pips. I walk down the platform, drop my bag and sit on it, unaware that I'm adopting the local style. Another hour to go, almost. I don't want to go out into the station forecourt until the appointed time. I don't want to feel that Charlie might at any moment descend on me from an unexpected angle. I realize I am nervous of our meeting. The sun breaks through the mushy sky in a brief spasm. Many rainbows appear, glow, and disappear; gold sweeps the platform and is gone. I become aware of a dark green, leaning towards me beyond the farthest buildings. The green is powerful and insistent. With a start I realize this is

248

the jungle. For some reason I felt myself to be in a maritime region but I am of course in the heart of an enormous land mass with the jungle pressing the town on all sides. Not far away the miles-wide surface of the Amazon slides past the town accounting for this maritime sensation. My mind clouds with anxiety but I shake myself and push back the jungle to where it belongs, in the realm of conquerable things.

4.45 p.m. I go for a pee. The latrine is noisy with rats and an old Indian masturbates mechanically and ineffectively in one corner, humming and swaying a little with eyes closed. The latrine smells of stale urine and rust. The whole of Manaos smells of urine and rust and when it doesn't it smells of mould.

Just after 5 I was standing in the forecourt looking about, not knowing what in God's name to expect, when a battered jeep pulled out from a row of parked vehicles and shot towards me. My heart clenched, I fell backwards, and the jeep stopped with a screech about a foot from where I'd been standing. A head leant out. 'Quick, jump in,' she said. I just gasped. 'Quick!' she repeated.

Dumb with incredulity, I obey and we tear out of the station and hit a fast-moving stream of traffic on a badly built motorway. 'This gets us out of town fast and down to the big river. Manaos is technically on the Negro. But we want the other one.' she says. All I can get out is 'Oh . . .' I gaze at this prodigy behind the wheel in crumpled battle dress. She looks fantastic – flushed, strong, clear-eyed, smiling. 'I know what you must be thinking,' she says after some time. But I had not begun to think. I'd been stopped dead in my tracks, my whole sense of reality had shuddered. Cause, effect, space, time, the very bases of our grip on the phenomenal world, went reeling through my head like numbers smeared out of cognition by the spin of a roulette wheel. What on earth was going on? Talk about the last person I'd've . . .

'You're thinking she's the last person I'd've expected to find here,' said Jill in her familiar Cockney tones, tilting up her familiar noble nose. 'You didn't think I had it in me, did you? We office girls – you boys mustn't underestimate us. It was all ticking away, Guy, in here, just waiting for the right moment. Well, my moment came and wham! I was off like a shot. Last time you saw me—' She swerved to overtake a beaten-up car overstraining its engine and hovering uncertainly between the 2 outside lanes. 'Get out of the bloody way!'

she yelled, and put her foot down and left the jalopy way behind. 'God, they're barmy out here, Guy, just you wait and see. The last time you saw me I was in a bit of a state. And now you're in a bit of a state!'

'I was in a bit of a state then too,' I said. 'But – how are you here?'

'How? Oh God – how he says. You got a couple of years free? How . . . in a nutshell – Tcherenkov tried to recruit me at the Computer Monitor. He didn't succeed, but he did introduce me to Rudolfo da Silva – Rudolfo and I had an affair that lasted 10 minutes but it was enough to get me involved with this little band.'

'You had a scene with Tcherenkov too, didn't you?'

'I went to bed with him once. That's all. It was Charlie I hit it off with best.'

'And now you're here. I always thought it was Trevor who dreamed of getting away.'

'Yes, bless his heart. But that's all he did – dreamed of it.'

'He had a terrible time afterwards. Why didn't you leave a note or anything?'

A shadow passed over her face. 'But I did. Of course I left a note, on top of the fridge. You mean there was no note?' She was distressed and didn't speak for some minutes. Then she said 'We collect Charlie at a small station some miles up river. After that we journey into the interior.'

'But I thought we were already in the interior.'

'Oh no, love. By no means. This is the big city. This is still up west. The interior is ahead of us.'

As if to underline her statement she swerved sharply across the oncoming traffic and down a narrow street, down another street, down ever narrower, shabbier, more rickety streets until we debouched from this shanty warren and bang! a great expanse of water, so great that the curve of the Earth could be seen upon it, opened before us. Jill pulled up on the waterfront and we got out.

'There it is,' she said with awe in her voice, 'the Amazon . . .'

There was something monstrous about it, so terribly out of scale from everything one associates with the word 'river'. It gleamed white beneath pregnant cloud. But after a while a thick putrid brown could be deduced as a mighty toiling mass beneath the silvery sheet, disclosed only by narrow blades of darkness opening in tiny rents upon the surface and immediately closing again. And in this roundabout way too, one felt the presence of the jungle, a prehistoric immensity of vegetation rioting and compacted, so limitless in every direction that a greenness suffused the sky as if the jungle had reached up with insatiable tendrils, clutched at it and pulled, and the sky had succumbed and been drawn down into this blind vegetable embrace and was now held there trapped and panting, close against the earth for evermore. Occasionally the evening sun came out and went in, casting huge rainbows.

A man shook Jill's hand. They conversed briefly in Portuguese. He climbed into the jeep and drove it off. 'Come on,' she said. I picked up my bag and she took me by the other hand. Every few yards the waterfront seemed to be on the point of giving way and collapsing slimily into the turbid depths. We descended a shaky wooden staircase to a pontoon. A small steamboat, with the air of a veteran campaigner, bumped against the side, painfully squeezing 3 used car tyres. The captain and crew amounted to 1. She introduced me to him. Down a few steps, sunk amidships, was a small cabin with 4 bunks. Jill turned on a light. 'You sleep here,' she said, 'and I'll sleep there. Use this spray to keep everything off you.'

'I'm bitten to death already,' I said lugubriously.

'Well, this is the equatorial jungle,' she replied with a slight swagger in her voice as if she half owned the place. 'And don't worry, for anything bigger I've got a gun.' I hadn't been worrying – until that moment. My mouth dropped open as if someone had pulled a lever in my back. She stared at me. Then something clicked and we laughed and laughed and laughed until the tears streamed down our faces.

Jill disappeared on an errand and when she came back it was night. 'Have some chocolate,' she said, handing me a bar from a carton. The hold was stocked with provisions. An orange glow arose from Manaos and in the other direction – blackness, strange sounds, dark water. I suddenly felt very tired and went to bed. It was not exhaustion but in fact the release from exhaustion, as if a great fatigue which had been accumulating for years, now had the confidence to step forward and declare itself and drown one's whole being in rest. It was a profound exhalation of tensions, and many tensions of which I'd been unaware, including muscular ones, now became apparent by their leave-taking. As I lay on the bunk, the engine started. It sent out a regular comforting throb which sank into my recumbent form and

251

loosened it like an opiate. I felt the steamboat push off from the steadying hand of the wharf – I had the distinct sensation of dropping over the edge of something. Then nothing. Nothing at all . . . . .

When Jill roused me with a cup of coffee, the cabin was filled with a stale brightness which suggested the light of afternoon. 'You've had enough dreaming,' she said, 'and the river station's up ahead.' Dark interlocking masses of foliage slid past the cabin window. Trees overhung the water in a deep fringe so that it was impossible to make out the actual riverbank or see any great way into the forest. Here and there, alarmed by our passage, colourful birds took to the air, crashing through the interstices of the trees. At a lower level, roots fought each other for any available foothold and then sent out fast growths which wove backwards and forwards among themselves, forming a matted texture, both rotting and rich with life, through which a pungent vapour percolated. The jungle, in a constant suck and exudation of vital juices, palpitated perceptibly to one's senses. It was curiously refreshing – so long as one didn't set foot in it.

The slide-past came to an end. There was a small clearing with a few cabins and scattered people. Charles was standing alone at the end of a short jetty. I recognized him at once, though he was far more, how shall I put it, tousled than I remembered him. In fact he looked terribly romantic. There was a suppleness to his stance and he held a bomber jacket over his shoulder with one finger. I went up on deck and waved feebly. He shouted 'Hey, you! It's me!' Like Jill, he was glowing. I felt travel-worn and insipid beside them. Also Jill told me that I'd slept for 17 hours which is not the sort of thing you come bouncing out of.

Anyway, here he was, my friend and superlative outlaw. It was a great occasion and so neither of us knew quite how to behave. We embraced awkwardly and he said 'How about some bacon and eggs? I'll get the boys to load up while we're eating, then we must be off. Time is short.'

Of course the food was exceptionally delicious but how Charles managed bacon at that remote site I daren't think. Perhaps it came out of a tin. The room where we ate was packed with tins, hundreds and hundreds of them.

'You look all right,' he said.

'I've never been to the Southern Hemisphere before,' I said. For some time this was the extent of our conversation – until he said 'Look what I found.' He crossed over to the corner, lifted the walnut lid of a wind-up gramophone, and put on an old 78 record with a plum label – Noël Coward singing 'Half Caste Woman'. We hardly dared to chew while it played, so terribly strange was its effect. After the food he said 'I'll explain as much as I can when we're aboard. Come on.' Jill, who'd been loading further provisions, came in and said 'Bring all the petrol you can, Charlie.'

As we took to the river again I felt we were returning to a safer place. The river has direction and was besides the umbilical between ourselves and the known world. But ashore, in the jungle, direction is meaningless. Jungle life would be entirely amorphous unless rooted very firmly in the self. In the jungle, direction and distance must be calculated not between locations but between men. The Indians go all over the place like small worms in a vast cheese. All their fundamental terms of reference are internal. To them a map would be sheer fantasy.

With a long pull on the siren, which flushed birds and animals from the immediate vicinity, the steamboat started upriver. The flow of water was powerful and of course contrary to our direction, so that an effort was felt in the engine – one knew that if the engine failed we'd be swept back, away from the source. This constant sense of effort added to my personal unease. We sat on Indian blankets spread on the deck, smoking cigarettes. Charles seemed content to do no more than this, so I opened the subject: 'Why?'

He looked at me with those eyes. They weren't really violet, but had glints of reddish brown in bluish grey, so that the effect was somewhat violet in certain lights. 'I should've thought,' he replied in a laconic manner that was rather typical, 'that the question was – where?'

'All right. Where is the Nineveh Codex?'

'In England of course. You don't think I'd come all this way with a thing like that under my arm? It'd be like travelling with a bomb. I tried to phone you before I left – but some joker kept playing silly buggers on the line.'

'Where in England?'

'Dick Tring's house. He wanted it. Desperately. It was the price I had to pay for his help. I thought Timothy Quaintance was onto us at one point. Tring was having some scene with Quaintance's wife –

all a bit near the knuckle. Perhaps Quaintance *was* onto us and Tring paid him off. I don't know. Anyway, we needed Tring's money and connections and his price was the Codex. Eventually his price went up and we had to drop him – that wasn't easy.'

'But money, connections – what for?'

'It was a stupid thing to do,' continued Charles, disregarding the question. 'But I'm not going back, so what the hell eh? And it was important to examine the Codex very thoroughly – to cut a piece off it for example for radio-carbon dating. That was how we discovered it isn't made from parchment as always thought but from human skin. Human skin, but not exactly – one of the doctors wants to build a clone off it in due course and we might all be in for a very weird surprise. We also worked out that the Codex is roughly contemporary with the Tower of Babel myth which we've also studied with interesting results. We certaintly weren't going to destroy it, so someone had to look after it and Tring wanted it – it's in an aluminium vault under the stables of his house in Worcestershire.'

'What's the important thing about this Codex?'

'It appears to be – and you'll appreciate that I've checked pretty exhaustively – the only document in the world which records an event parallel to that currently taking place among a group of Indians up ahead in the jungle. This was 3500 years ago and it's all dressed up in the usual religious mumbo-jumbo. But there was a great slaughter, it relates, of a certain group of people – men, women, some children too – for reasons which until recently seemed incomprehensible. It says things like they had to be killed because they wouldn't stop singing. It's an encoded artefact, all kinds of clues are hidden in it, like a modern banknote. We got a lot of money out of Tring but he wanted to be more and more involved, wanted to start running the show – that would have been a disaster – he was utterly moronic in many ways. There was trouble. He threatened to expose the whole thing by returning the Codex to the British Museum and posing as its recoverer. It would've been called the Tring Codex ever after – he liked the idea of that. So they did him in. I should say 'we'. I'm party to it, I plead guilty, and with no great pride either. A couple of the Snuffers kidnapped him from his yacht as it was making its way out of the Caribbean down towards us here. They mutilated the body and dumped it in the sea off Florida with sinks attached to his legs.'

'So he was that thing which came up with the lampreys?'

'Yes, afraid so. The bits sent to Bute and Tcherenkov – well, they are our opposite numbers. On behalf of their respective governments each tried to infiltrate us. And when they failed to do so, they tried to track down our headquarters and destroy us. I thought Tcherenkov was OK at first but I was wrong. The Senator's been seen off the map. That was a brilliant stroke. One of our agents does some dealing with the son and found out by chance about the fishing trip. It was the perfect opportunity for a frame – and so the guns were dropped. We didn't bargain on the Cubans being roped in – a call to the Florida coastal police would've been sufficient. As it was, Hurricane Juno removed you to another district. I had no idea you were on board of course, until I saw a newspaper. The Senator's role has been taken over by a right bastard called Brad Stretcher from the US Embassy in Brasilia. As for Tcherenkov, he's less easy to know about. He seems to have holed himself up in Havana like a lama in a monastery. He's obviously terrified of being murdered. It's all pretty dirty, I agree. But it's the Snuffers' show ultimately – they let me in, not vice versa. And they have their own way of doing things. In some ways, it's a paramilitary operation, so one has to turn a blind eye very often.'

'But that means you're involved with the people who tortured Kate . . . .'

'It doesn't mean that at all. Anyway the Snuffers have stopped that – they say they've more important things to do now. Your Kate was abused by a gang calling themselves the Quintomondists – they're a spin-off group who've caused us quite a few problems too. But the fact that Kate is alive to-day, you've got me to thank for that – although she doesn't know it .'

'Did you meet Tcherenkov in the Fountain of Youth the night you left England?'

'No. We thought he might be genuine at first, might be useful, so I arranged for a girl I know to do me a favour, go off to bed with him and clarify a few things. It then became obvious that he was a professional double-crosser to put it mildly. He's been trying to get hold of me ever since.'

'Listen, who else am I going to find up ahead? Is David Zoton involved in this?'

'No. He discovered a bit, but not enough to earn himself a

poisoned dart. Or a bag of seeds.'

'What about Henry Mountsavage?'

'Presumably you know of his gun-running activities?'

'David told me. I didn't believe it really.'

'Believe it. He's a pretty big boy in that field. He says that when he's got enough money he's going to build his own bomb and blackmail governments with it – that's Henry's idea of a good party. But the point about him is that he gun-runs for the British Government. Not officially of course. But when they want to support a terrorist group or an insurrection without being *seen* to, they phone Henry. He's not supposed to take matters into his own hands but of course he does. That note they found on the Quintomondist – the idiot – I told you they were fools – that note referred not to drugs but to arms. David Zoton's problem was to decide what the note meant. Did it mean that the British Government was secretly backing the Quintomondists? He didn't know. And at this very moment he's probably still working on it. Why for example didn't they jump on Henry? Could be they *are* backing the Quintomondists as a way of rocking our boat. Or could be Henry's too useful to ditch just for a bunch of dizzy gun-toting junkies who are quite capable of getting themselves caught anyway. In fact for me, it all begins with Henry, it was through him that I first heard about something strange in the jungle. He had fixed up a deal supplying the Snuffers with small arms via a man called Rudolfo da Silva who writes poetry in his spare time. This was paid for with Tring money (Tring was in on it before me) though Henry didn't know that. Soon after, Henry heard about Tom Kite's anthropological activities and certain pieces of geography started to overlap. He talked to me about it since I was acquainted with Kite and had corresponded with him on the Codex in more innocent days. One day Kite contacted me directly. Here I am.'

Charles lit a cigarette and coughed lightly. 'And why, you are probably wondering, should we go to all this extraordinary trouble for a bunch of Indians?' he said. I looked at him with a touch of petulance. 'Because we believe it's the only hope for our planet, the one way to avoid vanishing in that big puff of smoke they've got planned for us. Therefore we've nothing to lose. And when you've nothing to lose, you become very strong. Guy, these Indians represent an entirely new development in human life. A mutation has taken place, a new brain faculty has flipped into action. We call it the Fifth

World which sounds very grand but at the moment it doesn't amount to much more than a group of Indians doing some quite astonishing tricks in the jungle. But the Indians are utterly vulnerable and the protection and study of them have become the Snuffers' entire raison d'être to which all other considerations are subsidiary. We don't know where this new brain faculty will lead exactly but we do know that it is for the good. However, certain governments have got wind of something and their sense of security has been deeply threatened. Presumably they hope to do what they always do – capture the Indians and stick them in a laboratory. This would destroy everything. The Fifth World was destroyed before by frightened rulers and it took 3500 years to recur. It mustn't happen again. We don't have that sort of time any more.'

My mind was confused. It couldn't make the requisite jump, so I stuck close to the ground and said after a few moments 'Then you aren't in league with Tcherenkov?'

'Don't be silly. Tcherenkov tried to worm his way in by posing as a heroin dealer. He did quite a bit of business that way, hoping to convince us of his authenticity.'

7 or 8 years later, when by chance I ran across Tcherenkov in a secondhand bookshop off Great Russell Street, he said 'Mr Manners, did my eyes deceive me, or were you too down in the jungle when it happened?' I said nothing. 'Ah, very wise. You're keeping quiet about it. Just like me!' In other respects however he was quite brazen. I put it to him, I asked him if he still trafficked in heroin. He replied 'Sh, not so loud, the girl at the desk . . .' But she was scratching something in an old ledger – we might easily have filled shopping bags with desirable volumes and walked out. Tcherenkov pretended to examine a fine English language edition of Eisenstein's *The Film Sense* bound in black and yellow morocco while he said 'I enjoyed my little foray into the world of heroin dealing. I thought it pardonable to line my pockets and undermine the West simultaneously.' I said to him 'Did you kill Shropshire?' and he replied 'Why not! He was a very big, very unpleasant man. It was the perfect opportunity – no self-respecting agent with sound humanitarian principles would have passed it up. I even handed the gun to the police. "I found this, Superintendent, thrown into a corner. I'm sure it's important". "My God, thank-you very much, Mr Tcherenkov". Ha! But I didn't plant the bomb, Mr Manners.'

Charles lit another cigarette. He was far more nervous than I'd originally thought. The boat chugged on. 'The Americans and Russians are trying to reach the Indian camp and the Indians know it but it doesn't appear to bother them. The target murders carried out by the Snuffers, I think they were a mistake. Clearly they left certain clues. The Minever plant for example grows only in a certain region. Of course one's priorities then were not quite as clear as they are now.'

'The air's so heavy, Charlie, I'm soaked through with sweat.'

'It'll get worse.'

'I'm terribly thirsty.'

'Drink some water.'

Jill sat with her back propped against the side of the boat, reading a glossy magazine. 'Charlie, do you know a restaurant in Rio called Le Funambule?' she asked. 'It says here they do the most gorgeous crêpes.'

I said 'So I could be rotting in a Cuban gaol right now instead of . . .' I gazed at the passing jungle. Was this freedom? This solemn fear, this fragile excitement?

Charles made a contemptuous movement of his head. 'Senator Bute was on the US board of arms allocations. He had a lot of say about which countries got what killing power and on what terms – so of course he took a hefty cream-off. The Cubans don't realize it but this noise they've put out about Bute being a big gun-runner and which they think is a smart piece of propaganda – it's virtually the truth.'

'What's in it for the Snuffers?'

'Sense of purpose, sense of mission, sense of worth.'

'What's in it for you, Charlie?'

'Ha . . . . . Tom Kite will explain all the clever stuff. I'm a bit tired now.'

This Professor Kite was certainly a man with a reputation. Old golden eyes Kite! But many men greater than a Harvard professor have gone soft in the head. It is possible to see a great way into the design of life, to the perimeter of what is knowable. And when men such as Kite strike that perimeter, a sense of confinement oppresses them, an active claustrophobia. They long to burst out of their limitation and start casting about for an exit. In some cases any exit will do and this makes them susceptible to romantic fantasies of the soul while remaining thoroughly convinced that their feet are planted firmly on scientific ground – I felt that Kite was likely to be a man of this stamp. In due course he told me what he knew.

Suddenly the whole escapade filled me with revulsion, and in this recoil from overblown, even hysterical sentiment in an extreme landscape, and from the unrelieved sense of being in both physical and mental danger, I thought of David. What would he have said to Charlie? David too was my friend. Is my friend. He is alive and well in a dodgy world. He did me a great personal favour in leaving certain things out of his report. Of course a number of his conclusions were wrong – as he later discovered. Like all men with a talent for pulling the wool over other people's eyes, he could be quick to jump to the wrong conclusion.

We journeyed several more days by steamboat, then left the Amazon proper and followed one of its tributaries, the Purus, a hardly less mighty effluent, for 5 days or so. The days lost their distinction. They flowed into each other as imprecise phases of light and dark and these phases did not necessarily correspond to episodes of fitful sleep. As it did from the earth, the jungle had likewise a way of sucking power from the sun, so that even at noonday the sun when it came through the cloud cover did so as a token, like a dirty bulb in an attic. The air was the colour of dishwater. The river, with its heavy cargo of vegetable silt, was brackish and reptilean, occasionally stained with blood along its banks where alligators fed. An anaconda dropped out of an overhanging tree as we manoeuvred through a channel to avoid mud banks. I don't think it meant to. The monster was as disconcerted as we were. Jill shot it with a single bullet and cooked it on deck on a portable stove. It didn't taste of anything much.

The sun, flashing dully behind trees as we chugged along, went out unexpectedly and it started to rain. Drops the size of eggs fell on the deck with violent concussion and we had to pull over. The following day we reached a small station, the redoubt of a gang of Brazilian bandits. Here the steamboat turned round, taking 3 of the bandits downstream, while we transferred to canoes with Indian guides and porters. Squatting in a canoe hour after hour is extremely taxing on the joints. This stretch of the journey had a peculiar agony all its own. Our clothes were wet and dirty. Unlike the Indians, we were buttoned at neck, wrists and ankles. Even so my flesh was a mass of lumps, some of them suppurating, others orgasmically itchy. I was in need of a good wash but after a few days one's odour hits a balance and merges with the surroundings, ceasing to be offensive or indeed noticeable. Defecation and urination took place when periodically we came ashore. The Indians, all male and naked except for various adornments designed to emphasize not conceal their genitals, were rather more modest than we Europeans when it came to the bodily functions. Nor was it a modesty occasioned by our presence. Each of them went separately from the others into the bush to find a quiet place, and douched himself with river water on returning. Such prudery, originating no doubt in certain atavisms of hygiene, is often found in unsophisticated ethical systems. I asked Charles about their sexual habits since Jill appeared to have no interest for them whatsoever, and he said that all such enquiries were met with expressions of incredulity beyond which it was impossible to penetrate. Perhaps they regard such curiosity on our part as a great impertinence.

Luckily the canoe torture lasted only 2 days. We took to the land with porters and provisions, making our way on foot but following the river which had now become rapid and dangerous. The following day we cut inland with machetes at a point which struck me as arbitrary. We wore protective waterproof leggings but the Indians with boxes on their heads barged through unclad. They hardly worried about their bodies at all and their skin was in consequence covered with boils and swellings. The only thing they particularly dislike in this line is the bite of a rare fly which implants beneath the epidermis an egg which grows and one morning you wake up to find that the lump has opened and from its sticky orifice maggots crawl out one after another.

Fauna-wise, the most dramatic event was an attack from a pack of mandrills (only recently introduced to this continent). They came screaming at us out of the cavernous gloom without warning, obscenely ferocious, spitting eyes, wet fangs, purple anuses tumescent with hate. But they were easily dispersed by gunfire and went shrieking off as fast as they'd come, in a collective nervous breakdown. Gunfire was new to their *Weltpolitik*. We later heard from an Indian, who'd come upon the gasping remains, that in their consternation these mandrills had subsequently set upon each other in a grotesque self-massacre. As we sheltered one night under a dripping tarpaulin somewhere within this empire of plants, eating quietly from cold tin bowls (our food now was nutrition pills swallowed down with a carbohydrate porridge miraculously preserved from weevils + tea – the cognac and such niceties had long gone) I said to Charlie 'Don't you want to go back to England? Don't you long for the temperate mood?'

A quiver went through him and he said 'I don't think I want *that* any more.' Then added 'Who was it who said the English countryside is like a very beautiful, very gormless woman?'

One day, as we were hacking our way through the jungle, there was suddenly no longer anything to hack at. So thick is this vegetation, so infrequent the interruptions in it, that there is no feeling of approach to a space. You just find yourself in one, feeling naked and unprotected, the perfect target for an arrow or screaming mandrill. This is what happened now – the jungle fell away from us on all sides as if with vicious cracks of his whip a ringmaster had driven it back to a snarling perimeter where the jungle walls reared up, angry and resentful, in a wide circle about the glade. We had arrived.

Dark men in dark clothes surrounded us with machine-guns which fortunately they didn't seem about to use. Brilliant sunshine fell into the clearing, lighting it like a stadium. We'd been scrambling through the undergrowth for so long that this unexpected downpour of illumination gave to the appearance of things an hallucinatory twinkle which had at first a queasy effect on one. A number of gaily painted huts seemed to have been set down haphazardly in the glade. They were of a design peculiar to themselves, involving fretted gables, twirling apices and illustrated walls. They weren't at all Indian but resembled, if anything, the charming fancies of an 18th century exotic. No doubt like any English village, which looks at first glance to be a random collection of buildings, they would reveal in due course a social logic.

Greetings took place in a swaggering manner which I disliked, partly because I felt left out of it and partly because there was something bogus in the bonhomie. I now discovered that the cognac and such niceties, though depleted, had not been exhausted. They were received with great pleasure. All things considered, I was remarkably untired. The whole trek had been an exercise in endurance and heart and yet left one rather less drained than the psychological cannibalism of, say, half a dozen cocktail parties in London. We were served tea and slices of pink cake, with the promise of a more sub-

261

stantial meal in a few hours. There was little conversation in the camp and an atmosphere of unacknowledged nervousness. Everyone seemed preoccupied. But apart from the eccentricity of such a settlement existing at all, nothing particularly strange was going on. No levitating Indians, no transportations by telekinesis. The basic needs of food, shelter, warmth and companionship still seemed to apply.

Dinner was excellent but what it was I didn't enquire after congratulating them on the cheese with which it began. They said it wasn't cheese but the discharge of a tree, congealed and sliced. Afterwards everyone except myself had things to do, so I went and sat on the porch of the hut which had been allocated to me. It was painted yellow with red flames and pale blue flowers on it. These cabins were very pretty, lit up with lanterns. Here and there figures sat before small bonfires which glowed warmly in the night. Others passed to and fro, occasionally saying hullo or raising a hand, but that was all. There was an air of civility, that kind conspiracy between men – wherever it springs up, however deplorable the circumstances may be in other ways, something of man's nobility has sprung up too. A moon like a face behind a mourning-veil produced a patch of dim paleness overhead. I leaned back and rested against the wall of the cabin and relaxed. Quite slowly I became aware of a tiny crunching noise which came from a direction I couldn't determine. The reason for this was that it came irregularly from every direction, everywhere this tiny crunching – pausing – digesting – more crunching – without end. The worms! Already the worms were in this little house, eating it up.

By and by Professor Tom Kite of Harvard University joined me with the words 'Do you mind if I join you for a moment?' and he stood his complicated machine-gun, bristling with lights and switches and sensors, against the cabin wall. He was smaller than his name, much, but this is frequently the case with large names. Kite was completely bald and the strip of hair which remained growing round the base of his skull had been shaven off. A strong red face, jug ears, a large smooth hair-free mole where his right nostril turned into his cheek – as if a marble had been inserted under the skin. The squat wiry body of a monkey, about 60 years old. His least striking feature was the eyes, of a faded brown like weak tea. These were the famous 'golden eyes' of Tom Kite. Most disappointing. He took a

262

swig from a silver hip-flask then handed it to me second which I thought ill-mannered. 'It's yage & yacca brandy,' he said. I declined.

'Let me try and explain a little,' he began, adding ingratiatingly 'I think Charles would like me to.' I shifted my bottom as a gesture of attention. 'What's happening here,' he began, 'is something that hasn't happened for a long time, perhaps ever – an advance in man. Human progress as a moral advance has been discredited. Moral progress hasn't happened because it's been based on a wish, not on a fact. We'd like to be good but our make-up is such that etcetera etcetera. It's obvious therefore that there has to be a change in our make-up if human progress is actually to take place. And this is what is happening here. A group of Indians in remote jungle has mutated, the human mechanism has made that jump. No, you won't see anybody walking around with 3 heads or an extra set of hands. That's quantitative, not qualitative change. Man's essential power is not in the dexterity of his hands but in his brain. Many creatures are stronger than he, many can run faster, and so on. For man therefore, development – by which I mean essential change for the better – is neurological. Certain slow mutations have already been taking place, in laborious fashion, on our planet. For example, the world of electronics – which is an amplification of the human brain. It is clever, it is marvellous, but it's cumbersome. Pull the plug, and it's back to the axe. Take the world of computers – terrific, great – but self-limiting. Why? Because it encourages us to surrender our choice-making faculty to the machine because it's more convenient that way. Now these Indians have by-passed all that. Or one might say, they've incorporated it. Take for example just the mechanical considerations, without going too deeply into it – well, the Indians' faculties are much more powerful than they should be. They are capable of astonishing calculations. They communicate in their own language but it is enormously speeded up so that it sounds like a funny wobbly wail. It took us a long time to realize what that wail was. We made some tapes and slowed them down. We had to slow them down 280 times to reach normal speech patterns. Even so we often can't understand what they're saying – when form changes, so does content and they've invented a lot of new words. When you can process information 280 times faster than before, naturally you have different things to say. This factor of 280 keeps reappearing and we don't know why. They are incredibly intuitive – which is working out the obvious

263

option from the available information. In any situation they will be taking in 280 times the amount of information you or I can. Their integrating power is very high – therefore their filtering-out process is much reduced. They are hugely aware. And I don't mean this is any vague religious sense. If you can hear something ½ mile away, they can hear something 140 miles away. One of the results of this, which is a blessing for us, is they don't wanna move about much. If they can mentally penetrate 140 miles in all directions they've got a passable, albeit patchy, scan on an area 280 miles across. So unless they're going to move 300 miles or so, they're not much interested in moving at all. Anyway for their own safety we must keep them here. They accept this. We give them what they need. Which curiously enough isn't much. Their diet remains more or less the same but they like to eat constantly, in small amounts. All of which means they're getting very fat. This is one problem. The other is their stupendous complacency. They are very happy creatures. They know they are in danger – it's necessary to remind them of this – but it doesn't produce the normal emotional response. They giggle. So much for that. Now – a question you might reasonably ask is: how did this flip into high capacity come about? Which is to say, why the Indians and why now? We're not sure, we're working on it, but there are 2 broad lines of approach. The first line is: this mutation took place among a tribe who enjoy – well, that's not quite the word – certain cannibalistic traditions. It was this that attracted the Snuffers down here in the first place. The Snuffers gave them presents, patted the kids on the head, made themselves agreeable. They also filmed them. They began to participate in the rituals and to some extent direct them. One of the most important rites involves eating human brains, especially the pineal and pituitary glands. These 2 glands are very highly thought of hereabouts. Originally only men of honour were permitted to eat them. The Snuffers introduced the idea of allowing women to eat them too – with the result that several women have given birth to remarkable children. The mutation may be connected with this practice of eating brains. This is not a matter of like-affecting-like. I'm not saying that if you eat arms you'll develop big strong arms, or that if you eat eyes your eyesight will improve. That's ridiculous. But the point about eating brains is that you are taking in complex hormones and other generative agents. And we know what the consumption of hormones can produce very rapid and very radical

264

change. Take a course of oestrogen and you'll soon develop woman's breasts. The pituitary gland appears to govern the growth patterns of the body. What the pineal gland does nobody has the faintest idea. And there is some evidence that the cannibalistic eating of brains played a part in our earlier mutation from furry ape-type to furless man. The second line of approach is to examine how change itself actually takes place. What causes change? And the answer is: pressure. Which is an influence outside a given system forcing an adaptation. To an observer this change would appear to take place abruptly, as a stick subject to pressure suddenly snaps. And what is the pressure on the Indians? That's easy. Us. Technological man. They are an embattled species. Industrial advance threatens them on all sides. There is a very interesting parallel here to our own situation. Modern man is subject to a similar pressure: terrestrialism. Man has outgrown the planet. Now this pressure of terrestrialism can be resolved in one of 2 ways: either by nuclear destruction or by a psychological jump forward. Because expansion into space on the old-fashioned model of colonial settlement is not possible, these are our only options. The possibility of nuclear destruction is the specific factor forcing a mutation in modern man. We are part of an evolving universe. Nuclear power, it can be argued, is the agent through which the universe localizes and eliminates undesirable conscious impulses. In other words, if we destroy ourselves, a nest of "stupidity" or "evil" will rightly have been prevented from further participation in the evolving universe. This moment will occur in the history of every intelligent planet and only the truly intelligent will survive it. Those that do are perforce benign. This means, Guy, that if ever you encounter some intelligence from outer space you should not be afraid! And the ability to self-destruct will not go away, we can't uninvent it. From now on it will be ever-present in human culture, the price we pay for our cleverness. Earth is coming of age. Just as an individual attains personal awareness when he understands that unlike the animals he is not the victim of fate but has the power of life and death over his own existence, so it is now with the planet as a whole. You will understand why we all feel ourselves to be engaged upon an urgent task. If we cannot usher the planet into the Fifth World, that's it, the end of the human race. Before it was the dinosaurs. This time it could be us. But the process necessary to our survival has begun, here, deep deep in the jungle. The only discernible precedent we have for this occurs in the Nineveh Codex. The Tower of Babel story is a garbled version of it but clearly a pressure event. According to the Codex, the Tower of Babel gave rise not to a cacophony of tongues but to a race of "devils" who could understand every language. Our Indians here pick up languages with astonishing speed, simply because they are expert decoders. Thousands of years ago these "devils" terrified the population and the rulers – they were slaughtered. We don't want our Indians to be slaughtered. And do you know, there's another very interesting thing that's come out of all this: a further insight into the structure of the evolutionary or growth process. Which enables us to enlarge our concept of time. We have to whistle good-bye to the entropy-based outlook and its offspring. Take for example the tenet of Physics that non-living processes tend to destroy order. This is quite wrong. What can be said is that non-living processes tend to produce simplicity from complexity. But the universe is binary in structure. It exists because of the reciprocity between opposites. At any single moment a phenomenon is the product of 2 *contradictory* procedures. If something is true, its opposite is also true – given that the complete opposite is posited. From which we can draw our next statement: Living processes tend to produce complexity from simplicity. These 2 procedures, the living and the non-living, take place simultaneously. This gives us an entirely new model of evolution. It means for example that we are subject to 2 streams of time. In Physics, quantum signals are received from the future – 'indeterminacy' is a misnomer. In man, all significant decisions are based on future events, otherwise nothing would happen. All decisions based on past events reduce energy and performance: in Physics this is stability sliding into entropy, in human affairs it is passivity sliding into depression. Universal life is not characterized by decisions based on past events. The 2 streams of time, acting *simultaneously*, are:

1) Evolution towards simplicity, i.e. from
past cause to present effect.
2) Evolution towards complexity, i.e. from
future cause to present effect.

This is one of the key laws of binarism. Grasp the double nature of time and the implications are amazing. For example, let us return to our old friend, the secretive pineal gland. If you examine the pineal gland, which is something I've devoted a large part of my life to doing, you will find that—'

. . . Professor Kite continued in this way. My head was awhirl. When he'd finished with the pineal gland, he want on to various other glands including the sexual organs, then onto DNA, RNA, copper, zinc, the role of minerals in perception, diet generally, the differences between dualist and binarist thinking – dualism was simply wrong, I recall, worse than useless, therefore pernicious. The words grew longer and longer, the concepts more passionately recondite. There was something in it but exactly what . . . . . I needed to draw breath. So when a fat androgynous Indian walked past and winked at me, I winked back without quite realizing what I was doing. I then experienced a very bizarre sense of displacement. I was walking beside the Indian, then I was back on the porch, Tom Kite grinding in my ear with that Harvard drone (which when it gets into its stride must be the most boring sound ever made by man). This struck me as peculiar, because I hadn't moved. Then it happened again: walking with the Indian, back beside Tom Kite. I found that with an effort of concentration (though the effect appears to negate that word) I was able to hold myself in both places at once and, which was so odd, be aware of being in both places. The Indian said something which sounded like 'Very good, very good, maybe you can have some fun,' then he went out of my life. I was my old single self back on the porch. Kite was saying 'So I hope that when we go over to the Indian camp to-morrow, you'll now be able to understand a bit of what goes on.'

'You mean this isn't the Indian camp?'

'No.'

'You mean the Indians are somewhere else?'

'That's right. Their camp is about a mile in that direction. They never leave it.'

'But I just saw one go past. A fat androgynous type like you described.'

'You may have seen *an* Indian go past. But it wasn't one of *the* Indians. They're not allowed to leave their camp. We take good care of our Indians. They no more roam about here than you'd find the Crown Jewels dumped on the end of my bed. Now, to-morrow is an important day. It's my bedtime. And yours too. You'll need a clear head to-morrow. Everyone, Guy, must bring something to this enterprise. The least you can do is bring your attention.'

I entered the cabin and switched on the light. Several cockroaches the size of pigeons and the colour of dried blood squatted on the table, twirling their antennae, sensitive to hostile vibrations, human vibrations. They can survive almost anything, they can survive even a nuclear attack, but they cannot survive the lightning slipper of an alert human being. In the post-nuclear future, who will inherit the Earth, who will it be, the cockroaches or us? The cockroaches vanished – for the moment. Then that crunching noise, polite and implacable – the worms. I rolled myself in a sleeping bag on a settle, pulling it tightly up to my nose, aware that the whole room about me was alive and crawling with life.

Early the next day there was a rap on my door. A man with a pig-tail and a machine-gun entered and said, 'Wake up! It's Saturday!' I splashed my face with water, touched my toes, took a few deep breaths, and said 'Have I got time for a cuppa?' He replied 'whatever that is, you don't have time for it.' I snatched some bread from a sealed box and followed him out. About 20 people, apart from those in uniform, had assembled in the centre of the compound. There were 5 women including Jill. Everyone turned to look at me. Evidently I was the last. Charles raised his hand in greeting some distance away. He was talking to a large dangerous-looking fellow with black beard and paramilitary uniform and a dark younger man with fine features who seemed familiar. Charles eventually deferred to them. Black Beard said 'We go' and we all did, like boy scouts. In the course of the march, Jill introduced me to the fine-featured man who was Rudolfo da Silva. They seemed to be on excellent terms.

Where the Indians lived was in 2 round huts painted in various greens and blues which made them almost invisible in that setting. The larger hut was the domicile of the mutants or Neuros, and the smaller that of their attendants who also acted as intermediaries if necessary between the Neuros and their protectors. These 2 buildings rested on a large oval of – it looked extraordinary – of lawn. Smooth, soft, perfect. A circle of naked Indians sat on it. They were all very fat. This clearing was considerably smaller than ours and so it had been possible in its creation to leave a thin canopy of boughs and leaves overhead, making it undetectable from the air. This canopy of leaves, forming jigsawlike an almost continuous membrane, had in addition the property of translucence and allowed to filter down a soft green aquarium light, generally diffused, which had none of the characteristics of gloom. Here and there slender prisms of sunlight, solid and contained in the way that laser beams are, pierced the canopy at angles and shot into the earth like golden assegais. Round the perimeter guards in dark uniforms with machine-guns stood in relaxed postures looking towards the entrance of the larger hut. We waited in silence, as for the arrival of a potentate at the opening of an opera. There were a few coughs. Nothing happened. We stood for ages. Nothing happened. 'How long do we have to wait?' I whispered to Charlie. He turned with a twinkle in his eye and said 'Be patient. We wait. That's all.' We waited. And waited. And after what must have been almost an hour, 7 Indians came out of the hut. They were even fatter than those already on the lawn. 3 of them were children and looked very unappetizing, almost wider than they were tall, their bow legs ridged with excess flesh. The 7 formed a smaller circle within the others. It was difficult to assess their age because of their gross appearance but I'd say they were all under 30. Their hair was long and unbound and this enhanced the hermaphrodite aspect. In a number of cases the genitals were obscured by unsightly, hanging stomachs.

These 7 were apparently to be the 'performers' for to-day and their arrival on the scene changed the atmosphere completely. Firstly, they were fed by everyone's attention, which they enjoyed. Their demeanour was affable and amused. Secondly, the jungle noises subsided entirely, to be replaced by a light circulation of air among the leaves which set up a soothing rustle. This lulled us all delightfully and it was only after some time that one realized a wavering hum had become mixed in with it. Was this the high-speed converse to which Kite had made reference? Kite himself now intervened and painted a kind of silvery slime on the back of each of the 7. I was told that this contained a radio-sensitive metal which enabled him to monitor a series of analytical signals appearing on small screens to one side of the group. Kite's apparatus was not large but looked of infinite complexity. The 7 chuckled and sent ripples into the air.

Now something very impressive began to occur. The light in the glade started to alter. It didn't flicker or flash but went up and down in smooth but irregular phases, as if a child were playing with a dimmer switch. I felt extremely uncomfortable, the air between my skin and my clothes seemed suddenly charged with electrons, and a cold sweat sprung out of my back. 'Don't worry about the light,' whispered Charlie. 'Neurological activity concentrated to this degree sets up small magnetic disturbances. Remember that our ordinary human brain is a mighty sensitive thing too. It's picking up these disturbances and trying to perform corrections. The light isn't actually changing. It's our perception of it that's being interfered with. If you feel faint, just sit down. Kite thinks that participating in these sessions with one's physical presence alone could well be enough to effect a similar mutation in ourselves, through stimulation of the empathic response. That's basically why we are all here – not to observe but to participate. That's why we come every week to this place. That's the arrangement with the Indians. Once a week. No more. And look, don't feel you must adopt a special face for this. Just be relaxed and yourself. You can move about if you have to, go for a pee, but don't disturb others. If you get thirsty, the water's over there beside Kite's contraption.'

The 7 Indians were not exactly the picture of health, their skin looked damp and greasy and was a dirty dun colour, so that it was very noticeable when it glowed rose pink in slow flushes. A heat had entered into them. Sexual differentiation was now easier due to the men's erections and the intense flushing of the women's breasts. Several flashes of electrostatic sparked from a woman's hair. Patterns like the tattoos of Maoris appeared and disappeared on their skin in an ever-changing design. There was a weird smell, a harsh chemical smell mixed with a faint odour of burnt rubber. The light went out altogether, returned at once, then held itself fairly steady from now on.

But everything else got distinctly *un*steady. There was a tremendous roar which unnerved me. My stomach knotted tighter and tighter, as if someone were winding me up. I thought I'd better sit down. Also, I was terrified of shitting in my pants. I hadn't shat today and felt it might strike at any moment. One of the Indians produced a large transparent bubble, like a soap bubble with a rainbow smear on one side. He simply blew it out from his hindquarters. It grew and grew and detached itself, wobbling a couple of feet off the ground. The Indian then climbed into it and floated off across the glade and was gone. A fat little boy with a purple erection released a cloud of lavender butterflies by exhaling them from his mouth. Another child made a small seashell appear at the feet of everyone

270

present. I put mine in my pocket and have it to this day. One of the women stood up and stepped out of her skin and draped the skin over her arm like an expensive coat. My mouth was very dry. I desperately wanted some water but didn't want to move – the very thought of attracting attention to myself in this way filled me with acute anxiety. The woman once more stepped out of her skin and folded it over her arm. She did it 6 times, without getting any thinner, at which point she tired of this particular trick and flung the skins with a gesture of impatience up into the air. They went flying up and yanked her after with a comic, music hall effect. She went whistling up in the air, through the canopy of leaves, and vanished. I gave up trying to make sense of any of this – and the tension in my stomach relaxed appreciably. One of the Indians stood up and slowly sank into the earth until he'd totally disappeared. But he showed up again, popping out from behind a tree, and waddled back to his original position, vibrating with silent laughter. My thirst had gone – and was replaced by a horrible headache. I've never suffered from migraine but this must have been close. By the time one of the performers started growing feathers down his arm, the headache had turned to nausea. I was aware only of my vision, which was wavering like a badly tuned television picture, and the hot-cold nausea. He managed to cover one whole arm with feathers but couldn't do any more. He gave up, shrugged his shoulders and grinned. One of the children stepped forward – impossible to tell what sex it was – and started to speak to us in a familiar human voice. At the same time I felt my body cooled and refreshed by fine sprays of moisture, as if brought here on a sea breeze. I didn't understand the Indian language and don't know what the child was saying and this episode is very shaky in my memory, largely because of what happened next. The whole performance stopped at this moment. If was as if the lights had unexpectedly gone up in a theatre, making all hard and normal again, except that the Indians on the lawn looked terribly terribly tired. They seemed to cave in all at once, like punctured balloons. This was followed by complete confusion . . . . . A great flash of blue fire swept across the compound from one side to the other. There were screams, zipping sounds, the paltry crack of gunfire, clouds of black smoke. The leafy lid of the clearing was ripped quite away and became a ring of charred stumps. A large dish of blue sky showed overhead and the silhouettes of helicopters swam blackly

271

against it like aerial sharks. Blue electric fire shot out from their bellies, strafing the compound. People on fire ran in all directions and trailed the sickly sweet smell of burning flesh. Soldiers, real ones in real uniforms, ran everywhere killing. Blue electric flames burst from their guns and knives flashed. I saw Rudolfo da Silva running full pelt towards the jungle but a squad of troops coming out of it stopped him in his tracks. A soldier fired – a sheet of blue electric flame unfurled in the air. This illuminated the face of General da Silva leading the squad. As the flame travelled towards Rudolfo, the General recognized his son. Between them crackled an instant of love, horror, stupor. Then the flame struck and Rudolfo was a heap of smoking cinders.

Smoke rose in a grim tower above the jungle.

Killing, burning.

Could anything survive? I looked frantically about, recognized nothing and nobody I knew, escaped into the jungle. I turned round once – the devastation seemed total – then plunged in, ran, stumbled, crawled, got away. They released tracker dogs, I heard them, but these dogs were reluctant to go too far into the jungle without their masters. How did I survive? I hardly remember. I met 2 Snuffers. We travelled together for some days. I encountered a savage who gave me drinking water, led me to the river, and pushed me off in a canoe. I drifted downstream, out of that cruel dark world, and reached a station where one morning, asleep among the river weeds like Moses, I was discovered by a trader of the old school, a German named Plank. He fed me well and from there to civilisation was simple.

Civilization took the form of the private front door of Sir Michael Horrabin, the British Ambassador. His face was long-boned and ratty, with small dotlike eyes. 'Been on safari, Mr Manners? Wonderful country, isn't it. Lost all your stuff, I suppose, need an assisted passage home – try the Chancery division, it opens at 10 in the morning. This is my private residence, you know.'

I threw in the name of his relation, Iris Hatchett-Smith, and his eyes twitched so close together I thought they were going to coalesce. 'Haven't seen her in years,' he said. 'Well, I presume you won't be staying in Brazil much longer, so I shan't have an opportunity of inviting you to dinner. Bon voyage then. Pedro will see you out.'

Of these events I breathed not a word to a soul. And as I became absorbed in a more conventional world, I was increasingly at a loss to explain what had happened to me. I searched the Rio papers for any report but found only a reference to a terrorist incident in the jungle – and there was one of those virtually every day. One thing was certain – if I talked I was finished. The operation had been designed for no witnesses. And another thing – I'd committed murder myself. The 2 Snuffers I travelled some days with – one of them I'm sure was Kate's torturer, I recognized him from the film. I didn't explode or anything, just made my decision. When we set up camp and his friend went off to search for game, I stabbed him several times in the stomach with a knife. He made a curious little whoop of surprise, like a man coming across a friend in a crowded street. When the other returned I murdered him too and made off with all the provisions.

I expected my return to England to produce a strange mood in me, but it didn't – which was in itself odd. The atmosphere was curiously workaday. One of the first things I did was visit Trevor's old flat beneath mine and look for that note which Jill claimed to have left. It had, quite simply, fallen down the back of the fridge which was still there (full of Billy and Emma's health food – what a change in them too). So Trevor got Jill's note in the end. That was all that was left of her.

And me? I waited. I waited until I could make some sense of it all. I waited and one year became another and, well, they pile up without one's realizing it and now it's been over 30 years – at one time I'd have considered that quite a while, but now it's hardly anything at all. I waited but I didn't stay in one place. Staying in one place while you wait is the hardest form of waiting. I travelled, had a son, got married, got divorced. My mother and father died, still wondering why I wasn't a doctor like my brother. I managed to buy this rather too big vicarage not far from the district of my father's boyhood. I don't move in the smart world much but people come to stay because there's plenty of room. David Zoton comes down. Henry Flamingfield liked to come, until his recent death. He married an East European girl and she couldn't have kids so they adopted a little African boy – he's now the 15th Earl of Flamingfield and married to a white girl from South Africa. They still live at Risingtower, have a son, and are appealing to the nation for a roof. The Nineveh Codex was recovered when Dick Tring's death was finally established and his affairs opened up. The Codex business was his only major crime. Or since the Rt Hon. Timothy Quaintance headed the Committee of Enquiry, the only crime which saw the light of day. I often wonder if Quaintance thereby discovered his wife's infidelity, or whether he went to the grave congratulating himself on his power to command an exclusive devotion. The Codex is back at the British Museum (much to the annoyance of the British Library which was lobbying like hell to have it transferred) and is probably the most popular exhibit there, as a result of its peregrinations. It is credited with a mystical charisma by some and a paperback is available on the subject linking it to a persecuted magical sect in modern China. As for the bomb, one night on his television programme Lord Willywonky went berserk and confessed to being the author of the explosion. He went into a lunatic asylum soon after. Fanatical Muslims were actually convicted and imprisoned for the outrage – Margot's Jewish blood was usefully invoked by the prosecution – but a doubt lingers and sometimes in pubs late at night people will argue the matter still. And on my arrival back in England, I found a little seashell in my pocket.

One question remains. It tugged and still tugs. Kite had said to me 'Everyone, Guy, must bring something to this enterprise.' Indeed yes. But what had I brought? Why the telegram? Why ask me to join them? What had I to offer? Only now, at the end of this narrative, does a possible answer suggest itself. What did I bring to the enterprise? I brought – myself, my memory. They knew what would happen and they wanted a witness? Could that have been it?

Here the notebook stopped. Andrew lit a cigarette and didn't do anything else for a while. The fire had burned low. He closed the notebook with a grunt and stared ahead of him. He put it in a small cupboard to the left of the fire-place, locked it, put the key in his pocket, settled the guard in front of the fire, looked about him, grunted again, and switched out the lights. Passing into the hall he glanced at the grandfather clock and said 'Oh God, is that the time?' He searched for somewhere to stub out his cigarette, found an old chipped ashtray bearing the insignia of the Dorchester Hotel, and went upstairs to bed.